GREEK TYCOON'S MISTLETOE PROPOSAL

BY
KANDY SHEPHERD

First Published in Great Britain 2016
By Mills & Boon, an imprint of HarperCollins*Publishers*
1 London Bridge Street, London, SE1 9GF

© 2016 Harlequin Books S.A.

Special thanks and acknowledgement are given to Kandy Shepherd for her contribution to the Maids Under the Mistletoe series.

ISBN: 978-0-263-92032-1

23-1116

Our policy is to use papers that are natural, renewable and recyclable products and made from wood grown in sustainable forests. The logging and manufacturing processes conform to the legal environmental regulations of the country of origin.

Printed and bound in Spain
by CPI, Barcelona

CHAPTER ONE

LUKAS CHRISTOPHEDES HEARD the singing the moment he let himself into his Chelsea townhouse. The infernal sound of yet another Christmas carol. This time, infiltrating the sanctuary of one of his favourite homes. How many times had he heard a rendition of *Jingle Bells* already today? With only days until Christmas, canned festive music had followed him from the airport in Athens all the way to his disconcerting business meeting in east London. After the day he'd endured, he did *not* need *Jingle Bells* here.

The cleaner must have left a radio on. He had an on-going arrangement with the upmarket Maids in Chelsea agency to ensure his house was cleaned and aired daily so it would always be ready should he have to spend time in the UK. Perhaps they'd purposely left the radio on as a burglar deterrent? That could make sense—Chelsea was one of the most affluent areas of London. But the sooner it was switched off the better.

As he strode through the marble-floored entranceway the singing got louder—and more off-key. He winced. No radio would give airtime to this appalling rendition of *Jingle Bells* in that tuneless female voice. This was a live performance. He cursed in a fluent mix of Greek and English. A maid must still be here working—a particularly tone-deaf maid. At six p.m. he expected his house to be free of any domestic help. It was his escape and his refuge and

he demanded privacy. Strong words would be spoken to
Maids in Chelsea for this breach of protocol.

Lukas flung his cashmere coat and scarf onto the antique chair in the marble-tiled hallway and headed towards
the staircase that led to the next two floors. He wanted this
maid out of his house, pronto.

The tuneless singing was coming from the next floor
so he took the stairs two at a time. He wanted to plug his
ears with his fingers as he neared the master bathroom
that adjoined his bedroom. It couldn't be much fun getting
down on hands and knees to scrub out someone's bathroom but that was no excuse for this tuneless wailing. The
sooner this woman packed up her brushes and mops and
got out, the better.

The door to the luxurious bathroom, all marble and
glass, remodelled by one of the most in-demand interior
designers in London, was half open. He pushed it fully
open. Then stood, stupefied. *There was a naked woman
in his bathtub.*

She reclined in the freestanding rolltop tub. Although
a heavy froth of bubbles protected her modesty he could
make out the shape of high, round breasts, slender shoulders, a long pale neck. A mass of bright auburn hair was
piled on top of her head and fell in tendrils around a
flushed heart-shaped face. One slim leg pointed to the
ceiling as she used a long-handled wooden brush—*his*
new brush—to soap between toes tipped with a delicate
pink polish.

'Oh, what fun it is to ride in a one-horse open sleigh-ay,'
she caterwauled, her voice cracking on the last word as she
didn't achieve the high, extended note required.

Lukas stared in disbelief for a moment longer before he
exploded. 'Who the hell are you and what are you doing
in my bathroom?'

The woman turned. Her eyes widened and he saw they

were an extraordinary shade of blue. Then she screamed—an ear-splitting scream even more excruciating to his ears than her singing. 'Get out!' she shrieked.

Lukas glared at her. 'You can get out of my bathtub first.'

She waved the bath brush at him in what was obviously intended to be a menacing manner. 'Not until you get out of here.'

The movement of wielding the brush brought her breasts dangerously close to being bared. With a quick downward glance and a little gasp, she seemed to realise it and stilled. Then slid deeper down into the water, all bravado wilting like the foam bubbles on her shoulders.

'I… I guess you're Mr Christophedes. Even though I was told you weren't going to be in London until after Christmas.'

'And *you* are?'

The flush deepened on her cheeks. 'Ashleigh Murphy. Your daily maid. From Maids in Chelsea.'

'So, Ashleigh Murphy, what are you doing in my bathtub?'

She raised the brush again. 'I'm…uh…scrubbing it.'

Her audacity almost made him smile. Almost. He realised she was young, mid-twenties at most. And quite lovely. But she had taken an unheard of liberty for a maid.

'I think not,' he said. He shifted his weight from foot to foot, crossed his arms in front of his chest. 'Try again.'

'This is such a luxurious bathroom. As I cleaned it, I wished I could try out the tub—it's magnificent, isn't it?' The hand that wasn't holding the bath brush reverently stroked the side of the tub without, Lukas thought, her realising she was doing it. 'The slum of a hotel where I've been staying has the world's most disgusting shared bathroom. I had to disinfect it before I could even think about dipping a toe in the tub. And then the water was just a lukewarm trickle…' Her voice died away. She swallowed hard. She didn't meet his eyes but seemed to concentrate on the work-of-art tap.

'So the bathroom is no better in the place you're staying now?'

She crinkled up her nose in a look that expressed guilt better than any words could. 'Actually it is. Because, well, I'm staying here. In…in your house.'

'You *what*?' The words exploded from him and she cringed back into the water.

'You're getting a live-in maid at no extra cost?' she offered, in an obvious effort to placate him.

'Not good enough, Ashleigh Murphy,' he thundered.

She crossed her arms over her chest and sat up higher in the bathtub. The water fell away to reveal more of her slim, pale body. Lukas knew he should avert his eyes but it wasn't easy. In his thirty-four years, he had never encountered such a situation. Even though he'd grown up in a multi-servant household and kept a full-time staff in his Athens mansion.

'I had nowhere else to stay. My time ran out at the hotel; I was planning to couch surf with a friend but it didn't work out. London at this time of year is so expensive I couldn't find anywhere I could afford. I'd been hired as your daily maid so I—'

'Took advantage and moved in.'

'Took advantage? I suppose that's how it might look. But I was desperate. It was either bunk down in one of your guest rooms or…or go home.' Her voice trailed away.

'And home is?'

'Australia.'

He'd detected an accent but it wasn't strong and he hadn't been able to place it. Lukas frowned. 'Surely Australia is a good place to call home, especially at this time of year when it's summer there.'

Her eyes cast downward. 'Not…not when I ran away from my wedding. And if I go home again the family will think I've come back to…to marry a man I realised I don't love.'

She was a runaway bride? Lukas wasn't sure what to say about something so messy and totally out of his experience. But it was hardly an excuse to trespass. He cleared his throat. 'You'll be lucky if I don't call the police.'

Her eyes widened in alarm. 'Please. Don't do that. I assure you I haven't stolen anything. I've been doing extra cleaning in lieu of rent. And…and please don't tell Clio Caldwell at the agency,' she said. 'She knows nothing about me staying here. She's been so good to me and I don't want to let her down. And…and…well, she's having a personal crisis right now and doesn't need any extra worries.'

The fact that the intruder in his bathtub seemed more concerned at offending her boss than saving her own skin made Lukas soften towards her. Perhaps she was just young and silly, and desperate rather than dishonest.

'Then I suggest you pack your bags—'

'I only have a backpack,' she interrupted.

'Pack your *backpack* and get out of my house,' he said.

She caught her lower lip with her teeth. Lukas could not help noticing the lush fullness of her mouth, her perfect teeth. 'Now?' she said, her voice quivering a little on the word.

He tapped his foot on the floor. 'Now.'

'But…' Her voice trailed away and she hugged her arms closer to her chest.

Some dark part of him wanted to make her get out of the bath and watch as she fumbled for a towel. See for himself if her body was as slender and shapely as it appeared through the protective coating of bubbles. But he did not give in to base impulses. Not after having grown up with the consequences of his father's lack of self-control and indulgence in whatever appetites overcame him. Not when he'd been put at risk himself from the unbridled decadence of his family's lifestyle.

Lukas took a step towards the heated towel rail. Picked up a thick, pale grey towel and tossed it towards her. She went to catch it, her movement revealing the curve of the top of her breasts. Then, rather than risk further exposure, she stilled and let the towel slide to the marble tiles next to the tub. For a long moment she looked at him, her eyes wide, her mouth trembling. Lukas recognised the second a shadow of fear darkened her eyes as she realised the vulnerability of her position.

He stepped back to put a greater distance between them. He wanted her out of his house. But he would never want a woman to cringe from him in fear. Not that Ashleigh Murphy seemed to be the cringing type.

'Get yourself dressed and see me in my study on your way out,' he said curtly, turning on his heel. The sooner this opportunistic backpacker was out of his house the better.

Ashleigh towelled herself dry with trembling hands. Her encounter with Lukas Christophedes had left her shaking. Not just because she'd been caught trespassing by the owner of this multi-million-pound house but because of *him*. For that split second before she'd screamed, her senses had registered that the dark stranger in the bathroom was *gorgeous*.

As an Aussie girl from a country town, she had had no experience of Greek billionaires. If anything, she would assume they would be old, grey-haired and possibly paunchy—and there were no personal photos on display anywhere in this house to indicate Mr Christophedes was anything different.

The reality was that thirty-something Lukas Christophedes looked as if he'd stepped off the pages of an upmarket men's magazine—tall, broad-shouldered, dark-haired with a lean, handsome face. But his dark eyes had smouldered with fury, his mouth set tight when he'd discovered her in his bathtub. Gorgeous had suddenly seemed grim.

Thank heaven she didn't encounter him as she made her way to the bedroom she'd purloined, wrapped only in the towel he had tossed at her. Of course she'd been completely in the wrong to have abused her position of trust with Maids in Chelsea to squat at a client's house. She'd been desperate but, in hindsight, she realised she must have been crazy to do such a thing.

As she dressed, then shoved her few belongings into her backpack, her mind roiled with thoughts of what she could say to him. If, as he'd threatened, he got the police involved, she could end up with a criminal record. Even get deported. And all because her friend Sophie had mysteriously disappeared on the night Ashleigh had intended to ask her if she could crash on her sofa until she found somewhere to live.

They'd been waitressing at a posh party and Ashleigh had been dealing with some obnoxious guests who'd downed rather too much champagne. By the time Ashleigh had sorted them, Sophie was nowhere to be seen—and hadn't reappeared until the next day with an enigmatic smile and a refusal to explain where she'd been.

In the meantime, Ashleigh had had nowhere to sleep. In desperation, she'd thought of the house in Chelsea where she'd just accepted a two-month house-care job. The luxury residence was empty and, apparently, rarely used.

It had been after midnight by the time Ashleigh had let herself into the Christophedes townhouse and the smallest of the guest rooms. With an en suite shower, it might actually be earmarked for a housekeeper or nanny she'd told herself to quieten her conscience. That first night she'd slept fitfully, fully clothed on top of the bedcover, jumping in panic at any slight sound in the house. By now, the third night, she'd convinced herself she wasn't hurting anyone and no one need know. Wasn't it a waste to leave a house like this empty? And she *had* made herself useful by doing chores beyond the scope of a daily maid's duties.

But, however much she'd tried to convince herself otherwise, she'd known staying there was wrong. What an idiot she'd been not to have just left it at one night. If she had, she might have got away with it. She dreaded facing Sophie, her friend she'd known since they were teenagers, who had recommended her for the position at Maids in Chelsea. Not to mention Clio. The charismatic owner of the agency had taken a risk on employing her—an unknown Australian with little prior experience of hospitality or housekeeping work.

Ashleigh slung her backpack over her shoulder. It was light. When she'd run away from her wedding, she'd only intended staying in London for a two-week vacation and had packed the minimum required. But she'd loved being in London so much she'd decided to quit her job back home and stay longer. Maids in Chelsea was hard work but fun and she'd made friends with two other maids as well as Sophie: posh Emma and shy Grace. She planned on staying in the UK for as long as it took to make it very clear to both Dan, her aggrieved former fiancé, and her family that she had no intention of returning home to get married. In her mind the ceremony was permanently cancelled. In their minds they seemed to think it had been merely postponed.

Sometimes it seemed her family sided more with Dan than with *her*. 'Dan is like a son to us, we're so fond of him,' her mother was always saying of the guy who had been Ashleigh's off and on boyfriend for years. Huh. That was the trouble. She'd realised she was *fond* of Dan too. Just fond. Not the head-over-heels in love she needed to commit to marriage.

She'd explained that to her parents when she'd confessed she wanted to call off the wedding a month before she was due to walk down the aisle. In frustrated reaction to their shocked disbelief, she'd even gone so far as to call Dan *the world's most boring man*.

Instead of listening to her, instead of believing her, her mother had tut-tutted that she'd get over this little blip and that the stress of the wedding plans was messing with her mind. Her father had gone so far as to actually pat her on her head—as if she were seven instead of twenty-seven—and tell her there was nothing wrong with a bit of *boring* in a man. Boring meant steady and reliable. Ashleigh had gritted her teeth. Boring meant *boring*.

What did it take to get it into the heads of the folk back home that the engagement was *over*? She'd had every intention of going home to Bundaberg for Christmas. Her family celebrated Christmas in a big way and she'd never been away from them at this special time of year. But when the other day she'd video-chatted with her mother to talk about dates and flights, there was Dan, sitting beside her mum on the sofa. He'd blown her a kiss as if she still wore the engagement ring she'd consigned to the bottom drawer of her dressing table when he'd refused to take it back. *'You'll be wanting to wear it again,'* he'd said with pompous certainty.

Seeing him there, so complacent and cosy, had made her see red. It felt like a betrayal by her family. Then her mother had gushed that Dan would be with them for Christmas Day as both his mother and his father would be away. Without really thinking about the consequences, Ashleigh had informed her parents she was not coming home for Christmas and didn't know when she'd *ever* go back to Australia.

So here she was on a dark, freezing December evening, about to be booted out into the vastness of London without anywhere to stay. Except perhaps a police cell if she wasn't able to convince Lukas Christophedes to let her go.

She made her way up the stairs to the next level of the townhouse. There was an elevator, but she never took it, too frightened it might stall between floors and she'd be trapped in a house where she was staying illicitly. She sent up a prayer that the billionaire client would accept her grovelling apologies and let her go without punishment. Staying here had been a bad, bad idea.

She'd dusted and vacuumed around his already perfectly clean office so she knew where it was. Like all the rooms in this beautiful, luxurious house, it had been decorated with the most expensive of furnishings and fittings, yet still retained the cosiness of a traditional English library— the walls lined with books and Persian rugs on the floor.

The door was open. Lukas Christophedes sat at his desk, his back towards her. He'd taken off the jacket of his dark, superbly tailored business suit. The finely woven fabric of his shirt showed broad shoulders and a leanly muscled back. She knocked quietly and he immediately swivelled on his chair to face her.

She caught her breath, her trepidation momentarily overcome by heart-stopping awareness of his dark, Mediterranean good looks. He'd discarded his necktie and opened the top buttons of his shirt to reveal a vee of tanned olive skin pointing to an impressive chest. Rolled up sleeves showed strong, tanned forearms. His dark hair was rumpled as if he'd run it through with his fingers. For a moment, Ashleigh thought he seemed less intimidating. Until he turned his gaze to her, assessing her with narrowed eyes, his expression inscrutable.

A shiver travelled up her spine. This man had her in his power—and she had made herself vulnerable to him by her foolish behaviour. Talking her way out of this might not be easy.

CHAPTER TWO

LUKAS STARED AT Ashleigh Murphy as she peered around the door then stepped tentatively into his office. He schooled his face to hide his surprise. He'd been expecting a scruffy backpacker, the type travelling the world on a shoestring, seeking cut-price meals, free Wi-Fi and a cheap place to lay their heads. Backpackers of her ilk had filled the Greek seaside villages where he'd sailed and swam and partied as a student—before responsibility had grabbed him by the scruff and dragged him back to save the family business from his parents' gross mismanagement.

But Ashleigh Murphy seemed something more than that. True, she wore blue jeans that had seen better days, a sweater of some nondescript muddy colour and scuffed trainers. *Trainers.* His elegant mother would have hysterics at the sight of running shoes on the hand-woven carpet of a Christophedes residence. But there was something about this trespassing maid that transcended her humble attire and he found it difficult to drag his gaze away.

More petite than she'd appeared in his bathtub, fine-boned and slender, she moved with a natural grace. Her hair tumbled around her shoulders in a bright, untamed mass. It framed even features, pale skin flushed high on her cheekbones and those extraordinary blue eyes. Without even trying, she seemed *classy.*

He was still irritated by her outrageous incursion into his privacy. But Lukas's irritation began to dissipate as an idea began to form. An idea that could help him solve a particularly bothersome problem that, for all his business smarts, had him stumped. The problem had been plaguing him ever since his meeting at The Shard this afternoon. And it could impede the success of the business expansion he was determined to achieve.

But first he had to assess Ashleigh Murphy's suitability for what he had in mind. In the right clothes, her looks would pass muster. But he needed to find out more about her background, see if she was capable of what else was required.

Curtly, he indicated she take the chair on the other side of his desk. She put her backpack on the floor beside her and sat down. He made her wait while he tapped out some notations on his tablet. She sat up straight and appeared composed. Her attempt to mask her discomfort, perhaps even fear, at the situation in which she'd found herself was impressive. But she betrayed her anxiety in the way she shifted in her seat, her overly tight grip on the arms of the chair. In other circumstances, he would have put her at her ease. At this time, he felt it wouldn't hurt for her to squirm a little before he hit her with his demand.

He lifted his head to face her full on. 'I need to decide what course of action to take against the person I found basking in my bathtub instead of cleaning it.'

She flinched and the flush deepened on her cheekbones. 'Please, I can't apologise enough. I know how wrong it was to do what I did.' Her speaking voice, as opposed to her singing voice, was pleasant and well modulated.

'How long did you intend to stay here in my home?'

'Tonight. Then I—'

'You mean for as long as you could get away with it?'

'No!'

Lukas didn't reply. He'd learned silence often elicited more information than another question.

'Until I could find somewhere I could afford to live. I'm expecting a funds transfer from home any day. I... I haven't been working for Maids in Chelsea long enough to ask for an advance.'

She might not appear like the typical backpacker but it seemed she was as perpetually broke. That might play well into his hands.

'What kind of visa are you on that allows you to work in the UK?'

'No visa. My father is English by birth. I have an EU passport and the right of abode here.'

'Yet you live in Australia?'

'My grandparents emigrated when my father was a child. But we lived in Manchester for two years when I was a teenager while my father studied for his PhD.'

'Your father is an academic?'

'He's the principal of a secondary school in Bundaberg in Queensland where we live.'

'And your mother?'

'She's a schoolteacher too.' She tilted her head to one side in query. 'I don't know what that has to do with me doing the wrong thing here.'

'It interests me,' he said. *She* interested him.

She bit her lip, as if against a retort she wouldn't dare utter considering the precariousness of her situation.

'Have you always been a maid?'

'Of course not.' She spat out the words then backpedalled. 'Not that there's anything wrong with being a maid. In fact I consider myself to be a very good maid, and waitress and front-of-house person—all learned since I've been in London. But my real job is something quite different. I'm an accountant. I have a degree in commerce from the University of Queensland.'

'You—'

She put up her hand in a halt sign. 'Don't say it. If I had a dollar for every time someone told me I don't look like an accountant I'd be a wealthy woman.'

Lukas had to suppress a smile. That was exactly what he had been about to say. Of course there was no reason a woman so exquisitely feminine shouldn't be an accountant—it just made her even more interesting that she didn't fit the mould of an outmoded stereotype.

'You manage money for a living, yet you end up homeless in a big, ruthless city?' he said.

'Circumstances beyond my control,' she said, tight-lipped.

'Were you brought up by your family to be honest?'

Her eyes flashed with barely concealed outrage. 'Of course I was.'

'I could ask you to tip out the contents of your backpack for me to check, then to turn out your pockets.'

Her chin lifted. 'To see if I've stolen anything? I'd be more than happy for you to search my bag.' She gripped the arms of the chair and leaned forward. 'Go ahead. I have nothing to hide. But ask me to undergo a body search and it will be me calling the police.'

Lukas found he couldn't meet her fierce glare. He swallowed hard in distaste at his own actions. He had taken this too far. He had no desire to burrow through her personal belongings. Or undertake anything as intrusive as a body search. That would be…sleazy and he was not that kind of man. 'I'll take your word for it,' he said gruffly.

She nodded but her lips were pressed tight.

One of the reasons he'd been able to lift his family company from the verge of bankruptcy to a business turning over in the multiples of millions was his ability to read people. Every instinct told him this young woman had been foolish but not dishonest.

'I know Maids in Chelsea are scrupulous in the background checking of their employees,' he said. 'I assume the same was done for you.'

She rolled her eyes, just slightly, but he didn't miss it. It was an action he found unwarranted—but perhaps he would have done the same if he were on the other side of the desk.

'I can assure you I have no criminal record back in Australia,' she said. 'All I'm guilty of is an error of judgement. I know it was wrong of me and I reiterate my apology.'

'You admit you have slept under my roof. No doubt you were planning to spend tonight here too?'

'Yes. But it was only until—'

Lukas looked down at his tablet. 'I've calculated how much three nights at a West End hotel of equivalent comfort would cost you.' He named a figure that made her gasp. 'You owe me.'

Ms Murphy paled and he could see a sprinkling of freckles across the bridge of her nose. 'But I can't afford it. If I could pay that I would have gone to one of those hotels in the first place.'

He leaned back in his chair, steepled his fingers under his chin. 'That's really not my concern,' he said.

Lukas didn't like threatening her. But she could be a solution to his problem. And once he'd made up his mind on a course of action, he didn't stop until he'd got what he wanted.

'I... I can't,' she said. 'I just can't pay that.' Her lush, wide mouth trembled. 'You'd best call the police.'

Bravado or bravery? Whatever it was, he admired her spirit.

He narrowed his eyes. 'There's no need for me to call the police. I have a way you can pay off your debt to me without money exchanging hands. Something not very arduous that you might even enjoy.'

* * *

Ashleigh was up and out of her chair so fast she tripped on her backpack and had to steady herself against the desk. She could hardly believe what she'd heard. Sexual favours to pay off a so-called fabricated debt? Clio had warned her there was a certain type of man who considered maids and waitresses to be fair game. Already she'd had to fend them off—especially towards the end of the night at a party when they'd had too much to drink. But *this* man! She was shocked—and disappointed. Lukas Christophedes had seemed better than that.

'No,' she said. 'Never.'

He frowned, got up from his chair. The man was tall and powerfully built and she was glad there was a desk between them. 'You say "no" before you've even heard my proposition?' he asked, his frown deepening.

'Sex is sex, no matter which variant you want me to trade with you.' She glared at him then glanced at the open door, ready to bolt. 'And the answer will always be no.'

He frowned. 'You've got this wrong. I didn't mean that at all.' He wiped his hand across his forehead. 'I would never suggest such a thing. My English…'

His lightly accented English was perfect. It wasn't *what* he'd said but *how* he'd said it. Then she took in the bewilderment in his deep brown eyes and swallowed hard. Or could it be how *she'd* interpreted his words?

'Maybe I…misunderstood?' she asked hesitantly. Misunderstood big time, perhaps.

He came around the desk towards her. She took a step away, the back of her knees pressed against the edge of the chair. Just in case. After all, he was a stranger and she was alone with him in his house.

'Whether I did not get my message across correctly or you misunderstood is beside the point,' he said. 'I am not asking you for *sex*. That is not how I do business.'

'I… I'm glad to hear it.' He must think her hopelessly naïve. 'So…what is your proposition?'

'I want you to pretend to be my girlfriend.'

Ashleigh felt as though all the air had been expelled from her lungs. 'You *what*! How is that different from—'

He put up one large, well-shaped hand to halt her flow of words. 'Completely above board, I assure you. Just for one evening. An important business dinner tomorrow. I've decided I need a date to…to deflect unwanted interest.'

'And you want me to be a fake date?'

'Exactly.'

'Why? I can't imagine a man like you would have a shortage of real dates. You're wealthy, handsome. You'd just have to click your fingers for a multitude of women to come running.'

'Perhaps not a multitude.' He gave a wry, self-deprecating smile she found herself warming to. 'Of course I know a few women in London.' Ashleigh suspected that was a serious understatement. 'But none whom I want to involve in this. No one I want to get the wrong impression.'

'You mean the impression you're serious about her.'

'That is correct,' he said. 'This would be purely a business deal, with no continuing personal involvement. You are unknown in London and that suits me perfectly.'

Would being this man's fake date be any worse than being hired as a waitress for an upscale private party? The idea intrigued her. *He* intrigued her. Wasn't this why she'd come to London? To climb out of the deep rut she'd found herself in. To revel in freedom and independence. To be brave and take risks and open up to new experiences.

'So tell me more about this "proposition"?' she said.

Ashleigh stood by the chair close to her backpack, on the off chance she needed to pick it up and run. He paced up and down as he spoke.

'I met this afternoon at The Shard with a potential business partner, someone I very much want to work with.'

Ashleigh loved the beautiful old buildings in London where history was alive on every corner. But she was fascinated by The Shard—London's futuristic glass skyscraper. The first day she'd arrived, she'd stood at its base and craned her neck to gaze up at the incredible ninety-five-storey building, so tall its jagged top disappeared into the clouds. One rare free evening when they weren't working, she and Sophie had gone up to the bar for a drink—just one as they were so expensive—and gawked at the incredible views of London old and new.

Of course The Shard would be just the place for a visiting billionaire to hold his meetings.

'Excuse my ignorance,' Ashleigh said. 'But what exactly is your business?'

There was no point in pretending she knew anything about him—or in pretending she was anything other than who she was. Of course, if she agreed to be his fake date, that would take pretending to a whole new level. *He was so handsome it wouldn't be a hardship.*

'There are various arms to the Christophedes business but the one that concerns me now is electrical appliances. We dominate the Greek market, are one of the bestselling brands in mainland Europe, and export to Scandinavia and the Middle East. But the British market eludes me. I need a local partner.'

'You mean a distributor?'

'Yes. I did my due diligence and decided this woman's company would be the best fit for what I need. I approached her and today was our initial meeting.'

'Is she interested in doing business with you?'

'Yes.' He stopped his pacing, looked directly down at her. 'She is also interested in me.'

'That's good, isn't it?' she said, perplexed at the doom-laden way he said it. 'You would have to get on with her if you're working on such a big deal.'

He cleared his throat and shifted from foot to foot. Ashleigh was surprised at his display of discomfort. 'I mean she is interested in me as not just a business partner but as a man.'

For the first time Ashleigh saw a crack in the billionaire's confident air of arrogance. She tried not to smile. Somehow she doubted that was the reaction he would expect. 'I see,' she said, trying to sound very serious.

'Do you? Tina Norris is a very beautiful older woman used to getting her own way.'

'So…she's a cougar and she wants you as part of the deal?' Who could blame the woman? The man was good-looking in the extreme. And, she suspected, when he wasn't glaring or shouting at misbehaving maids, he could be charming.

'That is the impression she gave me this afternoon.' He shuddered. Again Ashleigh had to suppress a smile. He was no doubt used to being the hunter, not the hunted.

'But you're not interested?'

'Not in the slightest. I found her…predatory. Besides, I would never get involved with a business partner.'

'I see your dilemma—you don't want to offend her.'

'That is correct. I want her on side for the business.'

'But not in your bed.'

He paused. 'That's a blunt way of putting it, but yes.'

'Hence the fake date. It would be diplomatic if she could see you had a girlfriend.'

'Exactly,' he said.

'But you don't want to give the wrong idea to someone you might actually date.' Ashleigh felt she had to reiterate to make sure she completely understood what she might or might not be getting herself into. She was surprised at how at ease she felt with him.

'Yes.'

'And that's where I come in? If I agree, that is. What would my—' she used her fingers to make quotation marks '—*duties* involve?'

'Accompany me for the evening. Make intelligent conversation—I can see that won't be a problem—and behave as though we are a genuine couple. Convince Ms Norris that there is no point in pursuing me as I am already involved with a beautiful redhead.' He looked at her with what seemed like genuine admiration. She couldn't help but preen a little.

'So, act all lovey-dovey?'

'I'm not exactly sure what you mean by that but I think I get the gist of it,' he said with that ghost of a smile she was beginning to anticipate.

'You know, act affectionate and smoochy with each other.' *Why had she said that?* Because she realised that if she had met this man in different circumstances she would find the idea of smooching with him more than a touch appealing.

'It will be a business dinner,' he said. 'Anything… physical would have to be discreet.'

'I get it,' she said. Ashleigh wondered if he was subtly warning *her* not to form any expectations of anything other than a fake date with him.

He stood with his back to the window, his hands clasped behind him. The curtains were drawn against the cold of a December evening, but she knew the window looked down to a city-sized garden, perfectly maintained with formal clipped hedges and a centrepiece fountain. No doubt there was a team of gardeners to keep it in shape for when the absentee owner decided to drop into London.

She looked up at him, wishing she wasn't wearing flat shoes—he was so much taller than her and his superior height seemed to emphasise the balance of power that tipped firmly in his favour. The billionaire and the maid.

'If I agreed to your proposition, what would be the consequences for me?' she asked.

'No complaint would be made against you to your employer or the police.'

'And my "debt" to you?' That calculation of hotel rates rankled. She doubted he would be able to enforce something so spurious. But she was hardly in a position to question his methods. Not when he had every right to report her to the police.

'Of course your debt would be wiped completely.'

'In return for one dinner date with you and your potential business partner?'

'Yes,' he said.

Ashleigh didn't ask if she would continue to be his daily maid. She knew she'd flicked her last ever duster around this house. She'd have to invent a good excuse to give Clio for why she wanted to quit such a pleasant job.

'It sounds like it could be fun,' she said, forcing a smile. What choice did she have but to agree?

'As I said, you might even enjoy it,' he said. 'The dinner is at an excellent restaurant in Mayfair.' The kind of place maids usually didn't eat at was the implication. Or indeed accountants from Bundaberg.

She took a deep breath. 'Okay, I'll do it,' she said. 'But there's just one more thing.'

He raised a dark eyebrow. 'Yes?'

'How will we get around the fact that we're total strangers and know absolutely nothing about each other?'

CHAPTER THREE

'How do we get over the hurdle that we are strangers? We start finding out about each other,' Lukas said. 'We have until tomorrow evening to make our story sound feasible.'

He was pleased Ashleigh had acquiesced so readily. So he'd had to use some leverage to get her on board, but that was what it took sometimes to get a deal across the line. He'd learned that at twenty-one when he'd had to sort out the mess his profligate parents had made of the company. It had been a tough lesson—he'd discovered people he'd thought he could trust could not be trusted, that he had to be guarded, tamp down on his reactions and feelings. The episode had marked the end of his youth.

'You mean I get a crash course in Greek billionaire and you learn what makes an Aussie maid tick?' she said.

'Aren't you masquerading as a maid? That's just a vacation job, isn't it? I suggest you stick to Aussie accountant,' he said. 'We'll skirt around the maid thing as far as Tina Norris is concerned.' No doubt Ms Norris would have done her research, discovered he was a steadfast bachelor, would scrutinise the woman he chose to accompany him. He shuddered again at the thought of the predatory gleam in the older woman's eye when they'd met. Buried in his past was good reason for his revulsion.

'Actually, I don't much like being an accountant,' Ashleigh said. 'I was steered into it by my parents, who thought accountancy would bring a secure job. I've got my options wide open when it comes to changing career.'

'You'll need to brief me on all that,' he said.

The briefing would not be onerous—there was something about this girl that intrigued him. Ashleigh Murphy seemed somehow different to the women he usually met. Perhaps because she was Australian. More likely because she didn't move in the same social circles. He liked that she didn't seem intimidated by him or fall over backwards to impress him.

She shrugged. 'Not much to tell, really. I managed a flooring company back home.'

'You were a manager? That's impressive.' She didn't appear to be long out of university.

Her slight smile in response hinted at dimples and he found himself wanting to make her smile properly. Not that he was adept at telling jokes or funny stories. In fact he'd been accused of being over-serious. Since he'd been forced to swap his carefree life as a wealthy kid who'd known he would never have to work for a living, there had been little room for laughter. Or for love.

Where did that come from? Perhaps prompted by the knowledge that, at the age of thirty-four, he had to *pretend* he had a serious woman in his life. A wife, children—there wasn't room in his life for marriage. *He didn't want all that.* And, he told himself, he didn't miss it. The Christophedes companies took up all his life. The business *was* his life.

'The title sounds more impressive than it is,' she said. 'It's a small company and I wore a few different hats. But it had a good product and I worked with really nice people. Truth is, you can't be too picky when it comes to getting a good job in a country town. There aren't many opportunities.'

Lukas couldn't imagine why a woman as smart and lovely as Ashleigh Murphy would want to bury herself in some far-flung country town. He would find out why tonight.

He glanced at his watch. 'Have you eaten?'

'No. I was…er…going to have something after my bath.'

'So you've been using my kitchen too?'

She nodded. 'I won't lie,' she said. 'Though it sounds like I might be doing a lot of lying tomorrow night.'

'Not *lying*.' He refused to contemplate that he was planning anything that smacked of dishonesty. 'Think of it as role playing.'

Her auburn eyebrows rose. 'Not a bad idea. I've done some acting—amateur, of course—so I'll think of this as preparing for a role.' She pulled a face. 'You might have to help me with the script.'

'Starting from now,' he said. They had until tomorrow, but a good part of his day would be, as usual, taken up with work. 'You haven't eaten and I haven't eaten. Come out to dinner with me and we'll start the get-to-know-you process.'

'Uh, okay,' she said, obviously disconcerted. 'But…but I need to find somewhere to stay tonight. I have to phone around my friends.' She looked at her feet, obviously uncomfortable at the reminder of her transgression. As well she might be.

'You can stay here tonight,' he said.

She looked up. 'As part of the deal?'

'Yes,' he said. Whatever she might think of him, he would not let a young woman risk being alone in London without a safe place to sleep. 'Though you can steer clear of my bathroom.'

'And what about tomorrow night?' she said, audacity trickling back into her demeanour.

'Tomorrow night too.'

For the first time since he had encountered her in his bathtub Ashleigh smiled. Delightful dimples bracketed her cheeks and light danced in her eyes. He found himself dazzled by the warmth and vivacity that smile brought to her face. She really was lovely, in a wholesome, unsophisticated way.

'Thank you,' she said again. 'That will give me the breathing space I need to make other arrangements.'

'After that you'll be on your own,' he cautioned her.

'I'm aware of that,' she said. 'I realise I'm only here on sufferance.' She paused. 'Just checking I won't be charged accommodation fees for those two extra nights?'

'Of course not,' he said, an edge of impatience burring his voice. 'You're now an invited guest.'

'Just needed to be sure,' she said, but there was an impish gleam to her eyes that made him unsure if she was completely serious. He wasn't used to being teased.

He looked pointedly at his watch. 'I suggest you go back downstairs and change.'

She looked down at her jeans and trainers, as if seeing them for the first time. 'Yes, these clothes won't do, will they? I'm warning you, though, I don't have the wardrobe to be a billionaire's escort.' She flushed. 'I mean "escort" in the old-fashioned sense of the word, not…uh…the other.'

'I thought I'd made it very clear that this is strictly business.' Now he felt like rolling his eyes.

'Yes, you did,' she said. 'And I didn't mean…' Her words petered to a halt. She walked back to the desk and picked up her backpack. 'I'll go down to change now. Shall I meet you at the bottom of the stairs in ten minutes?'

He nodded, secretly sceptical about the ten minutes. Never had he known a woman to get ready for a dinner date in that small amount of time.

She headed towards the door. Again, he thought how gracefully she moved. It made watching her do something as simple as walk away a pleasure. But she stopped and turned on her heel to face him again. 'Mr Christophedes, before I go, I want to thank you for…well, for being so reasonable about all this. I appreciate it and I want to assure you that in return I'll do my very best for you with the fake date scenario.'

It gave him a jolt that she called him *Mr Christophedes*. The formal usage felt as if she had put him in his place—an older guy, an employer, someone of a different generation to be kept at a distance.

He didn't know why he didn't like it. But she couldn't keep calling him Mr Christophedes when they were together with Tina Norris. That would give away the game.

Ashleigh didn't wait for an answer and her quickened pace as she left the room made it clear she didn't expect one.

Lukas looked at the doorway for a long moment after she'd left. Who would have thought the maid in his bathtub would turn out to be such an interesting woman?

Ten minutes later, he was amazed to find Ashleigh waiting for him at the base of the staircase. She'd used the time to advantage. He was so taken aback by the result he was momentarily lost for words. Once again, she'd surprised him.

No trace of backpacker remained. She wore a simple black dress, buttoned down the front and belted at the waist, with elbow-length sleeves. The hem stopped just above her knees to display slender legs encased in fine charcoal stockings and finished with low-heeled black pumps.

'Do I look okay for the restaurant?' she said, aware of his overly long inspection.

Her hair had been tamed and pulled half back off her face. She'd darkened around her eyes, which made them look even bluer, and her mouth gleamed with a warm pink lipstick.

'You look very nice,' he said, then cursed inwardly that

he'd used such an overworked English word. *Eisai omorfi* were the words that sprang to his mind—*You look beautiful*. But that would be inappropriate.

'Great, because this is the only dress I've got with me,' she said with a sigh of relief. 'It's what I wear when I'm waitressing at posh parties. Maids in Chelsea doesn't have a uniform—a black dress is required for such occasions. My friend Sophie gave this to me when I started there. She's a fashion designer—when she's not a maid or waitress, that is—she'd made it for herself then adjusted it to fit me.' She smiled. 'But I guess that's too much information, isn't it?'

Lukas was still shaken by his reaction to how good she looked in that dress. It was discreet, modest even, but it fitted snugly and made no secret of her curves, a hint of cleavage in the open neckline, the belt emphasising her narrow waist and the flare of her hips. He had to clear his voice to speak. 'Not really. Now I know you have a friend Sophie who is generous and good to you.'

Ashleigh smiled—not her full-on dazzling smile but halfway to it. 'I went to school in Manchester with Sophie when we were teenagers and we've always stayed in touch. She got me the job too. Then introduced me to two of the other girls at Maids in Chelsea and we've all become friends.' She looked up at him, that smile still hovering around her mouth. 'But none with a sofa available when I needed it.'

Lukas smiled in response. He wouldn't go so far as to say he was glad she'd ended up at his house—but his outrage at her impudence had dissipated.

'You'll be cold when we get outside.' He noticed she had a coat slung over her arm. 'Get your coat on and we'll walk to the restaurant.'

She shrugged on her coat and once again Lukas stared at her, this time in what he feared was ill-concealed dismay. Of course she picked up on it. 'It's not great, is it?' she said of the shabby quilted anorak that didn't meet the hem of her dress.

'Is that the only coat you have?'

'A warm overcoat is not something you need in Bundaberg's tropical climate,' she said. 'I borrowed this from my sister from when she backpacked around Europe. I'm waiting until next payday to buy something more suitable for London.'

'In the meantime, you shiver?' he said.

'Let's just say I walk really fast when I'm outside,' she said. 'Oh, and these help.' From out of her coat pocket she pulled a hideous checked scarf and a pair of knitted mittens and flourished them in front of him. Lukas had to refrain from shuddering his distaste. He might have his issues with his mother but she was the most elegantly dressed woman he knew, and had set the standard for how he expected a woman to dress. He'd have to schedule a shopping expedition for Ashleigh in the morning so she looked the part for their fake date.

'You can't wear that out with me,' he said, too bluntly.

'Oh,' she said, suddenly subdued. Without protest, she slid the odious excuse for a coat off her shoulders. 'Then I guess I'll shiver in just my dress.' With great exaggeration, she wrapped her arms around herself and made her teeth chatter. 'I'll walk really, *really* fast to the restaurant.'

'No need for that,' he said, heading for the cloakroom under the stairs. 'My mother left a coat behind on her last visit. She's a little taller than you but I think it will fit.'

'Your mother won't mind?'

'My mother has so many clothes she's probably forgotten she has it,' he said.

Lukas flicked through the coats and jackets he left here for his own use. 'Here it is,' he said and pulled out a wraparound coat of fine wool in a subtle leopard print with a shawl collar. A faint whiff of his mother's signature perfume drifted to his nostrils. It brought memories of his glamorous mama kissing him goodnight before she headed out for yet another party, leaving him once again with his nanny. He'd grown up loving his nanny more than his mother. He held out the coat to Ashleigh.

'Oh, I *love* it,' she breathed, her eyes wide with admiration. 'Are you sure it's okay for me to wear it?'

'Would I offer if it wasn't?'

'It's just that it looks very expensive.'

'I'm sure it is,' he said. His mother's extravagance wasn't the sole reason his parents' management of the company had brought the business crashing to its knees, but it had certainly contributed to it.

He held the coat open. 'Here, let me help you into it.'

As Ashleigh slid her arms into the coat it brought her close to him. So close he could smell *her* scent—something fresh and light and appealing. Much like Ashleigh herself.

She shrugged the coat over her shoulders, headed to the large mirror on the wall opposite the stairs. There she tied the belt around her waist, adjusted the collar. Then fluffed up her hair and pouted at her image as she scrutinised her appearance, in a gesture that was instinctively feminine. She snuggled into the coat and closed her eyes in bliss. Lukas was stunned by the sensuality of her expression he saw reflected in the mirror.

'This is the most wonderful coat,' she purred as she stepped away from the mirror. 'I've never worn anything like it. Thank you, Mrs Christophedes.' She blew a kiss in the direction of the cloakroom. The warm tones of the leopard print were perfect for her colouring, making her hair seem to flame under the hallway chandelier, lifting her pale skin. She did a graceful little twirl and the hem of the coat swung open to show her legs. *She looked sensational.* 'And thank you too, *Mr* Christo—'

'Lukas,' he said gruffly, keeping his hands fisted by his sides.

'Of course,' she said. *'Lukas.'* His name sounded like a caress on her voice. 'I'll have to get used to calling you that. Be careful not to give the game away when we're on our fake date.'

'Yes,' he said.

He would have to be careful too. When he'd devised the solution to the problem with Tina Norris, he hadn't expected to feel any stirrings of attraction to his pretend girlfriend. *He could not let that happen.*

'You know, *Lukas,*' she said, exaggerating his name. 'You were right. I think I really am going to enjoy this… role playing.' She unleashed the full force of her dazzling smile. 'Let's get started straight away.'

CHAPTER FOUR

ASHLEIGH STOOD NEAR the top of the marble steps that led to the street, stamping her feet in her thin-soled pumps against the cold. It seemed surreal to be on her way out to dinner with Lukas Christophedes—billionaire, business-man, *fake boyfriend*.

As she well knew, it took time to attend to the various locks, bolts and security devices on the glossy black front door. She seized those few minutes to herself to try and sort her chaotic thoughts about the crazy deal she'd struck with him.

But as she watched him she started to shiver—not because of the cold but from delayed reaction as the full impact of her misconduct hit her. Security was vital to the high-end clients of Maids in Chelsea. She'd learned that London SW3 was one of the most desirable postcodes in the UK, possibly even the world. By handing her the keys to this house, Clio had entrusted her with the reputation of the agency—and she had betrayed that trust big time.

She felt she might hyperventilate when she realised how lucky she was to have got off so lightly. Had anyone other than Lukas Christophedes caught her in his bathtub she suspected she would right now be languishing in a police lockup. But his lenient treatment of her was only because she had something to offer him. If he changed his mind, or if she didn't deliver on her part of the bargain, she could still end up enjoying the hospitality of the Kensington and Chelsea constabulary.

Men like Lukas—no matter how charming—didn't get to be billionaires without being ruthless. She would have to play her assigned role to the nines. That meant getting as much as she could out of this evening so she could become the best pretend girlfriend ever. Then, after tomorrow's dinner date was over, she could put him and today's mortifying incident behind her. She took a deep breath to steady herself for the task to come.

Not that spending time with Lukas would exactly be a hardship. As he finished with the security device he turned to face her. Tall and imposing in a superbly tailored, deep charcoal overcoat, he was so strikingly handsome if she'd passed him in the street she would probably have tripped over her feet in her haste to turn and gawk at him. He was intelligent and interesting too. It seemed impossible that such a gorgeous man had to resort to a fake date. One thing was for sure—she could never think of Lukas Christophedes as *boring*.

He narrowed his eyes in the inscrutable way she had already come to recognise. 'You need boots in this weather,' he said. 'Tall black boots.'

She stopped stamping, berating herself for drawing attention to the paucity of her wardrobe. 'Yes,' she said. If he only knew how many of London's enticing shop windows she had lingered at, looking at boots she couldn't possibly afford. Running away from her wedding had cost her in more ways than one. 'Warm boots are on my shopping list.' To be purchased at the Christmas sales. She had to find somewhere to live first, before she bought boots.

He indicated that she go ahead of him down the steps. 'Do you like Italian food?' he asked.

Her tummy threatened to rumble in response. She hastened to speak over it. 'I like any food. Well, pretty well any food. I don't care too much for really hot curries, which is a disadvantage living in London when that's what my friends love best. But Italian? I love Italian. Wouldn't you like to eat Greek?'

'No one cooks Greek food as well as in Greece,' he said, his voice underscored with arrogance.

'I guess not. I've enjoyed Greek food back home in Australia,' she said. 'You know Melbourne is supposed to have the biggest population of Greek people of any city outside of Greece? Not that I'd recognise what was good Greek food or bad.'

Ashleigh knew she was chattering on too much, a habit she would have to curb if she were to be believable as the sophisticated kind of woman a man like this would date. *Lukas and her.* She had to get the script right. Because this might very well turn out to be one of the most life-changing experiences of her life.

'I'll take you to my favourite Italian restaurant on the King's Road,' he said.

'I'd like that,' she said.

As soon as she turned into the street, she gasped as a gust of cold, damp air hit her, burning her lungs, numbing her cheeks. Her eyes started to water and she blinked against the smarting tears.

'You're not used to the cold, are you?' Lukas asked.

'Not yet,' she said, rubbing her hands together then sliding them into the pockets of her glorious borrowed coat. 'I'm still getting acclimatised. Of course I spent very cold, wet winters in Manchester when I was younger but that was years ago. I've lived in tropical heat ever since.'

Immediately, Lukas unwound the finely woven grey scarf from around his neck. 'Wear this and keep it up around near your face.'

Dumbfounded, Ashleigh shook her head. 'There's no need—I can't possibly take your scarf.' It was all very well to wear his mother's clothing; to wear *his* clothes seemed way too intimate.

Did he intend to put it around her neck? She put up her hand to stop him and in doing so grazed his. At the brief contact, she dropped her hand—then regretted it immediately. A pretend girlfriend wouldn't react like that at such a casual touch. A pretend girlfriend *certainly* shouldn't feel such a zing of awareness.

'But you must,' he said, holding the scarf out to her. 'I insist.' It was not so much a demand but a statement not to be disputed.

Pretend girlfriend or not, it would be ungracious not to take the scarf when it had been so thoughtfully offered. Tentatively, she took it from him. The fabric was soft, cashmere and silk most likely, and warm from his body heat. She wound it around her neck, tucked it inside her collar and up around her chin, and immediately felt several degrees cosier.

'Thank you,' she said simply, too shaken to say anything else.

The scarf was scented with something spicy and woody—cedar perhaps?—and distinctly male. *Him.* The scent of Lukas Christophedes—the man she needed to get to know by this time tomorrow evening. The man she would have to fight crazy stirrings of attraction for. There was too much of a fairy tale feel about all this—she couldn't allow herself to believe any of it could be real.

'But now you'll be cold without your scarf,' she said.

'I'll have to walk really, *really* fast then,' he said, taking an exaggerated deeper stride.

She laughed, surprised at the unexpected touch of humour. Otherwise he seemed so *serious*.

'Does it get cold in Greece in winter?' she asked. 'I always think of it as a summer place, all blue skies and even bluer waters.'

'Even the islands get snow in winter,' he said. 'I live in Athens where it does get cold but not bitterly so. Then we have unexpected warm days—*halkionis meres*—halcyon days when the sun is shining and winter is temporarily banished.'

They were talking about the weather. She'd need to know more than that if she were to fool the astute businesswoman they'd be dining with tomorrow. But where to start without seeming to interrogate him?

They walked to the end of his street, turned into The Vale and then right into the King's Road, heading west. Far from walking really, really fast, Lukas kept his pace to hers. *As if they actually were a couple.* At this time of evening Chelsea was buzzing. Trees were strung with thousands of tiny lights, the shops decorated for Christmas, snatches of festive music greeting them as they walked by the buildings. London at Christmastime was magic—she was so glad she had decided to stay here.

'Where shall we say we met?' she asked, having to raise her voice over the sound of a red number eleven bus rumbling by. 'We can't say Greece, because I've never been to your country. I did a whistle-stop European bus tour when I was a student but we didn't go there.'

'We'll rule out Greece, then. I believe my potential business partner has vacationed on the island of Santorini many times and would immediately sniff out any fraud.'

'Have you ever been to Australia?' she asked.

'No. Although it is on my bucket list.'

'So "no" to Australia, then. Seems our common ground is England. We'll have to say we met somewhere on British soil.'

'But not in my bathroom.'

Was there a hint of teasing in his expression? Ashleigh couldn't see to be sure. She squirmed at the memory of their first meeting. 'No,' she said. 'Definitely not.' Maybe she would tell Sophie about that incident but no one else. She would never live it down.

'When were you in Manchester?' Lukas asked.

'When I was fifteen. Twelve years ago. And Sophie tells me the city has changed a lot.'

'Manchester won't work either.' He paused. 'So you're twenty-seven now?'

'You sound surprised.'

'I thought you were younger. Perhaps twenty-three, twenty-four.'

Ashleigh gritted her teeth. She couldn't let him know how much that assumption irritated her. 'People often take me for younger—and treat me as younger.' Especially her family—right now refusing to believe she knew how she wanted to live her own life. 'I'll be twenty-eight in March and am quite grown up, thank you.' She couldn't keep the tart edge from her words.

'I'll keep that in mind,' he said with that trace of a smile that lifted his somewhat severe face.

'How old are you?' she asked. If there'd been time, she would have looked him up on the Internet. As it was, she was flying blind. *He was a total stranger.*

'Thirty-four.'

'So you were okay with thinking I was more than ten years younger than you?'

'In my family it is not uncommon for the men to be much older than their women. My father is considerably older than my mother.'

'I see,' she said. She'd only ever dated men around her own age. It might be interesting to get to know a man six years older—even if they weren't *really* dating. 'There's so much I need to know about you if we're to appear authentic as a couple.'

'That is true. Ask me anything you need to know.'

'And you ask me anything too,' she said. Not that there

was a lot to discover. Her life had been anything but exciting. *Until now.*

They walked in silence while Ashleigh wrote herself a mental memo of questions. She fired off the one at the top of her list. 'I probably don't need to ask this, but I'm assuming you're not married?'

'I have never been married,' he said. 'I never will marry.'

His vehemence surprised her. 'That answers that, then,' she said. 'I'm…uh…sure you have your reasons.' He didn't rush to enlighten her as to those reasons. 'What about serious girlfriends?'

'Not recently. And none that should concern you.'

'Not married. No serious girlfriends. Okay.' *This wasn't going well.*

'My friends tell me I'm married to my work.'

'Really? That doesn't sound much fun.'

His laugh was short and cynical. 'One thing you would be expected to know about me is that I took over the family business when it was on the verge of bankruptcy. I was aged twenty-one when I set myself the goal of turning it around. There hasn't been much opportunity for *fun.*'

'That's quite a story. You must be proud of such an achievement.'

'Yes,' he said shortly.

'But what's the point of being a billionaire and not having any fun?'

Lukas stopped so abruptly she nearly crashed into him. *'What?'* he said.

'I said… I said… Well, I think you heard what I said. I mean, life's all about laughter and love and…' Her voice dwindled away. 'Forget it. On to the next question.'

He stared at her in what she could only describe as astonishment that she should be so impertinent. 'My life is about responsibility and hard work and righting the wrongs of the past,' he said.

She didn't dare ask what those wrongs might be. Not yet, anyway.

'I get that,' she said, even though she didn't. *They came from different worlds.* She forced her voice to sound bright and cheerful. *What the heck had she got herself into?*

'Moving on to my next question. You speak such perfect English. Did you study here?' His voice was deep and steady, with that hint of an accent to add to its appeal. She could close her eyes and just enjoy hearing him talk.

'I went to university here in London for a while. But I was already fluent. I had an English nanny from birth and studied the language all through school. My family considered it important that I spoke good English. There is another reason so many young Greek people speak English—American and English music and movies are not often dubbed into Greek.'

'That's a powerful incentive to learn a language. I wish I'd had something like that to inspire me.'

'Do you speak another language?'

'I studied Indonesian at school. But, apart from vacations in Bali, I've never really used the language so am not at all fluent.' She looked up at him. 'Maybe you can teach me some Greek?'

'There is not much I can teach you in the short time we will be together,' he said. *Putting her in her place.*

'Of course,' she said. 'But could you please just tell me the Greek for "darling"?'

He frowned. 'What for?'

She wanted to sigh heavily at his obtuseness but didn't dare. Wasn't it obvious? 'An endearment here and there might add to the authenticity of our…uh…relationship.'

'Agápi mou,' he said finally.

'I beg your pardon?'

'It means *darling*, or *my love*—*agápi mou*,' he said with an edge of impatience.

Ashleigh repeated the words. 'How did I do?' she asked.

'Not bad at all,' he said with an expressive lifting of his dark eyebrows.

'Thank you.' In her head she went over and over the phrase so it would seem natural should she get the chance to drop it into the conversation.

They walked further, past the fashionable restaurant that had in some earlier incarnation been a garage. She'd enjoyed a very expensive cup of coffee there with Sophie the first day she'd come to Chelsea to meet Clio and be interviewed for the position with the agency.

'How far is the restaurant?' she asked.

'A few blocks further down,' he said.

'Towards Land's End?'

He smiled. 'World's End is in Chelsea. Land's End is in Cornwall, right down at the southernmost part of England. They say if you walk from John O'Groats at the top of Scotland to Land's End you've walked the length of Britain.'

Ashleigh gave herself a mental slam to the forehead. 'Of course, what a stupid mistake. I've heard my English grandparents say that. You know more about this country than I do and I've got English blood.'

'I like London. That's why I bought the house here. Chelsea is so English but also cosmopolitan. I can enjoy a certain anonymity here.'

'I love it too,' Ashleigh said. She was about to tell him how she'd felt immediately at home in London when she'd got here but didn't want to remind him of how completely she'd made herself at home in his house.

The *ristorante* was large and noisy with clatter and chatter; delicious aromas wafted to meet her. Ashleigh wondered how she would be able to talk privately with Lukas. But he was greeted by name by the beaming *maître d'* who took their coats—she hoped hers wouldn't get lost because no way in a million years would she ever be able to afford to replace it—and ushered them to a quiet table in an alcove. Reluctantly, she handed over her borrowed scarf—already she missed its warm caress with the heady hint of his scent.

The waiter pulled out her chair for her. But before she sat down she rose up on tiptoe and deliberately planted a lingering kiss on Lukas's cheek, then trailed her fingers from his cheek, down his neck to stop at his collar. 'This is delightful, *agápi mou*,' she murmured in the throatiest, sexiest murmur she could muster. Then looked up into his eyes and pouted, as if inviting a kiss in return.

CHAPTER FIVE

TAKEN UNAWARES, LUKAS froze at Ashleigh's touch. For a heart-stopping moment she stayed intimately close, her curves against his chest, her sweetly scented hair tickling his face. She whispered in his ear, her voice laced with amusement at his reaction. 'Try to look like you're enjoying this—we're meant to be in love.'

Then she sat down on her chair opposite him, flashing a radiant smile to the waiter as she thanked him for his elaborate play at shaking out her linen napkin and placing it on her lap.

'Bella inglese,' the waiter murmured in Italian—*beautiful English lady.*

Lukas thought that was far too fulsome a compliment to *his* date. Besides, Ashleigh was Australian not English. Though he could not blame the waiter for his mistake; with her copper hair, pale skin and blue eyes, Ashleigh looked like she belonged in this country.

She had flung herself into playing her part as his girlfriend with gusto. Now *he* had to take up the role of doting boyfriend.

Ashleigh was right. Tonight was a rehearsal for tomorrow. He should react like a man smitten with a woman. Trouble was, that would be only too easy. He had allowed himself to get entranced by her closeness. By her fresh, warm scent. The touch of her lovely mouth on his cheek. By the sudden, sensual awareness her closeness had aroused.

He'd been too shocked by his body's reaction to respond in his fake date role. The waiter wasn't wrong—*she was beautiful*. And way more enticing than he had expected. He would have to rein in his libido if he were to remain as impartial as he needed to be to play this game. *It was all pretend*.

'Of course,' he said. He reached over across the table to take both her hands in his, look deep into her eyes. 'It's good to be here with you, *agápi mou*. I've had a long, stressful day.'

'My day has been quite exciting,' she murmured. 'Especially when you found me without any clothes on and...' He knew she was referring to the incident in his bathtub but, the way she murmured it, any person overhearing her would assume she was referring to something rather more intimate. If only they'd heard how she'd screeched at him.

'Now we can relax over a good meal,' he said. He released her hands, realising he had held them for a moment longer than was required for play-acting.

Ashleigh's lips curved up into a smile that hinted at her dimples. 'That's more like it,' she whispered. 'The more practice we get in this evening, the less we risk seeming stilted tomorrow. What if someone you know saw us behaving like it's a business meeting? Which I guess it is, in a way.' *Did she feel even the slightest stirring of what he was feeling?*

'Business? Yes, it is and the interplay between us must be believable,' he said. But he would have to remain on guard against the attraction he felt towards her. He did not want any distractions from the main game, which was—as always—the business. 'We have to get this charade right—it's important I seal that deal with Tina Norris.'

'Tina Norris? That's the...the cougar's name?'

He kept his voice low as he spoke. His business dealings were not for public broadcast. 'She's the CEO of a major distributor of domestic appliances and consumer electronic products to retailers, businesses, hotels, property developers and so on. Tina inherited the business from her father, then nearly lost it in a nasty divorce.'

Ashleigh's face softened with sympathy. 'The poor woman—how awful for her.'

Lucas put up a warning hand. 'Don't go feeling sorry for her. Tina Norris is a barracuda. But she is formidably effective in her business and I see a synergy between our two companies. I want to get on board with the Norris group.'

He thought of Ashleigh's perceptive comment. *On board* with Tina but not *in bed* with her. He could not share with Ashleigh—or anyone—the scars of an old aversion that made even the thought of sexual advances from cougar Tina send shudders up his spine.

He'd been fourteen, already tall and well-built with a man's body but still with the heart and soul and idealism of a boy. At one of his parents' infamous parties, his mother's friend had stumbled into his bedroom, drunk. He'd been too naïve to recognise she'd had seduction on her mind. When she'd made her intentions clear he'd been repulsed—and frightened. His shouts had brought his parents to his room. His mother—drunk herself—had found it amusing. His father had mocked him—he'd thought his son was a fool to pass up an opportunity for initiation by a skilled older woman. They had not protected him.

'That's what tomorrow night will be all about—securing a business connection, while playing down any personal relationship with Tina,' he concluded.

Ashleigh nodded. 'That's good to know so I have an idea of what she's like. Now I have to find out as much as I can about you. And you me, of course.'

He leaned over. 'There's one important thing you should know about me.'

Ashleigh quirked a perfectly arched auburn eyebrow. 'And that is?'

'I get irritable when I'm hungry.'

She smiled. 'Is that a hint that you'd like to order? Because I can't stop looking at that impressive antipasto display.'

By the time he and Ashleigh had returned to their table, their plates laden with a selection of Italian salami, prosciutto, marinated octopus, roasted vegetables, cheeses and olives, he was feeling more relaxed. The waiter took their orders for the next course and they settled back to eat.

Lukas noticed Ashleigh was hungry. Although she ate her starter slowly, he could see she was holding back, pretending restraint. If he wasn't there, he suspected the plate would be emptied very quickly and she'd be back up at the antipasto table for a second helping. He wondered when she'd last eaten.

'Why are you so short of money?' he asked her. 'You're educated, you held a responsible job.'

Startled, she stopped with a spear of asparagus that had been wrapped in prosciutto halfway to her mouth. She put it back onto her plate with a look of regret. 'Because I cancelled my wedding so close to the date of the ceremony. There were consequences. Hefty deposits on the venue and the catering that were not refundable. An unworn wedding gown to pay for. It was a considerable burden to bear on my own.'

He frowned. 'Surely your fiancé was also responsible for the debt?'

She shook her head. 'It was my fault there was no wedding. He didn't see that he should pay for my "rash" decision.'

'He was unhappy you called it off?'

'Very unhappy.' She looked down at her plate.

Lukas could understand that. Even on this short acquaintance he could see how a man could be captivated by Ashleigh Murphy. Not him, of course. He was beyond being mesmerised by a beautiful woman. Especially a woman like this. In his assessment, he realised she was not the type for a no-strings fling—which was the only kind of relationship he did these days. Yet there was something appealing about her. There were attractive women everywhere in this restaurant. But none that caught his attention. His eyes were only drawn to Ashleigh, the backpacker he'd found in his bathtub.

'Did your fiancé not try to get you to reconsider?' he asked.

'My *ex*-fiancé, you mean. He begged me to change my mind,' she said, with a twist to her mouth that spoke not of regret but of something else. Irritation? Contempt, even? 'But I wouldn't. No one would believe me that I didn't want to marry him. Not him. Not my family. Not even the marriage celebrant—whose fee I also had to pay, by the way.'

'That seems unfair.'

'I think so too. If Dan were the gentleman he claims to be, he would have paid his share. But it's the house that has really crippled me.'

'The house?'

'It seemed a good idea to buy a house together for us to live in after the wedding. I put up my share of the deposit, signed the mortgage documents. My savings are all tied up in the house.'

'Why don't you sell the house if there is to be no marriage?'

'Dan refuses to put it on the market. Why, I don't know. I will *never* live in that house.'

Lukas had some sympathy for her faraway fiancé. To be so close to securing this lovely woman as his wife, only to have her run away. No wonder the man was unhappy. However, he doubted the break was as final as Ashleigh said it was. He had learned from bitter experience that a woman could claim to be free while still being very much entangled with another man. Lukas would not be surprised if this Dan turned up in London to take her back. 'Perhaps he's hoping you will return.'

'He'll be hoping for ever, if that's the case. Ironically, it was buying the house that was the beginning of the end for me. I wanted to live at the beach. Can you believe when a house next door to my parents went on sale he wanted us to buy that? I had to fight for the beach house. Why I didn't back out then I don't know.'

She shook her head in disbelief and a strand of her bright hair worked its way free from its constraint and fell across her cheek. Lukas fought the urge to reach over and push it back off her face. If Ashleigh were a real date he wouldn't hesitate to touch her in such an intimate manner—but this was all pretend. He kept his hands firmly on his side of the table.

'In traditional Greek culture it would be seen as admirable for a woman to live close to her parents,' he said. He chose to live in central Athens, in the shadow of the Acropolis, away from his parents in the leafy green suburb where the wealthiest families congregated.

Ashleigh scowled—an expression that, far from being forbidding, looked cute on her. 'It doesn't work like that where I come from. I want to be independent of my parents, not living in their pockets. And wouldn't you think a husband would want his new wife to himself?'

Oh, yes. If he had a woman like this for his wife he would not share her with anyone. Not that he *ever* wanted a wife. The example of his parents and others in their social set had turned him right off marriage. The sickening hypocrisy of it all. That last summer of freedom on the islands, there had been a girl—a beautiful, vivacious French girl named Céline who had inspired in him thoughts of love and commitment and family. But the painful way it had ended had extinguished any such thoughts from his heart. Nothing and no one had since breathed life into those ashes.

'Most men would want privacy with their bride,' he said, in what he hoped was a non-committal manner.

Her scowl deepened. 'It was when he tried to bulldoze me into buying that house that I realised how stultifying it would be to be married to Dan,' she continued. 'He eventually agreed to the beach house but I knew even as I signed the documents that I shouldn't be. I'd be stepping straight into middle age. My dreams would be totally subsumed by his limited vision. I *had* to get away.'

'So you came to London?'

'And here I'm staying. Though of course my family don't believe me. They think I'll go crawling back to Dan.'

He frowned. 'Why would they think that?'

She looked down at her plate. 'Because I'd broken up with him before and gone back.' She looked back up at Lukas, her mouth twisted. 'More than once, actually. Mistake compounded by mistake, I see now.'

He paused. 'Then perhaps you will return to him.'

'Never,' she said with such vehemence her eyes seemed to spark blue fire.

He didn't believe her. A woman could lie so convincingly that the boyfriend or fiancé or ex-husband meant nothing. Never again would he let himself get caught up— even for the most casual of liaisons—with a woman who was still involved with another man. Not that Ashleigh's ties to her so-called former fiancé back in Australia affected him at all. He wouldn't see her again after tomorrow night.

Just then their main courses arrived—steamed sea bass

for him and organic chicken with balsamic vinegar reduction for her. The meal was complemented with a dry white wine from Tuscany. Ashleigh's eyes lit up at the sight of her plate. He doubted she would still be hungry after that.

When she pushed back her plate with a sigh of satisfaction and some food still left on it, he was pleased. She needed someone to care for her.

Ashleigh reached over and put her hand on his forearm in a gesture that to other eyes would seem affectionate and familiar. 'Thank you,' she said. 'I can't remember when I had such an excellent meal.'

Any meal more like it, from the way she'd polished off that chicken. He couldn't help but worry about her. How could she survive in one of the most expensive cities in the world on a maid's income?

'Would you like dessert?'

'Not for me,' she said.

'Or me,' he said. He was disciplined with his eating and exercise. And kept an iron-clad guard on his emotions. His heart had been battered once too often by the betrayal of the parents who should have protected him, by the careless cruelty of Céline.

Ashleigh treated him to her enchanting smile. 'I noticed you sneaking a glance at your watch. I know you've had a big day. But there are a few more things I wanted to ask you about yourself.'

'Fire away,' he said.

'Do you have brothers or sisters?'

'I'm an only child.' So often as a lonely, confused child he'd longed for a companion. Though it was as well his parents had not been entrusted with the care of a daughter. As an adult, he'd wished he'd had someone on his side to help sort out the mess of the once thriving business his parents had inherited from his grandfather. 'You?'

'An older sister. She's six years older than me. When I

was born she thought I was her baby. She still thinks I'm her baby.' The edge of irritation to her voice hinted at ongoing conflict with her family. She was older than he had at first thought. But she seemed to have the desperate need for independence of someone younger. It intrigued him, but he did not want to be intrigued by her. She was here to serve a purpose and that was all.

'How long have you been in London?' he asked.

'Three weeks,' she said.

'Good. That's long enough,' he said.

Her brow pleated to a frown. 'For what?'

'For us to have met and started to date—theoretically, that is,' he said. 'To try and pretend we've known each other for longer could be disastrous.'

She nodded. 'Good point. As far as Tina Norris is concerned, we met shortly after I arrived in London. Were you actually in London then?'

'No. But I could have been. She wouldn't know otherwise.'

'That's the timing sorted. What about the place we met—theoretically, of course?'

She screwed up her face in a delightful expression of concentration. 'I'm thinking about where I went as soon as I got here. All the tourist places, of course. The museums and art galleries. Big Ben. The Tower of London—I adored the Tower. Oxford Street. Not likely to be places where you would be.' She paused. 'I did a lot of walking around, just taking in the atmosphere, the Christmas lights, the shop windows. It's feasible we could have bumped into each other.' She smiled. 'I've had a light-bulb moment. Didn't you say you were at The Shard today?'

'My meeting this afternoon with Tina was there, yes.'

'How about we met in the bar at The Shard? One time I went there with Sophie. There were guys like you in suits, guys who—'

'Wanted to buy you a drink?' *Of course they did.*

'Exactly. Why couldn't one of those guys have been you?'

'Did you accept a drink from one of them?' This could *not* be an inexplicable surge of jealousy.

'No. I'd just run away from my wedding and was in no mood to meet men. Getting picked up by a guy in a bar—even such a salubrious bar—was the last thing I wanted.'

'And now?'

'I want to be single. Being half of a couple for so long was like being caught in a trap that was slowly strangling me. I'm happy to *pretend* to be your date. In real life, I'm not interested in dating anyone. I just want to be *me.*'

More and more, Ashleigh sounded like the ideal pretend date. He couldn't have found anyone more suitable if he'd gone looking. She would not make any demands on him. Not want to turn fake into real. There'd be no dramas and wounded feelings when he ended things with her. He would take her to dinner tomorrow night, let her stay the night at his house and then *goodbye, Ashleigh.*

'Meeting at The Shard is an excellent idea for a cover story,' he said.

'That's settled, then,' she said. 'Next step is to get things straight about how it all went down.'

He thought for a moment. 'I was visiting London and met a business associate for a drink. He went home. I noticed you with your friend.'

'You asked me would I like a drink.' Whether unconsciously or not, Ashleigh had adopted a flirtatious manner, eyes widened, head thrown back, lips pouting. *Enticing.* That was the word for her.

'And you immediately said yes.'

'How could I refuse?' she said. 'I was so impressed by your Greek handsomeness and charming manner.' The flirtatiousness came naturally to her. He could see how a man could become ensnared. Lucky this charade was only for two nights.

He smiled. 'Is handsomeness actually a word in English?'

'If it isn't it should be. You are very handsome. In real life if you'd asked to buy me a drink I might even have said yes.'

'I'm flattered.' Oddly enough, he was. He tried to think of a compliment he could return to her without seeming overly effusive. Whatever he came up with sounded either mundane or too much.

She tilted her head to one side. 'I'm waiting.'

He frowned. 'For what?'

'I'm giving you a prompt: now you're meant to say you were smitten by my beauty.'

He hadn't thought of that. 'I was smitten by your beauty,' he repeated in a monotone, fighting the smile twitching at the corners of his mouth.

'Not like that! With meaning,' she said, a little crossly. Then stopped. 'You have to take this seriously, you know. It won't work if you don't. After all, it was your idea and it's your business deal at stake.'

He was grateful for the reminder. *This was just a business deal.* He leaned across the table to her. So close their heads nearly touched. He looked deep into her incredibly blue eyes, purposefully made his voice a tone deeper and seductive. 'I was smitten by your beauty, your gorgeous hair, your perfect skin, your shapely body. Then intrigued by your Australianness.'

'I…er…don't think that's an actual word,' she said and her voice wasn't quite steady.

'It's a word now,' he said.

Then he reached out and smoothed the errant lock of bright hair from her face, his fingers lingering on her smooth skin as he tucked it behind her ear. She flushed and shivered at his touch. Her eyes glittered all shades of blue. He couldn't help but remember how she'd looked in his bathtub, naked but for those bubbles. At the powerful rush of awareness, he withdrew his hand as if he'd come much too close to a flame.

'Th...that's more like it,' she said. 'I think we can...can make it look like we are actually attracted to each other without too much trouble.'

'Indeed we can,' he said. It would be *hiding* his attraction that would be the problem. He leaned back in his chair, still shaken by his reaction. 'One more thing,' he said. 'What were you wearing when I met you in the bar at The Shard?'

She indicated her black dress. 'This dress.'

'Not jeans?'

'No.'

'Or trainers?'

'Of course not.'

'And your anorak?' He couldn't keep the distaste from his voice.

'It was in the cloakroom.' She frowned. 'Where is this leading to?'

He shook his head. 'Your clothes. They won't do. A woman like Tina Norris would never be convinced you're my girlfriend if you dress like a maid.'

'This is actually my waitress dress but I get what you mean,' she said, with a downward droop of her mouth.

'It's a nice enough dress, but you should be wearing designer fashion.'

'I can't afford—'

He didn't like the crestfallen look on her face that his words had caused. 'I know you can't. Which is why I will take you shopping tomorrow to ensure you're suitably dressed. At my expense.'

Her eyes widened. 'Take me shopping? Buy me clothes?

But you can't do that. I... I can't accept clothes from you. It wouldn't be right.'

A woman who didn't jump at the chance of a wealthy man wielding a credit card? Ashleigh really was very different from the women he usually associated with. Women who revelled in the lifestyle his wealth could give them. Who were placated by a gift of expensive jewellery when he ended things with them.

'I can and you will,' he said. 'I want this deal to go through. You have to be dressed appropriately. End of story.'

'I... I don't know what to say,' she said, raising troubled eyes to his.

'"Yes" will do,' he said. 'I will take you shopping in Bond Street tomorrow morning.'

Then he leaned over to kiss her lightly on the cheek. 'Relax and enjoy it, *agápi mou*.'

CHAPTER SIX

ASHLEIGH WAS NOT the kind of person to be easily intimidated. But she'd learned on her first few days in London that a look from the snooty shop assistants on London's super-posh Bond Street could shrivel her ego to the size of a thimble.

Her friend Sophie lived and breathed fashion. Ashleigh was as interested in clothes and shoes as most women, but her knowledge of luxury, high-end labels extended to what she saw in glossy magazines at the hairdresser.

Sophie had taken Ashleigh window-shopping not long after she'd arrived. Together they'd traipsed the length of combined Old Bond Street and New Bond Street— Ashleigh looking around her in awe. She'd rubbernecked at the opulent elegance of the Victorian era Royal Arcade. Stopped to stare at the Christmas decorations. Sophie told her that Bond Street was one of the most expensive shopping streets in the world and she could well believe it. It was lined with elegant shops, each more luxurious than the last. Each showcased luxury labels—some of which Ashleigh had heard of, others she'd had no idea existed. Not just clothes but accessories, shoes, jewellery, even chocolates.

'I can't afford to buy anything in these designer shops,' Sophie had explained. 'But I like to look. Not to copy ideas for my own designs but to note details like the cut of a collar or the placement of a pocket and to swoon over the beautiful fabrics.'

'One day it will be your designs people will be swooning over,' Ashleigh had said loyally. She had always believed in her friend's talent—right back to when they were schoolgirls in Manchester and Sophie had been so welcoming to the new girl from Australia.

On that shopping day with Sophie, Ashleigh had dared to venture into one shop to ask the price of a belt she thought her sister would like. She'd nearly fainted at the price the saleswoman had quoted—and the look of disdain delivered at her along with it.

'Big mistake,' Sophie had hissed on their way out. 'These people think if you have to ask the price you can't afford to shop there. The way to behave is to look at everything with equal disdain—be as snooty as they are right back at them.'

Ashleigh had laughed. 'I don't know that I can do disdain. Especially when everything in these shops is so wonderful. I can only dream that I could ever buy anything here.'

Now she was discovering that shopping on Bond Street in the company of billionaire Lukas Christophedes was an altogether different experience.

It started with the discreetly luxurious limousine and chauffeur that picked her and Lukas up from the townhouse to drive them into the heart of London. 'The driver will keep the car somewhere nearby, ready to load with your parcels,' Lukas explained.

'Parcels? Aren't we buying just a dress for me to wear tonight?' Ashleigh asked.

'You're out with me in public as my girlfriend. You have to look the part. Our first stop will be for clothes for you to change into immediately.'

'You mean shop for clothes to go shopping in?'

'Yes.'

Was he serious? A thrill of excitement ran through her. She'd seen so many clothes she'd coveted that day with Sophie. Now she might get to try them on.

She was sitting next to Lukas in the back seat of the car, the seat so wide there was no danger of any accidental touching. Not that she was worried that Lukas would cross boundaries. She'd locked her bedroom door last night, just in case she had misread the situation with him, but she need not have worried. It was she who had lain awake for some time, imagining him lying alone in the enormous bed in his room down the corridor, his long limbs and power-ful body sprawled across the sheets. *Did he sleep naked?*

At the *ristorante* when he'd leaned across to tuck her hair back from her face, she'd felt a jolt of attraction so powerful that it had rendered her momentarily speechless. When she'd agreed to his deal—not that she'd had much choice—she hadn't expected *that*. It was disconcerting, to say the least.

But he had shown every sign of being a gentleman. It was her who'd been bothered by fantasies of him naked in bed just a few rooms away. But when she'd eventually drifted off to sleep it was with a warm sense of security and she'd slept better than she had on her first illicit two nights alone in his house.

'Is that really necessary? I'll be wearing your mother's gorgeous coat when I get out of this nice warm car.'

'But when you take it off your black work trousers give you away.'

'They're not bad trousers,' she protested. 'And the shirt is new.'

'Straight from the high street,' he said.

'Yes,' she said, her voice trailing away. Up until this mo-ment she'd thought shopping in the big high street chains was as exciting as her shopping would ever get. Now, the way Lukas said it, 'high street' sounded like an insult. Did she really look that bad? The answer would have to be yes if she was to be mingling with billionaires.

He seemed to sense her sudden stab of insecurity. 'If you're performing in a play, you have to be in the right costume, yes? Think of this as getting your wardrobe right and enjoy it.'

Lukas as wardrobe master? Why not?

'Let the fun begin,' she said, determined to put aside any qualms she had about a man who was still very much a stranger buying her clothes. After all, she would move out of the maid's bedroom tomorrow and leave her borrowed finery behind her. Then she would never see him again.

For the first time she felt a pang of regret about that. He was an extraordinarily attractive man. She wished... *No.* There was no point in wishing they had met under different circumstances. That would never have happened—not the maid and the billionaire.

Excitement began to buzz through her as the car turned into Bond Street. When she'd visited with Sophie, they'd come by Tube. Did coming with Lukas in a chauffeur-driven car make the Christmas decorations shine brighter? She stared in wonder at the sight of a famous jewellery store completely wrapped in glittering Christmas ribbon like a multi-million-dollar festive parcel. Other shops glittered and shone with decorations in among the flags that flew above to proclaim the famous labels. She craned her head to see if the theatrical works of art in the shop display windows had changed since her last visit. Regent Street with its famous Christmas decorations was only a street away. She must come back soon in the evening to see this area at its festive best.

The closer it got to Christmas, the more people there were on the street. Everywhere she looked, fashionably dressed people—men as well as women—swept past on the narrow pavements, their arms strung with shopping bags emblazoned with famous designer labels. Whatever dress she ended up with, Ashleigh vowed, she would keep the bag as a souvenir.

The limousine dropped them off outside the starkly minimalist store of a well-known European designer label. It glided off, no doubt to join the other limousines double parked along the street. Ashleigh wrapped the beautiful leopard print coat around her like armour. Last time she'd been here she'd been wearing the past-its-use-by-date anorak.

'We should be able to quickly find something for you to change into in here,' Lukas said as he swept her into the shop with arrogant assurance. She thrilled at the feeling that nothing and no one intimidated this man. Certainly not a shop assistant. That particular brand of wimpishness belonged to Ashleigh.

Lukas exuded an air of wealth and confidence. A well groomed young female shop assistant almost tripped over her stilettos in an effort to reach him before her colleagues did. She'd probably assessed the cost of his suit and the value of his watch as he'd walked through the door.

Ashleigh stood meekly by his side—not that she usually did meek but she was too overwhelmed to be anything but subdued. She shifted from foot to foot, not sure of how this would work. She glanced up at Lukas. Would he choose what she wore or would she have a say in her play-acting wardrobe?

The assistant welcomed Lukas almost to the point of fawning on him. But Ashleigh didn't miss the sideways narrowed glance directed at her. The woman actually folded her arms in front of her and looked her up and down—out of the line of Lukas's sight, of course. As she did, Ashleigh recognised her as one of the people who had been dismissive of her and Sophie when they'd ventured into this shop on their window-shopping day. That crossed arm thing had annoyed her then and it annoyed her now.

'My friend has just arrived from Australia and needs some winter clothes,' Lukas said. It went without saying that he would be picking up the tab.

Again that sideward glance. Ashleigh realised the woman couldn't place her. She had immediately sized up her bargain basement shoes and clothes, noted the anomaly of the designer coat and speculated about her relationship to Lukas.

She thinks I'm his mistress, Ashleigh realised. Or worse—that he was buying her in some way. She got the distinct impression she was being judged as inferior to the handsome tall man beside her.

While Ashleigh might have been intimidated into *meek* she was never going to do *inferior*. And right now, as Sophie had suggested, she determined to muster up an attitude of disdain.

She straightened her shoulders and lifted her chin. Schooling her face into a mask of critical indifference, she let her gaze wander across the featureless mannequins dressed in various minimalist garments in tones of grey and winter white. She took a step towards the chrome racks with their artful displays of just a few garments, not deigning to pull anything close for an inspection.

Then she looked back up at Lukas. 'Nothing appeals, I'm afraid, darling,' she said finally. The clothes were fabulous but Bond Street was full of shops like this and surely her presence by Lukas's side demanded a better attitude.

His dark brows rose. 'Are you sure? We've only just got here and I wanted you to have a complete new wardrobe more suitable for this cold weather.'

She dimpled up at him. 'Quite sure.' She met the barely disguised dismay of the assistant. She hoped the woman regretted her bad manners as much as she was no doubt regretting her lost commission.

'Whatever you want, *agápi mou*,' he said, turning on his heel.

'I think I'll find what I want a few doors up,' Ashleigh said, naming an equally well-known designer. Then she tucked her arm through Lukas's and stalked out of the store.

Back out on the pavement, she smiled at him. 'Sorry about that, but I didn't want to give any business to someone who was so judgemental and downright rude. Did you see the way she looked at me?' She kept her arm tucked in his, liking the feeling, unable to stop herself from wondering what it would be like to have the real-life right to walk arm in arm with him.

'My mother always swears you get better service if you already look the part,' he said. 'I guess she's right.' Ashleigh appreciated that there was no hint of *I told you so* in his voice.

'Your mother sounds interesting,' Ashleigh said. 'Her taste in coats is excellent, that's for sure.'

'She's certainly an expert shopper,' he said drily.

The reception was so much better at their next stop. A courteous sales associate introduced herself first to Ashleigh and then to Lukas and listened as Ashleigh explained her needs.

The woman handed Lukas over to another associate, who settled him in a comfortable chair and asked him if he would like a coffee. Ashleigh found herself ushered into a roomy, beautifully furnished changing room. Her sales associate returned with a choice of garments for her to try. She felt giddy at the number of zeros on the price tags but reminded herself that, as far as Lukas was concerned, anything he purchased was an investment in a potentially lucrative business deal. *Enjoy every minute of this,* she told herself, *it will never happen again.*

Finally, she settled on a pair of perfectly cut slim black trousers with a narrow belt, and a fine knit cashmere and silk sweater in a flattering shade of charcoal. They were perfect under the leopard print coat. She didn't dare look at the price tags—though she had a very good idea of what just the belt alone would cost.

The sales associate asked if she would like to show Lukas what she had chosen. It was her only discreet reference that she realised who would be paying the bill.

Ashleigh tiptoed out of the changing room. Lukas was engrossed in the thoughtfully provided newspaper. What if this were for real and this handsome man waiting for her really was hers? That he would notice she was there and give her that slow smile she already found so compelling? The thought gave her an unwarranted shiver of excitement. But she could not let herself forget for even an instant that this was all a charade.

'What do you think?' she asked.

He looked up, startled. She couldn't read all the expressions that flashed across his face but admiration was certainly one of them. She flushed at the intensity of his gaze. 'Good,' he said. 'But you need boots. Black high-heeled boots.'

Ashleigh and her helpful sales associate were only too happy to oblige.

Lukas was both pleased and amused at the way Ashleigh sashayed into the designer shops with so much more confidence. She looked sensational. The tight trousers showed off her shapely behind and slender legs, the boots gave a sexy sway to her walk—and he wasn't immune to the effect.

He wasn't the only one to notice. Heads turned to watch

the beautiful, stylishly dressed redhead. Lukas realised that it wasn't just her that commanded attention—together they must make a striking couple. The realisation made him feel proud. He congratulated himself for seeing the potential in the scruffy backpacker.

But, with an unlimited credit card at her disposal, he couldn't understand why she needed to go into so *many* shops in search of an appropriate dress for the dinner tonight.

He wanted Ashleigh to get it right—both for his sake and her own as she could wear the dress on future occasions. Those occasions could well be far away in Australia when she got over her snit about her wedding and went back to her fiancé. Lucky guy, he thought, a touch morosely.

But shopping was far from Lukas's favourite pastime. He was going to have to call a halt to it. 'Surely it can't be that difficult to find a suitable outfit for tonight,' he grumbled. 'I can't endure any more hanging around while you look at every damn dress the shops stock.'

Her eyes widened. 'You did tell me to relax and enjoy it,' she said. 'And enjoy it I am. But if you're getting bored there is a dress I could go back to. It's not perfect but I like it and—'

'I'm not bored,' he said.

Actually, he *was* bored by the interminable waiting around. When he shopped, his mission was to spend as little time as possible with the shop assistant or the tailor and he made instant decisions. But he wasn't bored with Ashleigh. Not in the slightest. In fact her enthusiasm and pleasure in the experience was refreshing and somehow endearing. Then there was her total lack of greed.

'One more shop, okay?' she said beguilingly.

'I've created a shopping monster,' he grumbled again, though he didn't really mean it. Shopping with Ashleigh was the closest thing to fun he could remember having with a woman.

He followed her to the next shop and realised it was the one where his mother must have bought the coat Ashleigh was wearing. She realised it at the same time, her face lighting up. 'This is a good omen,' she said.

It seemed it was.

Once inside the store, his fake girlfriend looked around her and sighed a happy sigh. 'I love everything in here,' she said. 'I think I'm in fashion heaven.'

Even the poker-faced sales associate cracked a smile at that and was soon leading Ashleigh away to the fitting room.

Just minutes later Ashleigh emerged. 'I think I've found the ideal dress,' she said, giving her model-like twirl. 'It comes in black but I prefer the plum. What do you think?' She paused, waiting for his reaction.

Lukas caught his breath at how lovely she looked. The short, deep purple dress was deceptively simple. But it clung subtly to her curves and hugged her waist and her pale skin was luminous in contrast. He must have stared too long without comment.

'Do you like it?' she asked, a note of uncertainty creeping into her voice.

'Yes,' he said.

She pointed her foot in front of her like a dancer. 'And the shoes? Do you approve?'

The dress was discreetly sensual but the shoes were sexy as hell—a staggeringly high-heeled stiletto in narrow, multi-coloured leather stripes that buckled around her ankles.

He had to clear his throat to answer. 'Yes,' he said again, unable to choke out anything more.

'I'll take that as approval,' she said with a curve of a smile to him and a nod to the sales associate. 'Please tell me you're not just saying that because you're sick of shopping?'

'No. Just buy the dress. And the shoes.'

Then the sales assistant—no doubt scenting a generous credit card—came bearing a selection of glittering jewellery—semi-precious stones but still expensive.

'May I suggest these?' The woman fastened a necklace of large purple stones set in silver around Ashleigh's throat, a smaller version around her wrist. The jewellery lifted the simple dress and was perfect with her blue eyes and red hair.

'She'll take them,' he said.

'Thank you,' she breathed. 'Thank you, *darling*,' she remembered to add.

Ashleigh's new look was classy and discreetly sensual—a most appropriate look for his consort. Tina Norris couldn't possibly imagine he could be interested in another woman when she saw him with Ashleigh. He couldn't endure the thought of having to repel unwanted advances from the older woman. It brought back all those unpleasant, frightening memories.

'Is that it?' he asked Ashleigh.

'I…uh… I still need to buy the right underwear for this dress. I can get it here.' She flushed high on her cheekbones and couldn't meet his gaze.

What kind of underwear? A sheer, lacy bra cupping her breasts, the triangle of skimpy panties defining her hips? Or might she emerge from the fitting room in nothing but a tightly laced black corset, a tiny thong and those high-heeled black boots—then do a slow twirl and ask him, all wide-eyed: *What do you think?*

Lukas clenched his fists by his sides. *Damn it.* If he hadn't first seen her wearing nothing but bubbles, thoughts like this might not plague him.

Perspiration broke out on his forehead and he had to

drag a finger around a collar that felt suddenly tight. The shop was overheated. He had to get out of here. She needed a watch to replace the chunky digital thing more suitable for a tracksuit than an elegant dress. Time could be saved if he chose one for her.

'You get what you need—' he couldn't actually utter the word *underwear* '—while I shoot out to another shop.'

The associate held up an unstructured wool coat in a delicate shade of lavender that would complement the dress perfectly. '*Yes* to that too,' he said. 'And leather gloves.'

Ashleigh leaned forward, giving him a glimpse of the swell of her pale breasts in the clinging dress. *She wasn't wearing a bra.* Her fresh sweet perfume wafted up to him, heady and exciting. 'Are you sure about the coat? It's expensive and not really necessary for one night and—'

'Just get it,' he said through gritted teeth before he strode towards the door.

By the time he got back with the watch in the pocket of his coat, Ashleigh was covered up again in her new black trousers and top. But once he'd imagined what she might look like in her underwear it was difficult to get the sensual images out of his head.

He paid for Ashleigh's purchases and picked up the collection of heavy paper bags emblazoned with the designer label. 'I'll carry these out to the car.'

She put her hand on his arm to stop him. 'Please, let me,' she begged. 'I'll probably never shop here again in my life and I want to enjoy every bit of the experience.'

Ashleigh walked back out of the shop in triumph, bearing her haul of bags like trophies for all the other well-heeled shoppers to take note. She seemed exhilarated, cheeks flushed, eyes glinting in triumph and Lukas realised she was on a shopping high, fired by a pleasure that was almost orgasmic.

He had to force away thoughts of what she might look

like flushed with ecstasy in his arms. He gritted his teeth. This awareness of her as a woman rather than a pawn in his business strategy with Tina Norris could not go on.

Lukas signalled to his driver and the car pulled up in front of them. With her hovering around him, he placed Ashleigh's parcels in the boot, obeying her admonishments to be careful with the precious cargo.

Then he turned to her. 'This is where I leave you,' he said, more abruptly than he'd intended. He didn't know whether to be pleased or perturbed at the disappointment that drooped her expression.

'Where are you—?'

'I have business to attend to in the city,' he said.

'Oh. I can catch the bus back to Chelsea,' she said. 'That is, if it's okay for me to be there while you're not there. I—'

Lukas put up his hand to halt her flow of words. He'd known enough high maintenance women to realise that getting the clothes right wasn't the end of it.

'The driver is at your disposal. First to take you to a hairdresser and beauty salon in Mayfair, just near here, where I've made you an appointment. Then back to Chelsea.'

He was treated to the full dazzle of her dimples. 'Seriously? I was worried about my hair; it really needs styling and I—'

'Get done whatever you need get done,' he said with a dismissive wave. 'The driver knows where to take you. Just be home in plenty of time for our dinner date with Tina Norris.'

'Of course I will. I mean, that's what it's all about. Your business deal.'

He turned to walk away but was stopped by her hand on his elbow.

She looked up at him, her cheeks still flushed pink with excitement. 'Lukas? I know this will all be over in the morning. But thank you. This has been one of the most wonderful experiences of my life. Like a fairy tale. I'll never forget my day shopping on Bond Street with my fairy godfather.' She paused. 'Well, not *fairy* godfather. I didn't mean you... Heck, you know what I mean.' Then she flung her arms around him and kissed him on the cheek. 'Just thank you.'

He was too bemused to do anything but watch while she slid gracefully into the car as if accustomed to being driven in luxury around London. Shoppers brushed past him but for a long time he just stood there, remembering the warmth of her arms, the touch of her lips, and feeling dazed and inexplicably bereft. Then he turned on his heel and strode into the crowd.

CHAPTER SEVEN

POWERFUL, POISED AND PREDATORY—that was Ashleigh's first impression of Tina Norris.

The glamorous forty-something woman narrowed her eyes when Lukas introduced her as his girlfriend. There was speculation and suspicion there, but also a flash of disappointment. Ashleigh smiled a greeting but immediately felt on guard. She took a deep breath to steady her nerves. An award-winning performance would be required of her tonight. Thank heaven she was dressed for the part, with her new designer clothes and the confidence of newly styled hair and professional make-up.

As a child, Ashleigh had known of Mayfair in central London as the most valuable stop on the board in the game of Monopoly. Since then, she'd heard the area described as a haven for the international super-rich. That certainly fitted the description of Lukas. And while Tina was as British as could be, she too was very wealthy. Lukas had chosen the restaurant for tonight's dinner because Tina had an apartment nearby, although her home and company headquarters were in Liverpool.

And then there was Ashleigh Murphy—recently of downtown Bundaberg, more recently of no fixed abode, tomorrow to have no abode at all.

As the waiter led them from the bar area where they'd met Tina to seat them at their table, Ashleigh managed to catch Lukas's eye. The message was clear—they'd better get their story right.

The critically acclaimed restaurant was elegant, the Christmas decorations subdued in shades of silver. Their table was set with crisp linen and gleaming crystal, the floor carpeted so it was quiet enough for a non-shouted conversation. Unobtrusive waiters glided silently between tables.

'Nice,' said Tina, looking around her with critical brown eyes. 'Although I'm not too sure what to expect from the Scandinavian-Japanese fusion menu.'

'It's not a cuisine I've tried,' said Ashleigh.

'I don't think too many people have,' said Tina.

Did that imply criticism of Lukas for his choice of restaurant? Ashleigh decided to let the comment go. It was her role to support her pretend boyfriend, not to be combative on his behalf. She would just watch, listen and play her part when required. And not order the fried fish skin.

It didn't take long for Ashleigh to decide Tina was a little too much—too blonde, too tanned, too much cosmetic intervention and too blunt for comfort. Did that bluntness come from an overdose of self-assurance or because Tina knew it would put her on edge? The older woman started her inquisition as soon as they were all three seated at the circular table. 'So why have you kept Ashleigh a secret, Lukas?' she asked.

Lukas looked stunned at such a directly personal question so early in the evening. Ashleigh jumped in to rescue him. She placed her recently manicured hand over his where it rested on the table.

'Hardly a secret,' she murmured. 'It's just so new we've wanted to spend all our time…well…alone together.' His hand was warm and strong under hers—she liked the feeling. Liked it too much.

Tina's perfectly pencilled brows rose. 'How new?' she

asked then back-pedalled as if she realised her question could be construed as intrusive. 'I mean, when I do business with people I like to get to know their partners. I wasn't aware you had a lady in your life, Lukas.'

'I didn't until recently,' he said.

Ashleigh had decided that the closer to the truth their story, the better it would stick. 'We've only known each other for three weeks,' she said. 'I was meant to be in London for a two-week vacation. Then I met Lukas quite by chance.' She curled her hand over his and edged as close as she could to him. Would it be too much to drop a kiss on his cheek? Perhaps it would be overkill at this early stage. 'I decided to stay in the UK.'

'As you would,' said Tina with a cynical twist to her mouth that made Ashleigh cringe. The implication was clear. *Gold-digger.* 'Where did you two meet?' The question was quick and direct, as if intended to put Ashleigh on the spot. Terror choked her and she was unable to answer. *Tina didn't believe them.*

'At the bar in The Shard,' said Lukas smoothly. 'She'd practically just got off the plane when I spotted her.'

His confidence allayed her fears. *They could do this.* 'I was dying to see that view of London,' said Ashleigh—which was no lie. 'Then I saw him and forgot all about the view.' *He was a view worth gazing at all on his own.* She looked up at Lukas in what she hoped was besotted admiration. Resisted the temptation to bat her eyelashes. Or to giggle at the thought of what this tough executive would think if she told her that her first view of Lukas had been from his bathtub.

'Me too,' he said. 'I was smitten. We've been together ever since.' *Well done, Lukas.*

Tina's eyes narrowed shrewdly. 'I didn't take you for the "love at first sight" type, Lukas. You struck me as more of a lone wolf. A challenge to the single women of Europe, with your good looks and fortune being quite the prize.'

Lukas froze. Ashleigh gripped her wine glass so tight she thought it would snap.

'Really?' he said. Ashleigh had known him long enough—was it really only twenty-four hours?—to know Lukas was stalling. Immediately, she took over.

She leaned over the table to engage more with Tina. The trouble with dinner for three was the risk of someone feeling excluded. And she didn't want that person to be Lukas's prospective partner in the deal he so badly wanted to close.

'Sometimes it comes when you least expect it, doesn't it?' she said. 'That bolt from the blue, Cupid's arrow, whatever you want to call it. You're not looking for love but it finds you. Then everything else falls away. You just want to be with that one special person. You feel only half alive when you're apart. You live for them.' Her voice trailed away.

Ashleigh had only ever felt that craziness once. She'd broken up with Dan when they'd both graduated from high school and left Bundaberg for different universities. In her first year she'd had a ball, making new friends, dating different guys. Then in second year she'd taken drama as an elective and met Travis. Gorgeous, heartbreaking Travis. They'd been cast in the same production, playing lovers. Travis. The love of her life—in real life as well as on stage. It had been like an addiction—frantic, feverish. Nothing else had mattered except being with him. Not her studies, not her friends. She'd barely scraped through her other subjects. Then the play had ended. No sooner had the audience applause faded than Travis had dumped her.

Now, she realised she was clutching Lukas's hand way too hard. It was a wonder he hadn't yelped at the pressure on it. She released her grip. Thinking back to Travis always brought a rush of pain—even though it had been so long ago.

She looked over to Tina, saw a flash of what looked like regret in her eyes. Tina pursed her unnaturally full lips. 'I remember that feeling,' she said slowly, then briefly closed her eyes as if returning to a happier past. *She's lonely*, Ashleigh thought. 'But it's all stuff and nonsense,' Tina brusquely added, shattering the momentary illusion of vulnerability.

Ashleigh refused to be cowed. 'I don't think it's nonsense at all,' she said. 'I feel like that about Lukas.' She looked up at him, smiling, though she felt her smile was a bit wobbly at the edges. His eyes gave away nothing. 'He feels the same about me, but I don't expect him to say so in public.'

'Uh…no. I'm not good at that kind of stuff,' he said. 'But yes. I… I feel the same.'

His hesitation made it seem more authentic, Ashleigh thought with relief. They hadn't rehearsed anything like this. But it seemed natural to kiss him, her lips pressed lightly against his. She meant the kiss to be brief—mere punctuation to her confession of infatuation for her pretend boyfriend. But Lukas held the kiss, increased the pressure on her mouth until her whole body responded in a wave of dizzying awareness. She broke away, shaken, but determined not to show it. *She should not have enjoyed that so much.* But she had. If she wasn't in a posh restaurant under the narrow-eyed scrutiny of a dragon lady she would not have stopped the kiss.

She looked away from Lukas, not wanting him to see her confusion, and then back to Tina. 'So I guess whether you're a lone wolf like Lukas or a runaway bride like me, you don't know when Cupid's arrow is going to hit and—'

'Just hold it right there,' said Tina, her eyes gleaming. 'You're a runaway bride?'

Why the heck had she brought that up? Lukas's barely audible groan only echoed the groan Ashleigh felt inside. Her salacious bridal history was hardly relevant to Lukas's business deal with Tina.

'You actually bolted from the altar?' said Tina. 'In your wedding gown? I've never known anyone who actually did that.' Was that a sneer or genuine interest from the older woman?

'It wasn't quite that scenario,' said Ashleigh, not daring to look at Lukas. She explained to Tina how she'd cancelled everything just weeks before the wedding then run away to London to escape the flak of being in a town where everyone seemed to know her and Dan and have an opinion about her action.

'Good for you,' said Tina. 'It takes a special kind of guts to do that. Like knowing when to pull out of a business deal your instinct tells you is not going to work. Less messy in the long run.'

Lukas paled under his tan at her words and their possible implication. Ashleigh cursed under her breath. Had her impulsive words ruined the deal for him?

'Does that mean…?' she asked Tina, her eyes imploring the older woman not to blame Lukas for her indiscretion. Tina was obviously used to having power and knew how to wield it.

Tina frowned. 'What? You think I'm referring to my doing business with Lukas? Of course I'm not. I'm still doing due diligence before I come to any final decision.'

Ashleigh couldn't help her sigh of relief. 'I'm so glad to hear that. I…' She was going to say she knew how important the deal was to Lukas but realised that might be construed as showing his hand.

'You're being so supportive, *agápi mou*,' Lukas cut in, as if he had guessed she could be heading towards a blunder.

'And very entertaining,' said Tina. 'A runaway bride! Who knew?'

Ashleigh's mouth felt dry and her heart started pounding. Was Tina mocking her? She had a horrible feeling the older woman was trying to undermine her in front of Lukas. 'You…you wouldn't tell anyone about that, would you?' Ashleigh said. 'I came here to put it behind me.'

'You mean "Billionaire Greek Tycoon Romances Runaway Bride"—that type of headline?' Tina said with gleeful exaggeration.

Ashleigh couldn't help her gasp. All the deception would come out under media scrutiny. She didn't dare look at Lukas. Why, oh, why hadn't she kept her mouth shut?

But Tina continued. 'Trust me, my lips are firmly zipped when it comes to scurrilous gossip. I've been burned by it myself.'

Tina seemed totally genuine. Again pain shadowed her eyes and Ashleigh thought about the nasty divorce Lukas said she had endured. She felt really bad she had called her a cougar. 'Thank you,' she said. But still, she knew she wouldn't be able to relax until the evening was done and her role played out.

Their starters arrived then and it brought a welcome change of conversation. The food was innovative but satisfying with an emphasis on seafood and vegetables. Ashleigh managed a connection with Tina over their shared surprise at how excellent their meals were. Lukas pretended to be offended. Why would they think he would take guests to a restaurant he hadn't first approved? Both she and Tina laughed. But Ashleigh was not surprised when, during the main course, the spotlight shone back on her.

'You're from Australia?' asked Tina. 'I've been to Sydney. Great city.'

'I'm from Bundaberg in Queensland,' said Ashleigh.

'I've not heard of it,' said Tina.

'I guess not many English people would have. Unless you like rum, that is. Bundaberg is famous for its rum. We grow a lot of sugar cane.'

'Your town is famous for rum and sugar? That's kind of fun.'

'It is, isn't it,' said Ashleigh with a grin. She could see how in a different situation, when so much wasn't riding on the outcome, she might enjoy Tina's company.

'You never told me about the rum,' said Lukas.

'You never asked,' she said with a flirtatious tilt of her head.

'What did you do back home, Ashleigh?' asked Tina.

'I managed to evade the family profession of teaching—my parents and my sister are all schoolteachers—and did a degree in accounting. Then somehow ended up managing a flooring company in downtown Bundaberg.' She pulled a face. 'Not very glamorous.'

'The company I run isn't glamorous either,' said Tina. 'Your background would give you an appreciation of a down-to-earth business like retail distribution.'

'Or manufacturing,' said Lukas.

Since when had this turned into a job interview?

'I'd like to hear more about both your businesses, and how they could work together,' Ashleigh said. 'We haven't had a chance to talk much about how your company operates, have we, Lukas?' She climbed her fingers up his chest in flirtatious provocation.

'No,' he said hoarsely.

Tina explained briefly how her father had started their company from small beginnings, then ten years ago had died suddenly and she'd had to step in. She had adored her father; he'd brought her up after her mother had died when she'd been aged ten. 'Fortunately, I'd trailed around the warehouses and transport depots since I'd been a toddler. I knew how it all worked.'

'Tina is being modest,' said Lukas. 'In her time at the helm she's expanded the business beyond anyone's expectations.'

'You took over your parents' company too, didn't you, Lukas, and did much the same thing?' Ashleigh asked.

'Yes,' he said. 'Only Tina's father left a thriving business. Ours was in a horrendous state. No secrets there. It's all a matter of public record.' The way he said *no secrets* made Ashleigh wonder just what secrets he'd buried. It was a shame she wouldn't get a chance to find out. She would be saying goodbye to him in the morning.

She refused to let herself acknowledge the mixed feelings that swept through her at the prospect of that parting. That kiss had aroused a longing for Lukas she had not anticipated. It was going to be very difficult to forget him.

When Ashleigh got up to go to the ladies' room Lukas couldn't help but let his gaze follow the sway of her hips as she made her graceful way to the back of the restaurant. *She was beautiful.*

If he really *had* met her at a bar, he might have been tempted to seduce her. Even in her anorak and simple dress she would have attracted attention.

But tonight there wasn't a trace left of the scruffy backpacker. She wore her brand new designer clothes with assurance—as if famous labels were all that was in her wardrobe. That confidence gave her a sensual presence that couldn't be purchased in the most expensive shop in Bond Street. It was pure Ashleigh. And along with it came her warmth and charm.

Did she feel his gaze on her? She turned back briefly and smiled at him over her shoulder. Her hair tumbled rich and sleek past her shoulders, rivalling the Christmas decorations with its vivid gleam. Her face was heart-stopping in its loveliness, her eyes expertly made-up to emphasise their extraordinary colour, her mouth lush and naturally pink. *That kiss.* It had taken a monumental effort to control himself and not take the kiss deeper, exploring her with lips and tongue. It was only the inappropriateness of a passionate kiss in front of Tina that had stopped him.

'She'll be back in a few moments, you know,' Tina said wryly.

Lukas realised he hadn't heard a word she'd said, too lost in watching Ashleigh. 'I'm sorry,' he said. 'That was unforgivably rude.'

'I notice you haven't taken your eyes off her all evening and I don't blame you,' she said. 'She's lovely. Beautiful to look at, of course, but also smart and fun.'

'I think so,' he said. His plan had worked out so much better than he had hoped.

'Can you be sure she's not a gold-digger?' Tina said. 'Wealth is a privilege but can also sometimes be a burden. I've been burned a few times by someone I thought was special but was after the money, not me.'

Lukas's first reaction was to tell Tina to mind her own business. But he wanted to work with her. 'She's no gold-digger,' he said. 'Of that I'm certain.'

'You're quite sure?'

'Yes,' he said. He'd met enough of the real deal gold-diggers to be sure Ashleigh was not of their kind.

'Then be careful with her,' Tina said.

Lukas bristled. 'What do you mean?'

'She's a romantic and could be easily hurt.'

'I have no intention of hurting her,' he said through gritted teeth. If he didn't want this partnership with Tina so much he would tell her what he thought of her interference.

Hurt was never going to come into it. His arrangement with Ashleigh was a simple repayment of debt. And when she left tomorrow she would be well ahead of the game. She would take it all with her—the dress, the shoes, even the watch, the value of which she seemed to have no idea. It was quite a haul for one evening's work.

'I hope you mean that,' Tina said, her eyes narrowed. Was this a test? Perhaps she was not as hoodwinked by the charade as he'd thought.

'Of course,' he said.

Hurt could go two ways. So he might feel some regret when Ashleigh walked out of the door. But he'd get over it. Ashleigh was too dangerous for him to be around. She was starting to make him feel things he didn't want to feel. Feelings he'd locked away long ago. Not for her. Not for any woman. Especially not for a runaway bride who'd soon be on her way home to her forgiving fiancé.

He would never fall for that particular story again. That last summer of freedom on Mykonos was when he'd met Céline. They'd spent the season together, only getting out of bed for her to go to work as a waitress and him to crew on a yacht. She'd seemed so different, and he'd let down the barriers he'd erected so early as protection against the cynical arrangements that passed for relationships among his parents and their set. He'd thought it would be for ever for him and Céline. But on the morning she was leaving the island—when he was just about to propose—she'd told him she was going back home to France to the soldier boyfriend she'd told him was off the scene. Lukas's trust had been irrevocably shattered.

Now, he forced his attention away from painful memories and back to Tina.

'I'd like to see you again—and Ashleigh,' she said. 'I have a table for the Butterfly Ball on Friday night. By then I'll have a decision on our potential deal. Can I count on seeing you both there?'

Lukas bit down on his frustration and dismay. This

dinner was supposed to be about keeping Tina at arm's length on a personal level. Ashleigh was to be his fake date just for the one night. He'd intended to give a vague answer about her in the unlikely event Tina ever asked after the lovely redhead. Hell, the way he'd planned it, Tina should be jealous of Ashleigh, not wanting to see her again. The sudden change of agenda was unsettling. Ashleigh wouldn't be around by Friday.

At that moment she returned to the table. Her lush mouth was slicked glossy pink, making it look even more kissable. He had to fight the urge to pull her to him and kiss that lipstick right off. Instead he schooled his face to look neutral and stood up to greet her.

'You're back just in time,' he said. 'Tina has invited us as her guests to the Butterfly Ball on Friday night.'

'Oh,' Ashleigh said, obviously as shocked as he'd been. 'Th…that's very nice of you, Tina, but I—'

Tina looked from one to the other. 'I expect to see you both there.' There was steel in his prospective business partner's voice.

Lukas caught Ashleigh's eye, gave a slight nod. He'd noticed they seemed to pick up on the other's slightest variation in body language. She gave him the same signal back to signify her understanding.

'Thank you, Tina, that would be wonderful,' Ashleigh said. 'I was going to say I don't have a suitable dress for a black tie event. But I don't really need an excuse to go shopping in London.'

'Splendid,' the older woman said. She was used to getting her way.

'It's very kind of you to invite us.' Then Ashleigh deliberately wound her slender arms around his neck and looked up into his face. 'Lukas and I have never danced together. This will be a real treat. Won't it, darling?'

He gritted his teeth again. Anger at Tina's manipulation

mingled with an overwhelming awareness of Ashleigh's nearness. Did she realise she was playing with fire? He placed his hands around her waist as a good fake boyfriend would. Just what underwear did she have on under that body-hugging dress? The thought had preoccupied him ever since their shopping expedition this morning.

'Yes. A treat,' he said, forcing himself to sound unperturbed by the bombshell Tina had dropped on him.

And even more unperturbed by Ashleigh's curves pressing against his chest.

Ashleigh sensed the tension building in Lukas but he kept it tamped down until after they had said goodnight to Tina outside the restaurant. Tina had declined his offer of a ride in his car, saying she preferred to walk.

Lukas waited until Tina was well out of sight before he slammed his hand against the support of the restaurant portico so hard the force of it must have juddered up his arm. It was lucky it didn't come crashing down on top of them. Thank heaven there weren't any other patrons leaving the restaurant.

He unleashed an impressive stream of what she could only assume were formidable Greek swear words, ending in a very English 'Damn, damn, damn.'

'I'm guessing you're not pleased about the invitation to the Butterfly Ball.'

He glowered dark fury. 'Don't be smart with me, Ashleigh. What do you think? Of course I'm not pleased. This arrangement was supposed to end tonight.'

'But we did well, didn't we? Tina thinks you're taken. You won't have to walk away from your deal because of any embarrassment about Tina wanting more from you than your product distribution agreement.'

'Maybe I imagined her interest in me,' he growled. 'She seems enchanted with *you*.'

'I don't think so. The first thing she felt when she saw me was disappointment. She's lonely. You're hot. You're both rich.'

Lukas grimaced. 'Don't go there. She reminds me of my mother and her friends.' He swore some more, his expression dark.

He was usually so serious, so restrained, so in control. She liked this Lukas, furious he'd been outsmarted. His explosion of dark energy excited her and made her wonder what he'd be like out of control in the bedroom. It was all she could do not to push him up against the wall of the restaurant and kiss him senseless.

Instead he put his hands on the wall behind her. The action brought him very close, effectively trapping her with his body. All this pretend flirting was having an arousing effect on her libido. His dark eyes glittered as he looked down and for the first time she wondered if it might be having the same effect on him.

'So now I'm being coerced into this ball,' he said.

Ashleigh knew he'd shaved before they'd left for the restaurant yet already there was a dark growth shadowing his jaw. She found it incredibly sexy. What would he do if she reached up and stroked it? She ached to feel its roughness against the smoothness of his olive skin. Better, to feel its roughness against the smoothness of *her* skin.

'You feel you've been manipulated and steamrollered,' she said, fighting for the breath to fuel her words. To force herself to appear unaffected by his closeness, the sense of tightly leashed passion that, if it exploded, might carry her along with its force on a wild ride of sensual discovery.

'After all that, Tina still hasn't come to a decision.' His mouth set in a tight line. What would he do if she teased it open with the tip of her tongue? But he was still obsessed with his business deal. More than likely, he'd still keep on talking about Tina through her kiss.

The passion was obviously staying strictly on its leash. This feeling was pure fantasy on her part. She sighed and directed her thoughts back to where they should be. 'If I can be the voice of reason here, it's still early days. Tina said she still had to complete due diligence. Would you really be interested in a business partnership with a person who took your company evaluation at face detail?'

'Of course not,' he said, his thick dark brows drawn together. Would he look the same in passion as he did in anger?

'Maybe we overdid the lovey-dovey act?' she said. But my, how she'd enjoyed it. He'd given her a taste of what it might be like to go further than that interrupted kiss that had so taken her by surprise.

'Who were you thinking about when you were gushing about being hit by Cupid's arrow?' he growled. 'Your fiancé?'

'I've told you he's my *ex*-fiancé. No. It was someone I fell for when I was too young and naïve to recognise a player for what he was. Not a mistake I ever intend to repeat.'

Ashleigh could sense by his expression he didn't believe her. She shrugged away from him. Stood at a distance with her arms wrapped around her chest. Why should she care?

He shoved his hands deep into the pockets of his overcoat. 'So will you come to the ball with me?'

'You mean more play-acting?'

'If you want to call it that.'

'I don't like the thought of making a fool of Tina. Okay, she's intimidating and I'm not sure she bought our story one hundred per cent. We'd be wise to remain wary of her. But she's not some voracious cougar. I think she's a lonely woman who has suffered a lot of loss in her life.'

He rolled his eyes in an expression of male disgust. 'This is about business, Ashleigh, not bleeding hearts. So the initial plan backfired. Now I realise Tina's one of those managers who likes to interview the partner of any person she plans to work with. And she's taken a shine to you.'

'I took quite a shine to her too. As a fluttery fledging to her full-grown eagle, that is. If it's so important to you—and I'd like to know why one more deal is so important to you when you're already so wealthy—I'll do it.'

He slumped with relief. 'That's good. I—'

She put up her hand to stop him from going any further. 'On one condition.'

He frowned. 'Condition?'

'I want to stay at your townhouse until after Christmas.'

'You *what*?' The words exploded from him.

'I've got a deal to sleep on my friend's sofa but that's hardly comfortable or convenient for me or Sophie. If you want me to go to that ball and schmooze with scary Tina, that's my price.'

Price mightn't have been the most appropriate word to use. But Lukas was so furious at what he obviously saw as further manipulation he didn't notice the implication. Fact was, she couldn't be bought.

'That's blackmail,' he said.

'And a phony invoice for three nights' accommodation at your house wasn't?'

He glared at her and she glared right back. 'So is it *yes* to letting me stay?'

'Yes,' he said grudgingly.

'And of course you're aware I haven't got anything suitable to wear to a ball?'

'More shopping?' he groaned.

'You don't need to come with me. I've got two days to find something.'

'You can take my credit card. I have one I give to domestic staff for their use in running the household.'

That put her squarely back in her place. 'You might have to up the limit, considering the prices on Bond Street.'

'Can I trust you—?'

Insult upon insult. 'With your credit card? Are you questioning my honesty?'

He scowled. 'I meant can I trust you to buy something spectacular without worrying about the cost? No penny-pinching. I haven't been to one of these big charity balls for years. You'll have to do me proud.' He looked down at his feet in their handmade Italian shoes. 'Like…like you did tonight.'

Her indignation dissipated like the fog of her breath into the cold night air. 'Thank you. I… I did my best.' It had been surprisingly easy to pretend to be in love with him. To imagine… *No.* It was just business between them and she could not forget that. *Even though he set her heart racing just by his presence.*

'It was a very good best. You handled Tina better than I could have imagined.'

'But you're not happy about me hanging around, are you?'

'You're right about that,' he grunted. 'Tina was right when she called me a lone wolf. That's the way I like it.'

And wolves could not be tamed. His message could not be any clearer.

They spent the ride to Chelsea in an uncomfortable silence, with Ashleigh squashed against the car door to put as much distance between them as she could. She twisted the strap of her elegant new evening purse so tight it was in danger of snapping as she worried about what she might be getting herself into by living in close proximity to Lukas Christophedes.

Because she had really, really wanted to kiss him into a passionate frenzy against that wall.

CHAPTER EIGHT

THE NEXT DAY, Ashleigh leaned back against her chair in a swish café on the Duke of York Square in Chelsea and subjected herself to her fashion-crazy friend Sophie's scrutiny. She and Sophie had met earlier in the swanky square at the top end of the King's Road. Sophie had been quick to agree to help Ashleigh with a day of shopping for the Butterfly Ball. 'You mean actual shopping in posh shops, as opposed to window shopping?' she'd said. 'Count me in.'

Ashleigh had called in more troops for moral support—Emma and Grace were due to arrive soon. It was a perfect winter's day in London, crisp and clear with a bracing chill. People were talking hopefully of snow.

'You look…different,' Sophie said with a quizzical expression.

'Probably because I'm wearing a few thousand pounds' worth of coat and boots,' Ashleigh said with a laugh. Only the jeans she wore were her own. The black boots, lavender-coloured coat and charcoal top all belonged to Lukas.

Sophie narrowed her eyes. 'It's not just that. Your hair. The make-up.'

'All courtesy of a salon in Mayfair yesterday. They showed me a few tricks that really make a difference. And threw in some samples for me to take home.'

Sophie's eyes widened when Ashleigh named the salon.

'You have got to be kidding. I'd have to take out a mortgage just to have a manicure there.'

'I know. This whole pretend girlfriend thing is surreal. It was like the fairy godmother waved her magic wand over me yesterday. I took a selfie as proof it really happened. Look.'

Ashleigh pulled out her smartphone to show her old friend the snap she had taken of herself in her borrowed finery, just before she and Lukas had left for the restaurant.

Sophie took one look and identified the designer of her dress. 'You look so glamorous,' she said. 'And that fairy dust magic is still lingering. It's difficult to put a finger on it. It's not just the way you look. I think it's a new confidence after all these years of the dreadful Dan undermining you.'

'Maybe. It went well last night. I think I really pulled off the role of billionaire's girlfriend. I kept up with the business talk too. I… I fitted in.'

'Of course you did. You're beautiful and you're a brilliant actress. You were the best by far on the stage in the school productions. But is any of that fairy dust to do with Lukas? Don't tell me you don't fancy him!'

Ashleigh picked up her coffee cup and put it down again. 'Who wouldn't fancy him? He's the handsomest man I've ever met—and *hot*. But I'm just playing a role. So is he.' Not even to Sophie could she admit how much of her thoughts Lukas occupied. Wondering about what it would be like to go on a real date with him. To kiss him for real. To go further than kissing.

'He's not trying to make a move on you?'

Ashleigh shook her head. 'It's strictly business. He's got a real "don't get involved" barrier around him. Which is for the best, really. You know me, a one-night stand isn't my thing. And that's all it would be.' But who knew what might have happened to her scruples last night if that passion she'd felt for him had had a chance to flame?

'Er…of course not,' said Sophie, shifting in her seat.

'It's a tricky situation, but so far I'm managing to keep my cool.'

'Are you sure it's a good idea to be living in his house?'

'I'm perfectly safe there, if that's what you mean.'

'Good. But it sounds like at the moment he really needs you to carry out his plan. Have you thought about afterwards? As soon as that contract is signed he might boot you out.'

'I don't think so,' Ashleigh said slowly. 'My impression is that he's an honourable man in his own way.'

'The offer of my sofa still stands, wonky springs and all,' said Sophie.

Ashleigh smiled at her friend. 'Thank you. It's reassuring to have that safety net. But I know how important it is for you to have your own safe, private place. After what happened with Harry, I mean.'

Sophie put up her hand. 'You know I just want to forget that time in my life.'

But the episode with the Manchester bad boy had scarred her friend, Ashleigh thought. Thanks to email and phone calls, they'd kept their teenage friendship alive. She considered Sophie to be one of her best friends. It had been frustrating to be so far away when Sophie had been in trouble. But they were both in London now, looking out for each other. If Sophie ever needed her, Ashleigh would be here for her. 'I understand, of course,' she said.

'So, on the agenda today is shopping for the role of billionaire's girlfriend for one of the most prestigious events in the London fund-raising calendar,' Sophie said, in an obvious attempt to change the subject. 'And hey, how great you're actually going to a ball as a guest rather than a waitress.'

'I'll be well and truly back to waitressing by the time The Snowflake Ball rolls around on New Year's Eve.'

'I wish there was time for me to make you a gown for tomorrow night,' said Sophie.

'Oh, Sophie, so do I.' Sophie was a talented designer and preparing to open an online store selling her lovely vintage-inspired designs.

Just then Ashleigh looked up to see Emma and Grace heading towards them from the direction of the Saatchi Gallery. She waved to attract their attention. Then turned back to Sophie. 'Please, don't tell them about the bathtub. You're the only one I'm sharing that particular incident with.'

'And the rest of it?'

'The pretend girlfriend thing? So long as they swear not to say a word to Clio, I'll tell them everything.'

'Clio will find out, you know. She knows everything. Though she seems preoccupied at the moment.'

'Maybe because of that wedding on the weekend. The long-time client who insisted she organise his daughter's wedding—even though she hates weddings, as you know, and isn't actually a wedding planner.'

'Maybe that's it. I'm waitressing at that wedding; are you rostered on?'

'No, thank heavens. Otherwise I would have had to cancel to be free for the Butterfly Ball. And I don't want to mess Clio around.'

'The good news for you is that we're going down to Surrey tomorrow to start setting up for the wedding on Saturday. That means Clio won't be at the Butterfly Ball to spot you with Lukas. You know her rules about dating clients.'

Ashleigh swore under her breath. 'I sure hope the girls are good at keeping secrets.'

Sophie smiled enigmatically. 'Don't worry. We're all very good at that.'

Ashleigh didn't have time to demand an explanation about what secrets Sophie could possibly be keeping when Emma and Grace arrived at the café.

She stood up to greet them in a flurry of cheek kisses and hugs. It wasn't often the four friends were rostered all together on the same jobs for Maids in Chelsea and so they were determined to make the most of this opportunity to catch up in their own time.

Ashleigh had been a little in awe of gorgeous blonde Emma with her posh accent when she'd first met her. But now she couldn't imagine not being friends with her. They'd bonded at a big party where they'd all been wait-ressing and Emma had panicked at seeing her ex there. Her ex, whom she'd said was her teenage boyfriend but had actually turned out to be her secret teenage husband—the son of a marquess and now the Earl of Redminster in his own right. Their reconciliation had been cause for drama and played out in front of the media. But Emma was re-ally happy now with her beloved Jack. Of course, as the Countess of Redminster, Emma was no longer working as a waitress. But she was the kind of girl who liked to keep her friends close.

'Am I meant to curtsey?' Ashleigh joked as she said hello. 'And do we call you Lady Emma now? Or Lady Redminster? You know we Aussies aren't up on aristo-cratic etiquette.'

'Of course not,' said Emma in those cut-glass tones. 'No curtseying and I'm just Emma, as I've always been.'

'Have you ordered?' asked Grace. 'I've been looking forward to coffee and cake.'

'Just coffees,' said Ashleigh.

'We were waiting for you guys,' said Sophie.

'Sorry we were a little late,' said Grace. 'You know how much I love Christmas decorations. I was admiring the way the square is decorated. And there are some fabulous festive knick-knacks in the shops too.'

Ashleigh had found willowy, brown-haired Grace quite shy when she'd first met her but had soon discovered the warm, generous person behind her gentle smile. People had warned her London could be a hostile place—she was so lucky to have made such wonderful new friends here.

'Shall we look at the cake menu?' Ashleigh asked. 'Choose whatever you want. Because morning coffee is on me—or rather on my pretend billionaire boyfriend.'

When the squeals had died down, Emma and Grace demanded to know more.

'We had no idea what to think when you asked us to help you shop for a gown for the Butterfly Ball,' said Emma.

Ashleigh proceeded to give them an edited version of how she came to be Lukas Christophedes's fake date. She left out her presence in his bathtub and her unsettling urge to kiss him last night. She hadn't admitted *that* even to Sophie. 'So I need a ball gown for tonight and Lukas is so relieved he doesn't have to hang around in shops with me he told me to treat my friends to lunch,' she concluded.

'That's great about the lunch,' said Grace. 'What worries me is you having been stranded in the middle of London after the party on Sunday with nowhere to stay,' she added with a frown.

Ashleigh shrugged. 'I was meant to be catching the bus with Sophie but she disappeared on me. What actually *did* happen, Soph?'

'Er... I waited for you at the bus stop then thought you must have made other arrangements,' said Sophie, looking a bit shamefaced, her brown eyes looking down at her coffee cup.

'That's not like you, Sophie,' said Grace.

'I'll let you off the hook this time,' said Ashleigh. But

something about Sophie's expression didn't sit right. She'd ask her again later what had happened that night.

'So that means you're definitely not going home to Australia for Christmas?' Emma asked after they'd ordered coffee and a selection of decadent-looking cakes.

'That's right,' Ashleigh said.

'I'm so glad you'll be around in the next few weeks,' said Emma. 'Because—' she paused dramatically '—Jack and I have decided to renew our wedding vows and I want you all to be my bridesmaids.'

Shrieks of delight greeted her announcement but while Ashleigh uttered heartfelt congratulations she remained subdued.

'Are you okay with that, Ashleigh?' asked Emma.

'I'm honoured,' said Ashleigh. 'But we've only known each other a few weeks and I don't want you to think you *have* to ask me because you've asked the others.'

'You should know by now I don't do anything I think I *have* to do. I want you there.' Emma sounded her most imperious countess.

'In that case, I would be delighted to be your bridesmaid,' Ashleigh said, blinking back sudden tears.

'Where are you going to hold the ceremony, Emma?' asked Grace.

'Do you remember we scouted out that funky boutique hotel not far from here, The Daphne?' Emma asked. 'We've booked there.'

'Perfect,' breathed Grace.

Emma turned to Sophie. 'Sophie, I would love it if you could make my wedding dress—I didn't have one for the "real" wedding. And the bridesmaid dresses, of course. There's you three, and my friend and sister-in-law Clare will be chief bridesmaid.'

'There's nothing I'd love more,' said Sophie. 'But Emma,

you could have a top designer. You're a countess. Honestly, I won't be offended if you choose to do that.'

'But I want *you*,' Emma said. 'Not only do I think you'll give me just the look I want, the wedding will give you good exposure too. We want to keep it small and private but we'll have to release some photos to the media. The thing is, the ceremony is six days from today so I know it's a big ask. Jack and I had planned to wait till the new year, but really what's the point? We can't wait to make it official all over again.'

'I can get the dresses done. Even if I have to stay up every night.'

'No need for that,' said Emma. 'We'll need to get you some assistance.'

Ashleigh looked at Sophie and saw the glint of tears in her eyes too. This could be the break her friend needed.

'We should have champagne,' said Grace, her voice also not quite steady.

'There'll be time enough for champagne,' said Emma. 'Right now we need to help Ashleigh find a gown for the Butterfly Ball. King's Road, you said, Ashleigh?'

Ashleigh nodded. King's Road was lined with fabulous shops. She'd been captivated by the windows every time she'd walked by.

'Not so fast,' said Sophie. 'King's Road and here, The Duke of York Square, do have amazing shops. But time is short. I think we need to look at a designer runway collection for Ashleigh's night at a ball with a billionaire. That means changing direction and heading for Sloane Street.'

Ashleigh didn't have a clue what a designer runway collection was, but it sounded exciting—and exclusive. That was what Lukas would want—and she really wanted to play her role for him as best as she possibly could.

It was only a hop and a skip through Sloane Square to Sloane Street—another of London's exclusive shopping streets that ended up in Knightsbridge, home to the posh department stores Harrods and Harvey Nichols.

'I've got the credit card, girls, and I know how to use it,' Ashleigh said. 'Let's finish our coffee and go shopping.'

CHAPTER NINE

LUKAS DIRECTED HIS driver to stop the car outside the imposing entrance to one of London's most famous grand hotels, the venue for the night's Butterfly Ball. The limousine was at the head of a line of chauffeur-driven luxury vehicles and taxis dropping off guests all dressed to the nines in the requisite formal wear.

'Ready?' Lukas asked as he opened Ashleigh's door.

'Shifting right into girlfriend mode as we speak,' she said.

As she emerged from the car he caught his breath at how beautiful she looked. She wore an exquisite silk gown in shades of lavender, topped with a theatrically flamboyant ivory velvet cloak lined with purple. Her hair was piled up on her head with little tendrils escaping to fall down her slender pale neck, purple stones glittered at her ears. *They should be real jewels.* But she could not have chosen anything more perfect for her colouring and for the occasion.

Once more she looked the part he had cast her in, exceeding all expectations with a new level of sophistication and elegance. He could not keep his eyes off her.

'You look magnificent,' he said as he offered her his arm. He ached to say more—so much more—but had to remind himself that they were both playing roles. *It was strictly business.*

'All thanks to your credit card,' she murmured, tucking

her hand into his elbow. The action brought her close, so close he could breathe in her sweet scent, feel the warmth of her body. He kept her by his side as they walked into the ornate foyer of the hotel with its show-stopping Christmas tree that soared to the ceiling.

'Thanks also to your good taste,' he said. 'No amount of money can buy that.' Not to mention her innate grace and style—which he'd spotted even when she'd been wearing jeans and trainers. He'd said she should do him proud— and she'd done that in spades.

'You look magnificent yourself,' she said, her dimples flirting in her cheeks. 'Born to wear a tuxedo.' Her compliment pleased him. The women he usually dated were all about accepting compliments—and anything else they could grab from him—rather than bestowing them.

'Nobody is looking at me, I assure you,' he said. 'All eyes are on my beautiful date.'

'I feel like a princess,' she said. 'When I look in the mirror, I can't believe it's me looking back.'

'You outshine any princess,' he said. Did he really say that? He wasn't usually so fulsome. He was rewarded with a display of her dimples.

'I know you're only saying that as part of the act, but thank you,' she said. 'It's just the clothes—you know what they say: clothes maketh the pretend girlfriend.'

He'd meant every word of the compliment. It was an effort to keep the conversation at a superficial level when he found it difficult not to stare at her in admiration. 'You shopped well,' he said.

'I had enthusiastic help,' she said.

It had been the right thing to do but Lukas had regretted letting Ashleigh go out yesterday with her girlfriends instead of him. He could not admit to the time he'd spent imagining her coming out of a fitting room and asking him for his reaction, *What do you think?* Then imagining what it would be like to *show* her what he thought. *He should have been there with her.*

The truth was, he'd missed her. Even though she was now living legally in his house, he hadn't seen much of her. He suspected she'd kept purposefully out of his way and then she'd been at the hairdresser all afternoon. The house had seemed so empty without her.

But these thoughts of missing her, of wanting her, of—God help him—being given the privilege of carrying her parcels, could not be allowed to flourish. She was a beautiful, intriguing woman but what he had with her was just a business arrangement. Besides, she had given no indication that she felt any of the attraction he felt for her. The flirtatious looks, the kisses, the seductive smiles had all been with the aim of impressing Tina Norris—not *him*.

As they waited in the crush of people to get into the ballroom, he took the opportunity to update her on the negotiations with Tina. After all, the deal with Tina was the sole reason they were at the ball.

'Her finance people have talked to my finance people, so I'm hoping the agreement is progressing.'

'What do you want me to do?' she asked.

He had to lean nearer to hear her soft voice over the chatter and hum of hundreds of people. She had divested herself of her cape to leave in the cloakroom and he was tantalisingly close to her smooth, pale arms and shoulders, the swell of her breasts above the strapless dress. *Just like she'd looked in the bubbles.*

He had to clear his throat to speak. 'Just do what you did at our last meeting with Tina. You made such a good impression.'

'It won't be a hardship,' she said. 'I quite like Tina and this hotel is so magical. I feel like I'm in some kind of fairy tale.' Fairy tale to her, concrete business opportunity to him. He wanted it. She could help him get it. That was what all this was about.

As they approached Tina's table near the front of the ballroom, Ashleigh halted him with a hand on his arm. 'Come here,' she said. She made a show of straightening his already perfectly straight bow tie, tweaking it with fingers that feathered over his neck as she did so. It was an intimate caress that only a lover would attempt and, as such, was an inspired gesture on her part. He caught her hand and kissed it, holding the kiss for a beat longer than required. 'Thank you,' he said huskily.

'All part of the job,' she murmured, looking up at him with her wide blue eyes.

Of course that was all it was to her. *And to him*. He was crazy to entertain for one head-spinning moment that it could ever be anything else.

The trouble with a fake date was that you couldn't tell what was real and what was just part of the pretence, Ashleigh thought.

It made it difficult to know just how to respond to Lukas's compliments. He seemed so sincere in his admiration. But then perhaps he was as good an actor as she was. Businessmen of his stature did not get to be where they were without being able to put up a good façade when required, to bluff and feint. She had to stop herself from longing for his admiration to be real.

She was seated by his side as Tina's guests at the older woman's table, Tina to his left, she to his right. The other guests around the circular table were business associates of Tina's, some of whom Lukas was acquainted with. She, of course, knew no one. But she was soon chatting with the other guests. The story about Bundaberg being famous for rum usually went down well.

For a sudden, breath-stealing moment she realised some

of the people at this ball might have attended some of the high-end functions where she had worked as a waitress since she'd been in London. 'What if someone here recognises me as their waitress or maid?' she whispered to Lukas.

He snorted his disbelief. 'When you look more beautiful in your finery than the rest of the women here put together?'

'That's patently untrue,' she said with a smile, enjoying the flattery, at the same time wishing it was real.

'I'm entitled to my opinion,' he said, which made her smile deepen. Then he had to go and remind her of the gulf between them by adding, 'Besides, who *ever* notices the help?'

'I guess not,' she said, her voice trailing away. *Unless he finds them naked in his bathtub.*

She looked around her, admiring the splendour of the ballroom with its period style glamour. The room was elaborate yet elegant with panelled walls, ornate ceiling and outsized chandeliers all in the style of a bygone era. The hotel sat on the north bank of the Thames and the windows revealed a splendid view of the river. She felt entranced by the myriad lights of the city she was growing to love, the iconic London Eye slowly revolving through the dark.

It made her remember Emma's glow when she'd told them how Jack had taken her up on the Eye to toast her with champagne at midnight. Emma had gone through hardship and humiliation to get to the happy place she was now, yet Ashleigh could not help a twinge of envy.

She had got engaged to Dan for all the wrong reasons and ended the engagement for all the right ones. Yet for all her brave move in running away, for all her words about independence, deep down she longed for love with the right man one day. But here she was in the most cynical of sham relationships with the only man she'd found attractive since she'd arrived in London.

But it was difficult to feel maudlin in Tina's down-to-earth company. 'We're here to help support this wonderful charity,' she said. The charity funded research into premature and stillbirths. 'But we're also here to enjoy a Christmas get-together,' the older woman said. 'Let's eat, drink and be merry.'

It was a good deal more than that, as far as Lukas was concerned, and Tina knew it. But who was Ashleigh to question her reason for being here at such a glamorous occasion in the most beautiful dress she had ever worn? And—if the look in Lukas's eyes was genuine—a dress in which she looked her best.

Her shopping expedition in Sloane Street had been beyond her wildest expectations. As soon as the sales associate—giving awesome service with a countess as part of the party—helped her slip into the designer gown, Ashleigh had known it was the one.

'This is the dress,' Sophie had said, echoing her thoughts.

Ashleigh had been grateful for her friends' presence to help her shop. But she had felt a moment of wrenching disappointment there was no tall, dark-haired man waiting outside for her to watch her twirl the skirts around and ask, *What do you think?* She'd missed him. Looking back on that wonderful day in Bond Street, much of the magic had come from being with Lukas. And it was nothing to do with him being a credit-card-wielding billionaire—it was Lukas the man she was so unwisely growing attached to.

At the same shop she had found delicate shoes in purple suede, high-heeled, that wrapped around her ankles with soft suede ties. Pinprick-sized diamanté were scattered over the suede. Then they'd found outsize teardrop-shaped earrings that went perfectly with the dress and the faux amethyst bracelet.

No wonder she felt like a princess. And she was determined to enjoy every moment of this evening with the man more darkly handsome than any prince. Even if under ordinary circumstances he would never have noticed her. She refused to admit how much that hurt.

Lukas tried not to look bored as he sat through the inevitable talks about the good work of the charity and the speeches from its patrons. He pledged a hefty donation to the appeal. He refrained from pressing Tina for a decision—that would be poor form at a social occasion. And he begrudged the amount of time Ashleigh spent chatting with the other people at the table. Especially the men. It was irrational, he knew, but he wanted her to himself. She was *his* pretend girlfriend.

After the main course had finished, a show dance by professional ballroom dancers was announced. The dancers were stars of a popular television dance show and there was much applause.

The male dancer, slender and dark, and his partner in a flame-coloured spangled dress drew gasps from their audience with their skill. Lukas could see Ashleigh was entranced. She watched the dancers' every move, swaying to the rhythm of the music, tapping her feet. Lukas, in turn, watched her. He should warn her that her obvious interest would make her a target for when the dancers selected someone from the audience to dance with them. Ashleigh, with her beauty and enthusiasm, was a prime target. And if she danced like she sang… He would hate to see her humiliated.

But, before Lukas could say anything, the male dancer was by Ashleigh's side. She protested, saying her dress wasn't right but if he insisted she would love to dance with him. He took her by both hands and drew her to her feet. Flushed and laughing, she turned her head to Lukas. He nodded. She didn't need his permission. 'Good luck,' he said as she was led away by the handsome dancer.

Tina turned to Lukas. 'Don't look so woeful; he won't steal your lady away.'

His lady.

Ashleigh was *not* his lady. She had a man back in Australia—not for a moment did Lukas believe she wouldn't reconcile with him. Besides, he hadn't changed his mind about commitment. He liked his life exactly the way it was. His mansion in Athens. His townhouse in Chelsea. The private Ionian island that had belonged to his grandmother and now belonged to him.

He had the freedom to come and go as he pleased without answering to anyone. Sailing in summer. Skiing in winter. Women when it suited him. The type of women who knew the score and made no demands—if they did, he disentangled himself immediately. Once the women got his gift of jewellery they knew it was over.

He didn't date women like Ashleigh Murphy.

Not that he'd ever met a woman quite like her. She was unique. Special. At the spontaneous burst of applause Lukas sat up straighter in his seat and stared, astounded. *And she was a fabulous dancer.*

Ashleigh was not at the level of the polished professional but she was not far from it. Her partner stepped her into a sweet, simple waltz, slowly gliding Ashleigh around the floor. She gracefully dipped and swayed with utter confidence, her skirts swirling around her, revealing her slender, strong legs. *Dancer's legs.*

Lukas could see the astonishment on the professional's face. Then, after a murmured consultation with Ashleigh and a signal to the band, the music completely changed tempo to a sensual Latin rhythm. Ashleigh tossed back her head—haughty, sensuous—slowly entwined her fingers with her partner's and launched into a sinuous, sensual tango. This was a different Ashleigh, accomplished, confident, radiating sensuality and passion—the backpacker banished for ever. Lukas could not keep his eyes from her.

It was just a dance. But while Lukas joined Tina and the other guests in murmurs of amazed admiration, under the table his hands clenched into fists at the sight of Ashleigh in another man's arms. He wanted to wrench the man's hands from where they splayed against her bare skin. Even though common sense kept reminding him it was just a dance.

The performance was no longer about the expert toting the amateur around the room as entertainment. This had become another show dance—a showcase for the talent and skill of his pretend girlfriend. Her hair gleamed copper-bright under the lights, her pale skin and pastel dress in contrast to the black trousers and shirt of her dance partner. Tiny lights twinkled from her shoes, her feet in constant motion.

Ashleigh put emotion as well as skill into the dance that was once banned for its blatant sexuality. Her lips were parted seductively, her eyes gleamed with passion and desire, her hips swayed in invitation as she danced. Lukas saw a stranger at the same time he saw sweet, funny Ashleigh. A sensuous, beautiful woman with a life quite separate to his: not his maid, not his fake date, rather a woman with her own agenda. An exciting woman.

He wanted her. Lukas wanted her so much he ached. He would deny it to her. Deny it to anyone else. But he could no longer deny it to himself.

The vertical expression of a horizontal desire—that was what Lukas's mother used to call the tango after she'd had one too many flutes of champagne at those parties that used to fill his parents' house. Only now did he understand what she'd meant.

He knew Ashleigh had no interest in the other man.

It was all about the performance. But she made her passion for her partner disconcertingly believable. He realised what a skilled actor she was—how much could he believe of how she reacted to *him*?

She ended the dance bent backwards over her partner's leg in a symbolic gesture of sensual surrender. Then the dancer swept her to her feet and waltzed around with her as the guests were invited onto the dance floor.

Lukas didn't wait around for pleasantries at his table. He had to get to Ashleigh before any other man claimed her as a partner. Within seconds he was at her side as she thanked the professional with a hug. He heard her talking to him about a dance school in east London as the guy departed.

For a moment Ashleigh was stranded on the dance floor, alone and uncertain. Lukas could see her hesitate about what to do next. She was a newcomer to London, surrounded by a sea of strangers. He felt an unfamiliar surge of protectiveness towards her.

'Ashleigh,' he called, staking his claim.

She turned and her face seemed to light up in delight as she caught sight of him. 'Lukas!' He smiled with pleasure at her reaction, then reminded himself how skilled she was at playing a role. 'Did you see us?' she asked a little breathlessly. 'I adore the tango. The dress held me back a bit—I should have been wearing something shorter and slinkier.'

Lukas had to close his eyes against the image of her body on display in something *shorter and slinkier*.

'You were incredible.' He took her arm, making it known to the entire room of people that she was *his*. 'The next dance is mine,' he said with a fierce surge of possessiveness.

Her eyes widened. 'Of course it is. I'm yours.' Words spoken in character as his make-believe girlfriend. Yet he responded to them with something visceral from a place deep inside his soul that he had repressed for so long he'd denied it existed. *He wanted to make her his.*

Her face was flushed, her eyes bright, more of her hair had escaped from its confines to tumble around her neck. *Like she would look after passionate lovemaking.*

'Why didn't the fact you were a professional dancer come into our get-to-know-you sessions?'

'You didn't ask,' she said with a provocative tilt to her head.

'So it was your secret?' He realised how little he really knew about her. How much he wanted to know. How many other secrets did she hold?

'No secret. It just didn't seem relevant. I studied dance as soon as I could walk. Ballet. Tap. Jazz. Then ballroom. I'm qualified to teach. I thought about going professional at one stage.'

'What stopped you?'

'Injury. My right knee.' She looked down towards her leg without seeming to realise she did it, held out her foot in its twinkling purple shoe. 'I'll pay for this tomorrow—my knee will be swollen and throbbing. But it was worth it. To dance with such a skilled partner in this beautiful room.'

They were now standing in the midst of other people dancing around them, accidentally bumping into them, apologising in the way English people did, even when they were not at fault.

'Shall we dance?' he said, holding up his hands to her.

Her eyes lit up. Was that genuine delight at the prospect of dancing with him? Or part of the act? Without hesitation she put one hand in his and placed the other on his shoulder. 'With pleasure,' she said.

He swung her into the waltz. Immediately, she followed his lead as they fell into the rhythm of the dance. He was intensely aware of her closeness, her hand clasped in his own much bigger one, his other hand resting on the small of her back. *It was as intimate as a kiss.*

'Hey, you didn't tell me you could dance,' she said. 'You're very good.'

'My parents considered learning to dance part of my education.'

'Do you do traditional Greek dancing?' she asked as he whirled her around. She was so adept at the waltz it was obvious she didn't even have to think about what steps she took.

'But of course. Many Greek men enjoy *horos*. Dance is part of our traditional celebrations.' He realised he hadn't taken part in the traditional dances he'd enjoyed so much for a long time—rarely since his time on the islands when a day's sailing had ended in a *taverna* where all the men had joined in the dance, much to the delight of the tourists. He'd thought one day he would pass on the traditional dances of his ancestors' islands to his son—a dream long locked away.

His dreams and hopes had been frozen that night of the incident with his mother's friend, when he'd realised his parents cared too much for their decadent lifestyle to protect their son from the lascivious gazes of their guests—men as well as women. Up until then, he'd still sought their approval. But the scales had fallen from his eyes that night. He'd put a lock on his bedroom door and on his emotions.

The waltz came to an end and the music changed to a jazzy quickstep. The dance was energetic and lively and he swung Ashleigh into it, gliding and hopping where required. 'You really know how to dance,' she said, almost accusingly, as if he'd withheld such vital information from her. 'This is such fun.'

Fun. She'd accused him of putting work over enjoying life. Since when had work become an obsession, a shield?

Having fun with her was opening chinks in that shield and he wasn't sure how he felt about it.

At the end of the dance she collapsed against him, relaxed, uninhibited, laughing. She was all soft curves and warmth. He felt exhilarated by the energy of the dance, by her nearness, and he joined in her laughter. He realised he had laughed more in the days since he'd met Ashleigh than he had for a very long time.

His dancing teacher at school had berated him for his mechanical correctness in his dancing. 'It's not enough to get the steps right,' she'd said. 'You have to *feel* the dance.'

Dancing with Ashleigh, he finally felt it.

'What's next? Foxtrot? Cha-cha? Bring it on,' he said.

She looked up at him with a quizzical expression, her eyes still warm with laughter. 'You're full of surprises, Lukas Christophedes—and I'm enjoying discovering them.'

Did she mean that? Or was it all part of the act? He realised how much he wanted her to mean it.

Then the music changed to something slow and smoochy and contemporary. The kind of music that didn't call for steps but a sensual swaying, a pressing of bodies close to each other—a couple's dance.

Ashleigh took a step back from him. For a long moment his gaze locked with hers. Traces of laughter lingered in her eyes, to be replaced by something moodier that seemed to be an echo of the want that coursed through him. She wound her arms around his neck and pulled him close— breast to chest, thigh to thigh—in what was sanctioned as a dance but felt more like an intimate embrace, a prelude to a passionate kiss. He captured her thigh between his legs and they moved slowly together. *Did she want to be closer as much as he did?*

Lukas. Ashleigh gave herself over to his embrace, his arms holding her tight, his strong body pressed as close as her full skirts allowed. She ached for him to kiss her. Ached for so much *more* than a kiss. She wanted him badly. So badly she might make an utter fool of herself if he didn't feel the same. She thought she'd seen a new light in his dark eyes, a recognition of desire, a *connection*. But was it just part of the fake date—a touch of passion to add authenticity? She had never felt more uncertain of a man.

But dancing with Lukas, the waltz, felt so right—their rhythms so in step. She gasped out loud at the thought of how it might be if they became lovers. Lukas pulled away from her. 'You okay?'

'F...fine,' she stuttered. He seemed so calm, unaffected by this intimate dance—while she was a quivering wreck of want. Had she misread him entirely?

Over his shoulder, she noticed Tina making her way towards them. Ashleigh edged closer to Lukas, pressed her lips near his ear in what would surely look like a kiss to Tina. 'Tina alert—better look convincing.' Back to work on her role as a loving girlfriend—which was becoming more and more difficult as she started to want it to be for real.

But, instead of holding her tighter, Lukas stiffened, disengaged himself from her arms and abruptly stepped back from her. 'You're right to remind me. I should ask Tina to dance,' he said gruffly without looking at her.

Baffled and shaky, Ashleigh pasted a smile on her face and watched him walk away. She was still warm from the heat of his body but was rapidly cooling. Of course it was all still about the game for him. All about business. It would all be over tomorrow. She'd been a fool to even imagine it could be anything more. But he had aroused a tumult of feelings and desires in her that would not easily dissipate. *She would not let him see how it hurt.*

While Lukas danced with Tina, Ashleigh danced with Tina's business associate and made polite small talk with a huge effort. Then she danced with Tina's other guest while Lukas danced with the guest's wife. But even while Ashleigh did her duty dances her eyes were on Lukas, hungry for any glimpse of his sternly handsome face, his surprisingly graceful body. She only danced with him once again, at arm's length. She looked up at him and smiled so much the corners of her mouth ached. Pretend girlfriend was all he wanted—and she would continue to put on the best act she could. She would not give him any hint of her growing feelings. It would only embarrass both of them.

All pretence of a relationship was dropped after the ball was over and Lukas's driver drove them back to Chelsea. It became so awkward and uncomfortable that Ashleigh slumped back against her seat and pretended to be asleep.

She didn't think she fooled Lukas one little bit.

CHAPTER TEN

WHEN ASHLEIGH AWOKE next morning, Lukas's townhouse seemed very quiet. She lay back against the pillows and listened to the sounds of the house—the clock ticking, the slight shifting of old timbers, the occasional clank from the central heating. But there were none of the muted footsteps, the doors shutting, his muffled voice on the phone in the distance that she associated with the master of the house being in residence.

He must be out at one of his meetings, perhaps even with Tina Norris while his prospective business partner was still in town. Good. Ashleigh would find it hard to be chirpy and upbeat this morning. Unusually for her, she felt down, even a touch depressed. This was how Cinderella must have felt when her carriage turned back into a pumpkin and her footmen into mice. Oh, and her touched-by-fairy-dust wardrobe shrivelled back into a hand-me-down anorak and jeans.

The glorious lavender ball gown hung outside the closet where she'd left it to air last night. It looked like a work of art. The shoes had been kicked off haphazardly when she'd staggered into the room, her feet protesting against so much dancing in new leather. Those shoes! Of all the wonderful clothes Lukas had bought to outfit her for her role as pretend girlfriend, the purple suede shoes were the one thing she wished she could afford to buy from him to take with her when she left.

All around her London was fizzing with Christmas spirit. She felt like a balloon that had lost all its gas.

Fact was, Lukas had no further use for her. If Tina signed the deal—and all indications had looked good last night—the pretend girlfriend could be shunted backstage. And maybe onward to Sophie's sofa. Their paths were unlikely to cross again and she felt immeasurably sad about it. She'd become hyper-sensitive to his mood. He'd already started to distance himself from her, if the way last night's ball had ended was any indication.

Ashleigh swung her legs out of bed. Felt a twinge of discomfort from her right knee—no more dancing for a while. There was a fluffy white bathrobe in the closet that she'd been wearing, thoughtfully left there for guests. She slipped into the robe and a pair of multi-striped socks and headed downstairs.

As she neared the basement kitchen the aroma of coffee reached her. A step closer and she heard the hiss of steam from the coffee machine. When she stood at the threshold she saw Lukas. He sat at the table with his broad back to her, his laptop open in front of him and a mug of coffee nearby. He was wearing a dressing gown too, thick velour in a geometric pattern of burnt orange and chocolate brown. It came to his knees and his legs were bare—strong, tanned with just the right amount of dark hair.

From somewhere—*not her heart...surely not her heart*—came the fierce urge to loop her arms around him from behind, to nuzzle into his neck, drop a kiss there and say how wonderful the ball had been last night. How much she'd loved dancing with him. How awesome he'd been. As if he really was her man. But she couldn't do that. And she couldn't mention the ball. Because then she would have to acknowledge the feelings he'd aroused in her as he'd danced her around the room in his arms.

Ashleigh paused, uncertain whether or not to creep back

up the stairs and stay out of his way. But she wasn't a person to run away from an uncomfortable situation—the exception being her ill-fated wedding.

She remembered the excruciating silence in the car on the ride home from the ball, the stilted 'goodnight's when they'd got back here. The refusal on either side to acknowledge the sizzle of attraction between them that had burned up that dance floor. Or had the way he'd held her, the hunger in his eyes been all part of the game of pretend?

'Good morning,' she said, attempting chirpy but resulting in croaky. 'Any chance of a coffee?'

'Of course,' he said. He went to get up. She caught her breath at how handsome he looked, his jaw shadowed with dark growth, his hair unruly and falling over his forehead. Of course it wasn't her *heart* that reacted to him—it was her body thrilling to the sight of him, remembering last night and the erotic sensation of the dance. *It was her body wanting him, not her heart.*

'Stay there. I can make my own.'

She prepared the coffee in silence. Then sat down two chairs away from him, nursing her mug in her hands. 'I didn't expect to find you here. Thought you'd be gone off to a meeting.'

'It's Saturday,' he responded, with more of a grunt than words. Did he have a hangover? She hadn't seen him drink more than a few glasses of wine.

'Oh. Of course,' she said. The last days seemed to have merged into each other with that feeling of a life that wasn't quite real.

'Lukas?'

'Yes,' he said, barely looking up.

'If it's Saturday, why are you working?'

Finally, he took his eyes from the screen. The dressing gown had fallen open to reveal rather more sculpted male chest than she felt able to deal with right now. She flushed and forced her eyes away as she remembered how good it had felt to be crushed against him while they were dancing. He had felt it too, she'd convinced herself. But she'd obviously been wrong—very wrong.

Too late she realised how intimate it seemed now, both of them in their dressing gowns drinking coffee. She should have gone back upstairs and changed. She had boxer shorts and a T-shirt under her dressing gown. His legs were bare, his chest was bare. What else was he wearing—or not?

'Because I'm *always* working. Anyway, how do you know I'm working? I could be playing chess or reading the newspaper online.'

'You could be, but you're frowning so deeply it could only be work. What is it? A problem with the Tina deal?'

His frown deepened into a scowl. 'Running a business like mine means problem-solving twenty-four-seven.'

'That doesn't leave much room for *life*.'

'My work is my life; I've told you that. Every day is a work day for me.'

'Even at Christmas?'

'Why not? Christmas Day is just like any other day to me.'

She gasped. 'You can't mean that.' His words would have counted as heresy in her family.

'I most certainly do.'

'I didn't take you for a Scrooge.'

'*Humph,*' he muttered.

'Actually, that grumpy noise did sound a lot like Scrooge. Though a *bah, humbug* would have been better.'

The ghost of a smile lightened his scowl. 'You will not get me to say *bah, humbug*. Christmas is as big a deal in Greece as it is here. But not for me. My parents weren't religious and Christmas was just another excuse for a round of parties. They gave the lavish presents, but there was never any real feeling in it.'

'That's such a shame. Even when you were a little boy?'

'My English nanny did her best but she always went home for Christmas. I used to beg her to take me. One year my parents let me go with her and—'

'They let their little boy go to a different country to stay with strangers?' She didn't try to disguise her shock.

He made the *humph* noise again. 'My parents were the strangers. My nanny was more family to me than they ever were. They wanted to go on a cruise where a little boy would have been an inconvenience. That Christmas in her family's very ordinary house in a suburb of Birmingham was the best I ever had. I still remember it. Sadly, never to be repeated.'

Ashleigh felt stunned by the image of the lonely little boy with dark hair and unhappy brown eyes, unwanted by his family at Christmas. But she knew Lukas would not respond well to pity. 'My family has always made a big deal about Christmas. The tree. The presents. The dinner. Because my father is English, we always have the full-on traditional meal with all the trimmings—even in the sweltering heat of a Queensland summer.'

'Christmas in summer? It doesn't seem right.'

'It doesn't really, does it? The two winter Christmases we spent in Manchester were magic. But there's something to be said for a hot Christmas too. My family has a swimming pool and some years we'd take our food outside and eat in the pool.'

'You sound very close to your family.' There was a note of wistfulness in his voice that grabbed at her heart.

'I am.'

'So why are you staying in London and not going home?'

Why would she go into detail about Dan's infiltration of her family—and their disloyalty to her in encouraging it? Lukas wouldn't want to hear all that; he'd probably find it boring. She'd give the easy answer. 'Because I want to enjoy the full English Christmas experience. I'm just hoping it's going to snow.'

'It doesn't often snow in London for Christmas.' His voice was blunt, negative. Had his unhappy childhood squeezed out all the joy of Christmas? Now she felt sad, not just for the little boy but also for the adult Lukas. He deserved so much more. She wished she could be the person to give him the happiness and joy that would lift those dark shadows.

'Well, I hope it will for me.' She got up from the table. 'Can I make you some breakfast?'

'No, thank you.' He pointed to the coffee. 'That's all I want.' Everything he said, the way he kept his gaze on his screen, indicated he didn't want more from her than their agreed upon charade. She should probably grab something from the fridge and take it back to her room. But her hours with Lukas were limited and she was not going to squander them—no matter his not so subtle message of *leave me alone*.

'I'll make toast for me.'

'The toaster is—' He paused. 'I forgot. You know your way around the kitchen. Probably better than I do.'

'Uh…yes.' She still cringed at any reminder of her misdemeanour.

'About that. The day you were out shopping, I contacted Clio at Maids in Chelsea and told her I needed your maid service full-time while I was in residence.'

'You did? I haven't had a chance to do much housework while I—'

'I didn't expect you to. You've been working for me in a different way. But Clio won't be booking you for other assignments. Saves any messy explanations about what you're doing here.'

'Thank you,' she said. She paused for a long moment—

too long as it began to feel uncomfortable. 'I know I'm here in your house under sufferance.'

He didn't disagree.

'And I'll stay out of your way as much as I can. Christmas Day is next Friday. I'm a bridesmaid for a wedding on Wednesday. Well, it's really a renewal of vows. My friend got married in secret when she was eighteen and didn't have a proper wedding. But now—'

He made an impatient wave of his hand. 'Okay. I get it.' Then, seeming to realise how abrupt—even rude—he'd sounded, he said, 'I'm sorry. Weddings hold no interest for me.'

His words came back to her: *I never will marry.* He was happy to be labelled a *lone wolf.* What was the point of even imagining there could ever be anything between them?

'Okay,' she said through gritted teeth. 'No wedding talk. But I'll be out all day tomorrow doing bridesmaid duty.'

He nodded. 'Okay.'

'Any word from Tina?'

His deal with Tina was his only interest in her. Of course he didn't want to hear about her friend's ceremony—even if the bride was a countess and married to an earl. She was dying to tell someone about being Emma's bridesmaid. But she couldn't even call her best friend back in Bundaberg as she was yet another person annoyed with her for walking out on the wedding.

Lukas shook his head. 'Tina doesn't work on weekends if she can avoid it, she says.'

'Like sensible people,' Ashleigh said pointedly.

He did the *humph* thing again.

'So I'm still playing my girlfriend role?'

'Until I tell you otherwise,' he said.

The kitchen ended in a wall of French windows looking out onto the garden. 'Look at the beautiful day out there,' she said, indicating the garden. 'I'm told those clear blue skies

aren't the norm for London at this time of year. As your official pretend girlfriend, I suggest you get outside and enjoy
this crisp winter day instead of working all the time.'

'That's beyond the scope of your role,' he growled.

She took a deep steadying breath. 'Lukas, look at me,
please.'

Grudgingly, he raised his head from his laptop. His dark
brown eyes didn't give anything away.

'We get on well, don't we?' she said. 'Perhaps it's only
the pretend versions of ourselves that get on but I've enjoyed the time I've spent with you. In spite of…of an awkward beginning. And unless you're such a good actor you
should be playing in the West End, I don't think you've
found my company objectionable.'

It certainly hadn't seemed that way on the dance floor.

He frowned. 'Where are you going with this?'

'I'm finding this…awkward. Couldn't we actually pretend to be friends in the time we have left in each other's
company? I mean, just between you and me. When we're
anywhere in public we can keep up the boyfriend/girlfriend
thing until the deal with Tina is finalised. But when it's
just us, do we need to put barriers up? It's the festive season. Each of us is on our own. London must surely be one
of the most magical places in the world to be for Christmas. Can we enjoy some of it together? As…as friends?'

She knew she wanted so much more than that from
him. It would be like a scrap thrown from the master's
table but at the moment she just wanted to grab any time
with him—no matter the circumstances.

Lukas stared at her for such a long moment she started to
shift from foot to foot in her crazy striped socks. He could
see regret dim the astonishing blue of her eyes. Regret
and *rejection*. He didn't want her to feel that kind of pain.

He was being boorish to her. She didn't deserve that

just because he'd woken up irritable and out of sorts after a bad night's sleep. Just because she'd made it clear last night that the surprising intimacy of the dance had just been part of the game he'd staged between them to fool Tina. When he'd found himself wanting so much more.

Those exhilarating moments when he'd been dancing with her, he'd been convinced she'd felt it too—the feeling that was infiltrating in a matter of a few days the barriers he'd erected years ago around his emotions. But then she'd brought him crashing back to reality with her murmured reminder that they'd better *look convincing.* He'd known this woman for such a short time but it had gone way beyond a game for him. He should brush her off. Protect himself. But he could not pass up the opportunity to spend more time with her.

'Friends? Great idea.' He forced enthusiasm into his voice, and was rewarded with a sighting of her dimples.

'You mean that?'

She was offering him something *real.* Not pretend. He doubted she was capable of fake friendship. But how could he be *friends* with a woman for whom he felt such an intense attraction?

'What do you suggest that *friends* might do on a day like this?' he said gruffly. He knew what he'd like to do, but imagining her naked with him in his bedroom, her back in his bathtub this time with him, went beyond any platonic concept of friendship.

'Do you need to buy any gifts? It's the last Saturday before Christmas; the shops—' Her cheerful, practical voice put paid to any lingering thoughts that she might share any of the same sensual fantasies.

'My personal assistant in Athens has organised all that.'

'Even for your family?'

'Yes,' he said, tight-lipped. 'She knows my family's tastes better than I do.'

'That seems so…impersonal.'

'But efficient.'

'Whatever works for you,' she said. Was there implied criticism there? If so, he didn't bite.

Christmas with his parents was impersonal and soulless and left him feeling sad. The last few years had been particularly depressing. Once he'd hit thirty there were constant hints from his parents that it was time for him to settle down—they wanted children in the house for Christmas. It seemed as they'd aged they had turned to traditional family life but he couldn't believe they were sincere. The scars from their neglect ran too deep. Even though his mother had gone into rehab for her drinking, apologised for her neglect, expressed her horror at the incident with her former friend. That was why he'd decided to spend Christmas this year in Chelsea. Being on his own couldn't be worse than being lonely in the company of other people.

'It works,' he said dismissively. He'd already revealed too much to Ashleigh. She was turning his long-established life of avoiding emotional commitment upside down with unwarranted hopes and longings. Not only did she still have a man in Australia but she'd also stated she wanted to stay single.

Could he entice her into a no-strings affair? He immediately dismissed the idea. Not just because she was not the type for casual and carnal but neither was *he*. Not with this woman. The realisation shook him to his very core. *It terrified him*.

Ashleigh went on, determinedly cheerful. He was so shaken he barely heard her. 'What about Christmas decorations? Do you have any packed away here? Maybe in the attic?'

'No. I've never spent Christmas in this house. I always spend it in Athens.'

'It's a shame not to have at least a tree in this fabulous

house. There's a Christmas market in the King's Road today. I'm sure they would have decorations and—'

'Too crowded. The shops will be packed. If you want decorations buy them at Harrods during the week and have them delivered. You still have the credit card I gave you, I assume?'

She snatched her hand to her mouth. 'I'm sorry. I forgot to give it back. But I assure you I haven't used it since—'

'I meant you to keep it. Until after…after—' Whatever he said would sound offensive.

'Until I'm no longer useful to you.' Her eyes dimmed and her mouth turned down.

'I didn't mean—' He hated the look of hurt on her face but struggled to find the words to suggest there could be a different direction for them.

She put up her hand to halt him. 'Of course you did and it doesn't matter. I know the score. I never assumed—'

She was right. She didn't assume, she didn't take advantage. And she wanted to be *friends*. For the few days she would spend in this house before she went back to her own world, so very different to his. How could he have imagined, even for a fleeting moment, that it could be any different?

'You made an excellent impression on Tina. Anything you spent on the credit card was worth it. If you want to buy Christmas decorations just do it.'

'Thank you, I will. The house doesn't feel festive without at least a wreath at the front door.'

'Or a pomegranate hung there.'

'A pomegranate? Is that a Greek custom?'

'For good luck,' he said.

Ashleigh smiled. 'We might have to settle for an English wreath,' she said.

We. They were not a couple. They would never be a couple. So why did it send such a warm feeling through him when she referred to them as *we*? Ashleigh Murphy was turning everything he'd been so sure of completely upside down.

He closed the lid of his laptop. There were no problems there that couldn't be solved at a later time. 'Perhaps you're right. I should go out with my friend. Where do you want to go? Apart from shopping, that is?'

'Seriously?'

He nodded.

'I want to go ice-skating at the Natural History Museum.'

CHAPTER ELEVEN

ICE-SKATING WASN'T AS easy as she had imagined, Ashleigh thought, as she slid and slipped on the ice while other skaters whizzed by her to the sound of recorded Christmas carols. She had visited the Natural History Museum in South Kensington for the first time as a teenager when she'd been living in Manchester and been enthralled by its displays of dinosaurs and whales. When she'd heard there was an outdoor ice rink set up in the grounds of the museum during winter she'd put it on her wish list for when she was in London.

It didn't disappoint. While she and Lukas waited for their session to start she'd been mesmerised by the beauty of the imposing Victorian buildings of the museum reflected in the ice, surrounded by winter-bare trees and a towering Christmas tree. However, her skills on ice were a definite disappointment.

'Why didn't you tell me this was your first time skating?' said Lukas. But he seemed more amused than angry as he steadied her with his arm around her.

'I'm a dancer, I've skied—I thought it would be easy.'

'It is, once you get the hang of it.'

'Then what am I doing wrong?' she yelped, as her right foot went the opposite way she wanted it to. 'I'm just not getting it.'

'Bend your knees, use the edges of your blades, lean forward and don't look down—I said don't look… Ashleigh, don't look—' *Oomph*. His words were lost in a gasp of expelled air as she came down on the ice, pulling him down with her. 'Protect your fingers from other peoples' blades—make a fist,' he said urgently.

Ashleigh had come down hard and was too winded to reply. 'Sorry,' she finally gasped.

'Let's get you off the ice,' he said, hooking his arms under hers and hauling them both back upright. That was where her balance and strength did help her get back on her feet. 'Come on, we'll take to the side, where you're out of the way.'

'So sorry,' she said. He was so accomplished, so confident and she felt foolish he was having to help her. But she loved his protectiveness, his strength, the sure way he held her. *Lap it up, Ashleigh, enjoy being friends.*

'Stop apologising,' he said. 'You're a learner. You fell. No big deal. You're wearing hired skates too, which are not ideal.' He, of course, had his own skates.

She leaned in relief against the low wall that enclosed the rink. 'Thank you.'

'Ready to go again?' he said.

'Sure.' She put weight on her right foot and winced.

'Something hurting?' She was surprised at the concern in his voice.

'My knee. This wasn't the brightest idea I've ever had. Not after all the dancing last night. I should have put ice on my knee, not put my knee on the ice.'

He put his arm around her shoulder and she leaned back against its strength and comfort. That made it almost worth crash-landing on the ice.

'It's a shame,' he said. 'You were doing well.'

'No need to be kind,' she said with a wobbly smile. 'I was a disaster.'

'You weren't bad for a beginner. If it wasn't for your

knee, I'd insist you got right back on the ice. But, as it is, you need to rest that knee,' he said.

'I need to sit down; you don't,' she said. 'You're a marvellous skater and you must be itching to do more than you did shepherding me around the rink. Go back and skate.'

He didn't argue and once he had settled her in an observation seat he glided back onto the ice.

There were a lot of people on the rink—some demonstrating incredible skill. But Ashleigh only had eyes for Lukas. In black jeans and a black roll-neck sweater that showed off his athletic physique, he skated fast and skilfully around the perimeter of the rink. As he zoomed past her he raised his hand in a wave and grinned. She waved back, stopped herself from blowing him a kiss. *A friend wouldn't do that.* Somehow he looked younger, more relaxed, happier even. More a regular thirty-four-year-old guy enjoying a physical challenge. The kind of guy she really would like as a friend.

Who was she kidding? She wanted him—more than she had ever wanted a man. In reality, she couldn't be just friends with Lukas. She fancied him too much for there ever to be the comfortable, easy friendship she had with men for whom she felt no attraction. She hadn't lost that urge to push him up against a wall and kiss him—she'd just got better at denying it.

She thrust her hands deep into the pockets of her coat— the lavender one. Thank heaven she hadn't torn or stained it in her fall. Lukas had forbidden her to leave the house in the anorak, which she'd thought was more suitable for ice-skating. Eyes riveted to the rink, she watched him glide and spin and gasped her admiration when he jumped and landed perfectly on the ice.

He was magnificent. She wanted all that energy, all that vigour and passion directed to her. Her body ached for him so much a shiver of pure desire rippled through her. But her heart clamoured for airtime too. This wasn't just about physical attraction—an awareness that had been there from the moment she'd first met him shouting at her to get out of his bathtub. This was so much more.

She was falling in love with him. Against all reason, against all common sense she was falling for him. A lone wolf who had told her he was married to his work. A man who was prepared to manipulate and lie—and coerce her to lie—to get what he wanted. Who was so good at dissembling she didn't know what was real or play-acting.

Ashleigh drew in a breath of the chilly air in an effort to calm the tumult of her emotions. She had to fight this with all her being or she could end up as wounded as she had with Travis, her university heartbreaker, all those years ago. Then she'd been too naive to recognise Travis for what he was. Now Lukas had made it very clear he wasn't the kind for a happy-ever-after. And she wasn't the kind for a meaningless fling. Heck, Lukas hadn't given any indication he was interested enough even for a fling. He had stuck to the letter of their agreement. That passion she'd sensed on the dance floor, coiled ready to be unleashed, had obviously been a figment of her imagination. He was every bit as good an actor as Travis had been.

Lukas skated around the rink more slowly then glided to a halt with an impressive spray of ice. By the time he'd taken off his skates and joined her where she was sitting, she was shivering. He noticed straight away and went to take off his down jacket to put over her shoulders.

'I'm not that cold,' she protested. 'Please keep your coat. Really.'

'Delayed shock from your fall,' he said. 'A hot drink might help.'

She needed a lot more than a hot drink to cure what was ailing her—a kiss would work as a starter—but that was all he had to offer. She would grab what she could in the time she had left with him. *Just friends*, she reminded herself.

Lukas sat opposite Ashleigh in the café that overlooked the rink. He watched the colour return to her cheeks as she sipped on rich, sweet hot chocolate then nibbled on a *churro* dusted with cinnamon and powdered sugar. It left a smear of sugar on her lower lip. He wanted to reach over and wipe it away with his finger. Better, to press his mouth against hers and lick it, to test which tasted sweeter—the sugar or her delicious mouth.

'Feeling better?' he asked.

She nodded. 'Although my pride might take a while to recover from its battering.'

She took another sip of her chocolate. To his intense disappointment it washed away the smear of sugar.

'May I suggest you get some tuition from a professional next time you hit the ice?' he said. 'A lesson or two to get you started and, with your dancing skills, you'll soon be spinning with the best of them.'

'Thank you for that vote of confidence,' she said. She didn't like to fail, he realised. 'You were awesome on the ice.'

'I learned as a kid. I guess you didn't get much opportunity to ice-skate in your home town.' Curious about her background, he'd looked up Bundaberg on the Internet.

'You're right there,' she said. 'There are indoor ice rinks in Brisbane, where I went to university, but I wasn't really interested. It's here that's the attraction. London. Even though I was a dud on skates, the experience of being here counts for everything.'

'Yet surely you must miss being home for Christmas. From what you say, you're very close to your family.'

That closeness and sense of belonging was something he found himself envying. Christmas seemed to magnify the sterility of his own family life. Not that he should care. That little rich boy who had to fly to a council house in Birmingham to experience a loving family Christmas had long grown up into a man who had given up hope that the festive season would ever mean anything to him again.

'Of course I do,' she said. 'This will be the first Christmas I've spent apart from my family. It will feel weird not to be with them.'

'Why not fly home for a few days and come back to London?'

She rubbed her thumb against her first two fingers together to signify lack of cash. He could pay for her fare if she really wanted to go. 'But it isn't just the money. It's... complicated.'

'How do you mean?'

She paused and he could tell by the expressions that flickered across her face she was debating whether or not to tell him. 'Because my family are insisting on inviting my ex for Christmas and I don't want to be there if he's there.'

He frowned. 'Your family would choose your former fiancé over you?'

'So it seems,' she said, her lush mouth trembling with hurt and betrayal.

'Why would they do such a thing?'

'In some misguided attempt at getting us to reconcile, I suspect,' she said, compressing her lips to a tight line.

'They must believe that there's a case for that.'

Her pale redhead's skin flushed. 'Please don't tell me you're another one who doesn't believe a twenty-seven-year-old woman who decided she didn't want to marry a guy would have cancelled a wedding and burdened herself with debt if she didn't really mean it.'

'So tell me why your family thinks this way. It puzzles

me.' He remembered how convincing Céline had been that everything had been over with her boyfriend back home.

Ashleigh rested on her elbows and leaned across the table towards him. 'Let me tell you about Dan. His mother was friends with my mother. The mums were delighted when they had babies within six months of each other—Dan being born first. We were destined to be together, according to them. Actually, we were thrown together so much we did become childhood friends. Dan was the closest thing I had to a brother. But he was always teasing me and it bugged me. As we got into our teens it got worse; he was trying to get my attention I see now. I avoided him. The joke that we'd get married when we grew up wore very thin. Then we went away to Manchester. When I got back for my final year of high school Dan had grown up into the handsomest boy in the school.'

'And you fell for him.'

'He was hot. I was flattered he still only had eyes for me. We dated. But we were kids. I didn't want just the one boyfriend.'

'High school is much too young to be serious,' he said. Yet some of his friends had married their teenage sweethearts and were happy. In fact, they felt sorry for him, single at thirty-four. He was only alone because he wanted to be, he reminded himself. Or because he had never met a woman who made him think otherwise. Until now. Until *this* woman, who was still entangled with another man.

'I broke it off with him when I went to university,' she said, continuing her story. 'I wanted to explore new interests, new friendships.'

'How did he take it?' It was difficult for him to hear this, to think of her with that other man. He forced himself to act the disinterested friend.

She shrugged. 'Okay, I thought. But it didn't seem to change things with him. "I'm always here for you," he'd say.'

'To cut a long story short, I had my heart badly broken at uni, then made a few rotten choices that also ended badly. But when I went home to Bundaberg on vacation, there was always Dan waiting there with a shoulder to cry on and to bolster my ego. I began to think I couldn't do better than Dan. He wouldn't hurt me. We started dating again. Our families were delighted. I... I chose the safe harbour rather than the wild, tumultuous waves that had thrown me so painfully on the rocks when they'd finished with me.'

'Were you happy with him?' He hated the thought of her with another man yet he had to ask.

Her mouth twisted. 'If happy meant the absence of pain and angst. If happy meant comfortable and predictable. If happy meant being bored but telling myself that was the price for security.'

'And Dan?' The man had kept taking her back—and Lukas would bet he would do it again. It wouldn't surprise him to find the Australian on his doorstep in Chelsea wanting to know where his bride was. Then he, Lukas, would be pushed aside.

'Here's the weird thing—he was the son of my mother's best friend. When his parents split up it was like he moved onto family number two. It became like he wanted to marry into my family as much as he wanted me. The more certain of me he got, the more he bonded with my parents and sister. The teasing started again. I began to feel undermined, disrespected, ganged up on. They'd laugh off my protests as if I was a kid. In the end I'd had enough. You know the rest.'

'Yet your family seem convinced you'll go back to him. Again.'

'Aaargh!' She mimed tearing out her lovely red hair. 'Even you don't believe me. I will *never* go back to Dan. *Ever.* I started to drown in that safe harbour. And now...

Well, now I want the wild sea. I want the passion. And I want a man who'll ride those waves with me and only *me*.'

Her eyes sparked that blue fire that excited him. She held his gaze. Was there a message there for him? Or was he seeing what he wanted to see? Eventually, she dropped her eyes. He remembered just days ago she'd sworn she wanted to stay single. Now she wanted a man to give her passion. Why had she changed her mind? Because of *him*? A tiny flame of hope flickered to life in his heart that had been so cold for so long.

'So now you know why I will not be going back to Bundaberg for Christmas,' she said emphatically.

Lukas still wasn't sure he believed her. She drained her hot chocolate. Picked up the remaining crumbs of her *churro* with her finger and licked them off with the tip of her pink, pointy tongue accompanied by a throaty little murmur of appreciation. Was she doing this to provoke him? Or did she just like *churros*?

'What about you, Lukas? When do you fly to Athens?'

'I don't,' he said. 'I'm staying here in London.'

Her eyes widened. 'But you said you always spend Christmas in Athens.'

'This year is the exception. Rather than endure another of my parents' idea of a festive celebration, I decided to spend Christmas Day on my own in one of my favourite houses in one of my favourite cities.'

'Oh,' she said. 'I was planning to travel to Manchester to spend the day with Sophie and her family but if you're here on your own I'll—'

'Please don't change your plans on my account. I'm happy to be here on my own. I *want* to be here on my own.' But, once planted, the thought did not go away. Christmas Day with just Ashleigh and him in the house…

'I don't like the thought of you being in London all by yourself,' she said. But he only saw friendly concern in her eyes. He could not read more into it—that would only lead to disillusion and the kind of pain he had protected himself against for so long.

He glanced down at his watch. 'I enjoyed today. Thank you for getting me away from my computer. It did me good.'

She smiled. 'I'm glad. You see, I'm on a mission for you to stop being such a workaholic and enjoy life. As I said earlier, what's the point of being a billionaire if you don't have fun?'

'Work is fun—maybe you have yet to learn that,' he said.

She was right, but he wasn't going to admit it. He was too used to guarding himself, to not admitting to anything that could be perceived as weakness. A kind of myth had developed around him in his country—the invincible young man who had modernised a product, turned around a company, transformed loss into soaring profit and created sorely needed jobs at a time of economic disaster. If the distribution deal with Tina worked out, and his marketing people did their work—which they would or they would lose those jobs—a new market meant more opportunities for his company and his people.

'Perhaps,' she said. 'In the new year I'll have to seriously think about what I'm doing here. Waitressing is all very well in the short term but it's not a career.' She dimpled at him. 'Nor is being your maid.' He wanted her as so much more than a maid. But the thought that she intended to stay in London further fanned the new hope in his heart.

'Will you look for work as an accountant?'

'Probably. You know Tina offered to help me?'

'No. You didn't tell me that.' He felt uncomfortable at the thought that Ashleigh might step out of line. Dealing with Tina Norris was not her place. And he didn't trust Tina's motives.

'Don't look so annoyed,' she said. 'Of course I thanked her but obviously it will never happen. I won't ever see her again.'

'No,' he said. And very soon he'd be saying goodbye to Ashleigh.

It was not a happy thought.

CHAPTER TWELVE

ASHLEIGH SPENT A delightful day on Sunday with Emma and the other two bridesmaids, Sophie and Grace. She also met Emma's childhood friend and sister-in-law, Clare, who was to be Emma's chief bridesmaid. Ashleigh liked Clare immediately. She felt she was building real friends—important if she were to stay indefinitely in the UK. Bundaberg seemed a long way away, a different world. *And too far away from Lukas,* an insistent voice from deep in her heart reminded her.

They enjoyed the morning at Sophie's tiny flat in the furthermost edge of Chelsea, trying on their bridesmaid outfits, exquisite vintage-style dresses in a dusky pink silk trimmed with antique lace. When the others marvelled at how quickly she'd got the dresses to fitting stage, Sophie explained she'd already had the fabric, purchased ages ago at a market.

The four bridesmaids braved the Christmas crowds to shop for shoes in Oxford Street and had a delightfully girly lunch in the stylish café in Selfridges department store. Ashleigh couldn't help contrasting Emma's confidence and joy in making plans for her renewed marriage to how she'd felt planning her wedding to Dan.

She'd been irritable, snappy, picking fault with the dresses, the caterer's menu, with everything. Deep down she'd known marrying him wasn't right. She should have listened to her instinct earlier. That same instinct that was telling her that if she ever had a chance to be with Lukas it would be earth-shatteringly wonderful—wild waves the like of which she had never imagined existed. If only she had even an inkling that he might feel the same.

But when her friends asked her how things were going with the 'pretend boyfriend' she just described the Butterfly Ball and the show dance and told them how well the outfit they'd helped her buy had been received. Her feelings for Lukas were something to be hugged to herself.

After she said goodbye to her friends she went back to Chelsea via Harrods, where she bought decorations for Lukas's house—exquisite glass baubles and ornaments and a beautifully crafted artificial tree.

He wasn't at the house so she put them up alone, giving in to the indulgence of imagining how very different it would be if they were decorating his house together. Lukas and her getting into the spirit of Christmas, Lukas reaching up to help her put the star at the top of the tree, Lukas manoeuvring her under the mistletoe she'd hung in the hallway.

Her sigh echoed through the empty living room. *Wasn't going to happen.* But at least he would celebrate his solitary Christmas Day with some of the festive trimmings in his fabulous house. Maybe, just maybe, they might inspire thoughts of her.

The next morning, Ashleigh lay in Lukas's guest bed for longer than she should have. She counted down the remaining days until she'd have to kiss its featherbed luxury goodbye and head for the dubious comfort of Sophie's sofa with the broken spring. The plan was she would pack her bag on Christmas Eve, head up to Manchester with Sophie and then return to her London flat with Sophie the day after Boxing Day. All her borrowed finery would stay behind in this room. With one exception. There was just one thing she was determined to take with her—too bad the possible consequences.

Her smartphone buzzed the presence of an incoming text message. If it was Dan or her parents or her sister begging her to reconsider her decision to come home for Christmas she'd throw the phone at the wall. But it was from Lukas, asking her to meet him in his study at her earliest opportunity. Her heart sank right to the level of the basement kitchen. So this was it. Eviction time.

She got dressed with hands that shook so much she could barely pull up the zip on her jeans and drag a long-sleeved black T-shirt over her head.

Then she was in his office, back where they'd started—him handsome and imposing on one side of the desk, her the intruder on the other.

But he got up to greet her with the biggest smile she'd seen on his face. Her heart seemed to flip inside her at how handsome he looked, his dark eyes lit with excitement. 'Good news. Tina has signed our agreement. We'll be doing business.'

'That's great news,' she said, forcing enthusiasm into her voice. 'Congratulations.'

'Our strategy paid off,' he said.

Now he had no need for her—she was meant to be delighted about that? 'So it's over. The pretend boyfriend and girlfriend thing, I mean,' she said dully. In truth, she was glad about that part. Keeping up the charade had become too difficult. Not when she wanted it to be something unscripted and genuine.

'Not quite,' he said. 'Tina has invited us to celebrate with her tonight at her Mayfair apartment for drinks.' How casually he included her as the other half of the *us* equation.

Panic threatened to choke her reply. She couldn't do

this. Not now. She could no longer pretend feelings for him that had become so painfully real. Her gaze darted around the room, to his rows of books in both English and Greek, the blue paperweight on his desk that was a Greek charm against the evil eye—intrigued, she'd looked it up when she'd first dusted his desk—anywhere but at him. 'I… I can't… I just—'

'Just one more time, Ashleigh. Please.' Finally, she faced him to see an expression she hadn't seen before on his features. A subtle shift. Not pleading. Not demanding. Just asking a favour of an equal. 'Because we're friends now,' he said.

How could she refuse when he played that card? She nodded, still having difficulty with her words.

'Thank you,' he said, with a sincerity that was new to her. 'This deal is important. Not just to me and my company. But to my country, which needs the employment and the tax revenue it will bring. These are troubling times.'

Again she nodded. There was so much more to this man than she had imagined on that first meeting in this room when he had threatened her with jail. She ached to know him better. Would she ever get the chance?

'This will mean more shopping, I'm afraid,' he said.

She managed a wobbly smile. 'You're afraid?' she said. 'When you've just uttered words that are magic to a woman's ears?'

He smiled back and for a long moment her eyes locked with his. Surely there was something new there. Amusement? Affection? Whatever it was, it warmed her. *Even if it was only friendship.*

She would love to be able to hand him back his credit card and tell him she would buy her own new clothes for the drinks with Tina. But she needed every penny for when she had to find accommodation in the new year. And he wanted her to look the part of his consort. She looked down at her jeans. 'So I guess I'd better get into my shopping outfit,' she said.

'You'll enjoy it more if you do,' he said.

She held her breath, hoping he would say he would accompany her. When he didn't, she let it out on a sigh that was disappointment edged with relief. Maybe it was for the best. Having him there with her, assessing her choices through narrowed, sexy eyes would only make her life more difficult than it had suddenly become. *In love with her billionaire boss.* How could she have been so foolish to let this happen?

'A dress, do you think?' she asked.

'You've done everything right so far,' he said. 'I'll leave it to you.'

Now that her use to him was nearly at an end he didn't care. She forced a smile on her face as she thanked him.

Of course Ashleigh had got it right, Lukas thought that evening as Tina welcomed them to her apartment. As she'd done from the get-go. Poised and elegant, Ashleigh wore a fitted black dress with strategically placed sheer panels that sent a man's imagination into a frenzy but didn't actually reveal anything. She'd bought new shoes too—sexy black stilettos with a flat bow on the front and laced around her ankles. With his mother's coat flung over the top, she looked perfect for the part she was about to play for the last time.

'Welcome,' Tina effused. 'I'm so glad you two were available to toast the sealing of our deal.' As if he'd had a choice—this deal was too important to risk offending her.

Tina air-kissed Lukas on each cheek then did the same to Ashleigh. 'I'm so glad we'll be doing business together,' Tina said.

But Lukas wasn't sure if she was directing her words to him or to Ashleigh. Both of them, he supposed, as Tina made such a big deal of vetting people's spouses. He didn't trust the way the older woman had suggested she could help Ashleigh find a job. That was not part of the remit. It could be ulterior motive on her part, but then again she seemed to genuinely like Ashleigh.

Tina might even be disappointed when, after a decent interval, he informed her that Ashleigh had decided he was merely a rebound guy and had moved on. A cold sweat broke out on his forehead. Forget Tina. *He* would be gutted when she was no longer around.

A pleasant-looking young man offered them champagne flutes from a silver tray. Lukas grabbed one. *He needed a drink.* Lukas took the guy for a waiter. He was shocked when the waiter took a glass for himself. Even more shocked when Tina smiled and introduced him as her boyfriend, Gary.

Lukas caught Ashleigh's eye. She discreetly raised her eyebrows, obviously as surprised as he was. Lukas's first reaction was relief. So the cougar had found herself a toy boy. That took him completely off the hook. He still shuddered at the memory of that older woman friend of his mother's invading his bedroom.

But then, when both couples were seated together on the cream sofas in Tina's small but elegantly appointed living room, he noticed the body language between Tina and Gary and wondered what was really going on. There was something genuine there. Not something to make fun of.

'Your apartment is beautiful,' said Ashleigh to kick off the conversation.

'Couldn't afford it now,' said Tina with typical bluntness. 'My father bought it as a pied-à-terre back in the nineteen sixties. These days Mayfair is a cosmopolitan outpost of Moscow and Dubai and prices are astronomical.'

'Indeed,' said Lukas. He didn't like to discuss his personal finances with anyone other than his bankers. In fact he felt uncomfortable discussing *anything* personal with anyone.

Gary squeezed Tina's hand and got up from the sofa. 'I'm sure you'd like some food,' he said. He shared Tina's Liverpudlian accent.

'Gary is a chef,' Tina explained as her eyes followed the younger man from the room. 'He works for the catering company I use in Liverpool. But he's cooked for us tonight as my man.' She seemed to take extraordinary pleasure from the words *my man*.

'He seems very nice,' said Ashleigh diplomatically.

'That he is,' said Tina. 'I've known him a while. Always liked him. He liked me. But he's twenty-five and I'm forty-five. It seemed impossible.'

'No one would blink an eyelid if your ages were reversed,' Ashleigh said. 'Why should it matter? Besides, you don't look older at all.' *Well done, Ashleigh*, Lukas thought. Though she was only stretching the truth a little. No way did Tina look forty-five.

'I began to realise that,' Tina said. 'But it was you who finally made me see it.'

'Me?' said Ashleigh.

'Ashleigh?' said Lukas at the same time.

Tina addressed Ashleigh. 'The night we met for dinner when you said love comes when you're not looking for it. When that person comes along who makes you feel only half alive when you're apart. That's how I felt about Gary. And, happily, how he felt about me. I didn't invite him to the Butterfly Ball, too worried what people might think. I missed him so much all night. Seeing you two so happy, so in love, made me realise there was no running from what I felt any more.'

We're not in love. Lukas had to stop the words from blurting out. He noticed Ashleigh frown. Because she didn't like the idea of him being in love with her? Or because he didn't acknowledge Tina's words?

'That's such a lovely story, Tina,' said Ashleigh with a warm, genuine smile. 'I'm glad I was of some help, even inadvertently.' Not only was Ashleigh beautiful, she was kind and warm and supportive—everything he'd thought he would never find in a woman.

One thing was for certain—he intended to politely eat some of Gary's superb hors d'oeuvres and then get the hell away from this place. He had to be alone with Ashleigh. Once and for all, he had to see if there was something real between them.

It was as if all Ashleigh's fantasies had come to life. As soon as she and Lukas reached the pavement outside Tina's apartment, he turned her to him, looked deep into her face. She thrilled to the intensity of his eyes, the way they narrowed as he searched her face, the sensual half curve of his mouth. Then, without a word, he pulled her close to him.

Finally, the truth—no words required. His quickened breathing told her all she needed to know. *He wanted her as much as she wanted him.* Her gasp of impatience, of *want*, no doubt sent the same message to him.

Then his mouth was on hers, hard, warm, exciting, demanding a response. She parted her lips, welcomed him, kissed him back. It felt as if she'd waited all her life for this. For *him*. It hadn't started sweet and gentle and went straight to deep and demanding—an urgent meeting of mouths and tongues, of bodies straining hard against each other. His overcoat was open. She splayed her hands on his hard chest and pushed him to the wall behind him. *At last*. This. *Lukas*. Her heart thudded loud and fast. He slid his hands inside her coat, to pull her close—as close as she could be to his body through layers of winter clothes. Her nipples tightened as desire pulsed through her in a wave that demanded more. He held her so close to his body she felt his response, hard and insistent, which further inflamed her. *She wanted him.*

'Lukas,' she moaned. 'Why did we wait so long for this?'

He stilled. She knew immediately she'd said the wrong thing. 'We didn't,' he said, his voice hoarse and strained. 'I've only known you a week.'

'That's long enough,' she said, her voice raspy with desire.

'For what?'

'For this,' she said, lifting her face to his, hungry for his mouth to possess hers again.

'For a one-night stand?' He broke away from her. 'Because that's all I can give you.'

'Not even a two-night stand?' she asked, trying to lighten the tension, succeeding in making it worse.

He made his *humph* sound but it didn't sound in the slightest bit amusing.

'I scarcely know you but you're making me feel things I don't want to feel, feelings I've lived without for a long time,' he said roughly. Was that an edge of panic to his voice? 'I can't give you what you want.'

She could feel a red flush rising on her neck. 'How do you know what I want? How do you know I don't just want to drag you into the back seat of the car and make crazy, heart-pounding, toe-tingling love with you—then walk away from you when it's over?'

'Because you'll want more.'

'I might. The way I feel about you, once wouldn't be enough. I mean, if it was really toe-tingling...' Her voice trailed away at his desolate expression.

'I meant more than I can give. Commitment. Marriage. Presumably children.'

Ashleigh stared at him in disbelief. 'I'm sick of people

telling me what I want. You included. How can you possibly presume to know what drives me? I want you— I want you desperately. I won't lie about that.'

'I want you too,' he muttered.

'But not enough to believe it might be worth taking a risk on me? That there might be *more*? You're from a different world but I don't think this kind of…of *feeling* comes along very often whether you live in Athens or in London or in Bundaberg. Maybe…maybe only once in a lifetime.'

She turned her face from him, not wanting him to read the depth of her despair that this might be all she would ever have of him. Knowing she could not even hint at *love*. 'Or maybe we've made such a good job of pretence it seems real, when…when in reality there's nothing there.'

A group of people turned the corner into Tina's street and headed towards them. Mayfair was full of clubs and restaurants. It was a miracle there'd been no one around to witness their exchange. She stood in silence looking up at Lukas, until the group staggered by with generalised greetings of 'Merry Christmas' fading away with them.

'Merry Christmas,' she responded in a low choked voice she wondered if the revellers even heard.

Lukas's face was set like granite, his mouth a grim, hard line. 'All my life I haven't known who was genuine or what their motives were.'

'Well, please don't dump me in the same basket as people who…who might have injured you.' Ashleigh cursed her redhead's temper after the words slipped out—she hadn't meant to be hurtful.

She wiped her hand over her forehead. Wrapped her borrowed coat tight across her. Forced away the memory of how exciting his hands had felt on her body through the fine fabric of her dress. How much more she wanted than those brief, passionate moments. 'I'm sorry. I… I think I had too much champagne and not enough of Gary's snacks.'

In truth she'd been too eager to get away from Tina and Gary and to be alone with Lukas to bother with eating. Only to be lifted up on a wild wave of desire and exultation that he wanted her, then to crash painfully back down on the rocks to whimper and nurse her wounds. But she wasn't the whimpering type. She would not give in to the tears of disappointment that burned behind her eyes. Instead she tossed her head and strode as fast as she could on her stilettos away from him.

The car was a few houses away, the driver sitting patiently waiting for them. She headed towards it, was aware of Lukas close behind.

Why did she get the feeling that it was going to be another journey back to Chelsea—she could never think of the townhouse as *home*—with her and Lukas sitting in grim silence? Especially when thoughts of what she'd told him she'd like to do with him in that very back seat would not be easy to suppress.

Ashleigh checked her watch in the dark. Three a.m. She'd gone straight to her room when they'd got home, wanting to avoid Lukas at all cost. Now she was hungry.

She used the light from her phone to guide her down the stairs to the kitchen. The elevator might be too noisy and alert Lukas to her presence. If he was still in the house, that was. He could easily have gone out and she wouldn't have heard him.

He hadn't left the house. As she pushed open the door of the basement kitchen she saw him sitting in the same chair where he'd been last time, in a dim pool of light from the pendant lights that hung over the table. He had his head resting on his arms on the table. The back of his neck looked somehow vulnerable—not something she had ever expected to think about Lukas Christophedes. A great rush of tenderness for him swept over her. *Oh, she had it bad.*

'Lukas,' she said softly. 'Are you awake?'

He nodded.

This time she didn't resist the urge to go to him, this the last night she would spend in his house, maybe the last time she would ever see him. She stood behind him, leaned down, circled her arms around him and placed her cheek against his. His stubble was deliciously scratchy against her skin. She breathed in his already so familiar scent. Felt the wave of want for him that she doubted would ever go away. Silently, he reached up to put his hand on her arm.

'You okay?' she asked, emboldened because she couldn't sink any lower than she already had with her suggestion of having her way with him in the back seat of his car.

'I felt hungry,' he said. 'But I got down here and it all seemed too much effort.'

'I guess you're used to having staff,' she said. Staff like *her*.

'I actually don't need staff to toast a piece of bread,' he said gruffly.

She released him from her arms and stood up straight. 'The staff is on board now. Let me make you some toast. There's pizza in the freezer if you want me to—'

He got up, blocked her with his body from heading to the freezer. 'You're not staff.'

She looked up at him. His eyes were bloodshot and weary. 'I actually am. You pay Maids in Chelsea for me to be your full-time maid.'

'You are *not* my maid. Not any more.' He didn't touch her, just looked down into her face.

'Then what am I, Lukas? Not your pretend girlfriend— the need for that is over; you've done your deal. Not your friend either. I want you too much to keep up the pretence of being a platonic friend. Not even your lover—despite the...the desire we so obviously feel for each other.'

He swore under his breath in Greek. She didn't understand a word of it, which was probably just as well. 'I don't know who you are to me,' he said finally. 'I don't know who the real Ashleigh is. You are such a good actress. You fooled Tina, you confused me. Sometimes I think you could transform my life; other times I'm not certain I know you at all.'

'I have been no one but myself,' she said. 'What you've seen are different facets of me. I was never dishonest with you. Ever. Except when I hid my attraction for you, not dreaming you felt anything for me. But tonight...well, tonight I bared my heart to you. Yet you can't seem to trust me.'

He acknowledged that with a slow nod. 'I have an issue with trust—especially with women.' Would he ever share what had put those shadows behind his eyes?

'I've got every reason not to trust you either,' she said. 'You're not bad at pretending to be someone you're not. You made our fake date scenarios as real as I did. But I liked everything I saw about you. I *like* you, Lukas, as well as being crazy attracted to you.'

'How do I know what is real about you and what is façade?' he asked. 'I thought my mother was a devoted wife. Until I walked in on her with another man at one of the decadent parties my parents were famed for in Athens. I discovered both my parents had multiple affairs. My father from the beginning of the marriage. My mother in retaliation when she found out about his. I grew up shielding my mother from my father's lies—and vice versa. I knew more than a child should know about my parents' private lives. I learned to hide my feelings. They only stayed together for my sake, so they told me. Though why they are still together now, I don't know.'

'I'm sorry,' she murmured. Not in a million years could she imagine her parents holding decadent parties and finding lovers. In spite of the gravity of it, she smiled to herself. There'd be no holding onto those kinds of secrets in a country town.

She brushed past him, thrilling in the contact no matter how brief. Put a saucepan of milk on the stove to boil. Hot chocolate might be required if she was ever to sleep again tonight. She put thick slices of wholewheat bread in the toaster.

'That must have been difficult for a kid to cope with.'

'The worst was to come,' said Lukas with a grimace. 'A few days before I turned twenty-one I discovered they had totally mismanaged the company that my grandfather had spent his life building up. It was on the verge of bankruptcy and yet they still kept on spending, milking the company to fund their lavish lifestyle.'

'And it was up to you to save it. Still a boy. What had you intended to do instead?'

'All my life I had wanted to be an architect. Growing up in a city where everywhere there are reminders of our great civilisation, I was inspired to make my own mark on the landscape.'

'But you had to give up your studies?'

'Yes. And my dreams.' Disappointment and regret threaded through his words.

'From what you've told me, you've made your mark in a different way. You must be proud of what you accomplished.'

'My family were very grateful. They got to keep everything. They didn't care that I had to remove them as directors.'

'That must have been difficult.'

'You can't imagine what it was like to unravel the mess

they'd made—the lies, the deception, the payments to mistresses, even blackmail.'

'No wonder you have an issue with trust,' she said. 'But now, as an adult, having gone through all that, surely you feel able to make your own judgement of who is genuine and who is not?' *Surely you could believe in me?*

He shrugged. 'Perhaps my judgement was distorted.' He told her about a girl named Céline who had deceived him and broken his heart. 'I believed in her yet she turned out to be not the person I thought she was. Like my mother. Like my father.'

'We've all had our hearts broken,' Ashleigh said. 'But we have to learn from it. Not that I'm any great example; look how long I took to do the right thing with Dan. The right thing for him too, I now realise. He's actually not a bad guy and deserves someone who genuinely loves him. I wasted his time as well as mine because I was scared of getting dumped by the waves.'

'How do I do that?' He seemed genuinely puzzled.

'You have to listen to your instinct; you have to *feel* what is right rather than try to intellectualise it or, worse, block it with fear.'

'Like when you're dancing,' he said slowly.

'Exactly. The steps are nothing without the emotion. You have to feel the dance.'

He frowned. 'How do you trust your feelings when they are so abstract?'

'Is that a trick question?' She took the milk off the stovetop. 'Why is a successful billionaire asking me that?'

He shook his head. 'I genuinely want to know.'

'Surely you trust your instinct when it comes to business? You couldn't have got to where you are without doing that.'

'Success involves facts and figures and market analysis and—'

'Knowing when to take a risk or make a gamble?'

'That too,' he said. 'I can trust a gamble informed by research. I will never be able to make life-changing decisions based on something as ephemeral as *feeling*.'

'You're serious about that?'

'Of course. What other answer could I give?'

The toast popped out of the toaster. 'Peanut butter?' she asked. The pantry was packed with jars of an American brand so she assumed it was his favourite.

She spread both pieces of toast thickly, cut them in half, put them on a plate and slid it across the table to him.

'Aren't you having any?' he asked.

'I'm not hungry any more,' she said. 'A milky drink will do me fine.'

The illusion of intimacy in the semi-darkened kitchen was seductive. But she could not stay here. She was beginning to believe he was right. *He could not give her what she needed.* He would destroy her if she kept on throwing herself against an emotional brick wall. *Maybe he didn't know how to love.*

She waited for him to finish his toast. Her drink stayed untouched in the mug.

She took the plate and the mug to the sink and rinsed them like a good maid should. Delaying. Wanting these last moments alone with him. Until the tension made her feel nauseous.

'Lukas, I've packed. I'm leaving in the morning.'

Was that relief that flashed across his face? Not regret or hurt or anger? She felt as if he had plunged a knife into her heart.

'You don't have to do that,' he said. It *was* relief. Her stomach roiled.

'I promised you could stay until after—'

'Christmas. I know. But you have no further use for

me. And I… I have to get on with my life.' *Beg me to stay, Lukas, beg me to stay.*

But he didn't.

'Where will you go?' he asked. The knife twisted deeper.

'The renewal of vows ceremony is on Wednesday at The Daphne Hotel in Cadogan Gardens. My friend has booked rooms for her bridesmaids for Tuesday and Wednesday nights. Thursday is Christmas Eve and I'll go to Manchester with Sophie.'

Silence hung between them for a long, uncomfortable moment.

'If you decide you want to go back to Australia for Christmas, I'll buy you a ticket.'

She stared at him. '*What?* Why would I want to do that?'

The expression on his face told her everything.

'After all I've told you—you still think I want to go back to Dan? You still don't trust me? Yet I have more cause not to trust *you* and I was prepared to take the risk. You just don't get it, do you, Lukas?'

She took his hand and placed it on her chest where her heart was furiously pounding. 'Do you feel that, Lukas? Do you? That's my heart pounding for *you*. Not Dan. Not any other man. But *you.*'

She kept his hand over her heart for a long moment. *Can't you feel it breaking, Lukas?* Then dropped his hand and turned on her heel.

Ashleigh lay on her back on her bed until the light filtered through the curtains. Then picked up her backpack and the one Bond Street shopping bag she'd vowed to save and left it all behind her. The clothes, the shoes, the watch. *Lukas.* They had never belonged to her.

The only thing she would take with her that she hadn't come with was Lukas's scarf he had loaned her that first night. Her breath hitched as she buried her face in its soft warmth and breathed in his scent before she wrapped the scarf around her neck and tucked the ends over her heart.

CHAPTER THIRTEEN

YOU JUST WANT to be with that one special person. You feel only half alive when you're apart.

Ashleigh's words echoed through Lukas and made the weight in his chest feel even heavier. Now he knew exactly what she'd meant. *Too late* he knew what she'd meant.

She had been gone a day. And it was as if a light had been switched off—not just in his house but in his soul. How could one woman make such an impact on his life in such a short time? She had urged him to *feel* it—to feel her heartbeat as if it might somehow kick-start his own. But there was a void there. Why was it that some part of him that processed emotions seemed so shut off and in-accessible?

Until Ashleigh had breezed into his life on a cloud of bubbles and opened just a crack that was slowly, painfully being pushed apart.

He sat at his desk and tried to work—his great solace, his great distraction. Had he actually told her that work was *fun*? But the more he tried to focus on the overall strategy for his move into the UK market, the more thoughts of Ashleigh kept slamming into his mind and knocking his concentration sidewards.

Fun was stumbling on the ice with Ashleigh. *Fun* was feeling the rhythm of the dance with her. *Fun* was holding in his arms the loveliest woman he had ever met—lovely in both face and spirit.

She spoke of trust. He realised he had an abiding distrust of women. His mother, the first betrayal. Then his nanny, falling in love and marrying a Greek boy from a town too far away for the young Lukas to visit. She hadn't abandoned him completely. He was still in touch with her, even now. But he had loved her more than anyone and had not been allowed to express it for fear of offending his mother. Then he had allowed Céline to shatter his trust—foolishly now, he saw. He should have treated that as the fling it so obviously had been for her. But Ashleigh had not lied to him—he had asked her to lie *for* him.

Nevertheless, the fear was there. If he made himself vulnerable to her—the first woman since Céline to make him want to—he could end up wounded beyond endurance. With all the responsibility for his family on his shoulders—the son holding up the parents instead of the usual way of things—he could not afford the distraction. Yet if he did not—what kind of empty life stretched out ahead of him?

By his persistence in thinking she would betray him and return to her former fiancé, had he driven Ashleigh away? Had he ever really heard her?

The house was very quiet. Too quiet. He usually took delight in solitude. But he longed to hear the most tuneless version of *Jingle Bells* ever sung coming from his bathroom. Instead there was nothing. The ticking of the grandfather clock in the hallway below had always sounded comforting. Now it sounded ominous. Each second taking her further away from him.

He gave up on work. Found himself heading in the direction of her bedroom. He pushed open the door—almost expecting her to be there. A remnant of her scent danced in the air—fresh and sweet. Lukas closed his eyes the better to inhale it.

When he opened them, he was shocked to see she'd left everything he'd bought her behind, neatly packed in the closet. It was bitterly cold today; snow was predicted for Christmas Day. He was angry at her for not taking at least the coat and the boots. She would be freezing in that old anorak.

But she had left something else behind. A small gift-wrapped box on the dressing table. He picked it up, was stunned to see it was for him. He read the tasteful Christmas tag.

To Lukas—good luck.
A xx

With hands that weren't steady he tore open the wrapping. It was a hand-blown glass ornament in the shape of a pomegranate, its rich colour picked out with gold. Lukas remembered telling her about the Greek tradition where a pomegranate was hung above the front door for Christmas. He was touched by her thoughtfulness. Of the many lavish gifts he had been given over the years, this was the most precious by far.

Lukas turned the card over.

P.S. This was not *paid for with your credit card.*

He was *feeling* it now all right. Loss. Regret. A deep, aching need for her. And, overriding it all—*hope.*

She did not intend to come back. He'd found her keys and the credit card on the hallway table. He hadn't needed to see them to know she was gone. He had *felt* the emptiness of the house.

But if she felt a fraction of the emotion that was building in him he might be able to convince her to come back. He had to find her. Apologise. Explain. Grovel if he had to. And he had to go armed with something to convince her of the truth about how he felt.

He thought of the many kiss-off pieces of jewellery he had purchased to signal the end with a woman who had started pushing him for more. The only kind of jewellery he wanted to buy for Ashleigh was something she'd wear on the third finger of her left hand and that he'd be around to admire until death did them part.

She'd told him where she was staying. He had to go find her. He wanted her. And he didn't stop until he got what he wanted.

But then the phone rang.

Ashleigh stood with the other bridesmaids, lined up alongside Emma under the elegant floral arch in the main reception room at The Daphne Hotel. She was enthralled as she witnessed Emma and Jack renew their vows six years after they had married in secret as teenagers. There was something heart-wrenchingly beautiful about celebrating a relationship that was already deeply committed and had been forged through hardship and separation. These two deserved their happiness.

They were the Earl and Countess of Redminster, high up on the social scale that was the English aristocracy. Yet today, here, they were simply a man and a woman in love, celebrating that love with a select few family and friends. Ashleigh felt honoured to be part of the bridal party.

Jack was so tall and protective, Emma slender and golden in the strikingly elegant white dress designed by Sophie, with flowers twisted through her blonde hair. Love and trust and faith shone from their eyes as they made promises to each other. To love. To honour. In sickness and in health.

Could she have felt that for Lukas? The painful lurch in her heart told her *yes*. Or had she fallen for a man who didn't really exist? Real or not, she'd been grateful she'd had the wedding preparations to distract her. Because that man she had only known such a short time had left a big, aching gap in her life. All this happiness, all this talk of love made her feel that loss even more. For the first time since she'd been in London, she felt lonely.

Emma and Jack concluded the ceremony with the sweetest of kisses that made the bridesmaids sigh. Then the couple was immediately surrounded by well-wishers—including Emma's mother and her second husband, who had come from France. Clio Caldwell was there too, in the company of an intriguingly handsome man who could rival Lukas for dark, Mediterranean good looks. Was that an engagement ring flashing on Clio's finger? Standing at a distance, emanating disapproval, were Jack's parents. Apparently, they would never forgive Emma for the scandal that had enveloped her father and dragged her along with it.

Parents, Ashleigh mused. Here they were in their mid-to late twenties—Lukas in his thirties—still being affected by their parents and their behaviour. It sounded as if Lukas's family had been dysfunctional at best; no wonder he'd learned to tamp down on his emotions for self-protection. Except for their inexplicable obsession with Dan, Ashleigh's parents were almost boringly normal and she wouldn't have them any other way.

The thought struck her that perhaps she'd been striving for the kind of marriage her parents had when she'd agreed to marry Dan. Thank heaven she'd run, because now she'd tasted fireworks with Lukas, she knew nothing else would do. *Ever.*

Lukas had no trouble getting past reception at the quirky Chelsea hotel and through to the ballroom where the renewal of vows ceremony was being held for the Earl and Countess of Redminister. Another thing he didn't know about Ashleigh—he'd had no idea she had connections with the cream of this country's aristocracy. She could hold her own anywhere, as she'd proved again and again. But all he wanted was for her to find her place in his heart.

The ceremony was concluding as he made his way quietly to the back of the room. His eyes immediately arrowed in on Ashleigh, standing in a row with three other bridesmaids. Out of the five beautiful women in the bridal party he saw only her—the smallest of them, luminous in a dusky pink dress, her bright hair pulled up off her face and entwined with creamy flowers. Her gaze was intent on the bride and groom. Even from where he stood, he could see the expressions flit across her face. Joy for her friends. Happiness. And a poignant longing that echoed how he felt as he gazed at her.

His longing was fierce, possessive. He wanted to see her dressed not as a bridesmaid but as a bride—*his* bride— with all that longing and joy lighting up her face for *him*. Now he had to convince her to trust him, to believe that he had left behind him any play-acting or pretence, and pray that she felt the same way he felt. He slid his hand in his breast pocket for the reassurance of that important piece of jewellery that he hoped would seal the most important deal of his life. And summoned up the courage to reveal his true self to her.

Lukas watched as the ceremony concluded. He had always prided himself on his lack of sentimentality. But when he watched the tall blonde bride and the dark-haired groom exchange a lingering kiss he felt overwhelmed by an agony of longing. *Yes.* This was what he wanted for him and Ashleigh.

He wanted to propose to her right now. But she was surrounded by people congratulating the happy couple. He considered himself a brave man. It had taken courage to make the difficult decisions required to save the family company. He was fearless in sport. But what if he asked Ashleigh to marry him in front of all these people and she said 'no'? Humiliation wasn't something he could wear lightly. He had to get her on her own, away from here.

'Ashleigh.' The voice was low and urgent. Did she want to be with Lukas so much she was conjuring up his voice at her shoulder? But no. Ashleigh turned to see him standing just behind her.

'You've gatecrashed my friends' wedding?' she hissed, while trying to deny the way her heart leapt at the sight of him. Tall and imposing in an immaculately tailored dark suit, he put the rest of the male guests to shame—including the incredibly handsome groom.

'I told the gatekeepers I was your significant other,' he said in a low voice.

'So we're back to the pretend now, are we?' she said through a sickening sense of disappointment. 'I thought that was what gave you such cause to doubt me? Maybe we should try sticking to the facts. You could have told them you were my boss and they would have let you in. Though the security is pretty tight. My friends have had a problem with paparazzi in the past.'

'I didn't realise you had friends in such high places,' he said. He seemed…nervous. Lukas Christophedes *nervous*? Surely he wouldn't be intimidated by the grand company here? Or was he intimidated by her less than friendly welcome?

She had no idea what he was doing here—not when he'd been so relieved to see the last of her that heartbreaking night of Tina's drinks. The night she had humiliated herself by revealing her feelings. Feelings he'd made so clear were not reciprocated. But if it went on past performance he must want something from her. Something related to his business—the work that meant more than anything to him. Certainly more than *she* could ever mean.

'You told me you weren't interested in weddings, so the titles of the bride and groom didn't come into it.'

'It's true I've never been interested in weddings. Though I could get interested if the circumstances were right.' Was he trying to tell her something? If so it was in some kind of male-speak code she had no idea how to decipher. But his tortured expression didn't give her any clues.

'That still doesn't explain why you're here,' she said. Hope leapt in her heart. Had he missed her? Come to ask her to come back? It had hurt, the way he'd let her go so easily, had seemed so relieved she'd decided to leave before Christmas.

He cleared his throat, took a step closer. She glanced over her shoulder. 'Try not to look too friendly,' she warned. 'And no need to act lovey-dovey—Tina's not here. However, Clio Caldwell is here and it's against Maids in Chelsea rules to fraternise with clients.' Not to mention push them against a wall and kiss them in a frenzy of want. Lukas was attracting a few interested looks. She had to be careful; she didn't want lose her job.

'I came to ask you…to ask you a favour,' he said finally.

Business again. Why had she thought it would be otherwise? She sighed. Hid her plummeting disappointment behind a matter-of-fact manner. 'What is it this time? And does it involve me requiring a complete change of wardrobe?'

'Just the clothes waiting for you back at home,' he said. *His* home, he meant. It could never be hers. Although, the way she felt about him, anywhere he was would be home. Why was he here, stirring up impossible feelings?

Ashleigh took a deep breath to steady herself. She really couldn't endure any more make-believe; it would be cruel of him to expect it of her. Not when she yearned for him to take her in his arms and tell her…oh, tell her impossible things like he'd fallen in love with her the way she'd fallen for him. That he wanted their relationship to be genuine. *Get real, Ashleigh*, she told herself. There was a far more likely explanation for his presence.

'Is Tina offering invitations again?' she asked. 'Maybe a double date with her and Gary that you think you can't refuse?' Unable to meet his gaze, she looked down at the floor, at a pattern in the carpet that seemed appropriately like a jagged red heart torn in two. 'If so, I think it might be time to tell her…to tell her you've crushed my heart and moved on.' Which wouldn't actually be far from the truth.

'It's not that.' There was a note of urgency to his voice that made her look up to find his dark brown eyes lit by something unfamiliar and unsettling as he searched her face.

'Then…then what is it?' she asked in a voice that came out shakier than she had meant it to. For a long moment her gaze met his and it seemed as though everything around her faded away—the chatting of the guests, the music, the happy laughter of the reunited bride and groom. She had the feeling that her world was about to change for ever.

'It…it's something personal. I… I want to ask you to… to…' She wasn't used to seeing Lukas this uncertain, as if he were unable to get the words out.

'Ask me what, Lukas?' She clasped her hands behind her back so he wouldn't see they were trembling with nervous anticipation.

He took a deep, shuddering breath. 'Ashleigh, I…' he choked out.

'Yes?' she said.

One of the groom's friends, bearing two flutes of champagne, brushed past them, murmured an apology.

Lukas glared at him, then muttered something under

his breath in Greek that didn't sound like a curse word, rather that he might be berating himself. Whatever it was, Ashleigh got the distinct impression he had changed his mind about what he was going to ask her—and that she might never know what it would have been.

She looked up at him, forced her voice to sound steady. 'Lukas, are you asking me to help you with something?'

He responded to her question as if to a lifeline. But his answer took her completely by surprise. 'Yes. My parents called to see when I'd be arriving in Athens for Christmas. When I told them I was spending Christmas in London they insisted on coming here to join me. They're arriving tomorrow morning, Christmas Eve.'

She frowned. 'And that involves me, how?'

'I want you to spend Christmas Day with me.'

Ashleigh was so astonished she was momentarily lost for words. 'So you want to hire me as your hostess?' she said eventually. *Work, after all.* 'If so, you need to talk to Clio.'

'No! I'm not saying that at all. I need someone there so I'm not outnumbered.'

Ashleigh almost choked on the nausea that rose in her throat. 'So you want to trundle out the pretend girlfriend again to make Christmas Day easier for you?' she managed to get out, aware she needed to keep her voice low so interested bystanders couldn't hear her. 'Well, I don't even have to think about it. I've paid over and over for my mistake in squatting in your house. The ledger is balanced; as a matter of fact, there's probably credit in my column. My answer is *no*. The deal is *off*.' They were equals here. Ashleigh and Lukas. Not the billionaire and his errant maid. In fact *he* was the intruder into *her* world.

He paled beneath his tan and she could see a pulse throb at the corner of his mouth. 'You couldn't be more wrong. I need someone to give me moral support. Watch my back. I want someone to be on my side.'

'And that's me?'

She saw a new vulnerability in his eyes, an appeal. 'Right now, Ashleigh, I can't think of anyone more on my side than you.' He looked and sounded so sincere—but then he'd proven himself to be a top-notch actor.

'Really?'

'Yes. I… I need you. Not for business reasons. This is…this is personal.'

He *needed* her. The word flashed out a warning that if she went along with this she was heading into danger. Danger to her heart, danger to her sanity. Because the thought of him needing her was alluring beyond reason. She wasn't at all sure what this was about. It was far from the declaration of devotion that would have sent her heart singing. But she had missed him. There wasn't a minute since they'd parted that she hadn't missed him.

He needed her.

Spending Christmas Day with him would be a cruel torture. How could she endure having to fall back into the easy repartee, the flirtatious fake kisses, the pretence of being someone special to him when she ached for it to be real? When it could never be real. Why had she let herself fall in love with such an unattainable, difficult, *damaged* man? A man who had given no indication he reciprocated her feelings. He had admitted he was attracted to her. But that wasn't enough. Her heart would be breaking knowing that once her usefulness had expired, his parents back on a flight to Athens, it would be *goodbye, Ashleigh.*

And yet… He needed her. She kept coming back to that. No matter what his motivation for having her back in his house, she wanted to be with him. And it would be a milder form of torture than if she was without him. If she said 'no' to his proposition, she would most likely spend the most miserable Christmas Day of her life wondering what he was doing.

Sadly, it seemed he thought he could just pick her up and put her down again as he chose. But if she went into this with her eyes open, knowing the likely consequences, knowing it would be for the last time, she would say yes. For his sake, but also for her own.

'I actually have plans for Christmas Day,' she said.

'Surely you could change them,' he said, with the arrogant assurance of a man used to getting his own way.

'I'll have to talk to Sophie.' In between their bridesmaid preparations, she had taken her friend into her confidence about her feelings for Lukas. Sophie wouldn't think she was blowing her off for a better offer if she accepted Lukas's invitation. But it would be good manners to check first.

'Of course,' he said. He waited, obviously impatient if the tapping of his foot had anything to do with it, while she went to look for Sophie. She found her with Grace, who had seemed subdued all through the renewal ceremony. The friends all knew it was Grace's first Christmas on her own since her beloved grandmother had died. Ashleigh joined Sophie in giving her a big hug and suggesting they catch up over Christmas.

'All okay,' she said to Lukas when she got back. 'I'll be there.'

'Please convey my thanks to Sophie,' he said in a formal way that made her smile. But there was gratitude underscoring his words.

'Shall do,' she said. 'You know I'm needed here on bridesmaid duty and will be staying at the hotel with the others tonight?'

'As long as you are with me on Christmas Day.'

She still wasn't sure what this was all about but she looked up at him, willed him to believe her. 'Now I've committed to this, I won't let you down, Lukas. You can trust me.'

He placed his hand on her cheek, gently, tenderly, and she didn't care if Clio saw it. 'I'm beginning to believe that,' he said.

'Good,' she said, placing her hand over his. Was this a subtle change in direction for them? If so, she realised they would have to take it step by step. Or was it just him manipulating her for his own ends?

But, in spite of her confusion, there were practical considerations surrounding Christmas Day in Chelsea. 'What about Christmas dinner?' she said. 'You say you're good at making toast, Lukas, but how are you going to handle a meal for four people?'

'All sorted. Everything is coming from Harrods. It's being delivered tomorrow.'

'How the other half lives,' she said with a sigh. 'They say the rich are different.'

'I'm not so different, am I?' he said.

'You're actually quite nice,' she said with a grudging smile. *Back to the mock flirtation.*

'Quite nice? I think I'll take that as a compliment,' he said, returning her smile and holding her gaze with his own.

'Please do,' she said.

For one long moment she thought he was going to kiss her, there in the middle of the wedding party with all eyes on them. Instead he took both her hands in his and drew her closer in a gesture that seemed almost as intimate. 'Thank you,' he said. She felt he was thanking her for so much more than a compliment—but she wasn't sure what it was.

'Just one thing—how will you introduce me to your parents?' she said. 'As your maid?'

'As my friend,' he said. 'Maybe we can work up from there.'

Which didn't actually make his intentions any clearer.

CHAPTER FOURTEEN

WHEN THE DOORBELL rang at noon on Christmas Eve, Lukas thought it was a delivery from Harrods. But it wasn't.

Ashleigh stood on the threshold. 'I know you said Christmas Day but I thought I could make myself useful on Christmas Eve,' she said. 'Is that okay?'

Her smile was tentative as she looked up at him, fresh faced, her cheeks pink from the cold, the pale winter sunlight dancing off her hair in sparks of gold. She was wearing jeans and the dreaded anorak and she had never looked lovelier. On first impression, he had thought Ashleigh to be wholesome and unsophisticated. She had proved to be so much more complex than that.

'More than okay,' he said.

Much to his mortification, he hadn't been able to get out the words he'd wanted to at the wedding party. It wasn't that he'd been scared to propose for the first time in his life—of course he hadn't—it had been too public for something so momentous and private. Now she was here and he would have another chance when the time was right.

He wanted no more pretence, no more lies—no matter how well intentioned—no more hiding behind his workaholic barrier. So he followed his first impulse. 'Come on in,' he said. 'I'm so glad you're here.' Then he pulled her to him in a hug. He tightened his arms around her and closed his eyes in sheer joy and gratitude that she had come back to him. She stiffened against him at first, then relaxed into his embrace.

'You have your backpack,' he said, pointing out the obvious as he'd actually hugged that too.

'Yes,' she said. 'I'm calling in the offer of accommodation until after Christmas. Sophie's sofa will be there for me after that.'

'Your room is waiting for you,' he said. If he had his way she would never sleep on her friend's sofa again. Or indeed that bed in the guest room.

'Are your parents here?' she said, peering around him into the hallway.

'I sent them off in the car for some last-minute shopping. My mother loves Peter Jones in Sloane Square.'

'I seriously am here to help,' she said, slipping off her anorak to reveal the long-sleeved black T-shirt. He couldn't help checking for trainers—the huge hate of his mother's. Even though his parents exasperated him, he wanted Ashleigh to make a good impression. *As herself.* But trainers would get her off to the wrong start. Thankfully, he saw neat ankle-length black boots. The kind of shoes his mother would approve of being worn in the house.

Ashleigh had followed the direction of his glance. 'The sales have started,' she said by way of explanation.

'My mother will be in heaven,' he said.

'Not when she has to elbow her way through the crowds, she won't,' said Ashleigh with a flash of dimples.

'I appreciate your offer of help,' he said. 'But you're not here as a maid, you know. You're a guest.'

'What kind of a friend would I be if I didn't check to see if all is okay?'

'When you actually were the maid you did such a good job everything is in perfect order.'

'Fresh towels and toiletries in the bathrooms?'

'I guess so.'

'But do you *know* so?'

'Not something I would think to check.'

'So I'll do the checking. And all the other stuff you mightn't have thought of because you're used to having staff.' It wasn't a criticism; she was smiling at him. 'It's a routine I got used to here.'

'Thank you,' he said. 'I'll take your backpack up to your room.'

'Great,' she said, already turning away to head towards her self-imposed chores.

He paused. 'Ashleigh, wait,' he said.

She turned back, her hair swishing around her shoulders. He wanted to run his hands through it, tilt her face up for his kiss. But there would be time for that if all went to plan. 'Yes?' she said.

'The clothes in your room. They're all yours, you know. To wear them, to give them away, to sell them, whatever you wish to do with them.'

'I… I can't think of them as mine. They belong to the pretend girlfriend. The wardrobe you bought for her to play her role as your fake date.'

'Didn't you say every Ashleigh I saw was a facet of you?'

'Yes,' she said, eyes downcast.

'Doesn't that glamorous Ashleigh like those clothes?' he said quietly.

'She loves them, of course she does. But they don't belong to her. I would be wearing them under false pretences.'

He placed his fingers under her chin to tilt her face towards his. 'You should wear them. Please. I'll throw the lot out if you don't.'

'I'm sure a charity would welcome them.'

There wasn't a gold-digging bone in her body. She still hadn't figured out that the worth of the watch, if sold, would buy her a considerable number of nights in one of those West End hotels he had 'billed' her for. But he didn't intend she'd be sleeping anywhere but under his roof. Ever.

'You might need to wear them while my parents are here.'

'You're right,' she said. 'For one last spin of the pretend girlfriend.' She put up her hand to block his protest. 'Because if your parents are anything like my parents, they will immediately look for a relationship whether or not one exists.'

Now. He should say something now. But his pause lost him his chance.

Ashleigh continued. 'I would make a better impression for you in designer clothes.'

'True—when you meet my mother you'll see just how true,' he said. 'But you look perfectly fine in what you're wearing. I… I like whichever facet of Ashleigh I see.'

'Even anorak Ashleigh?' she said with, at last, a teasing glimpse of dimples.

'Maybe not that Ashleigh,' he conceded. 'Though it's the anorak, not the Ashleigh I object to. It's not warm enough either. Snow is predicted. Would you please keep the warm coat?'

She hesitated. He could see the indecision ripple over her features. 'Okay. Thank you. I'll keep the coat.'

'And the anorak?'

'It shall be burned, thrown on the Yule log and consigned to the flames,' she said dramatically though her voice wasn't steady. He realised what an effort it was for her to keep up the façade. His indecision was hurting her. 'Though I'd better check first with my sister, who owns it.'

'You do that,' he said. *She was adorable.* She turned away again. 'One more thing before you go,' he said. 'Thank you for my gift, the beautiful pomegranate ornament.'

She flushed high on her cheekbones. 'You found it. I'm so glad you like it.'

'I will treasure it,' he said. 'It's too fragile to hang over the front door. Perhaps you could help me hang it on that amazing tree you set up in the living room?'

'I... I would love that,' she said, looking up at him.

Then Lukas realised she was standing right under the mistletoe she had hung from the chandelier above them. He saw an invitation to a kiss in the gleam of her blue eyes, the slight parting of her lush lips. This couldn't wait.

He dipped his head to claim her mouth. She responded immediately and wound her arms around his neck to bring him closer, to press her body close to his. She made a little murmur of pleasure deep in her throat. With an answering groan he deepened the kiss. He wanted to hear more: whimpers of need, sighs of pleasure, moans of ecstasy from this wonderful, perfect woman. *His woman.* He slid his hands down her back, her waist, to come to rest cupping the curves of her bottom.

That, of course, had to be the moment his parents burst through the front door, laden with parcels and complaining about the London traffic.

Ashleigh dropped her arms from around Lukas's neck, felt the hot tide of a furious blush colour her cheeks.

The older couple froze. It would almost be comical if she didn't feel so mortified. She had hoped to meet Lukas's parents under more dignified circumstances than this. Although this was certainly more dignified than the way she'd met their son.

Lukas stepped forward. 'Mother,' he said, indicating the beautifully groomed woman looking at her in wide-eyed astonishment. 'Father,' Lukas said, indicating the broad-shouldered man with iron-grey curly hair and thick black eyebrows. 'This is Ashleigh,' he said, indicating her.

Ashleigh stepped forward. 'Hello, Mr and Mrs Christophedes. Er… Merry Christmas.' What had that kiss been about? It had seemed real. Fired by genuine passion. By— dare she hope?—genuine *feeling*. This was getting more confusing by the second.

'Ashleigh is the…the friend I told you about who will be staying with us for Christmas,' said Lukas. 'She has arrived early.'

'To help,' she jumped in. 'I've come early to give Lukas a hand with the Christmas dinner and…and anything else he might need.'

That didn't sound right. Not when he'd had a possessive hold of her bottom. So much for the *friends* theory. The parents would be as unsure as she herself was about how she fitted in to Lukas's life.

His mother had the same deep brown eyes as Lukas and they gleamed with curiosity. She offloaded her parcels onto her already overburdened husband and made a beeline for Ashleigh.

She held out a perfectly manicured hand for Ashleigh to shake. 'I am Efthalia—my friends call me Effie. I hope that is what you will call me.'

Ashleigh returned the older woman's handshake. 'Thank you, Effie. It's a pleasure to meet you.'

'My husband is Dimitris,' she said, indicating Lukas's parcel-laden father.

The man shrugged to indicate his inability to free his hands from the multitude of parcels so he could shake hands. Instead he nodded. 'Hello, Ashleigh,' he said, with a warm smile and a glance to his son.

It wasn't just his mother who was curious. *What had she got herself into?* A new game called by Lukas, of which she was uncertain of the rules.

'Can I help you with those parcels?' she asked. 'You've done a lot of Christmas shopping.'

'Most of it is for her,' Dimitris said, indicating his wife with a raising of his dark brows.

'Why else would I come to London except to shop?' Effie said blithely. Then she turned to Lukas. 'And to see my beloved son for Christmas,' she said, her voice breaking.

'He's thrilled that you're here,' said Ashleigh diplomatically, sensing the sincerity—and pain—in his mother's voice.

Lukas took some of the shopping bags and parcels from his father. Effie was wearing a superb red coat. Ashleigh recognised it as the same label as the leopard print coat, as her lavender ball gown. She could see why Lukas saw a resemblance to his mother in Tina. Effie had the same cleverly tinted blonde hair, the same look of a very well maintained older woman. But she was more beautiful. And there was a depth of pain and remorse in her eyes when she looked at her son.

'Where do you want these put, Mother?' Lukas asked.

'Some to my room, others I need to gift wrap.'

'May I suggest the kitchen table for a gift-wrapping station?' Ashleigh said. 'Let me take some parcels down for you.'

Lukas shot her a grateful look.

'While I'm there, I can make tea or coffee,' she added. 'I'll bring it upstairs here to serve.'

'I can drink tea in the kitchen,' said Effie. 'I will come with you.'

Ashleigh suspected she would be subjected to a vigorous grilling about her relationship with her son. She decided to stick to the truth as closely as possible.

Later that day, in the dimming light of late afternoon, she walked up Sloane Street with Lukas, heading for Knightsbridge. The chauffeur had dropped them when she'd suggested it would be quicker to walk than drive in the practically stalled Christmas Eve traffic.

Lukas had said he had some last-minute shopping to do at Harrods for provisions and had *insisted* she go with him. She hadn't needed much convincing. The situation had become so awkward she'd welcomed the chance to escape the house. And to be alone with him. They'd left his parents bickering over their gift-wrapping in the kitchen.

Now she would have a chance to call him on the way this day was panning out. What his invitation to share Christmas with him really meant. But she had to pick her moment.

'I like your parents,' she said. 'I didn't expect to, after what you've told me about them, but I did. They're charming and warm and good company.'

Lukas's mouth twisted. 'They're the kind of people you'd like to chat with at a party rather than have parent you.'

'Maybe they didn't know how to parent. That's why they made such a mess of it. But they love you. There can be no doubt about that. Now your welfare is of utmost concern to them. Maybe…maybe they've grown up too.'

'I know,' he said. 'That's why I let them come for Christmas.'

'They're desperate for grandchildren.'

He cursed under his breath. 'My mother didn't harass you about that, did she? She saw through the "friends" thing straight away.'

'Considering how she caught us kissing, that shouldn't surprise you. I didn't deny we were more than friends.'

'What did you tell her?' he said. 'So we keep our stories straight.'

More play-acting and pretence. She was over it. Lukas either let her in on the new game or she was off to Sophie's flat the moment dinner was over. Her friend had given her the spare key, just in case. And she hadn't unpacked her backpack.

'I told her the truth—well, nearly the truth. That I'd run away from my wedding in Australia. That I was working for Maids in Chelsea until I found a position as an accountant, and got a job as a live-in maid in your house. That's how we met. I did not mention the bathtub.'

'Good,' he said. 'That most memorable of meetings will stay strictly between us.'

'Talking about memorable, what was that kiss back there all about?' she said.

'You seemed to enjoy it,' he said evasively.

'Of course I enjoyed it. It was a wonderful kiss. It felt like a *real* kiss. Was it real, Lukas?'

He cleared his throat. 'This is hardly the time and the place for a discussion like that.'

'When *will* be the time and the place for it?' she said. 'Because I'm confused. And I'm getting cranky about being confused.'

'After we get to Harrods. It closes at five so we need to rush.'

She stopped in the middle of the pavement and let the Christmas shopping hordes of humanity pass by her. 'Seriously, Lukas. You'd better have some explanations for me. Not only for my sake. But to make it easier for me to talk to your parents without making an utter fool of myself.'

'You will get an explanation,' he said. 'Come on. We have to keep moving.'

She had to quicken her pace to keep up with him. 'I'll hold you to that. Your mother told me I was the first "female friend" you've introduced them to for many years.'

'That's true. I didn't consider my private life any of their business. Be wary of what you say to them.'

'For what it's worth, I think they'd be wonderful grandparents. Perhaps they want to try and get it right the second time around.'

'*Humph,*' said Lukas in typical manner. No doubt warning her that she was not in the running as consideration as the mother of the grandbabies. Did he realise how hurtful he was being?

They neared the top of Sloane Street and Ashleigh stopped to admire the Christmas lights. 'I can't wait to see Harrods all lit up and—'

She paused as she felt something cold and damp drift onto her cheek. Then looked up to see a flurry of snowflakes cascading towards her. 'Lukas. It's snowing. It's snowing for Christmas! I can't tell you how exciting this is for an Aussie girl.'

She did a little jig of joy on the pavement. People walking by them laughed, but in a good-natured way—a spirit-of-the-season way.

Lukas picked her up and whirled her around. 'You are enchanting, Ashleigh Murphy. Has anyone ever told you that before?'

She thrilled to the light in his eyes. *What was this about?* 'Actually, they haven't.' Something about him was very, very different. Something exciting. Something she could not bring herself to believe. Again she felt that sensation of impending change.

'I'm telling you now. Ashleigh, that kiss was real. I kissed you without any pretence. As me, Lukas, kissing you, Ashleigh.'

She caught her breath. 'Are you feeling it, Lukas?'

'I'm feeling it,' he said. 'Thanks to you, you beautiful woman.' And he picked up her hand and placed it on his chest, just like she had done to him the other night. She couldn't feel a thing through his overcoat except a wall of muscle. But she felt the pulsing of something strong and perfect and life-changing in her heart.

'I wasn't going to tell you this. But your mother asked me was I in love with you,' she said.

His dark eyebrows rose. 'And what did you say?' Again, she sensed his vulnerability, that he needed answers from her as much as she did from him.

This was no time for pretence on her part either. 'I… I told her the truth.'

'And that was…?' She got the distinct impression he was holding his breath for her reply.

'That I was head-over-heels in love with you.' She reached up and pulled his head to hers, looked up into his eyes. 'I love you, Lukas.'

He looked down into her face with relief, joy, and something else so wonderful and exciting her heart started a furious beating. He let out his breath on words she had never imagined she would hear. 'I love you too, *agápi mou.*'

His voice sounded rusty, as though he hadn't said those words for a very long time. Or maybe it was because he was finally letting himself feel the emotions he had blocked for so long.

He kissed her, long and sweet and tenderly, to the sound of cheers and clapping from the circle of well-wishers who had formed around them.

Ashleigh broke away from the kiss, looked around her and grinned at the expressions of goodwill on all the different cosmopolitan faces around them. It was only then that she realised they were standing in each other's arms in front of the most famous jewellery shop in the world. Tiffany. Fingers of excitement marched up her spine. Were they in this particular spot by accident or by Lukas's design?

She looked up to him for an answer.

'We didn't get it clear the other night about what you actually felt about commitment, about marriage, about children,' he said. 'Is it what you want?'

She had to clear her suddenly choked-up throat to reply. She forgot they had an avid audience hanging onto their every word. 'With the right person. Yes.'

'I never wanted all that before. In fact I've run from it. But I want it now. With you, Ashleigh. Will you marry me?'

Dan had hounded her for years to get her to agree to marry him. With Lukas it took all of two seconds. 'Yes, Lukas, yes,' she said. 'I will marry you.'

His smile was wide with relief and happiness and he had never looked more handsome, with snowflakes frosting his dark hair. He took a small velvet box in a distinctive pale blue from his pocket. Then flipped it open to reveal a huge diamond, simply and elegantly set on a platinum band. 'What do you think?' he asked. 'If you don't like it we can go inside and choose another more to your—'

She stopped him with a swift kiss. 'It's perfect,' she breathed. 'I love it.' He picked up her left hand and slipped the ring on her third finger, where it sparkled in the glow of the Christmas lights that twinkled all around them. 'And I love you more than I can say.'

Lukas kissed her again. The man who would be her husband kissed her long and slow and thoroughly and she, his wife-to-be, kissed him back with all her heart as the snow drifted down on their heads and the Christmas shoppers of London cheered their approval and delight.

CHAPTER FIFTEEN

AT CHRISTMAS TIME Australia was nearly a day ahead of London. It was already Christmas morning there as Ashleigh prepared to video-call her family in Bundaberg. She would have left it at a phone call if Dan had been there—anything else would have been most inappropriate. But, thankfully, he had decided to join his father at the Gold Coast.

Ashleigh sat alone behind Lukas's desk in front of his large-screen computer and keyed in the family code. When the screen came to life, her family were grouped on the sofa, her father in shorts, her mother and sister in brightly coloured sundresses. Her sister's husband was there too and her aunt and uncle. Yes, her mother was wearing her glittery antler-shaped earrings that played *Rudolph the Red-Nosed Reindeer* at random intervals. Ashleigh prayed they were switched off.

'Merry Christmas,' she said through sudden tears she had to choke back.

'Merry Christmas,' her family chorused as they all waved. Her sister picked up the family tabby cat from a cushion beside her and made him wave a paw too.

'Are you okay, sweetie?' her mother said. 'That doesn't look like Sophie's parents' house behind you. It looks like a library. You're not on your own, are you? Not lonely? Not cold?'

Ashleigh laughed. 'It's a study, Mum. And I'm not alone.' She beckoned to Lukas, who was standing out of range of the camera with Effie and Dimitris, to join her. Ashleigh shifted in her chair to make room for him beside her. He brought his head to the same level as hers, his cheek against hers. She looked into his face and smiled her love and happiness. The expression on her family's faces was priceless.

'This is Lukas Christophedes,' she said.

'Merry Christmas,' said Lukas with a big smile and his slight Greek accent.

Her mother was obviously too stunned to say anything but her sister jumped in with a tentative 'Hi, Lukas.'

Her father was more forthcoming. 'And who is Lukas Christophedes when he's at home?' he growled.

'He's the man I'm spending Christmas Day with,' Ashleigh said. 'And the man I'm going to spend the rest of my life with.'

Then she splayed her left hand with the beautiful diamond ring on her third finger in front of the computer's camera so it filled her family's screen.

When all the excited squeals and expressions of disbelief had died away she spoke again. 'Mum. Dad. Everyone. I know you all love Dan. But I didn't. Not enough to marry, anyway. I love Lukas more than I could ever have imagined I could love a person. This is real, this is for ever. I want you to accept him into the family.'

Her family all looked at each other and then back at the camera. Her mother was the first to speak. 'Whatever makes you happy, sweetie. Congratulations. Welcome, Lukas.'

'Thank you,' he said.

'There's a couple of other people I want you to welcome too,' Ashleigh said. She beckoned Effie and Dimitris to the camera and introduced them as her future parents-in-law.

'So when will the wedding take place?' asked her mother.

'In summer. I don't see myself as a winter bride,' Ashleigh said. 'We'll get married in London.' She wanted to make that clear from the start.

Dimitris beamed expansively. 'Of course Lukas will fly you all over for the wedding. Then for a big party on our family's private island in Greece.'

That caused a flurry of excited reactions. Her father glared at the camera. 'We'll pay our own way to London for our daughter's wedding, thank you very much.'

Her mother jabbed him in the ribs with her elbow. 'And to the private Greek island, don't forget that.'

Lukas put up his hand. 'I understand that you are concerned you do not know me. And that this has all happened very quickly. But I can assure you I love Ashleigh and will look after her and cherish her for the rest of her life.'

'While letting me be my own person at the same time,' Ashleigh added.

'We are also planning to come and visit you in the new year,' Lukas said. 'That is, if it meets with your approval.'

Lukas turned to her and smiled. She smiled back and hoped her family could see the intensity of her joy. Perhaps they did. Because when he kissed her it was to a chorus of approval and applause from the other side of the world.

* * * * *

"If you're gonna hate me anyway—"

She barely had a chance to frown before his mouth hit hers.

She went rigid with shock, yanking away. But only two inches away. Maybe three. Just far enough to stare into his dark eyes while her chest heaved.

Then his mouth was on hers again, and she wasn't sure if she'd moved first, or if it had been him.

But what did it really matter?

They were once more in the shadows on the side of the high school gym, Caleb's weight pressing into her while his hands raced down her sides, delving beneath her short leather jacket. She felt devoured by his kiss.

Why was it always that way? His lips on hers, and she'd forget all rhyme or reason. She'd forget every single thing but the taste of him, the smell of him, the weight of—

A burst of laughter accosted them and they both pulled apart. It was hard to tell who was breathing harder.

"Some things don't change, eh, Caleb?"

Kelly's cheeks burned. The sooner she and Tyler could get back home to Idaho Falls, the better off they all would be.

A CHILD UNDER HIS TREE

BY
ALLISON LEIGH

MILLS & BOON

First Published in Great Britain 2016
By Mills & Boon, an imprint of HarperCollins*Publishers*
1 London Bridge Street, London, SE1 9GF

© 2016 Allison Lee Johnson

ISBN: 978-0-263-92032-1

23-1116

Our policy is to use papers that are natural, renewable and recyclable products and made from wood grown in sustainable forests. The logging and manufacturing processes conform to the legal environmental regulations of the country of origin.

Printed and bound in Spain
by CPI, Barcelona

A frequent name on bestseller lists, **Allison Leigh**'s high point as a writer is hearing from readers that they laughed, cried or lost sleep while reading her books. She credits her family with great patience for the time she's parked at her computer, and for blessing her with the kind of love she wants her readers to share with the characters living in the pages of her books. Contact her at www.allisonleigh.com.

For sweet baby David Rae—born the same day
I began this story—his parents and his "Glama,"
who is my dearest and oldest friend.

Prologue

Six years ago

"**Y**ou're *pregnant*?"

Startled, Kelly hid her hand down by her side, but it was too late. Her mother had already seen the distinctive plastic stick and snatched it out of her hand.

This is what Kelly got for not waiting until she was back at work on Monday to take the test. But she'd been too anxious. Too worried to wait through the weekend, to wait another two days when she already knew.

After a glance at the stick, where a huge blue plus sign broadcast the results, her mother pitched the test into the faded pink trash can that had been in Kelly's room since she'd been ten. "Well? What do you have to say for yourself?"

She wished she'd waited until Monday, that's what she had to say.

She wisely kept the sarcastic thought to herself. Kelly was twenty-three. Old enough to deal with the consequences of her actions, but not old enough to deal with her mother's reaction.

Evidently unsatisfied with Kelly's silence, her mom grabbed her by the shoulders and shook her slightly. "*Well?* At the very least, tell me it's the Buchanan boy's baby."

Kelly looked away from her mother's face. "Why? Caleb and I broke up two years ago." She was only buying time, though. Because she knew why.

Her mother made a disgusted sound and let her go. "Because you'll be set for life, obviously!" She propped her hands on her skinny hips. "He'll marry you. Even when it doesn't work out, you'll be taken care of. Those people take care of their own. Always have. Always will."

Those people.

Kelly felt nauseated. More from her mother's words than from the baby inside her that hadn't even existed five weeks ago. By *those people*, her mother meant anyone connected to the wealthy Clay family. The family who possessed everything that Georgette and Kelly Rasmussen did not.

Money. Plentiful land. Education. Class.

Georgette envied everything they possessed, even as she seemed to hate them for it.

"I don't want to marry Caleb."

Her mother made another disgusted sound. "Since when?"

Since he dumped me more than two years ago? Again, Kelly kept that answer to herself. She was over Caleb Buchanan. Had been for a long while now. Sleeping with him thirty-four days ago had been her way of proving it. Convoluted thinking, perhaps, but it was true, nevertheless. Which only seemed to confirm that the Rasmussen nut didn't fall far from the tree.

"You'll marry that boy," her mother said into the silence. She pointed her finger at Kelly's face. "You're not going to get stuck raising a baby on your own the way I was. You'll marry him. He'll provide for you both." Her eyes narrowed, and she smiled tightly. "They'll provide for *all* of us."

"You hated when I was dating him when we were teenagers! Now you're all for me marrying him?" Kelly wanted to throw herself on the twin bed that also hadn't changed since she was ten and pull the pillows over her head.

"I knew you'd mess it up. Same as I did when I was that age." Again the disgusted sound from her mother, accompanied by a hand swiping dismissively through the air. "And you did. He went off and found someone else."

Someone better. That's what her mom had said at the time.

Kelly pushed away the hurtful memory and put the width of the twin bed between them. "Exactly." She didn't throw herself on the bed. She wasn't a teenager anymore. She was an adult. With a baby inside her. "He found someone else. A brilliant premed student just like him." She left out the part that Caleb had also broken up with that woman. "Why on earth would you think this baby is his, anyway?"

"He was home here in Weaver for Christmas. If not his, then whose? God knows you're not much of a catch. Only boy who ever came sniffing around for you was that Buchanan kid."

"Ever think that's because I didn't want boys coming around here to meet you?" She couldn't believe the words came out, even if they were true.

"All right, then," Georgette challenged. "Whose baby is it?"

Kelly's eyes stung. She wasn't a liar by nature.

But she lied. She lied because she wasn't going to get foisted on Caleb Buchanan just because he and his people took care of their own. She wasn't going to end up a wife out of his sense of responsibility. Not when she'd been raised by a mother who'd only acted out of responsibility instead of love.

Caleb might have wanted her once, but he'd cast her aside.

Until one night thirty-four days ago when he'd wanted her enough to get naked in the front seat of her pickup truck, just like they'd done back when they were in high school. Back before he'd left her and gone off to college. Back before he'd chosen another woman.

"It was just a guy, Mama. Nobody you know at all."

The determined brightness in her mother's eyes dimmed, and she got the same disappointed, dissatisfied, discontented look she'd had all of Kelly's life. She sank down on the foot of the twin bed as if she couldn't stand the weight of her own body. "The only chance you had of making something of yourself—snagging a fancy, educated surgeon like that Buchanan—and you take up with some guy just passing through town?"

Her mother was editorializing. Adding details that Kelly had not. Embellishing the story with her own experiences. It wasn't the first time, nor would it be the last. "Caleb has years to go before he'll be a surgeon! And I don't need to make someone like him marry me in order to make something of *myself*, Mama. I've got a good job working with Doc Cobb!"

"Sure, answering his phones and putting out the trash. You think that old coot is gonna want his receptionist parading around with a pregnant belly and no ring on her finger? Times may have changed since you were born, but people in this town still expect mamas to be with the daddies. All you're gonna earn is a lot of gossip and speculation. You ought to have been smarter than to ruin your life the same way I did!"

Kelly stared at her mother and vowed right then and there that she'd make sure *her* child never heard such hateful words. "I'm sorry you feel that way."

Georgette just snorted, not seeming to notice Kelly pulling out her ancient suitcase from the closet until it lay open on the bed. "What fool thing are you doing now?"

"Packing." Kelly kept moving, pulling open her top drawer and dumping the contents into the suitcase, quickly followed by the second drawer, and the third and last. She had to push down hard on the suitcase when she closed it to get the lock latched, but she managed.

Georgette was watching her with an annoyed look. "Gonna go chase after the guy, I suppose. Fat lot of good that'll do."

Kelly didn't have a second suitcase. But she had an oversize beach bag that managed to hold several pairs of shoes and her favorite pair of boots. "Why? Is that what you did?" She propped the bulging canvas bag against the faded pink suitcase and went back to the closet again. "Fruitlessly chase after my father?" She snatched two handfuls of hanging clothes from the single wooden bar in her closet. "Is that why you've always hated me?"

Her mother answered with a huff. "I've always said you had a crazy imagination."

"Yes." Kelly draped the clothes over her arm. She was leaving behind stuff, but she was beyond caring. "It's my imagination that I can count on one hand the times you've ever shown a lick of caring for me."

Georgette's frown deepened. She'd never welcomed other people's opinions, and Kelly's was no different. "Kept a roof over your ungrateful head, didn't I?"

"Yes, you did, Mama." She awkwardly looped the beach bag strap over her shoulder and wrapped her fingers around the suitcase handle, dragging it off the mattress. It bumped hard against her knee. "You did your duty, that's for sure." Tears glazed her eyes. "But I'm not going to raise my baby like that." She shuffled toward the door with her heavy load precariously balanced.

Georgette followed, arms crossed tightly over her chest. "Go ahead and think you're not just like your mama. Was a time I thought I wasn't just like my mama, too. But here you are. Knocked up by some walk-away joe. Just who do you think is going to take you in when they learn you got yourself pregnant?"

Kelly blinked hard and kept going, carefully navigating the creaking steps that she'd pounded up and down all of her life. "I can take care of myself." She wasn't going to allow herself to think otherwise. If she did, she'd want to curl up and disappear. And she wouldn't do that now, not when she had a fledgling life inside her.

Behind her, Georgette gave that I-told-you-so huff of hers. "Guess you proved that, all right." She followed Kelly right out to the front porch of the small two-story house Georgette had inherited from her mother.

There was a deep ache inside Kelly's chest. She blamed it on the weight of carrying all of her belongings in one single trip and quickened her pace down the porch steps. The suitcase banged against her leg, and a few hangers slid out of her grasp. "I guess that's *my* problem, isn't it?"

She stepped over the dresses lying in the dirt, aiming blindly for the pickup truck that had been old even when she'd bought it five years earlier with the money she'd earned working at the grocery store. She set down the suitcase long enough to open the door and shove her hangers and beach bag across the threadbare bench seat.

"When you learn you can't handle your problem, don't come crawling back to me," Georgette yelled.

"Don't worry, Mama." Her voice was choked. She hefted the suitcase into the truck bed. It landed with a terrible bang, but at least the latches stayed closed. "I won't be back."

Georgette wasn't listening, though. "You'd be better off at least *trying* to pass off that kid as Buchanan's baby! Least you'd get some money outta *your* mistake!"

Kelly's chest ached even more.

She got behind the wheel, turned the key with a shaking hand until the engine cranked and drove away. When she dared a glance in the rearview mirror, all she saw was the plume of dust kicked up from her tires.

She swiped a hand over her wet cheek. "I won't be back," she said through her teeth.

She didn't know where she was going.

She just knew that anywhere was better than her mother's house.

But where could she go? She'd been working at Doc Cobb's for a year now since leaving the grocery store and had saved up some money, but with a baby on the way, she would need to conserve every penny she could.

She braked when she reached the highway and stared down the empty road toward Weaver.

She could find a place to live in town. Keep working for Doc Cobb. He was a pediatrician. Nobody liked babies and children more than her genial boss. But whether Kelly wanted to admit it or not, her mother was right about one thing. Gossip was going to dog her every footstep when it became obvious that she was pregnant and there was no daddy standing by her side. More important than that, though, was the baby. And that same gossip was going to follow her child the same way it had always followed her.

She was not going to repeat her mother's mistakes.

And she damn sure was not going to beg Caleb Buchanan for one single thing.

She exhaled, wiped her cheeks again, looked down the empty highway one more time and hit the gas.

Chapter One

"Dr. C shouldn't be too long." The nurse—a young blonde Kelly didn't know—smiled as she ushered them into an empty examining room. She winked at Tyler. "Be thinking about what color cast you want this time." She slid the medical chart she'd started for them into the metal sleeve on the door that she closed as she left them alone.

The door had barely latched before Kelly's son gave her a plaintive look. "How come I gotta get another cast?"

She dumped her purse and their jackets on the chair wedged in one corner of the room. "Because your wrist still hasn't healed all the way and you cracked the cast you already have."

"But—"

"Be glad that you didn't hurt yourself even more." She'd seen the X-rays herself on the computer screen just a few minutes ago. Not only had Doc Cobb hired several new faces since Kelly'd last been there, but he'd gotten himself some state-of-the-art equipment, as well. She patted the top of the examining room table. The thin paper covering it crinkled. "Want me to lift you up here, or—"

Tyler didn't wait for her to finish before he scrambled up onto the high table by himself. Then he stuck out his tongue and stared at the cast circling his right forearm. "Stupid cast," he grumbled.

She brushed her fingers through his dark hair, pushing the thick strands away from his forehead. He needed a haircut, but there just hadn't been time enough to fit one in before they'd left Idaho Falls. Not between arranging her vacation days, talking to his kindergarten teacher about his absence and packing up what she thought he'd need during the two weeks she'd allotted to get things settled. She had a day before the funeral, though. She'd get him to the barber before then. "Maybe next time you'll think twice before climbing a tree," she said calmly.

"Had to climb it," he argued. "Gunnar did."

"And you have to do everything that Gunnar does?" She didn't really expect an answer. Her five-year-old son and his best friend, Gunnar Nielsen, were like two peas in a pod. What one did, the other had to do, as well. Fortunately for Gunnar, he had climbed down the tree, whereas her daredevil son had decided to jump.

Thus, the broken wrist.

"So think twice next time about the way you get out of the tree," she added.

Tyler was swinging one leg back and forth, looking from the closed door of the small examining room to the sink and counter on the opposite side. "What's in all those drawers?"

"Bandages for little boys who don't listen to their mothers when they should." She tapped her finger pointedly against the crack in his cast then pulled a fresh coloring book out of her oversize purse. If she knew Doc Cobb—and she did, even though it had been nearly six years since she'd last seen him—it would be a good while yet before he made his way to Tyler. Given the nature of the doctor's pediatric practice, the later in the afternoon the appointments were, the farther behind he was likely to be. "Want to color?"

Tyler scrunched his face and swung his leg a few more times before nodding. She set the thin coloring book on the table beside him and rummaged in her purse again until she found the plastic baggie full of the washable markers he preferred over crayons. "Which color first?"

"Red."

She extracted the red marker and handed it to him. She knew from experience that if she gave him the entire pen collection, he'd have them scattered everywhere within seconds and she wasn't particularly in the mood to scramble around the floor in her dress and high heels picking them up. She would have changed out of the outfit she'd worn to the lawyer's office if there had been time before Tyler's appointment. But they'd worked him into the schedule as a favor when they could have just as easily referred him to the hospital to have his cast repaired.

"Was I born yet?"

"Were you born yet when?"

"When you used to work here." He stretched out on

his stomach and attacked the robot on the page with his red pen.

"You were born in Idaho, remember?"

He giggled. "I don't remember being *born*."

"Smarty-pants." She pushed the jackets over the back of the chair and sat. "I worked for Dr. Cobb before I moved to Idaho. Before you were born. Before I became a nurse."

"What was Grandma Gette?"

"Grandma Georgette had the farm," she reminded him calmly. Small as it had been. Her mother had grown vegetables and raised chickens, though the lawyer had told Kelly the chickens had gone by the wayside a few years earlier. Which explained the broken-down state of the coops now. "The bedroom you slept in last night was my bedroom when I was your age." She hadn't been able to make herself use her mother's room. Instead, she'd slept on the couch. It was the same couch from her childhood, with the same lumps.

"But then we went to Idaho."

"Yes." It had been one of the best decisions she'd ever made in her life. She held up the baggie. "Want another color yet?"

He stuck the tip of his tongue in the corner of his mouth, considering. "Green."

They exchanged the markers. "Your robot is going to look like a Christmas robot."

He grinned, clearly liking that idea. "Santa robot." He held up his cracked cast. It, too, had started out a bright red. But in the weeks since he'd gotten it, the color and the various drawings and signatures on it had all faded considerably. "Santa's gonna know where I am, right?"

"Santa doesn't come until Christmas. That's almost two months away. We'll be home long before then."

"Not before Halloween, though."

She shook her head. Halloween was less than a week away. "I don't think so, buddy. I'm sorry."

"Gunnar's gonna trick-or-treat without me."

"I know." She rubbed Tyler's back. "I'll figure out something for us to do on Halloween." It wouldn't be answering the door to trick-or-treaters, that was certain. Even back when she'd been a kid, children didn't voluntarily knock on Georgette Rasmussen's door. Not unless they were on a dare or something.

"I wish we didn't have to come here."

"I know." She propped her elbow on the table and rested her head on her hand. "I wish that, too. We'll only be here in Weaver for a little while, though."

It felt like months since she'd had a moment to draw breath, when it had really only been three days since she'd gotten the call about her mother. One day to absorb the news that the woman she hadn't spoken to in six long years had died of a sudden heart attack. One day to pack up and drive nine hours from Idaho Falls to Weaver, Wyoming. One day to meet Tom Hook, the attorney who'd contacted her in the first place.

That's the way she meant to continue. Dealing with things one day after another until she and Tyler could go back home where they belonged in Idaho. Then she could examine her feelings about losing the mother who'd never wanted to be her mother in the first place.

She pushed away the thought and started to cross her legs, but the doorknob suddenly rattled and she heard muffled voices on the other side of the door. She sat up straighter and brushed Tyler's hair back from his eyes again. "You'll like Doc Cobb. He's one of the nicest men I've ever known."

"Is that why my middle name is Cobb?"

"Mmm-hmm." Considering everything her onetime boss had done for her, she should have stayed in better contact with him. She held up the baggie. "Put your marker away for now."

Tyler rolled onto his side and sat up but missed the bag when he dropped the marker. It rolled under the table.

"Good aim, buddy," she said wryly and crouched down to reach blindly beneath the metal base.

She heard the door open behind her just as her fingertips found what she was looking for. "Sorry for the wait," she heard as she quickly grabbed the marker.

She was already smiling as she straightened and turned. "Doc—" The word caught in her throat, and all she could do was stare while everything inside her went hot.

Then cold.

Not because good old Doc Cobb, with his balding head, wildly wiry gray eyebrows and Santa-size belly was standing there.

But because he wasn't.

Instead, the man facing her was six-plus feet of broad shoulders and very lean, un-Santa-like man. Sharply hewn jaw. Unsmiling mouth. Dark, uncommonly watchful eyes. Even darker hair brushed carelessly back from his face.

Seeing Caleb Buchanan was like being punched in the solar plexus.

She hadn't seen him face-to-face in nearly six years. But there was no mistaking him now.

And no mistaking the fact that—while she was blindsided at the sight of him here in Weaver, when he should have been a surgical resident somewhere else by now—

he didn't seem anywhere near as surprised by the sight of *her*.

Well, duh, Kelly. Her name was written plainly in Tyler's medical chart. How many Kelly Rasmussens could there be, particularly in the small town of Weaver?

The young blonde nurse stepped between them as she rolled the cast saw unit into the room.

Panic suddenly slid through Kelly's veins and she snatched up their coats from the chair.

"You can stay," the nurse assured, looking as cheerful as ever. "The machine looks more intimidating than it really is."

Kelly's mouth opened. But the assurance that she was perfectly comfortable with the saw stuck in her throat. She didn't dare look at Caleb. And Tyler was starting to look alarmed.

How could she explain to any of them her urgent need to flee?

Caleb took a step past her, approaching the exam table. "I'm Dr. C, Tyler. We'll have you fixed up in no time."

The nurse patted Kelly's arm comfortingly as she moved the saw next to Caleb. "He's going to cut off your cast and put the new one on," she chirped. "Did you decide what color you want?"

"Red."

"Again?"

"I like red."

One part of Kelly's brain observed the scene. The other part was imagining herself grabbing Tyler and running for the hills.

"I was expecting Dr. *Cobb*," she blurted.

The nurse blinked, clearly surprised. Kelly felt an insane urge to laugh hysterically. The practice was still clearly Cobb Pediatrics. The sign on the outside of the building said so. When Kelly had called for an appointment, that was the greeting she'd received.

"He's on sabbatical," Caleb said. "Put your coats down, Kelly. It's been a long time, but you're here and your son's cast needs to be replaced."

Your son.

She let out a careful breath, finally daring to glance his way as he set the medical chart on the counter next to the sink before flipping on the water to wash his hands. He was wearing an unfastened white lab coat over blue jeans and an untucked black shirt. "How'd you break your cast, Tyler?"

"Sliding down the banister at my mother's house," Kelly answered before Tyler could say a word. She knew it was silly not to want her son talking to Caleb, but she couldn't help it. And she felt sure that Caleb would have already read the information the nurse had recorded in Tyler's chart. "I would have taken him to the hospital if I'd known the doctor was away," she said to the nurse.

"No need for that." Just as Kelly had spoken to the nurse, Caleb aimed his comment at Tyler. "Banisters *are* pretty cool. How'd you break your arm in the first place?"

"Jumping out of a tree," Kelly answered again. Even though it took her closer to Caleb than she wanted to be, she edged closer to Tyler. Every day that she looked at her boy, she could see his father in him. How could Caleb miss the similarities that were so obvious to her? "Sabbatical where?"

"Florida," the nurse provided. "Six more months yet. He'll miss all of Weaver's lovely winter." She widened her eyes comically. "Poor guy." She draped a blue pad over Tyler's lap. "You're lucky today," she told him.

"Dr. C is going to take your cast off himself. He doesn't do that for just everyone."

Kelly's nerves tightened even more. But she could see Tyler's alarm growing as he stared at the saw. She dumped the coats on the chair again and rubbed her hand down his back. No matter what she felt inside, her son's welfare was first and foremost. "It's a special kind of saw, buddy. Only for cutting through casts. It won't hurt a lick."

His eyes were the size of saucers. "How do you know?"

"I had a broken wrist once, too. Remember I told you that?"

"She did," Caleb concurred. In a motion steeped in familiarity, he reached out his long arm and snagged two gloves from a box next to the sink. "She was fourteen years old." As he worked his fingers into the blue gloves, she hated the fact that she noticed he wore no wedding ring. Not that the absence of one proved anything.

Not that she cared, either way.

The lie was so monumental she felt herself flushing.

"Flew right over the handlebars of her bicycle," he was saying. "Saw the whole thing. I'm sure your mom remembers that day very well, too." His eyes snagged hers for the briefest of moments, and she looked away.

The nurse handed him the saw. "This'll be loud, Tyler, but your mom's right. It won't hurt," Caleb said. He turned it on and the loud whine filled the room.

Kelly didn't want to, but she moved out of the way so he had more room to maneuver. Only then did she realize she was still clutching the plastic marker. She it inside her purse then moved back to the opposite corner near the door.

The noise from the saw was short-lived. After only a few minutes, Caleb turned it off and handed it back to the nurse. Then he used the long-handled spreader to separate the gap he'd just cut in the fiberglass cast. "Doing okay there, Tyler?"

"Mmm-hmm." Tyler was obviously over his alarm and watched as Caleb worked. "You knew my mom before I was born?"

The knot in Kelly's throat doubled in size.

"Sure did." He took up a pair of scissors and began snipping through the padding next to Tyler's skin.

"That was a long time ago, huh."

"Sure was." Caleb flicked another glance her way. What he was thinking was anybody's guess. As a young man, she'd been able to read every thought he had.

Now his expression was completely unreadable.

Could he recognize his own eyes looking up at him from Tyler's face and not show any reaction at all?

Then he focused on Tyler again as he pulled open the fiberglass cast and slid it gently away from Tyler's forearm. "Still doing okay, buddy?"

"His name is Tyler," Kelly said tightly. *She* was the one who called her son "buddy."

"Tyler Cobb Rasmussen," Tyler piped proudly. "That's my *whole* name."

"Cobb!" The nurse exclaimed. "What a coincidence."

Hardly that. But Kelly had no desire to explain anything to the nurse. As it was, she wondered just how close Caleb and Doc Cobb had gotten over the years. Even though the elder physician had been the one to refer Kelly to a professional associate of his in Idaho Falls, she had never told him why she'd been so anxious to leave Weaver. Aside from her mother, Kelly had never told anyone in Weaver that she'd been pregnant when she'd left.

She crossed her arms tightly and returned Caleb's look with a hard-won impassive look of her own. Mentally daring him to make some comment. Some observation.

But none came.

Instead, with the nurse's assistance, he had Tyler's arm recast in short order. Leaving the young blonde to clean up the small mess that remained, Caleb threw away his gloves, washed his hands again and scribbled in the chart before holding it out for Kelly. She took it, but he didn't immediately release it, and her nerves ratcheted tight all over again. She tugged a little harder on the chart and he finally released it.

"I was sorry to hear about your mother."

Her jaw felt tight as she flipped open the chart to scan the contents. She wished she could find fault with the notes but couldn't, so she closed the folder with a snap. She wanted to ask him why he was sorry, but that sounded too much like something her mother would have said. "Thank you."

She wondered if she imagined his faint sigh before he went on to explain that the nurse would give them information on cast care.

"Think I've got that covered," Kelly said.

One corner of his mouth kicked up in an imitation of a grin. It wasn't a real one. Despite the intervening years, she could still tell the difference between real and fake with him. He turned back to Tyler and stuck out his hand. "Nice to meet you, Tyler Cobb Rasmussen."

She felt vaguely dizzy but her little boy giggled as he manfully shook the offered hand. "Nice to meet you, Dr. C."

"No more sliding down banisters, okay? At least for now."

Tyler nodded. "I promise."

Sure. Easy for Caleb to elicit the promise, whereas Kelly needed to be constantly on alert where her rambunctious, active son was concerned.

Guilt squeezed her stomach. If she'd been better at her job, Tyler wouldn't have been on that banister in the first place.

And they could have avoided this trip to Doc Cobb's office altogether.

She rubbed at the pain between her eyebrows.

"You all right?"

She dropped her hand. She didn't want or need Caleb's concern. All she wanted was to escape unscathed with her son. "I'm fine." She retrieved her purse from the chair in the corner and looped the leather strap over her shoulder before lifting Tyler off the table and handing him his jacket. She went ramrod stiff when Caleb cupped her shoulder. "It was good to see you." The touch was as brief as it was light and shouldn't have felt like it burned.

Yet it did.

Then he opened the door and left the room.

Kelly could have collapsed with relief.

"We all love Dr. C," the nurse commented as she tore off the protective paper from the table and rolled out fresh. "He's so great with the patients." She smiled impishly. "And pretty great to look at, but don't tell him I said so."

Kelly wrapped her fingers around her purse strap and clutched her own jacket to her waist. "How long has he been here?"

"Almost a year now."

The nurse didn't seem surprised by the question. But

then she probably fielded lots of questions from single mothers about the handsome Dr. C. Kelly's fingers tightened even more on the leather strap. "I'm surprised," she mused casually. "I'd heard he was on the surgical track. Didn't even know he'd switched to pediatrics. Is he here permanently?"

"We're all hoping so." It was hardly the definitive answer Kelly wanted, but the nurse pulled the door open wider as she led the way from the room, pushing the saw unit ahead of her. She smiled brightly at Tyler. "Take care of that cast like Dr. C said, okay?"

"I will." Tyler tucked his left hand in Kelly's. "Can we have ice cream?"

The vise around her nerve endings eased up as she looked down at his hopeful face. Everything she did in her life was worth it when it came to her precious boy.

Even facing his unknowing father.

She leaned over and kissed Tyler's nose. "After dinner."

"When's dinner?"

"Trying to tell me you're already hungry?"

He nodded.

She led him through the rabbit warren of hallways until they reached the exit where the billing desk was located. The white-haired woman sitting at the desk was a welcome sight. "Mary Goodwin! You're still here? You were threatening retirement even when I used to work here."

The woman laughed. "I tried a few years ago. Went stir-crazy after only a few months and begged Doc Cobb to give me back my job. I heard you were back in town. Haven't changed a single little bit, either. Still as pretty as a picture. How's married life?"

Kelly faltered. "Excuse me?"

Mary looked awkward for a moment. "I… Nothing.

You know how word gets around in these parts." She focused quickly on the paperwork in the chart. "No follow-up appointment?"

Kelly hesitated. Had Doc Cobb told people that she'd gotten married? It was far more likely that such a story had originated with her mom. Though for what purpose, Kelly couldn't imagine. "We're only here for a few weeks. I'll take Tyler to his regular pediatrician back home when it's time." She handed over her credit card before pushing her arms into her jacket sleeves. "You can put the co-pay on that."

Mary ran the card. "I saw your mother's obituary in *The Weaver Weekly*." She set the card and the printed charge slip on the desk in front of Kelly. "My condolences."

She quickly signed her name on the authorization. "Someone is still publishing *The Weaver Weekly*? Surprised that hasn't died off by now."

Mary shook her head. "Quite the opposite. Comes out twice a week now."

"Any other changes around town I should know about?" She managed to keep her tone light.

"Just drive on down Main Street and see for yourself," Mary advised. "Weaver's grown a lot since you left. There's even a—" she cast a quick look at Tyler "—a particularly popular fast food place on the other side of town. Bekins Road, right before the highway on the way to Braden. Arches on the sign," she added, raising her eyebrows for emphasis.

"Never would have expected that." Maybe in Braden. The town was a good thirty miles away and had always edged out Weaver in terms of available services. Kelly slid everything back into her purse and took Tyler's hand again before pushing on the exit door. "Take care, Mary."

"You too, honey."

They stepped out into the weak October sunshine and Kelly hauled in a deep breath.

"Mommy! You're squeezing my hand too tight."

"Sorry, buddy." Kelly quickly loosened her hold as they walked to the small parking lot that was full of vehicles. Hers was the only one sporting an out-of-state license plate. She let go of his hand and unlocked the car doors. He climbed into the rear onto his booster seat. He was particularly independent about fastening his own safety belt, and she waited while he worked at it, not closing the door until she tugged the strap to be sure it was secure.

Then she straightened, glancing back at the building over the roof of her car.

Six years had passed since that night she and Caleb had unintentionally conceived the brightest light in her life. Six years since they'd had any sort of contact. Intentional or otherwise.

She'd gotten over Caleb a long time ago.

He, of course, had never needed to get over *her*.

Six years.

That time had evidently brought a lot of changes to Weaver. But none of them mattered to her. She and Tyler had a life—a good life—in Idaho. One she'd worked darned hard to achieve. They had friends. They had a home where Tyler had never known anything but love. She'd returned to Weaver to do her last duty as Georgette Rasmussen's daughter.

She wasn't going to let herself think about anything else.

Caleb Buchanan included.

Chapter Two

"I heard Kelly Rasmussen and her little boy are in town." Caleb's sister, Lucy, leaned past his shoulder to set a bowl of salad on the kitchen table. "Staying out at her mother's place. I should take them a meal or something. Can't be easy for her."

"I'm sure she'd like that," Caleb answered smoothly. He wasn't sure if his sister was fishing or not, but knowing Lucy, she probably was. "Last time I saw Georgette's house it was practically falling apart, and that was years ago." He'd gone to see Kelly's mother only once after he and Kelly had parted ways for good. Only because he could hardly believe the story around town: that she'd moved to Idaho and gotten married. There were even stories about a kid.

Georgette had confirmed it, though. The woman had wallowed in her bitterness as she told him how Kelly had abandoned her in favor of her new life in the city.

She then told him about Kelly's new man and the baby they'd had together.

Georgette's attitude hadn't been particularly surprising. She'd always given new meaning to the word *ornery*. But the fact that Kelly really was married? With a baby, no less?

Even though there was nothing between them anymore, the confirmation had knocked him sideways.

He eyed the platter of pork chops Lucy put on the table. His mouth had been watering for her cooking since that morning when she'd called to invite him for supper. But his thoughts kept straying to his encounter with Kelly.

He'd seen Tyler Rasmussen's name written in as a last-minute addition on the schedule but hadn't thought twice about it. There were dozens of Rasmussens around Weaver. The family seemed to have more branches than his own.

Then he'd opened the boy's chart and Kelly's signature had all but smacked him in the face.

His only thoughts when he'd opened the examining room door after that were to keep his act together. He was a physician, for God's sake. Not a stupid kid who hadn't known what he had until he'd thoughtlessly tossed it aside in favor of someone else.

She'd always been pretty, with otter-brown hair, coffee-colored eyes and delicate features. But Kelly Rasmussen all grown up? She'd held herself with a confidence that she hadn't possessed before. She was still beautiful. More…womanly.

He pushed the disturbing image to the back of his mind and focused on his three-year-old niece bouncing on his knee. "What do you want more, Sunny? The salad? Or the pork chops?"

"Gravy," she said promptly. "And 'tatoes."

"You have to eat some carrots first," Lucy said firmly. She moved the toddler from Caleb's lap to her high chair and ruffled her daughter's dark hair. "She'd eat mashed potatoes and gravy morning, noon and night if I let her," Lucy said with a wry smile.

"Girl knows what she likes." He winked at the tot, who awarded him with a beaming smile. "Kelly's boy is cute," he commented casually. "Tall for his age."

Lucy stopped in her tracks and gave him a surprised look. "You've seen them?"

He knew from long experience there was no point hiding anything from his family, especially his sister. It was better to head her off at the pass than to keep things secret. Then he'd never hear the end of it.

"She brought him to the office today." He got up and brought the mashed potatoes and gravy to the table himself, giving Sunny another wink that earned him a giggle from her and an eye roll from her mama.

"You're as bad as a three-year-old." Lucy set a few carrot sticks on Sunny's plastic plate then went to the kitchen doorway and called, "Shelby! Come and eat."

Only a matter of seconds passed before Lucy's step-daughter raced into the kitchen. "Uncle Caleb!" The girl's light brown eyes were bright as she launched herself at him. Caleb caught her, wrinkling his nose when she smacked a kiss on his lips.

"Kissing boys now, are you?"

She giggled, shaking her head violently. "Boys are *gross*."

"Sometimes," Lucy joked. She filled Shelby's milk glass. "Caleb sure was for a long time."

"Spoken like a loving *older* sister."

She just grinned at him, forked a pork chop onto her plate and began cutting it into strips for Sunny.

"Mommy, when's Daddy coming home?"

"He'll be back from Cheyenne tomorrow night, sweetie." She transferred some of the strips to Sunny's plate.

"Good." Shelby sat up on her knees and attacked her own meal.

Caleb followed suit. "How's Nick doing?"

"He's twenty-five, as handsome as his daddy and spending the year in Europe, studying."

Like Lucy's stepson, Caleb had been studying when he was twenty-five, too. But medicine in Colorado versus architecture in Europe. "In other words, he's doing pretty fine. Is he going to go into business with Beck?"

"Beck certainly hopes so. Father and son architects and all. So, how was it?"

Caleb doused his plate with the creamy gravy. "How was what?"

Lucy whisked the bowl out of his reach when he went in for another helping. "Don't pretend ignorance. Seeing Kelly again, obviously."

With her mother otherwise occupied, Shelby slyly palmed some dreaded carrot sticks from her and Sunny's plates. Beneath the table, Caleb reached out and Shelby dropped them into his hand.

Lucy's eyes narrowed suddenly, darting from Caleb to her daughters. "What are you three grinning about?"

"Nothing." Caleb blithely folded his napkin over the carrots. He hated them, too.

"Who's Kelly?" Shelby was only nine, but she'd already developed the art of distraction.

"Uncle Caleb's old girlfriend," Lucy said. She smiled devilishly at him. "One of them, anyway."

"I don't rub in your old mistakes," he argued in a mild tone.

She blinked innocently. "Well, I wasn't the one going around breaking girls' hearts."

Not all that long ago, before an injury had sidelined her career, his sister had been a prima ballerina with a dance company in New York. Now she ran a dance school in Weaver, and despite her blessedly relaxed rules over her personal diet, she still drew admiring looks everywhere she went. "Pretty sure you broke a few hearts along the way, Luce."

"Then she met Daddy and I got to wear a beautiful dress." Shelby's expression turned dreamy. "When you get married can I be in your wedding, too, Uncle Caleb?"

He nearly choked on his food, and Lucy laughed merrily. "Sounds like a reasonable question, Uncle Caleb."

He ignored his sister and answered his far more agreeable niece. "Maybe I'll just wait until you're grown-up and marry *you*."

That elicited peals of laughter. "You're my *uncle*. I can't marry you!"

Far be it for him to explain the finer aspects of blood relations. "Then I'll just have to stay single," he drawled.

Lucy rolled her eyes. "Sure. Blame your loneliness on an innocent child."

Shelby's brow knit with sudden concern. "Are you lonely, Uncle Caleb?"

"No," he assured her calmly. "Your mom's just teasing. How could I be lonely when I have all of you around?"

To his satisfaction, everyone seemed happy to let the matter go at that.

He was wrong to think the reprieve would last, though.

Two hours later, after he'd told Sunny two bedtime stories and played two games of checkers with Shelby, Caleb was ready to leave. But Lucy trailed after him as he headed to his truck. "You never answered the question."

He set the container of leftovers she'd packed for him inside the cab before climbing behind the wheel. "What question?"

Coatless, she hugged her arms around herself, dancing a little in the cold. "What it was like seeing Kelly again."

"It wasn't like anything," he lied. "We broke up nearly ten years ago. She even married someone else, remember?"

"One of my students' moms works for Tom Hook, and she says there doesn't seem to be a husband in the picture. If Kelly's little boy were a few years older, he could've been yours."

"For God's sake, Luce!" If he hadn't known better, he'd have wondered himself about that boy. But even as impetuous as that night had been, they hadn't been irresponsible. He'd used a condom. They'd always used condoms. From the first time until the last.

"Hey!" His sister had lifted her hands innocently. "Don't blame me for what other people find interesting topics of conversation. So…no sparks between old flames?"

"It was just another appointment, Luce," he said smoothly. "Thanks for supper. Tell Beck I'll be in touch about the house plans."

"Have you decided where you want to build?"

"Not yet." He nudged her out of the way so he could grab the truck door. "It's freezing. You'll catch a cold."

"You're a doctor. You're supposed to know that being cold and catching a cold aren't related."

"Tell that to Mom. She still thinks wearing a scarf during winter keeps a cold away."

Lucy smiled and lifted her hand, heading back to the house while he drove away.

Lucy and Beck lived on the outskirts of Weaver, on the opposite side of town from the condo he'd been renting since he'd moved back home. Since he had nothing and no one waiting for him at home once he got there, he pulled into the hospital parking lot on his way. He didn't have to be there, but he also didn't have to be anywhere else. Might as well look in on the newborn he'd examined first thing that morning.

His presence didn't raise many eyebrows as he made his way to the nursery. The staff there were pretty used to him by now, ever since he'd joined Howard Cobb's practice. When Caleb entered the nursery, he washed up and pulled on gloves.

"Come to rock the babies, Dr. C?" Lisa Pope, one of the swing nurses, gave him a friendly smile over the minuscule diaper she was changing.

"Any who need it?" He glanced at the clear-sided bassinets. The majority of them were empty. It was a slow night in the nursery.

"Babies always need rocking." As if to prove her point, she cradled her freshly diapered charge and sat in one of the wooden rocking chairs lined up against one of the walls. "But none of them tonight are missing a mommy or a daddy."

"So a slow night *and* a good night."

Lisa smiled over the tiny head cradled against her pink-and-blue scrubs. "Pretty much."

He took his time looking over his newest patient— an eight-pound little guy who sported a head full of brown hair and a serenely sleeping face. Caleb didn't mind the nurses knowing that he came in sometimes just to rock the babies. Some didn't have mothers in good enough condition to rock their restless infants. Some didn't have any parents at all. Others had been born to perfectly normal moms and dads but were feeling outraged at finding themselves abruptly in a cold, bright world and didn't like it one bit.

He'd never particularly felt a need to let the nursery staff in on the real secret—that rocking those babies soothed something inside him, too. Truth was, most of the nursery staff probably felt that way themselves.

But he wasn't going to disturb the little guy's slumber just because he was feeling restless. He wasn't that selfish.

He said good-night to Lisa, disposed of the gloves and headed back out of the hospital.

What had it been like for Kelly when she'd given birth to Tyler?

Had she been alone? Or had the man she'd found— the husband Georgette had told Caleb about all those years ago—been by her side?

He walked briskly toward his truck, shaking off the pointless wondering. Whatever had happened between Kelly and Tyler's father—was still happening, for all he knew—it was none of his business. Just because she wasn't wearing a ring and she *and* her boy went by the name of Rasmussen didn't mean she was single again.

Available.

And even if she were, chances were she still wanted nothing to do with him.

Why would she?

They'd been high school sweethearts. They'd been each other's first. Even though they'd been just kids, it was a history. A history that had ended badly.

His doing entirely, and one he took full responsibility for.

But the last time they'd seen each other? When she'd told him flat out that she'd wanted to rock his world once more, simply for the pleasure of walking away from *him* afterward?

That had been all her.

He'd broken her heart once, and she'd proven just how well she'd recovered.

He could even understand it. Some. After Melissa had dumped him, he'd gone out of his way proving to her that he was over her, too. Last he'd heard, she'd married a thoracic surgeon out in California. Caleb wished them well. Was glad, even, that she'd been smart enough not to marry Caleb when he'd proposed. They'd been all of twenty-one at the time. She'd known what he hadn't, though—that they weren't going to last.

In the busy years since, he'd thought more about the girl back home whom he'd pushed aside in favor of Melissa than he had about Melissa herself.

"Which makes you sound about as lonely as Lucy thinks you are," he muttered as he got into his truck. He pulled out his cell phone and checked the signal. Near the hospital, it was pretty strong. Around Weaver, a steady cell phone signal was never a foregone conclusion. But whom to call?

His cousin Justin Clay and Tabby Taggart had gotten married six months earlier. When his cousin wasn't working at the hospital lab, he was practically glued to Tabby's side.

It would be revolting if it weren't so annoyingly… cute, seeing his two oldest friends so stinking happy.

He tossed his phone on the dashboard and drove out

of the parking lot. He didn't need company. For one simple reason.

He wasn't lonely.

If he wanted a date, he got a date. There was never a dearth of willing women when you were single and had the initials *M* and *D* following your name. They usually didn't even mind all that much when they came a distant third behind his studies and his patients. And if they did mind, they soon parted ways. No harm. No foul.

Definitely no broken hearts.

He'd learned his lesson well enough not to repeat it.

He drove down Main Street. Even on a weeknight, the lights were shining brightly at Colbys Bar and Grill. He abruptly pulled into the lot and went inside. "Hey, Merilee." He greeted the bartender as he slid onto an empty bar stool. Considering the crowded parking lot, the bar was pretty calm. Only two pool games going and nobody dancing on the small dance floor. "Grill must be busy tonight," he commented when she stopped in front of him.

"Have a school fund-raiser going on in there," she told him. "What're you having tonight?"

Restlessness in a bottle.

"Just a beer," he told her. "Whatever's on tap tonight."

She set a round coaster on the bar in front of him and a moment later topped that with a frosty mug of beer.

"Jane not working tonight?" Jane was the owner. Married to another one of Caleb's cousins.

"Thursdays?" Merilee shook her head. "Do you want a menu?"

He shook his head. "Just ate." He glanced around again. The beer didn't really hold any interest. Nothing in the bar held any interest. Not the trio of young women sitting at the other end who were nudging each other and looking his way. Not the hockey game on the television mounted on the wall.

The door opened, and Caleb automatically glanced over, then wished he hadn't, because the woman walking in looked straight at him. Pam Rasmussen was a dispatcher at the sheriff's office. She had been around forever and was one of the biggest gossips in town.

And she was married to one of Kelly Rasmussen's cousins.

He looked down into his beer, resigning himself to being courteous when she stopped next to him at the bar.

"Evening, Caleb. How're you doing?"

"Same as ever, Pam. You just get off duty?"

She nodded. "I came by to pick up Rob." She tilted her head toward the breezeway that led from the bar into the attached restaurant. "He's holding a fund-raiser thing tonight for his class at school." She pulled out the stool next to Caleb's and sat. "Heard you saw Kelly today."

He gave her a bland look. "Oh, yeah?"

She wasn't the least bit put off. "Shawna Simpson had her baby in your office today for her checkup. She told me."

"It's still Doc Cobb's office."

"Everyone knows you're going to take over his practice for good when he retires."

"He's not retiring. Just on sabbatical."

She shrugged, dismissing his words. "Shawna said Kelly looks just the same."

He slid a glance toward the restaurant, wishing her husband, Rob, would hurry his ass up. "I don't remember Shawna from school."

"Sure you do. She was Shawna Allen then." Pam's

eyes narrowed as she thought about it. "Would have graduated high school a year ahead of you and Kelly, I think."

Whatever. He pulled out his wallet and extracted enough cash to cover the beer plus a tip and dropped it on the counter.

"Leaving already?"

"Hospital rounds in the morning come early." Not that early. But as an escape line, it was pretty good. "See you around."

"Probably at the funeral, I imagine."

The wind was blowing when he stepped outside the bar, and he flipped up the collar of his jacket as he headed for his truck. When he drove out of the parking lot, though, he didn't head for his apartment.

He headed for Georgette Rasmussen's old place.

Even though it had been several years since he'd last driven out there, he remembered the route as easily as ever. When he turned off the highway, the condition of the road was not so good. More dirt than pavement. More potholes and ruts than solid surface. The fact that there had never been anything as convenient as streetlights on the road didn't help. If he were a stranger driving out to the Rasmussen place for the first time, he'd have needed GPS to find his way.

But Caleb couldn't count the number of times he'd gone up and down that road when he and Kelly were teenagers. Following the curves in the road still felt like second nature.

When he pulled up in front of the two-story house, though, he wasn't all that sure what he was doing there. It wasn't as though she'd welcome a friendly ol' visit from him.

He turned off the engine and got out anyway. Walked

up the creaking porch steps and stood in front of the door beneath the bare lightbulb above it.

She answered on the second knock.

She'd changed out of the formfitting gray dress she'd been wearing earlier. In jeans and sweatshirt, she looked more like the high school girl she'd once been.

"Caleb." She didn't close the door in his face, which he supposed was a good sign. But she didn't open it wider in invitation, either.

"Kelly." He wasn't used to feeling short on words like this.

Her lips were compressed. She'd let her hair down. It reached just below her shoulders. When they'd been teenagers, she'd usually worn it braided down to the middle of her back.

He'd always liked unbraiding it.

She suddenly tucked her hair behind her ear and shifted from one bare foot to the other. "What are you doing here?"

He balled his fists in the pockets of his leather jacket. It'd been too long since he'd had a date if he was so vividly remembering unbraiding her hair the first time they'd had sex. "Wanted to see how you were."

"Still standing." She held one arm out to her side. "As you can see."

"Yeah." He glanced beyond the porch. Light shone from a few of the windows, but otherwise the place was dark. "How's Tyler's arm?"

"Fine." Her tone was short. "He's asleep."

Caleb exhaled slightly. "He's a good-looking boy."

She shifted again, lowering her lashes. "What do you want, Caleb?"

He cleared his throat. Pushed away the memory of his hands tangled in her hair. "Where's Tyler's father?"

Chapter Three

Kelly felt the blood drain out of her face. She tightened her grip on the doorknob. Her palm had gone slick. "I beg your pardon?"

The porch light cast sharp shadows on Caleb's face as he looked down at her. "Sorry. That was blunt."

She let out a breathy sigh, which was all her throat would allow.

"There's just no tactful way," he went on. "You know. Asking."

"Right." Still breathy. Still faint. "I, uh, I—"

"Is he still in the picture?"

"Who?"

"Your husband." He took a step back from the doorway, pulling one hand from his pocket and running it through his hair.

"I don't have a husband!"

He didn't look shocked. He just nodded and studied the toes of his boots for a moment. "I wondered if you'd split up after I saw your name on Tyler's paperwork this afternoon."

She pressed her shaking fingers to her temple. "Who, uh, who told you I was married? My mom?"

"Yeah. She told me you eloped after you went to Idaho. That you had a baby."

Kelly's eyes burned. Her mother was dead. She hadn't been a part of Kelly's life since Kelly walked out all those years ago. So why did her mother's words and actions still have the power to hurt? Georgette hadn't felt a need to make up a fictional husband when she'd had Kelly. But she'd created one when it came to explaining an illegitimate grandchild? "When did she tell you?"

"Doesn't matter. A while ago." He pushed his fingers through his hair again. "Look, I'm not trying to stick my nose where you don't want it. I know this can't be easy for you, coming back like this. Regardless of how tough things were between you, she was still your mom. I just wanted to tell you that if you need anything, just ask."

Her nose prickled. She couldn't seem to get a word out. She managed to nod.

"Well." He took a step back. "It's late. Watch for any increased tenderness or pain in your boy's arm." Caleb went down the porch steps, and she had the feeling he was anxious to get away. "The films looked good," he went on, "but switching up the cast can still be jarring."

Her tongue finally loosened. "I'm an RN. I know what to watch for."

He stopped, obviously surprised. "You're a nurse?"

She lifted her chin. "Don't look so shocked. Even *I* managed to get an education."

"That's not why I—" He broke off. "I'm glad for you.

I didn't know nursing was something you were interested in. Doc Cobb never mentioned it."

"I wasn't interested. Or at least I didn't know I was when I was his receptionist. And I didn't know you were interested in pediatrics. Seems there was a lot about each other we didn't know." She smiled tightly. "Good night, Caleb." She didn't wait for a response.

Just shut the door in his face.

After a tense minute, she heard his truck engine start up, followed by the crunch of his wheels over the uneven, rutted drive as he drove away.

She shivered, leaning back against the door. "Oh, Mama. Why did you lie to everyone?"

What was worse? Admitting to everyone that it was a lie? Or admitting to Caleb the truth?

And why did she have to do either, when she was only there to bury her mother?

"Mommy!" Tyler's sleepy voice came from the head of the stairs, and she quickly swiped her cheeks.

"What is it, buddy?"

He came down the steps. He was wearing his footy pajama pants but—as was typical—had pulled off the matching shirt somewhere along the way. Didn't matter how chilly it was outside, her son liked wearing as little as possible when he slept. He was rubbing his eyes, and his hair stood up in a cowlick. "My stomach's growly."

She picked him up when he lifted his arms and smiled into his face. "I'm not surprised. You only ate half your supper."

He wrapped his legs around her waist and leaned his head on her shoulder. "Can I have ice cream?"

"Not at this hour, bud." She carried him into the kitchen. She'd spent two hours cleaning it, and there were still stacks of empty boxes and crates lining the small room. Among other things, her mother seemed to have become a pack rat.

Kelly set him on the counter next to the refrigerator and made him half a sandwich. "PB and J," she said, handing it to him. "Plus milk."

He swung his foot as he ate. "When do we get to go home?"

"In a few weeks." She brushed down his hair again. He definitely needed a barber. "We've talked about it, remember? We'll go home just as soon as we can."

He nodded, licked his finger and drank his milk.

Love for him swelled inside her. She cupped her hand under his chin. "You know what?"

"What?"

She kissed his nose. "I love you."

"To infinity and beyond!"

She smiled. "You betcha. Come on." He'd finished his milk already. "Gotta brush your teeth again, then back to bed." He wrapped his arms around her neck and circled her waist with his legs, clinging like a limpet as she carried him back upstairs.

"Can I have another story?"

She was a sucker where he was concerned. She rubbed her hand down his bare back. "A short one."

The short story spread into two, then part of a third before his eyes finally closed and she was able to slide off the bed. She turned off the light and left the room, leaving the door ajar so she could hear him if he needed her.

She passed her mother's room and hesitated at the closed door. She inhaled deeply, then quickly pushed it open. It was the first time she'd gone inside the room since her mother's death, and she did so now only because she still needed to choose an outfit for Georgette's burial. She'd promised the funeral home that she'd deliver it the next day.

The room hadn't changed during Kelly's absence, any more than Kelly's bedroom had, except that like the kitchen, here too Georgette had stored dozens and dozens of containers. Empty shoe boxes. Empty plastic bags. Even empty coffee cans.

Kelly was going to have to clean up all of it before she could put the house on the market.

She opened the closet. Typically, there were only a few choices. For Kelly's entire life, her mother had run her spit of land all on her own. She'd lived in jeans and boots. There was only one dress for those times when Georgette couldn't get out of going to church.

Kelly pulled out the dress. Studied it for a long while. Then she shook her head and hung it back up and chose a pair of clean jeans instead. Her mother was who she was. Burying her didn't change that. The metal hangers squeaked as she pushed them on the rod until she found a decent plaid blouse. It was cotton and obviously new, judging by the tag still hanging from it.

She set it on the bed along with the jeans and went to the chest of drawers. Georgette Rasmussen had never owned lingerie. For her, underwear was underwear. Serviceable and plain. Kelly chose socks and cowboy boots. The only pair in the closet that weren't run down at the heels. She bundled all of it together in her arms and turned to leave the room, stopping at the last minute to grab the small metal box sitting on top of the chest. Her mother's version of a jewelry box.

She left the room, closing the door firmly, and carried everything downstairs. She used a kitchen towel to polish up the boots as best she could. Shiny boots were another thing that Georgette had considered a waste of time, so Kelly knew better than to look for polish.

She set everything inside one of the plentiful boxes stacked around the room and flipped open the jewelry box. Her mother had only ever worn a plain gold chain necklace, but it wasn't there. The only things inside the metal box were a couple faded photographs of her mother when she'd been young and still smiling—which meant before Kelly—and a few rings. Old-looking and probably belonging to Georgette's mother. Kelly could barely remember her. She'd died when Kelly was little.

She pulled out a tarnished ring, trying and failing to picture her grandmother. All she knew about her was what Georgette had told her. Kelly had always assumed it to be the truth.

Yet Georgette had told at least one big lie in her life. She'd told Caleb—told everyone, it seemed—that Kelly had gotten married.

Why bother? Had she actually wanted to protect Kelly's reputation?

It was too late for an answer. She would never know what had motivated her mother now.

She dropped the ring back in the box, closed it with a snap and went to bed.

"Kelly! Kelly Rasmussen, hold up!"

"Hold on, buddy." Kelly caught Tyler's hand and stopped him from stepping off the curb as she looked back to see who was yelling her name. It had been a busy morning. Dropping off the clothes at the funeral home. Signing some paperwork at the lawyer's. Getting Tyler into the barbershop.

"But I'm hungry."

"I know." She barely got out the words before the

dark-haired woman reached them and caught Kelly's neck in a tight hold. "Pam," she managed to squeeze out. "It's been a long time."

"Rob and I are so sorry about your mama, honey." Pam finally let go of Kelly's neck and crouched down to Tyler's level. "Hey, there, cutie pie. I'm your cousin." More accurately, the woman was married to one of Kelly's distant cousins. Even so, Pam had known Kelly all of her life. "But you can call me Auntie Pam. How's that?"

Tyler cast Kelly a wary look. She gave him a calm smile. "Pam used to babysit me when I was your age," she told him.

Pam laughed, tweaking Tyler's nose lightly before rising. "Sure. Make me sound old, why don't you? I was only sixteen when I babysat you. Now I hear you're an RN even!"

"I see word still spreads as fast as ever in Weaver." She hadn't mentioned becoming a nurse to anyone but Caleb. And that had been just the night before.

"Time brings progress, but some things just stay the same and the grapevine is one of them. Puts all other means of social media to shame."

Kelly smiled despite herself. "I don't do any kind of social media. Never had the time nor the inclination."

"Which explains why we still need a grapevine in Weaver. How else would we keep up with anyone?" Pam grinned. "So proud of you, though. I'm sure your mom was, too, even if she couldn't bring herself to say so." Pam's smile softened. "I wanted to get by your place yesterday, but I was working a double shift at the sheriff's. Is there anything we can do for you?"

The offer reminded Kelly of Caleb's. Not that she needed any sort of reminder.

"The funeral's pretty well taken care of," she said. "The lawyer handled most of it. Evidently, my mother left him instructions a few years ago."

"Sounds like Georgette. Probably because she didn't trust anyone else to get things right, rather than not wanting to burden her loved ones." Pam made a face. "Sorry. Shouldn't speak ill of the dead. Especially to you."

Kelly smiled humorlessly. "It's all right. You've only said what everyone already knows."

Pam gave her a sympathetic look. "You and Tyler are welcome to stay with Rob and me at our place. We have plenty of room."

Kelly was genuinely touched. "Even though I haven't spoken to any of you in all this time?"

Pam clicked her tongue. "There's not a soul who knew your mom who blames you for that, hon. She made it pretty obvious she didn't approve of you eloping. She was so mad about it, all she'd say about him was his name was Joe."

Kelly opened her mouth, then closed it and smiled weakly. She rubbed her hand over Tyler's neatly cut hair. "It…it doesn't matter anymore."

Pam nodded sympathetically. "These things happen," she said. "I meant what I said, though. You're welcome to stay with us. We're right here in town."

"Thanks, but there's a lot to be done out at the house, and I only have a few weeks off work. I want to get the farm on the market as soon as possible."

"So you're going to sell it, then?"

"*If* it will sell." The house was in deplorable condition, and the farmland was equally neglected.

"Selfishly, we'd love to think about you moving back home. But I do understand. Your mom—" Pam broke off and shook her head. "Well, it was her way or the highway. She didn't want help from anyone."

And the state of the farm showed it.

"Mommy," Tyler said, "my stomach's growly again."

"I know, baby." She knew Pam's propensity for gossip. But she had never been anything but nice to Kelly. "I promised him lunch after we got his hair cut," she told Pam.

"Take him to Ruby's. It's still open until two." Pam gestured down the street. "Tabby owns the place now."

"Tabby *Taggart*?"

"Tabby Clay now. She and Justin got married earlier this year. Bubba Bumble's the cook. Do you remember him?"

She nodded, trying to imagine Justin Clay and Tabby as a married couple. From Kelly's earliest memories in school, they along with Caleb had been like the Three Musketeers. Kelly hadn't been part of that crew until she and Caleb started high school.

Until he'd picked her up and dusted her off after she'd done a header over her bicycle right in front of him.

She pushed away the memory.

"Good for them. I thought Justin was living back east somewhere, though."

"He was. He's in charge of the hospital lab now." Pam adjusted the scarf around her neck and glanced at her watch. "I've got to run, but remember what I said. If you need anything—"

"Thanks, Pam."

"See you later, peach pit." Pam poked Tyler lightly on the nose.

Tyler giggled, watching the woman hurry off. "I'm not a peach pit. I'm a *boy*."

"My favorite one," Kelly assured him. She had

thought about driving them out to the new McDonald's that Mary had told her about, but Ruby's Café was just down the street within walking distance. "Come on, buddy." She turned until they were facing the opposite direction. "Lunch is waiting."

They'd made it partway down the block when Tyler stopped and pointed. "What's that?"

She glanced at the sign hanging in one of the storefronts. It was a colorful thing, featuring a black-hatted witch and a grinning jack-o'-lantern. "It's an ad for a Halloween carnival," she told him.

"Can we go?"

"It's next week, bud. We'll see."

He ducked his chin. "That means *no*."

"That means I have to think about it. Come on. I thought your stomach was all growly. When I was young, Ruby's Café had *great* chocolate milk shakes."

His eyes widened. "I can have a milk shake?"

"If you eat your vegetables first."

"They won't be carrots, will they?"

"I'm sure they'll have something other than carrots." They were the one vegetable he really hated. She'd learned that when he'd been a baby and spit them right back in her face. "That's the café, right there." She pointed at the building near the corner. "Race you."

Tyler giggled and shot off ahead of her. Kelly laughed, keeping pace right behind him. There'd come a day when he'd outrace her. Of that there was no doubt. But for now… She caught him and lifted him off his feet just as he reached the door. "It's a tie!"

He wrapped his legs around her waist. "Uh-uh. I won."

She tickled his ribs with the hand she kept around

him and pulled open the café door. The little bell hanging over it jingled softly.

Walking into the café was like stepping back six years in time.

The red vinyl seats and linoleum-topped tables were the same. Even the waitresses still wore pale pink dresses as a uniform.

Despite herself, she smiled. Tabby might be running the show, but she was certainly staying true to the history of the place.

"Find a seat where you can," a waitress Kelly didn't know told them as she walked by bearing a round tray loaded with hamburgers.

Tyler wriggled until Kelly set him on his feet. "Can we sit at the counter, Mommy? Please?"

Four of the round stools were empty. She gestured at them. "Take your pick."

He aimed for the one closest to the old-fashioned cash register, climbed up onto it without waiting for her assistance and yanked off his hoodie sweatshirt. She caught it before it hit the floor and tucked it inside her bag as she sat down beside him.

It was plenty noisy inside the diner, between people's chatter, the clink of flatware against crockery and the slightly tinny country music coming from the kitchen. She still heard the bell jingle over the door and automatically glanced over her shoulder. A white-haired woman came in and headed for one of the few empty tables. Kelly focused on the specials written on the chalkboard in the corner. The bell jingled again. Kelly was glad they'd come when they had. The place was hopping. She angled her head toward Tyler's. "Would you rather have a hamburger or a grilled cheese sandwich?"

"Hamburger." He swung his legs, making the stool

rotate one way, then the other. "And a chocolate milk shake. Don't forget."

Another waitress, who looked like she was about fifteen years old, set glasses of water on the counter in front of them. "Y'all need a menu?"

Kelly shook her head. "We'll have two burgers. One with cheese. No onions on either. French fries on the side. And a small salad."

"And the milk shake," Tyler whispered loudly.

"And a chocolate milk shake. Two straws."

"That's a familiar-sounding order."

Kelly started in surprise, rotating her stool all the way around to see Caleb standing behind them.

"Dr. C!" Tyler held up his cast. "I didn't break it again."

Caleb smiled slightly. "Glad to hear it, Tyler." His gaze went from Kelly's face to the empty stool beside them. "Mind if I sit there?"

She did. But saying so would have revealed more than she wanted. So she shrugged. "Open seating."

He swung his leg over the stool and leaned his arms on the counter, looking past her at Tyler. "I like the haircut. Looks sharp."

Tyler beamed. "I hadda get it cut 'cause of the funeral."

Caleb's gaze flicked briefly to Kelly's again. "Your grandma would have been impressed."

Kelly shifted. Despite everything, she'd sent cards every year to her mom with a new picture of Tyler inside. Her mom had never responded. And so far, Kelly hadn't seen any evidence that Georgette had kept them.

Apparently, she'd valued hoarding her empty oatmeal cartons and shoe boxes more.

"I never been to a funeral before," Tyler was saying.

"That's a lucky thing," Caleb told him.

"Mommy says they're sad."

Caleb nodded. "Usually."

Kelly grabbed her water and drank half of it down. It *was* sad. Especially because she didn't feel much of anything in the face of her mother's funeral. And wasn't that a horrible realization for a daughter to make?

She unfolded Tyler's big paper napkin and tucked it into his collar.

"I don't want a bib, Mommy!"

"And I don't want to wash ketchup out of your shirt."

The waitress delivered the side salad, and Kelly placed it in front of Tyler. She plucked out the two carrot matchsticks she spotted. "Eat at least half of it," she told him.

He made a face, but she drizzled ranch dressing on top and he picked up his fork and stabbed it into a cucumber slice.

She grabbed her water glass, focusing on it rather than the disturbing warmth of Caleb's shoulder brushing against hers when he reached over the counter and grabbed the coffeepot. He sat back, flipped over the white mug in front of him and filled it.

"Want some?"

She shook her head and watched from the corner of her eye as his fingers circled the mug. He'd always had long fingers. Deft fingers. And narrow, sinewy wrists that had become even more masculine and elegant all at the same time…

She took a quick sip of her water. He was numbingly good-looking. *Get over it already.* She set the glass down decisively. "Slow day at the office?"

"Had a cancellation. Figured I'd take advantage and grab some lunch."

She tapped her foot on the stool rung and hunted for something else to say.

"There's a picture I haven't seen in a long time." A brunette stopped in front of them on the other side of the counter, propping her hands on her very pregnant hips as she smiled at them. "The two of you sitting together right here in Ruby's. Almost seems like old times."

"Tabby!" Kelly stood up on the rung and leaned across the counter to give the other woman a hug. "Look at you! Pam told me you were still running this place, but she neglected to say you were pregnant!"

Tabby laughed wryly. "Maybe she forgot."

"You look marvelous. When is the baby due? Do you know what you're having?"

"We decided to wait to find out until the baby's born. Which, hopefully, will be in about three weeks." She dashed her hair out of her face and smiled ruefully. "Or less. Can't be soon enough for me."

Kelly chuckled. "I remember those last few weeks all too well. In one sense, time went way too fast, but in another it just crawled. I didn't know what my feet looked like. Couldn't even fasten my own shoes."

"That's what husbands are for." Caleb's comment was so abrupt, it unnerved Kelly. "To help fasten your shoes. So I hear, anyway."

Tabby wrapped a white apron over her belly, tying it below her breasts. "Imagine Justin's been complaining to you about that, Caleb."

He snorted softly. "Bragging, more like. He always has liked doing things first. Earning his PhD before I got my MD. Now he's having a kid before me."

Kelly sank her teeth into her tongue. She was pathetically grateful when Tabby shifted to one side so their waitress could deliver their hamburgers; it gave her something to focus on.

"Well, if you want a baby—" Tabby's tartness held the ease of lifelong friendship "—then find yourself a wife. I suggest you start by actually *dating* someone." She gestured toward Kelly. "Tell him I'm right."

Kelly's face felt hot. Tabby didn't have a hurtful bone in her body. She had no way of knowing about the knife she was twisting. "Um, she's—"

"For God's sake, Tab," Caleb muttered. "You're embarrassing her."

Tabby's eyebrows shot up. "Why? She beat us both on the marriage front by a long shot."

"I'm not married." Far too aware of the way her son was observing the exchange, Kelly nudged the milk shake toward him and kept her voice calm even though she felt like screaming inside.

If she didn't correct the ridiculous lie her mother had spread, it was only a matter of time before her little boy innocently did.

So she lifted her chin and focused on Tabby, even though the words were meant just as much for the man sitting next to her. "I never was."

Chapter Four

Caleb went still. He angled his head, giving Kelly a long look. "You said—"

"*I* never said anything." She looked defensive. "If you want to blame anyone, blame the person who spread that particular story."

Tabby's brows were knit together. "Your mom—" She broke off. "Oh, boy." Her gaze flicked from Caleb to Kelly and back again. "Let me get you the special," she said suddenly and turned on her heel to waddle through the swinging kitchen doors.

Coward, he thought.

He looked at Kelly's downturned head as she toyed with a crispy French fry. "Why'd you leave Weaver then? If there wasn't a guy involved."

She stiffened and gave him a tense look. "You think you held the market on wanting something more?"

"You never said you wanted to get out of Weaver."

"Well, after you told me you wanted to marry some-one else, we didn't talk about a whole lot of anything, did we?"

They certainly hadn't a couple years later, when they'd ended up steaming the windows of her truck. He'd thought she'd finally forgiven him for the Melissa debacle. It turned out she hadn't.

"Point taken." He twisted the coffee mug in circles. "Why do you suppose she—"

"—told a bald-faced lie about me? I'm the last person who could explain why my mother said or did anything. If I had to guess, I would say she was ashamed of me. Tyler—" she shifted focus to the little boy beside her "—stop playing with your hamburger. Are you full?"

"No." The boy poked his head forward so he could see past his mom to Caleb. "Are you and Dr. C fight-ing?"

"Of course we're not, buddy. Here." She dropped a few more French fries on his plate and squeezed out an-other measure of ketchup from the dispenser.

Caleb waited until she was finished. "Then you ended up in Idaho working for an old friend of Doc Cobb."

She didn't look at him. Maybe so that her observant son wouldn't pick up more of the tension between them. "He told you that?"

"He mentioned it once. I thought it was an office job, though."

"It was. For a while."

The same waitress who'd delivered the meals for Kelly and Tyler set a plate in front of him. Meat loaf special. Ordinarily, he liked that just fine, but his appe-tite had taken a hike. "And the nursing bug bit?"

She finally looked his way. Her amber-brown eyes

were fathomless. "It took a few months," she murmured. "But, yes."

"So what happened with the guy? The one you didn't marry."

She looked back at her meal. She'd gotten after her boy for playing with his food, but as far as Caleb could tell, she was doing the same thing. "He never asked me."

Caleb frowned. "And Tyler?"

She tilted her chin, giving Caleb a pained look. "What about him?"

"Did he *know* about Tyler?"

Her eyebrows rose slightly. "Should I have told him? Forced him into marrying me when he clearly didn't want to?"

He put down his fork. "People don't automatically get married anymore just because there's a baby on the way."

"Would you have?" Her expression got even more anxious. "Stepped up to the plate? Done the right thing? Sacrificed yourself in a marriage that wasn't based on anything but responsibility toward a child?"

His head suddenly hurt. "We're not talking about me."

"What if we were?" She gave up the pretense of eating and pushed aside her plate altogether. Color rode her cheeks, making her eyes look bright. "For the sake of argument. What if Melissa—that was her name, right? What if *she'd* come to you one day and said, 'Guess what? The rabbit died. The stick turned blue.'"

"That's different."

"How's it different?" Kelly didn't wait for him to answer. "Oh, that's right. You already wanted to marry her."

"Yeah, well, she didn't want to marry me, if you'll remember."

"Fun to learn you're not really what someone wants, isn't it?"

Tyler suddenly hung his arms over Kelly's shoulders. He'd climbed up until he was kneeling on the seat of the stool and was giving Caleb a stern glare. "Don't yell at Mommy."

Kelly's sigh was audible. She closed her eyes and patted Tyler's arms. "Nobody's yelling," she soothed, turning away from Caleb. "Now sit on your seat properly. Are you finished with your lunch?"

"Uh-huh."

"Wipe your face with your napkin, then." She didn't look at Caleb while she pulled her wallet out of her purse and glanced at the check the waitress had left. She yanked out some cash and left it on the counter. "Come on, Tyler." She lifted him down to the ground and quickly pulled his sweatshirt on over his head. "We still have things we need to do before tomorrow."

Caleb watched them walk straight out of the restaurant.

Kelly didn't look back.

He couldn't exactly blame her. He didn't appreciate people butting their noses into his business, either.

He turned back to the meal that he no longer wanted. Tabby waddled back out of the kitchen. Her timing was too perfect to be coincidental.

"Nice work, Tab."

She spread her hands. "How was I to know I was stepping onto a Georgette Rasmussen land mine?" She leaned back against the counter and rubbed her belly with both hands. "I always felt sorry for Kelly, being raised in that household. Seems like nothing she did ever satisfied the woman."

Caleb had observed that himself. If Kelly didn't get

good enough grades because she'd been helping so much on the farm, Georgette was mad. When she got the best grades possible, Georgette accused her of acting too big for her britches and ignoring her responsibilities at home. No matter what Kelly did, she couldn't have won where her mother was concerned.

"She wouldn't appreciate your pity," he told Tabby. He was positive that neither time nor distance would have changed that about her. "She left Weaver. Found a career she probably wouldn't have if she'd stayed."

"I know. But still." Tabby chewed the inside of her cheek. "You know, I always thought you and Kelly would end up together. You couldn't keep your hands off each other in high school. Caleb and Kelly, sitting in a tree. K-I-S-S-I-N-G."

The glare he gave her had no effect.

"You even stayed together for a while after you went to college," she continued.

"We were teenagers."

"If Tyler were a few years older, he could have been yours. Ever think about that?"

"Jesus, Tab." First his sister, now his old friend? "What?"

He shook his head. Of course he'd thought about it. Pointlessly. "He's not mine. Obviously." The timing could have been about right courtesy of their angry night of car sex, but they'd used a condom.

Tabby was silent for a moment. Then she sighed and nudged his plate. "Do you want me to box that up for you?"

He shook his head. "I have patients this afternoon." He pulled out his wallet, but she made a face.

"You don't need to pay for a meal you didn't touch."

"Not exactly the way to stay in business."

"Guess that's *my* business, isn't it?" Then she winced a little and pressed her hand to her belly.

"You all right?"

"Yup. Except for a kid who's already practicing to be a football punter." She waved him away then took his plate. "Go on with you now. Suppose I'll see you at the funeral. You *are* going, aren't you?"

"Yeah. Not that I figure Kelly will appreciate my presence all that much. She still hates me."

Judging by the way she'd looked at him, he didn't figure he had a chance of that ever changing.

He pushed off the stool and left.

"Thank you for coming."

The next afternoon, Kelly stood with Reverend Stone in the narthex of the Weaver Community Church, shaking hands as people left following her mother's funeral service. During a break, she glanced at the reverend and said, "I don't know what to do with all the flowers." She still couldn't believe the number of people who'd attended her mother's funeral, much less the quantity of plants and floral bouquets that had been sent. "My mother didn't have this many friends," she said under her breath.

He smiled kindly. "I think that you did."

She was more comfortable thinking that the outpouring of sentiment was for Georgette.

"Whatever plants and floral arrangements you choose not to take, you can leave here for worship tomorrow," he advised. "That's what most people do unless they're having a reception after the service." In this case, there would be no reception. Georgette's instructions to the lawyer had expressly forbidden one. Just as her instructions had been clear about the open casket and a cremation immediately after the funeral.

She'd left instructions about her death. She just hadn't bothered with a will.

"Thank you for coming." Kelly shook another hand. Submitted her cheek for another sympathetic kiss. Then she looked back at the minister. "I don't want to take any flowers," she said. Though she was going to be writing a lot of thank-you notes for them. She pinned another pleasant look on her face for the next person that stopped in front of her but felt it falter when she recognized the couple standing there.

Caleb's parents.

"Mr. and Mrs. Buchanan."

"Goodness." Belle leaned forward and kissed Kelly's cheek. "We're all adults now. It's Belle and Cage."

"Sorry about your mama, kiddo." Cage gave her a kiss on the cheek, too, followed by a paternal squeeze of her shoulder. "It's good to see you, but I sure wish it was under better circumstances."

Caleb's folks had always been nice to her. "Thank you. So do I." She felt guiltily grateful that she'd taken Reverend Stone's suggestion to let Tyler play in the nursery with the other young kids after having had to sit still for the funeral service. She wasn't sure she could take seeing Tyler through their eyes. "You're both looking well." To say the least. Belle Buchanan's long hair was as dark as ever; her face showed only a few lines. And Cage—well, Cage was an older version of his handsome son. He'd look good when he was eighty. He just had that kind of bones.

"You're as sweet as ever." Belle squeezed Kelly's hands. "Is there anything we can do for you?"

She immediately shook her head. Just as she'd been

shaking her head at all of the other similar offers of help she'd heard that day. "That's kind, but I'll be fine."

"Just don't be as independent as your mama was," Cage advised gently. "You know where we are." He squeezed her shoulder again, and the two moved off, making room for the next.

"Thank you for coming," Kelly said, focusing with an effort on the next face in the line. She was all too aware that Caleb hadn't come through yet. She'd seen him sitting in the back of the small, crowded church, alongside Tabby and Justin. Just like old times, except Kelly was pretty sure the three of them had outgrown their habit of scribbling notes and passing them back and forth.

Maybe he would take a different exit, she thought, as the mourners—which might have been a euphemism considering Georgette's lifelong habit of alienating the people around her—made their way past her. Maybe he'd be as reluctant to face her after their last encounter as she was to face him.

She still wished she'd just kept her mouth shut about having never been married. The conversation never would have gotten out of hand the way it had. Never would have gone down that dangerous road.

If there was tension between her and Caleb now, how much worse would it be when—*if!*—she told him the truth?

Her head ached and her stomach hurt from the internal debate that had been going on ever since coming face-to-face with him at Doc Cobb's office.

Everything had been fine up until then.

She and Tyler had a busy life. It didn't leave time for her to constantly second-guess the decisions she'd made six years earlier.

"Hey, there." Tabby and Justin appeared in Kelly's

field of vision. Tabby tucked her arm through Kelly's. "You're looking pale. Maybe you should sit down for a while."

"I'm fine."

"Where's Tyler?"

"Playing in the nursery downstairs." She pushed at the sleeves of her black sweater dress. Would Caleb be soon to follow after Tabby and Justin? "He was getting antsy and there were some kids already down there he was able to play with."

"He's about the same age as my brother's little boy," Tabby said. "I could set up a playdate for them if you want. I imagine you've got a lot on your plate trying to settle everything out at the farm."

"I'm sure he'd like that." Kelly was distinctly uncomfortable with it since Tabby's brother was married to one of Caleb's cousins, but that was no reason to punish her son. Aside from the toys she'd brought with them from Idaho, there was very little to entertain him out at the farm. She couldn't even let him outside to run and play without supervision yet, because the place was a wreck. The chicken coops were broken-down hazards; there were metal tools rusting in the overgrown weeds. And she wasn't sure there was going to be money enough to hire someone to help with the worst of it. "I have another meeting with Mr. Hook the day after tomorrow. I'll know more about what needs doing after that." She tried surreptitiously looking past the very pregnant Tabby into the church. All she could see were the backs of empty pews.

"Kelly." Reverend Stone discreetly inserted himself into the conversation. "The funeral director is here to take the casket. Would you like a moment alone with your mother?"

It was the very last thing she wanted. But she wasn't

up to shocking the kind minister by telling him so. And at least she wouldn't have to wonder if or when she was going to have to face Caleb again. So she nodded.

Tabby's eyes looked moist. "Do you want someone to stay with you?"

"No, it's okay," Kelly said. Tabby gave her hand a squeeze before leaving with Justin.

Reverend Stone escorted Kelly back into the empty church and closed the double doors, leaving her alone.

She exhaled and walked up the center aisle until she reached the casket. Someone had already closed it, and frankly, she was grateful. She set her hand on the glossy wood. Choosing a casket was another task that Kelly hadn't had to deal with, thanks to Georgette's advance orders.

"I wish things had been different, Mama," she murmured. Even now, her eyes were dry. Uncomfortably so. She'd given up crying over the relationship she'd never had with her mother when she drove away from the farm six years ago. "I wish you could have been happier in your life. I'm sorry if I was always the reason you weren't. Maybe now you really are at peace."

That's what Reverend Stone had talked about during the eulogy, at least. Maybe Georgette had found religion in the years Kelly had been away. Before that, her mother could hardly be bothered by what she'd called "church nonsense."

Kelly heard a noise and pulled her hand away from the casket. Two young men wearing black suits came in from the side entrance. "Ms. Rasmussen, are you ready for us?"

She nodded, perched on the edge of a pew and watched them wheel the casket out.

Then it was just her, alone.

Her eyes stung.

She sniffed. *So much for being beyond tears.*

She blinked hard and stood.

She wanted her son. And she wanted to go home.

The narthex was empty when she pushed through one of the double doors, though she could see through the outer glass doors of the church that there were still a few clusters of people standing around outside on the grass.

She took the stairs down to the basement where the nursery was located and found Tyler sitting on the floor. He was working on a puzzle. But not with Olive, the young woman who'd been watching the half dozen children when Kelly had left Tyler there.

Instead, it was Caleb sitting on the floor with him.

"Tyler," she said more sharply than she intended. "We need to go."

"Mommy, I'm almost finished." The little navy blue clip-on tie that had come with the child-size suit she'd bought for him was gone, along with the suit jacket. He had a smear of something red on his cheek, and one of his shoes was untied.

The mere sight of him made the tightness in her chest ease, even though the man with him made everything else feel worse.

"Tyler—"

"A few more minutes won't hurt, will it?" Caleb's voice was deep. Easy.

Her jaw clenched. "Where's Olive? Does she usually leave the children she's supposed to be watching in just anyone's care?"

He pushed himself off the floor and pulled on the charcoal-gray suit jacket that had been lying on top of a dollhouse. "Your mother's funeral ended forty-five minutes ago. I'll let you have that one." He shot his cuffs and yanked his loosened tie back to center.

The only time she'd ever seen him wear a suit had been at their high school graduation. Then he'd been a boy.

Now he was a man.

One who was plenty irritated with her.

"I'm sorry. That was uncalled for."

Tyler suddenly let out a whoop. "Finished it!"

"Good for you, Tyler," Caleb praised.

Her son shot them both a grin, then grabbed the puzzle with two hands and proceeded to gleefully demolish it.

The genuine smile he'd given Tyler was absent when he looked at Kelly. "Olive only left ten minutes ago. She was going to be late for her shift at Colbys."

Kelly felt even smaller. "So I owe you thanks, as well, for watching him."

She heard his faint sigh. "Kelly—"

"Can we go home now, Mommy?"

She nodded, glad for the interruption. Whatever Caleb wanted to say, she didn't feel the strength to hear. "We can go back to Grandma's house." There was a small part of her that felt ashamed using her son as her excuse to make a getaway. But there was a larger part of her that was pathetically grateful.

She pointed at Tyler's miniature blue suit jacket and looked in Caleb's general direction while their son darted over to get it. "It was nice of you to come."

"But you're surprised that I did."

Her lips parted, then closed again. She made some sound that was part agreement, part annoyance. "All right. Yes, I'm surprised. I'm surprised that you're in Weaver at all. Why is that, anyway? Couldn't cut it in the big city after all?"

"I came home because I realized I wasn't happy. I

came home because I realized my roots mattered more than I thought. Does that satisfy you?"

She let out another sound. One that even she couldn't interpret. "No. I—" She broke off and shook her head. Tyler had pulled on his jacket. "Where's your tie, buddy?"

He shrugged. "I dunno."

It was a clip-on. And if it hadn't come with the suit, she wouldn't have bought it. She didn't care if it was lost for good, but she also was trying to instill in him better habits when it came to keeping track of his personal belongings. "Go look," she suggested mildly.

His shoulders slumped dramatically, and his feet dragged as he slowly made his way around the perimeter of the room.

"He's constantly losing shoes and gloves and hats," she told Caleb defensively.

"Kids do that. You don't have to explain yourself to me."

How true that was. Yet she couldn't help herself. Probably because she was withholding the biggest explanation of all.

Her stomach churned. "Caleb, I—"

"Found it!" Tyler darted back to her side, waving the tie triumphantly.

"Good for you, pal," Caleb said before she could. He crouched down to the boy's level. "Want to put it on?"

"It's not like yours," Tyler said.

"Yeah, well, I wish mine were as easy as yours. Lift your chin a little."

Tyler did as he was told, and Caleb refastened the button at his neck and slipped the clip-on into place. "There you go. All set. Looking *GQ*-ready."

"What's *GQ*?"

Caleb laughed softly. "Nothing that matters when

you're five," he assured the boy. "And when it does matter, you'll have no worries. You got your mama's good looks."

Kelly closed her eyes. They were burning again. Tyler did resemble her. But she also could so easily see Caleb in him. In the line of his jaw. The set of his eyes…

"You've got to be tired after all this."

He had no idea. She nodded. "Yeah." She opened her eyes and found him standing again, watching her. He had the same expression on his face now that he'd had when she'd done a header over her handlebars right in front of him when she was fourteen.

And she was *not* going to cry now, either. "I feel like I could sleep for a week," she admitted.

"You want a ride back to the farm?"

She shook her head, quickly turning away from him. "I have my car."

"That wasn't exactly what I meant."

"Tyler." She held out her hand, but her son ignored it, instead running out of the nursery room on his own. "Don't go playing on those stairs," she warned him.

Then she looked back at Caleb. "I know that wasn't what you meant. Don't start being nice to me, Caleb. It just makes everything harder."

"Why does it still have to be hard?" His brows pulled together. "All that stuff between us was a long time ago."

And yet, right now, it felt just like yesterday.

"It was a long time ago," she agreed. "Just not long enough."

Then, because she could hear the distinct sound of her son stomping on the stairs, she grabbed hold of the excuse.

And escaped.

Chapter Five

"Are you *sure* Leandra doesn't mind?"

"Positive," Tabby declared.

It was Sunday afternoon, and Tabby had called Kelly to let her know that her sister-in-law, Leandra, would be delighted to have Tyler over to play with her son, Lucas. Tabby had insisted on coming to the farm to pick Tyler up, as if she was afraid Kelly would back out. It was on her way, she'd said, because she was heading out to her brother's place anyway after having Sunday dinner with Justin's folks.

"They'll have a blast," Tabby said for about the tenth time. "Most of Lucas's cousins are either older or younger." Her bright eyes took in the aging kitchen where they were standing. "You know, I would be happy to come back and help you with some of this stuff."

Kelly laughed with actual amusement. "If you were overdue with that baby, I'd say have at it. Dealing with the immense amount of *stuff* here would put you into labor for sure. But you're not overdue, so I'll say thank you, but no, thank you. I may work at an ob-gyn's office, but I haven't delivered a baby in a while and don't particularly want a refresher course."

Tabby grinned. She was rubbing her back. "All the aches and pains *do* go away, right?"

"To be replaced by a symphony of new ones," Kelly said blithely.

The other woman made a face. "Oh, thanks."

Kelly chuckled. "You're going to be fine. If the way he ties your shoes for you on a regular basis is any indication, Justin will be a lot of help. Plus, you have tons of family around who'll help. Your parents, your brother. All of your cousins." She put Tyler's plate from lunch in the sink. "You'll be lucky to have ten minutes a day to hold your own baby with everybody who's around to pitch in."

"Who helped you?"

Kelly shrugged. "I have friends in Idaho Falls, too. I wasn't alone." Not if she counted staff at the hospital where she'd delivered Tyler and the nurses at the medical complex where she'd gone to work, who'd brought meals for Kelly in those first few weeks. The nurses who'd inspired Kelly as she struggled to become one herself.

Tabby still didn't look convinced, but she dropped the matter. Instead, she went to the window over the sink and looked out. "I understand why you want to get this place off your hands, but it sure would be nice to think about you coming back to stay."

Kelly was shaking her head even before Tabby finished speaking. "I like Idaho Falls. I like my job there. I finally have steady hours at a practice with six physicians. My days are busy. Tyler is in a good school and he has friends."

"You could have that here," Tabby wheedled. Then she tossed up her hands. "Fine. I'll stop bugging you about it. Weaver's barely a dot on the map compared to places like Idaho Falls."

Kelly couldn't help but laugh a little. Because Idaho Falls was barely a dot on the map when compared to many other places.

Like Denver.

Where she'd pictured Caleb still living all this time.

She pushed him out of her thoughts. It was getting tiresome having to do so.

"Tell Leandra I'll pick up Tyler in a couple hours." Any longer, and her rambunctious son would likely be wearing out his welcome. "Where do they live again?"

"Out past the old Perry place. The barn's the only thing still standing, but you'll see it. Just keep going another mile or so till you get to the sign for Evan's veterinary practice."

The Perry place. Another unwanted memory. She and Caleb had spent many a stolen afternoon in that abandoned barn.

She went to the staircase leading from the kitchen and yelled for Tyler. "Bring your jacket," she called, and heard his footsteps overhead as he took a detour. Then he was racing pell-mell down the stairs.

"Slow down, buddy," she warned. "Fall down the stairs and you could end up with yet another cast."

He slowed, but only enough to jump past the last two steps.

"Hey." She crouched in front of him and tugged his jacket over his wriggling shoulders. "You need to behave yourself when you get there, okay? Use your good manners."

"Please and thank you," he chanted.

"Give me a kiss."

He bobbed forward to bestow a lightning-fast peck on her cheek. "Can we go now?"

Tabby stepped forward. "You betcha." She held out her hand to him, and they headed out the kitchen door. Kelly chewed the inside of her cheek, watching them.

The only other person she'd ever sent Tyler off with had been Gunnar's mother back home, and it felt odd doing so now.

She managed a cheerful wave, though, in response to Tyler's wildly enthusiastic one as they drove away.

When they were out of sight, she closed the door and stared at the kitchen around her.

Then she went to work.

She had two uninterrupted hours. She'd do well not to waste them.

And she didn't.

By the time she stopped to wash up and change out of her grimy clothes, she'd broken down most of the strange collection of boxes and containers. Half she'd already burned in the big metal drum out behind the house. The other half would need to wait for another time.

But at least she'd removed enough of them to allow her to get a few more rooms dusted and mopped. She planned to call a Realtor or two the following day and imagined they'd have plenty of ideas about the best way to list the house. At the very least, though, she wanted the place to be clean.

The sun was dipping a little low in the late-afternoon sky as she drove past the Perry barn.

She hated that her foot lightened up on the gas pedal as she passed it. She couldn't even blame it on the condition of the road. Unlike the one leading out to her mother's place, this one was smoothly graded with a fresh coat of tar.

She hit the gas a little harder until she saw the dark wood barn in her rearview mirror. Just as Tabby had said, another mile or so up the road, she saw the sign for Taggart Veterinary. She slowed and turned into the drive.

She spotted Tyler and Lucas immediately. They were climbing on the wooden play structure situated in a fenced yard next to a two-story house. She parked in the paved area next to the clinic a little distance from the house. As soon as she got out of her car, she could hear the boys' young, high-pitched voices.

Clearly, they were having a blast, and she was smiling as she headed toward the front door of the house.

She didn't get there, though, before she heard her name being called. She looked back toward the vet building and spotted Leandra Taggart standing in the doorway, waving toward her.

She about-faced and headed that way. "Sounds like they're having a good time," she said by way of greeting.

Leandra had been ahead of Kelly several years in school, so they'd never really been close friends. But the other woman hadn't changed a lick since the last time Kelly could remember seeing her.

She greeted Kelly with a quick hug as if it were the most natural thing in the world. "Sorry we missed your mother's funeral yesterday," she said, pushing back a short lock of bright blond hair from her forehead. "I hope you got the flowers we sent."

"I did. Thank you. They were lovely." Tasteful white lilies. She looked back toward the play structure when she heard Tyler's laughter. "It was really nice of you to watch Tyler like this."

"Are you kidding? Lucas was over the moon. His best friend from preschool moved away this summer and he's been mopey ever since. As you can hear, they've been getting along like wildfire." She looked over her shoulder. "Evan, we're heading over to the house," she called loudly, earning a muffled response in return before she closed the door and led the way toward the house. Her steps were quick, probably because she wasn't wearing a sweater or a jacket and the wind was blowing harder than usual. "So how have you been faring?"

Kelly gave what had become the standard answer. "Fine."

Leandra smiled slightly. Her gaze was sympathetic. "You've probably been hearing that question a lot."

Kelly hesitated. "Well—"

Leandra waved her hand, her smile widening. "How about some hot chocolate?" She pushed through the white-painted wooden gate, entering the grassy side yard where the boys were playing. "Lucas? You and Tyler about ready to go inside?"

"No!" Lucas's head popped up over the edge of the fort at the top of the structure. Tyler's was only a second behind.

Her boy's face was wreathed in smiles; his cheeks were rosy from the cold air and his hair stuck up in spikes from the wind.

She waved at him.

"We're playing pirates, Mom," he yelled, then disappeared again.

"They'll sleep well tonight," Leandra said on a chuckle as she bounded up the steps and darted inside the house. "Nothing like a couple hours of fresh air." She pushed the door closed and gestured toward the kitchen. "Come on inside and relax. J.D.'s got my daughter Katie for the afternoon, otherwise she'd be out there demanding to play pirates, too. She and J.D.'s son are both four. Katie thinks she's big—" she made air quotes "—like her big brother. Lucas, of course disagrees."

Since Kelly had concluded that she wasn't going to be able to make a quick getaway, she pulled off her jacket and sat on one of the iron bar stools at the granite breakfast counter. "How's Hannah?" She remembered from before leaving Weaver that Leandra and Evan were also raising his niece.

"She's great. She's with her cousin Chloe cooking something up for Halloween costumes. You remember my cousin Ryan, don't you? Chloe's his daughter."

She nodded weakly. The Buchanans and the Clays were related by marriage rather than blood. But if they knew that Tyler was one of them, he'd be absorbed right into the fold.

She closed off the thought.

Leandra was busily moving around the kitchen, pouring milk in a saucepan and pulling down a couple oversize blue mugs.

"Nice place you have."

"Thanks. We like it." She slowed down long enough to look out the window, and then reached for two more mugs, setting them on the counter, as well. "I've heard through the grapevine that you're planning to sell your mom's place?"

"Mmm-hmm. I'll call a couple Realtors this week.

Anyone in particular you can recommend?" She glanced at the door when it opened again and Leandra's husband, Evan, walked in. The smile on Kelly's face froze a little when she spotted the man following him, though.

"If that puppy pees on my floor, you're cleaning it up, whether you're a doctor or not," Leandra warned when she saw the blond puppy Caleb was holding. "Unless you want to go to Braden, there are only a few here in town to choose from," she said to Kelly without missing a beat. "Caleb, which real estate office have you been working with?"

Caleb lifted his chin away from the pup's tongue and switched her from one arm to the other. "The new one out by Shop-World. Why?" Maybe it was pure orneriness, but he deliberately pulled out the stool right next to Kelly.

She gave him a fulminating look.

"Careful," he murmured softly. "Don't want to scare my new puppy into peeing with that glare of yours."

"I didn't know you were here."

His cousin Leandra was either truly oblivious or chose to be when she cheerfully plunked two mugs in front of them, then turned and handed one to her husband. "See you found another sucker," she said to him.

Evan's smile was broad. He looked toward Kelly. "Still have three more pups available to good homes," he said. "They're rescues. Golden retriever mix. Make good family dogs."

"Please." Kelly was already shaking her head. "Don't say that in front of Tyler."

"All boys want dogs," Caleb said. He let the pup climb up his shoulder.

She didn't look his way. "All boys want them. Not all boys live in apartments that don't allow pets."

The door flew open, and Lucas and Tyler raced in.

"Door," Leandra said, and Lucas skidded to a halt, backed up three feet and shoved it shut.

Then the boys were running through the kitchen again. A moment later, they heard footsteps pounding on the stairs.

Leandra was standing at the stove, whisking something in a pan. "Axel and I were lucky," she said. "We always had lots of room for pets when we were growing up."

"How is Axel?" Kelly asked.

"He's great. Got married. He and Tara have two little boys. Aidan will start kindergarten next year."

"She brought Hank the tank in for a well check a few weeks ago," Caleb said. The puppy had climbed off his shoulder and was circling on his lap. "Kid's not even three and he's off the charts for height and weight."

"The Clays grow 'em big," Leandra joked. "Remains to be seen what y'all Buchanans do." She turned and poured creamy-looking hot chocolate from the saucepan into their mugs. "Marshmallow or whipped cream on top?"

Kelly shook her head, declining both.

"Marshmallow," Caleb said. "My niece looks like a mini Lucy. Bet she'll be taller, though."

He felt Kelly's sudden look.

"Your sister had a baby?" she asked. For once, she wasn't giving him a looks-could-kill glare. "Is she still dancing in New York? I remember she had a knee injury or something."

He plucked a fat white marshmallow out of the jar Leandra set in front of him. She made the things from scratch. He didn't know how, but they put the stuff you could buy in the store to shame. "She moved home to stay after that injury. Married a widower. But she still dances, if you count the dance school she runs in town."

"Wow. That's a big change." Kelly took the tongs from him and grabbed a marshmallow after all. "So who else has gotten married? Had babies?"

"Well." Leandra pursed her lips slightly, then skewered him with a sly look. "Everyone but Caleb there."

"Not for lack of trying," Kelly said. When he nearly choked on his hot chocolate, she gave him an innocent, wide-eyed look he didn't buy for a second. "What? I'm not saying anything they don't know."

The puppy on his lap let out a huffing snore. If Kelly was able to poke fun at him, maybe there was hope she wouldn't detest him forever after all.

"She's got you there, cuz." Leandra's eyes were laughing over the rim of her mug.

"We're only cousins because my grandmother married your grandfather," he reminded her.

"How *are* your grandparents?" Kelly directed her question at Leandra.

"Squire's ornery as ever," Caleb answered before she could. "By default that makes my grandmother eligible for sainthood."

"They've started spending part of the winter down in Arizona," Leandra told her.

"Or whatever cruise Gloria drags him on," Evan added.

"You know, Kelly, if you want a quick sale of your farm, just let him know it's available. Uncle Matt runs the Double C, of course, but Squire still likes to snatch up good property when he can."

Kelly's expression sobered. "That'd be a trick. You

know my mother would come back to haunt me if she ever knew her farm became part of the big, bad Double C Ranch." Whenever Georgette wasn't envying the cattle ranchers, she'd been sneering at them for being land-grabbers.

"She'd haunt anyone with the nerve to buy her farm, period," Evan said. "No disrespect, Kelly. But I got to know her a fair bit over the past several years." He shook his head slightly and gave a crooked smile. "She was a woman of…strong conviction."

"Stubborn as hell, I think you mean," Kelly said.

Leandra lifted her mug with one hand and squeezed Kelly's hand with the other. "To Georgette Rasmussen. May she rest in peace." She waited a beat. "And not tell too many angels how to do their jobs."

Caleb heard Kelly's faint laugh. Heard the bitter-sweetness in it. But she lifted her mug. "To my mother." As soon as she took a drink, though, she set down her mug and said, "I really should get Tyler home now. Leave you all to enjoy the rest of your evening."

"You could stay for supper," Leandra suggested. "It's not going to be anything fancy, but we'd be glad to have you."

"What about me?"

Leandra sent Caleb a look. "You never need an invitation." She patted his cheek as she passed him. "You're always more than willing to mooch a meal off your relatives."

"That's the doctor degree," he told her as she left the room. "Makes me smart enough to successfully avoid menial tasks like cooking." The puppy lifted her head from his lap, yawned and started licking his arm.

He got up. From his experience with puppies, he knew that it was pee time after nap-time. And he had as little desire to clean that up as he did in cooking his own meals. He carried her outside into the yard and set her on the grass.

She was still sniffing around, trying to choose her spot, when the door behind him opened again. Kelly and a dejected-looking Tyler came out. But the second the little boy's gaze landed on the puppy, his eyes lit up. He jumped off the steps and rushed over to her, falling to his knees as he patted her head. The puppy immediately tried climbing up on him.

"Is he one of Doc Taggart's puppies?"

"She is."

"Tyler, come on." Kelly held out her hand and waited impatiently for her son to take it. "It's getting late and we need to go home."

"But Mommy," he protested, "she likes me."

"I can see that." Kelly crouched down beside them. "But the puppy doesn't need a bath before bed, and you do. Gunnar's also expecting you to call him tonight, remember?" She rubbed her hand over the puppy's fluffy back. "So say goodbye."

"I wanna take one home, too."

"Buddy, you know we can't take a puppy home to live with us. We've talked about it a hundred times."

Tyler tilted his head back, looking up at her. "Then can we come back and visit her? Please?"

Finally, Kelly's gaze slid toward Caleb. But only briefly. "The puppy is Dr. C's. She's going to go home and live with *him*."

Tyler's bright brown eyes shifted to his face. "Can I come visit?"

"Tyler—"

"Sure," Caleb said over her immediate protest. "You can come and visit the puppy any time you like."

Chapter Six

The next afternoon, Kelly stared out her windshield at the apartment complex in front of them.

She still wanted to strangle Caleb, and since he wasn't available, her steering wheel had to suffice.

"Is this it?"

She glanced in her rearview mirror to meet Tyler's hopeful look.

"Apparently." The building hadn't existed when she'd moved away from Weaver. Caleb had seemed to take inordinate pleasure in giving her the address when she'd called his office earlier.

She put the car in Park and turned off the engine. She wanted to be there about as much as she wanted to have a hole drilled in her head.

"This is not going to become a regular habit," she reminded Tyler when she unfastened him from his booster seat. "One visit to the puppy." She still didn't know what had possessed her to allow it in the first place.

Too bad Evan had already found homes for the other puppies that morning; she'd have just taken her son back to his and Leandra's house to visit *them*.

Tyler pushed out his lower lip, and she lightly tapped it. "Don't pout. You wanted to visit the puppy and you're getting that chance. Do you want to enjoy it or pout your way through it?"

He sucked his lip back to where it belonged and climbed out of his booster, hopping down to the ground. She closed the car door behind them and reluctantly turned to face the building again.

The apartment was at the far end of the building. Inwardly, she felt the way Tyler did when he was facing an unwanted task; she wanted to drag her feet and let her shoulders droop. Outwardly, she hoped she was doing a decent job of hiding that fact.

They reached the door and she lifted Tyler up when he begged to use the door knocker. It was a decorative brassy thing shaped like a lion. As soon as he'd clanged the metal ring hanging from the lion's mouth, they heard a loud yapping from inside.

Caleb opened the door, immediately bending down to catch the dog before she bolted outside. He was barefoot and wet headed, wearing green hospital scrub pants and nothing else.

She tore her eyes away from the small scar on his naked shoulder blade and lowered Tyler to the ground. "This a bad time?"

He muttered an oath, brushing past Kelly to follow the wily puppy out onto the sidewalk when she escaped his grasp. He scooped the dog up and carried her back with him. "No. I told you when you called that this was about the only time I was free." He grinned at Tyler, who was receiving a face washing from the puppy who was straining over Caleb's grip to reach the boy with her tongue. "Looks like someone's glad to see you."

Tyler was giggling madly. "Can I hold her?"

"Let's go inside first," Caleb suggested. His dark eyes drifted over Kelly's face. "It's a little cold outside."

She kept her expression calm. She was a nurse. She'd seen lots of bare chests. Male. Female. Young. Old. Just because his was...well...*his*...it didn't make a difference.

Liar.

She ignored the taunting inner voice and followed Tyler inside, trying to keep from dwelling on the way Caleb's pants hung low around his hips. Then he reached past her to close the door behind her, seeming to surround her with his clean, spicy scent. While she was working hard not to ogle him, he didn't give her so much as another glance as he gestured to Tyler. "Now you can take her," he said, and handed the pup over to him.

Not surprisingly, the puppy immediately put her paws on Tyler's shoulders, slathering his face even more.

"Boys and dogs," Caleb murmured.

She adjusted the strap of her purse on her shoulder, looking anywhere other than at the wealth of bare skin he displayed. It was the end of October, for pity's sake. How could the man be so tan? It was brought into even sharper relief by the strip of lighter skin just above the low-slung drawstring waist of his scrubs.

But then, maybe he went around without his shirt all the time. How was she to know what his habits were these days?

Annoyed by her thoughts, she sat down on an over-stuffed leather chair, perching on the edge of the cushion where she was within quick reach of Tyler. He was now lying flat in the middle of the floor with the dog bouncing on his belly. "Don't let us interrupt whatever you were doing," she told Caleb. *Like getting dressed after a shower.*

He didn't take the hint. Instead, he sat on the couch right across from her. Wavy damp hair falling over his forehead, crazy-wide shoulders, ridged abdomen, slightly bony toes and all.

God help her.

She wanted nothing to do with him. Because he was the only man who could make her forget reason and good sense.

And the evidence was rolling around on the floor between her booted feet and his bony bare toes. Their little boy was turning red in his face from laughing so hard over the puppy's attention.

She never should have crumbled to Tyler's pleas to see the puppy.

"Tyler, take off your jacket. And be careful with your cast. You don't want to knock it into something."

Not that there was much stuff sitting about Caleb's apartment. Aside from the chair and couch, there was only a side table with nothing on it and a television mounted over the fireplace. She could see the kitchen from where she was sitting. It was separated from the living room only by a breakfast counter, and it looked equally barren. Not a single bowl or glass on the countertop. No bananas turning brown, no bowls of crisp fall apples.

"How long have you lived here?" She caught the jacket Tyler tossed to her and folded it over her knees.

"About six months, I guess." Caleb leaned down and lightly tugged the dog's tail. The puppy jerked around and proceeded to chase her tail, knocking right into the side of Kelly's chair. She barked at the offending chair, then pounced on Tyler's chest again. "Give or take," Caleb added. He got up suddenly and left the room.

She refolded the jacket and smoothed it over her knees. "Do you stay with someone else a lot?" she asked, raising her voice.

He reappeared with a white T-shirt in his hand. He had an amused look in his eyes. "What are you trying to say?"

She shrugged and stopped herself from nervously folding Tyler's jacket a third time. She set it aside before sliding off the chair to kneel next to Tyler and the puppy. It was better to stay focused on them than the sight of Caleb pulling on his shirt. For some reason, seeing him putting *on* clothes was more disturbing than if she'd seen him taking them off.

She yanked her mind out of *that* dangerous realm and back into the land of harmless animals. "Does she have a name yet?"

He threw himself back on the couch, spreading one long arm along the top of the cushions. "Haven't decided. Considering how she's already chewed through one of my tennis shoes and a bed pillow, Beastie would've been good, but Justin and Tab already snatched it up for their hound."

"You're the one who wanted a puppy."

"More like I'm the latest sucker for Evan's strays. I'm lucky because I've got a spit of a yard out back of the kitchen, but until I find a permanent place, I might have to get doggy day care or something at this rate."

"Weaver has a doggy day care?" She couldn't hide her skepticism.

"Weaver has all sorts of things these days. From tanning salons to Italian restaurants. The secret might be out that this is a pretty good place to live."

"That's what lured you back from Denver? Fake tans and eggplant parmesan?" She scratched behind the dog's silky ear. "Figured there'd be plenty of that available in Denver. But at least it explains the, uh—" she waved her hand in his direction "—the bronze pecs."

He laughed softly. "You spend a couple afternoons helping my dad string fence at the Lazy-B and see if you avoid getting some color."

The Lazy-B was his parents' cattle ranch. It was minuscule in comparison to the Double C, but it was still nothing to sneeze at. "You used to hate doing stuff like that."

"Yeah, well, he's my old man."

Calling Cage Buchanan old was a stretch. The man who'd greeted her at the funeral had been better looking than ever.

He suddenly sat forward. "What do you think, Ty? Have any good names in mind for the fuzzy blonde there?"

"Lucy?"

He chuckled. "That's my sister's name. Not sure how well that would go over with her."

"I don't got a sister," Tyler said. He rolled over onto his belly and put his head on his folded arms. The puppy wasn't discouraged; she just scratched at the carpet next to his nose and licked his ear. He giggled breathlessly.

"Well, maybe your mom will give you a sister one day," Caleb said. His gaze met hers.

Distinctly uncomfortable, she pushed to her feet. "So you actually have a yard with this apartment?"

He nodded. "All the end units do." He stood, as well. "I'll show you." He gave a short whistle. "Come on, dog. Ty, put your jacket back on."

The puppy and Tyler immediately scrambled after him, through the kitchen and out the door. Kelly brought up the rear.

He'd called it a spit of a yard. Which turned out to be a bit of an overstatement. *Postage stamp size* would have been a more accurate description.

There was grass—currently brown—and a spruce tree in one corner with a couple dozen Christmas bulbs hanging from the branches. "A little early for Christmas decorations, isn't it?"

He shrugged. "I was watching my nieces recently for Lucy and ran out of ways to keep them entertained."

Kelly took in the rest of the yard decor: a large metal cooking pot containing the dog's water, two tennis balls, a small stuffed rabbit with a torn ear and a short length of rope tied into knots.

"All these toys but the dog still prefers tennis shoes and pillows?"

"Go figure, right?" He watched Tyler snatch up the rope and swing it around for the puppy, then turned back into the kitchen. "Want something to drink?"

"No." She hovered in the doorway. Half in. Half out. A wood-paneled fence surrounded the yard, so it wasn't as if she was afraid of taking her eyes off Tyler for a minute. It just felt easier to breathe, despite knowing she was letting in some very nippy air. "Thank you, anyway," she added.

He leaned against the counter, crossing one foot over the other.

She looked away from his toes. Seeing his bare feet was harder than seeing his naked abs.

Clearly she should have been listening to her co-workers, who kept wanting to set her up on dates. She'd just had no interest. What with Tyler and work, her life was plenty full.

But after less than a week back in the same breathing space as Caleb Buchanan?

Her interest was back in full swing.

It had always been that way. Even when she'd wanted to wipe the floor with his gorgeous face, she'd wanted him.

Hence, the son he didn't know he had.

She looked out the doorway at boy and pup.

Her stomach tightened. "Caleb, there's something I—" She broke off when the cell phone sitting on the counter rang.

"Hold that thought," he told her and picked it up. "Dr. Buchanan," he said. His gaze held hers as he listened for a moment. Then he pushed his damp hair away from his forehead. "I'll meet you at the hospital. No, it's fine, Hildy. I'm glad you called me. See you in less than an hour."

Kelly stepped outside, pulling the door closed a little to give him some privacy as he finished the call. "Tyler, say goodbye to the puppy. We're going to have to go now."

"But Mommy—"

"I know you're having fun. But Dr. C has to go to work. So we need to leave."

Tyler leaned over and scooped the puppy up with both arms around her little round belly. The dog's tail whopped him in the chin. "Can't we babysit her, then?"

"Tyler—"

He pushed out his lower lip.

She hated that pout. It always made her feel like the meanest mom on the planet. Before she could deal with it, though, Caleb pulled the door open again.

"Sorry about that," he said. "One of the challenges of practicing in a small town. Everyone knows how to get hold of you directly when they want. No answering service to act as a go-between."

"Yet you chose to come here to practice. And pediatrics, even." Why he'd chosen to switch from his lifelong dream of being a surgeon was still a mystery that there was no point in pursuing. He was here, and that was that. It had nothing to do with them. Any more than their life had anything to do with him. Upsetting the status quo by telling Caleb the truth about Tyler would just turn her and Tyler's world on its ear.

It wasn't as though she believed Caleb could force her into marriage. Thanks to the last five years of single parenting, she was made of stronger stuff than that.

She hoped.

She beckoned to Tyler again. "Come on, buddy. Put down the puppy. She doesn't need us to babysit her."

"But Mommy—"

"He can take the pup with him," Caleb murmured so close to her ear that she nearly jumped out of her skin. She turned her head and found him only inches away.

Her mouth went dry, and she unconsciously took a step back, nearly losing her balance on the porch step.

His arm shot out and caught her. "I don't mean forever," he added. "Just until I take care of this call. I'd pick up the pooch in a few hours."

Even though he'd kept his voice low, Tyler still managed to overhear enough.

"Yes!" He somehow succeeded in keeping hold of the puppy and doing a fist pump at the same time.

"I didn't say it was okay, Tyler." Her voice was sharper than she intended, and she squelched a sigh when his victorious expression fell.

She rubbed at the sudden pain in her forehead.

It was just a puppy.

For an hour or two.

"Fine," she said on an exhale. "This is *not* going to become a regular habit."

The fact that she'd said that very thing twice in the span of thirty minutes, though, didn't bode well for her.

Man and boy had twin smiles on their faces.

She wanted to bang her head against the kitchen door.

"I've got a leash," Caleb said immediately. "Tyler, grab a couple of her toys." He yanked open one of the kitchen drawers, grabbed the leash and handed it to her before disappearing down the only hallway leading from the living room and kitchen area. When he returned, he was wearing clogs on his feet and carrying a smallish animal crate.

She worked with medical professionals all day long. She'd seen similar footwear on dozens of them.

She'd just never seen Caleb wear them.

Even when he'd changed Tyler's cast the previous week, he'd been wearing cowboy boots and jeans under his white lab coat.

"What's the emergency?"

"Mom with an asthmatic kid."

"Asthma attack?"

He set the crate on the counter, shaking his head. "Nervous mom. Ty, let's put the puppy in the carrier so she won't get freaked out in your car." He nudged the puppy inside, tossed in the tennis ball that Tyler handed him and secured the wire door.

Kelly reached out to take the carrier, but Caleb's hand brushed against hers, beating her to the handle. "I'll carry her."

She curled her fingers against her palm, managing not to rub them against her jeans. Taking Tyler's hand, she preceded Caleb out the front door to her car. While she buckled Tyler into his booster seat, Caleb tucked the crate on the floor behind the front seat where it wouldn't be jostled.

"Be thinking about more names," Caleb told Tyler before closing the car door and opening the driver's side for Kelly.

She'd forgotten that he'd always been that way about doors. Always opening them for her like that. School doors. Diner doors. Barn doors.

Truck doors.

Thank goodness she'd gotten rid of that old gas guzzler years ago.

As if he'd read her mind, he gave her sensible little four-door an assessing look. "Little more passenger room than in that pickup truck you used to have."

"Car seats need space." She quickly slid down into the driver's seat and jammed her finger against the push-button ignition.

"Drive safely."

"I managed to get through the Tetons between Idaho Falls and here without incident. I imagine I can drive back to the farm just fine, too." She sounded waspish but couldn't help herself. She grabbed the armrest and pulled the door closed. "If you're going to be longer than you expect, I'd appreciate you letting me know," she said through the window.

Just fire up that witch's cauldron, Kelly.

Her jaw clenched. "Please," she added.

He inclined his head an inch and backed away from the car. "Don't forget names for the puppy, Ty."

"I won't!" Tyler sounded so earnest, her chest ached. In her rearview mirror, she could see him waving at Caleb while she backed out of the parking space and drove away.

The puppy whined softly in her crate. *I know how you feel, puppy.* If Kelly could whine right now, she would, too.

"What do you think would be a good name, Mommy?"

"I don't know, buddy." They were very near the su-persized Shop-World, and if she didn't have the puppy in her car, she would have taken the time to stop. She needed more cleaning supplies and trash bags.

Her hands tightened on the steering wheel. Blaming Caleb for not being able to stop was silly, as well. She knew it. But it didn't prevent her.

Maybe because the more blame she could heap on his head, the less guilty she'd feel over keeping the truth about Tyler from him.

"Is Dr. C going to come get the puppy tonight?"

"Yes." She stopped at a traffic light. She could re-member the days when Weaver only had one. Now there seemed to be at least a half dozen. In her present mood, that didn't strike her as an improvement. They'd prob-ably all be red. It would take them more than an hour to get home. It would be dark by then, and she hadn't thought to leave any lights on in the house.

"I like Dr. C," Tyler prattled on. "I'm gonna ask him to sign my cast, 'cause he's my friend. Right, Mommy?"

The light turned green, and she hit the gas harder than necessary. "I suppose so."

"I wonder if he—"

"That's enough, Tyler!" The words burst out of her. "I don't want to hear any more about Dr. C!"

The silence from the backseat was deafening, and remorse cut her to the quick. She pulled off to one side of the road out of the way of traffic and put the car in Park before turning around to see Tyler's wounded expression.

Tears were welling in his eyes.

"I'm sorry, buddy." She stretched over the seat until she could touch his hand. "I didn't mean to be so sharp."

His lip jutted out, but it wasn't a pout. "Then why were you?"

How on earth could she possibly explain the emotions tangling inside her to her five-year-old son?

"Sometimes it's not very easy for Mommy to talk about...about Dr. C."

"Why?"

She squelched a sigh. "Because, well, we used to be friends. And now we're not."

"Did you have a fight?"

Her head began throbbing again. "Something like that."

"Then if you're sorry, just say you're sorry."

It was the advice she gave him when he and Gunnar had some sort of tiff. "Sometimes it's not that simple."

"Why not?"

For one thing, she wasn't all that sure she *was* sorry. Not where her decision about leaving Weaver was concerned. Yes, now that they'd run into Caleb again, she was going to have to either fish or cut bait when it came to telling him the truth about Tyler.

But would she have done anything differently six years ago?

It wasn't something she could answer.

"Because we're adults," she told Tyler. "And adult stuff isn't always simple." She rubbed her fingertip over his hand. "I shouldn't have yelled at you like that, though, and I am sorry for that. I love you more than anything in this world. Okay?"

He nodded. "I love you, too, Mommy."

One day, she knew he wouldn't say the words so easily.

But for now, he was still happy being her precious boy, and she was going to hold on to that with both fists.

And what about the day when he asks about his father?

She turned around in her seat, and deliberately ignoring the voice inside her head, put the car in gear and made her way back into the light traffic.

The next signal light she came to was red.

Naturally.

Chapter Seven

What should have taken Caleb all of thirty minutes at the hospital stretched into three hours. He'd barely finished soothing Hildy Hanson's nervousness over her daughter's asthma when a real emergency cropped up. He didn't even have time to phone Kelly himself and let her know. His cousin Courtney, who was a nurse at the hospital, took care of that for him.

It was close to ten when he finally pulled up in front of Kelly's house and stepped onto the bare-bulb-lit porch.

He figured it would be past Tyler's bedtime, so he didn't ring the doorbell in case the boy was sleeping. He knocked lightly instead. And the puppy immediately started barking like crazy.

Caleb couldn't imagine Tyler sleeping through that racket.

When Kelly opened the door, it was almost an exact replay of when he'd opened the door to her earlier that day. Only this time, it was Kelly who quickly crouched down to scoop up the excited pup before she could dart outside between Caleb's feet. Her hair was wet; she was wearing an oversize sweatshirt that reached halfway down her thighs and a pair of black leggings.

She was covered from neck to ankle, but he still had to stop himself from imagining the shower she must have just taken.

"*Hush*, puppy," she was saying to the still-barking dog. She didn't glance at Caleb as she turned back into the house. "If you're coming in, close the door. It's cold outside."

He'd had more enthusiastic invitations, but he stepped inside and closed the door. "Tyler asleep?"

"So far. If I can keep the puppy from barking, hopefully he'll stay that way."

The last time Caleb was there, he hadn't made it past the porch. Now, all he could do was stare as he followed her through the entry, where the dog crate was sitting next to the coatrack, and into the living room. Everywhere he looked, there were stacks. Stacks of magazines. Stacks of clothes. Linens. Dishes.

"I know," she said, setting the puppy on the floor in front of the same couch he remembered from their youth. The dog immediately hopped up onto the cushions. "There's a lot of stuff." She pushed up the sleeves of her faded sweatshirt and glanced around. "I dragged everything in here just because I needed room to work. I've been trying to sort what's salable and what's not." She gestured behind him. "That bigger pile there is what's not."

"Your mom had a lot of stuff in her closets."

Her lips twisted slightly. "I haven't even gotten to the closets yet. It's not *quite* an episode out of *Hoarder's Life*, but it is close."

"You need help with all this."

Her shoulders rose and fell with a huge sigh. "Tell me something I don't know." She sat down on the couch and finally looked at Caleb. "When Courtney called, I told her we could keep the dog overnight."

The puppy climbed on Kelly's lap and cocked her head as if she knew she was the topic of conversation.

His cousin hadn't shared that. But to be fair, there hadn't been time for a lot of personal chitchat between dealing with distraught family members, protective services and the innocent child at the center of it all.

"Tonight or tomorrow, I'd still need to get her." Kelly hadn't invited him to sit, but it had been a long damn evening. He sat in the chair her mother had always been sitting in whenever he came by to pick up Kelly.

He ignored the unpleasant sensation that Georgette Rasmussen was still there, glaring at him the way she'd always done, and focused instead on the clutter. "How do you plan to deal with all this stuff?"

"One room at a time?" Her tone was vaguely flippant, and when he just looked at her, she grimaced. "One room at a time," she repeated, but the tone was gone. She lifted her shoulder. "Same way you get through anything, right? One step, one day at a time."

"Looks to me like you've got a year's worth of days, then."

Kelly let out a wry laugh. "Yeah. It's a little overwhelming, to say the least. Particularly when I've only arranged to be gone from work for two weeks."

He couldn't help looking around skeptically.

"I know. I can probably arrange to stay longer, but that means Tyler's out of school longer."

"It's kindergarten."

"You're a pediatrician. You ought to know just how

much kindergarten counts these days. It's not like when we were that age. The teacher sent me with an entire package of worksheets just so he wouldn't fall behind."

"So put him in school here," Caleb suggested.

She looked alarmed at the very notion. "I'm sure that won't be necessary." She set the dog on the ground and rose. "Anyway, the lawyer told me about all the bills yet to be settled. The two different real estate agents I spoke with told me they can sell this place, but if I don't want to practically give it away, improvements are going to have to be done. And it needs to be cleaned out no matter what. But the auction house says not to get rid of a thing. One man's junk is another man's treasure and all that. They want to send over an appraiser, but the appraiser needs to be able to see more than just clutter." She picked up a sheet of paper from a side table. "They even gave me a list. Estate jewelry is evidently pretty big these days. When did you ever see my mother wearing jewelry? And since my mother didn't leave a will, I can't do anything about anything anyway until the court says I can." She tossed down the paper and headed toward the kitchen. "I need a drink. Do you want one?"

He figured she probably needed a hug more than a drink. But a hug from him wasn't likely to be welcome.

"Sure." He followed her into the kitchen. "Is that Tyler's infamous banister?" He gestured at the stairs.

"Yep." She plucked two clear glasses from a dish drainer and set them on the counter. Then she opened a cupboard and pulled out a bottle of whiskey. She uncapped it and sniffed it with a grimace. "Have no idea how long this has been in here," she warned as she poured some into the glasses. "Ice?"

"Please."

She recapped the bottle and opened the freezer, pulling out an old-fashioned metal ice cube tray that she banged once on the counter before yanking back the handle and freeing several cubes that she dropped into the glasses.

"Haven't seen one of those things in a while." His freezer had an automatic ice maker.

"Then maybe it'll go for more than ten cents when I am finally allowed to sell it." Kelly left it on the counter and handed him one of the glasses, lifting her own in an unsmiling toast. "Cheers." She took a drink and hissed. "Whoa, that burns."

"You have to sip whiskey," he advised, taking his more slowly. It wasn't the best whiskey on the planet, but it wasn't rotgut, either. By the time he'd broken up with her because of Melissa, he and Kelly hadn't even been of legal drinking age. The most they'd shared was a few bottles of beer sneaked from his folks' refrigerator and drunk down while they'd sprawled together on straw inside the old Perry barn.

The puppy had followed them into the kitchen and was sniffing around the bases of the table legs. "When's the last time she was out?"

"Probably too long ago." She opened the kitchen door. "Come on, puppy."

The dog didn't seem interested, so Caleb picked her up, carried her outside and set her down on the dry grass. "Tyler come up with any more names?"

"He's working on a list. So far, he's got Spot on it. You might do well to choose a name yourself." Behind him, Kelly turned on the porch light and stepped outside also. "Don't let her go too far out or we'll never find her in the dark."

That was true enough. Clouds had rolled in, obscuring the moon. Beyond the porch light, it was pitch-black. "Heard it might snow next week."

"I'd rather have snow than rain. But only if it sticks. I'd just as soon not have to deal with this place turning into a mud bog on top of everything else."

He followed the dog as she trotted around in circles. "Your mom never told you she was having trouble keeping the place going?"

"I hadn't talked to her in six years. Hadn't talked to anyone in Weaver in six years. So, no."

He stopped and looked at Kelly. She was leaning against the open door. With the oversize sweatshirt dwarfing her, she looked more petite than ever and hardly a day older than when they had been teenagers and couldn't keep their hands off each other. "You and your mother didn't talk even once?"

"No." She sipped her whiskey and gave another little hiss, though it wasn't quite as loud this time. "So, we can blame me for the state of affairs here."

"I wasn't." Finally, the dog found a worthy patch and squatted just long enough to leave a little dribble. "Are you blaming yourself?"

She lifted her shoulder, watching the puppy hop up the porch steps and trot back inside. "Who else is there to blame?"

"It was pretty obvious to me at the time that your mom was angry with you about leaving Weaver, but holding on to it for six years?" Even knowing the woman, it still boggled the mind. His mother wouldn't last six days, much less six years, if there were a grandchild in the picture. "You shouldn't blame yourself. This farm was her life, not yours."

"Spoken like the guy who strings fence for his dad

when he needs to." She was still looking out the open door. Cold air was filling the kitchen.

"That's different."

"Why?" She sipped her drink again. This time without the hiss. "A parent is a parent."

"A parent is someone that produces a child. Good parenting goes way the hell beyond that." He nudged her away from the door and closed it. "A good parent—whether by blood or not—is someone who loves and nurtures their child. I'm not saying your mom didn't love you, but—"

"Why not?" Kelly sipped her drink. "It was true. My mother did *not* love me. She was evidently so ashamed of me being a single mother that she made up a husband. And well before that, she blamed me for ruining her life. You know I'm not exaggerating. You heard her say it, too."

If it were anyone else, he would have given the "I'm sure she didn't mean it" spiel. But he had heard Georgette spew the bull Kelly was describing. More than once.

She'd meant it.

And not for the first time, he wondered what sort of welcome Georgette Rasmussen had received at the pearly gates.

"Ultimately, adults are responsible for their own lives," he said calmly. "The choices your mother made in her life were her choices. Same as the choices you're making are yours."

Kelly didn't put up any resistance when he pulled out one of the kitchen chairs and pushed her down onto it. Then he plucked the glass out of her hand.

"Hey!"

He dumped the liquor down the sink, rinsed the glass and filled it with water instead. "You're feeling sorry for yourself, and whiskey isn't helping. You're not your mother. You don't have to deal with all of this—" he made a sweeping gesture with his arm "—by yourself unless you want to. There are plenty of people around this town to help you. All you have to do is ask." Though she had an annoyed expression on her face, he bent over and kissed the top of her head anyway.

Why not? She was already peeved with him.

He set the water on the table in front of her. "Drink that, then go to bed."

Before she could react, he picked up the puppy and went back through the living room to the front door, grabbing the dog carrier along the way.

"Caleb."

Her voice stopped him just as he was opening the front door. He looked back. She was hovering near the couch, hugging her arms around her waist.

"What?"

"Do you ever think about—" She hesitated.

"About what?" The past? Her? About that damned night when he'd been changing a flat in the snow out on the highway between Weaver and Braden and she'd pulled up in her truck behind him? He'd gotten in her truck to warm up, then out of the blue she'd suddenly kissed him—

"A-about not becoming a surgeon?"

It was so far off from what he'd been thinking, it took him a second to adjust. "Not really. Why do you ask?"

She shook her head slightly. "Curious, I guess." Her arms unwound from her waist, and she lightly slapped her hands against her sides like she was putting a period on a sentence. "Be careful driving home. The road's worse than ever. I hit a pothole with my car and nearly bounced off the road." She lifted her hand, palm out.

"Not pitying myself," she assured him. "Just offering a word to the wise. Don't want you breaking an axle."

"I'll be careful." Carrying the dog under one arm and the crate in the other hand, he pulled open the door and left.

With the dog safely crated inside the truck, he drove away from the house.

But when he looked back, he could see Kelly standing in the front window.

Watching him go? Or just thinking about the tasks that were piled on her plate before she could leave Weaver, and everyone in it, behind once and for all?

"Mommy, who's that lady?"

Kelly looked up from the ragged wooden boards she was stacking and saw the petite blonde climbing out of a black SUV.

Lucy Buchanan.

"That's Dr. C's sister. She used to be a ballerina."

"Like Gunnar's sister?"

Kelly chuckled. "Something like that." Gunnar's sister was a three-year-old who liked to wear tutus all day long. Perhaps that was the way Lucy had started out, too.

Kelly pulled off her leather work gloves and shoved them in the pocket of the ancient jacket she was wearing. "I'm going to go see what she wants."

Tyler shrugged and turned his attention back to the bucket and gardening trowel she'd found for him. For the moment, he seemed happy enough to sit in the dirt and play.

As Kelly approached, Lucy waved and reached back into her SUV for something. "I didn't get a chance to talk to you at your mom's service, but I figured you must have your hands pretty full," she said when Kelly finally got to her. Lucy's hands were occupied by a big cardboard box, but that didn't stop her from quickly brushing her cheek against Kelly's. "I brought you a meal."

"You didn't have to do that." Kelly took the box when Lucy pushed it toward her. She then pulled a second box from the SUV.

"Is this Caleb's doing?" Kelly asked. She was still feeling more than a little undone from the night before. She'd come so close to asking him if he ever thought about them—about what might have been—that she'd lain awake for hours after he'd left.

Then, when she had finally fallen asleep, she'd been plagued by nightmares of him taking Tyler away from her as punishment for not telling him in the first place that he had a son.

It had not been a restful night.

"Caleb can't boil water," Lucy was saying with a laugh. "When he's not mooching meals off me twice a week, he's hitting up Tabby or Mom and Dad or some other sucker."

"I sort of doubt anyone's complaining too loudly," Kelly said drily. The Buchanans, the Taggarts and the Clays were all thick as thieves. They had more family connections than Carter had pills; they did business together, ran ranches together and socialized like the best of friends.

It was exactly the kind of family Kelly hadn't had. But only because Georgette had never given two figs about the rest of the Rasmussens living in the area. Kelly wasn't sure if Georgette's attitude would have been different if the other family members had been siblings instead of distant cousins.

And how different from your mother are you?

She pushed away the disturbing thought.

"This is awfully nice of you, Lucy, but you needn't have gone to the trouble."

"No trouble," Lucy assured her blithely. She turned and led the way toward the house, waving cheerfully at Tyler when she spotted him. "Shelby—she's my step-daughter—doesn't get out of school for another hour, and Sunny's home taking a nap with my husband, Beck. So I had the perfect opportunity." She darted up the porch steps and waited for Kelly to push open the door. "Nothing too fancy, mind you. Just ribs I tossed in the slow cooker, baked mac and cheese, and a chopped veggie salad."

"*Just?*" Kelly chuckled as they went inside the house. She was glad that she'd managed to haul off a load of trash that morning, as it left the living room looking a little less insane. "It definitely beats the heck out of frozen fish sticks. Kitchen's in the back."

"Always is, in these old houses." Lucy didn't seem particularly shocked as she picked her way through the cluttered room and into the kitchen, where she set her box on the table. "How're you holding up?"

Again, Kelly wondered what, if anything, Caleb had told his sister. "Fine. I've made more progress today than I expected. Tyler and I were just outside taking advantage of the afternoon sun." They'd both been happy to get out of the oppressive house.

She plucked a clear glass bowl containing the chopped salad out of the box. She could see the carrots in it, which meant getting Tyler to touch it would be impossible. But she would certainly enjoy it. "Looks delicious," she told Lucy as she popped it on one of the bare shelves inside the fridge. "I'll get the dishes back to you as soon as I can."

"There's no hurry." Lucy handed her two more covered casseroles and she slid them inside, as well. "You can warm those up in the oven or the micro—" She broke off, glancing around the kitchen.

"No microwave," Kelly confirmed. "This is really great, though, Lucy. Tyler loves macaroni and cheese."

"Doesn't every kid?" Lucy pushed up the sleeves of her pink sweater as she headed out of the kitchen. "Shelby would have starved some days if not for the miracle that is noodles and gooey cheese. Oh." She stopped short when she reached the couch and saw the pile of quilts that Kelly had left there. "Are these handmade?"

Kelly hesitated. "Yeah. Well…my mother always told me that her grandmother had made them. I assume that's true. I found them in a trunk in the attic."

"Do you mind?" Lucy barely waited for Kelly's answer before she pulled the top one off the pile and partially unfolded it. "It looks in perfect condition except for the stain here." Lucy rubbed her fingers against a faded circle marring the pale pink and blue wedding-ring pattern.

"Red Kool-Aid," Kelly told her. "I remember spilling it when I was not much older than Tyler."

"You had the quilt on your bed?"

"No. We used it once when my mom took me on a picnic." Kelly sat on the arm of the couch, drawing the corner of the quilt over her legs. "I'd practically forgotten that."

"Did you do that often? Go picnicking?"

Kelly shook her head. "Not ever." She narrowed her eyes, thinking back. "I can't even remember why we went on a picnic. She just picked me up from school one day. Had the quilt in the car, along with a picnic basket, and off we went. Drove out of town, even. I suppose it wasn't far, but back then it seemed like it was. She stopped at a spot with a pond and trees."

"Sounds like the hole out at the Double C."

"Sort of." Kelly had swum in the spring-fed swimming hole plenty of times with Caleb during high school. "I don't think it was quite that big. Mama spread out the quilt, and we lay on it after we ate fried chicken and chocolate cupcakes. And she wasn't even angry when I spilled my drink."

"It sounds like a lovely memory," Lucy said gently.

Only then did Kelly realize that tears were sliding down her cheek.

She blushed and quickly wiped them away. "Yeah." She pushed the quilt aside and stood. "Didn't mean to get maudlin."

Lucy tsked. "It's not maudlin to remember good times."

"Mommy." Tyler's voice accompanied the sound of the front door closing. "You always tell me to shut the door but you left it open." He came into the living room, smiling a little shyly at Lucy. "I'm hungry."

Kelly went over to him and tilted up his face with both hands, "Fortunately, Mrs.—" She broke off and looked at Lucy. "I don't even know your married name."

"Ventura," Lucy provided with a chuckle. "But you—" she crouched in front of Tyler and poked him lightly in the stomach "—can call me Lucy."

"Mrs. Ventura brought us macaroni and cheese," Kelly told him. "Wasn't that nice of her?"

He nodded.

"I also brought ribs and a veggie salad," Lucy added. "And you're going to have to help your mom eat up all of it, because I want the dishes empty when I get them back. Okay?"

Tyler nodded earnestly. "'Cept carrots. I don't like carrots."

Lucy laughed outright. "The hateful carrots. Neither Shelby nor Sunny will touch them, either, no matter how hard I try." She straightened. "Speaking of… I need to get back into town to pick up Shelby from school. We're finishing her costume tonight for the carnival tomorrow over at the high school. Sunny's is already finished. You should bring Tyler."

"Tyler saw a poster for the Halloween carnival in town last week," Kelly admitted.

"Mommy said we'll see."

"Ah. The dreaded 'we'll see.'" Lucy nodded sagely, though her blue eyes were laughing. "It *is* a school night," she allowed.

"Not for me," Tyler said immediately. His bright gaze zeroed in on Kelly's face. "Right, Mom?"

Oh, how she preferred his little-boy "Mommy" over the occasional "Mom" that seemed to slip out more and more these days. "That's true," she agreed and suddenly lost the desire and interest in keeping as far apart from the goings-on in Weaver as she could manage.

At least when it came to a Halloween carnival and her little boy.

"I guess we'll see you at the carnival then," she told Lucy.

Tyler jumped up and whooped, causing a minor dust storm in the untidy living room. "Can I wear a costume? Can I?"

She stifled a sigh, glancing around at the mess yet to be dealt with. "Sure," she said. "Why not?"

Chapter Eight

"I'm a good robot, right, Mommy?"

"The best, buddy." It was the best costume that could be made out of plastic butter tubs and broken-down cardboard boxes covered with two rolls of aluminum foil, at any rate.

She stopped at the table outside the high school gymnasium and paid their admission.

The teenager manning the table handed over a long strand of perforated red tickets. "You can buy individual tickets inside, too," she told Kelly. "If you run out."

Kelly laughed wryly. "You mean *when*."

The teen grinned, showing off a mouthful of braces. Then she focused on Tyler. "Smokin' costume, little man."

"I'm a robot," Tyler said so proudly Kelly just knew his chest was puffed out beneath the square top of his costume.

"I can tell," the teenager said, seeming suitably impressed. "Haven't seen too many robots tonight. Mostly cowboys and princesses. So be sure to enter the costume contest, okay?"

Tyler nodded so enthusiastically, the foil-covered tub on top of his head nearly slipped off. He quickly righted it and grabbed Kelly's hand, pulling her toward the gymnasium. "Come *on*, Mom. Wait until I tell Gunnar about this!"

It was hard not to be carried along by her boy's enthusiasm as they entered the crowded room.

The high school didn't seem to have changed appreciably since she'd walked the halls as a student. The paint was fresh. But the floors were still covered with the same industrial gray-and-blue-flecked tile they'd always had.

Inside the gymnasium, the bleachers were collapsed back against the walls to make room for the dozens of carnival booths that had been set up. She'd have thought with the bleachers put away she wouldn't be accosted with memories of getting detention when she and Caleb were caught making out beneath them when they were sixteen.

But she was.

Tyler led her excitedly around the room, stopping at one booth after another. He tossed beanbags through the grinning mouth of a gigantic jack-o'-lantern. He rolled a pumpkin like a bowling ball at stacked pins made out of toilet paper rolls. He shot squirt guns at bobbing balloons and climbed in the inflatable bounce house situated in the far corner of the room while she held his robot hat and the silly trinkets he'd won along the way. And when he finally came out, flushed and sweaty and happy, she steered him to the bingo game where they could both sit for a few minutes.

"Next game starts in a couple minutes," she was told when she stopped at the table to hand over more tickets in exchange for two bingo cards and two little bags of candy corn. "Candy corn are your markers," the attendant—another teenager—told Tyler. "So don't eat 'em up until you've finished playing your game, okay?"

He nodded. "Over here, Mommy." He darted to one of the long lunch tables that were set up in two rows in front of the gymnasium's low stage. She followed and sat next to him, smiling at some of the familiar faces around them. So far, they hadn't run into Lucy and her kids. "After bingo I want to bob for apples, okay?"

"Better you than me," she told him agreeably. Unlike the bobbing-for-apples game she'd grown up with—a barrel of water with a couple dozen apples floating in it—she'd already seen that tonight's version involved individual containers of whipped cream in which a small apple might or might not be hiding. Basically, it meant each kid got a chance to dunk his face in his own helping of whipped cream.

And she'd be cleaning whipped cream out of Tyler's ears for days.

"Here." She peeled open the bag of candy so it was lying flat on the table. "Don't eat them, or you won't be able to play. If one of your numbers gets called, you set a piece of candy on it, okay? And this—" she slid a candy into place on the center of the card "—is the free spot you get."

He nodded as he studied their two cards. "How come my numbers are different than yours?"

"Everyone's is different. When I was little, I used to

play at least two cards at once," she told him. "But we'll start you out with just one since this is your first game."

He wriggled around until he was sitting on his knees on his folding chair. "This is the best carnival I ever gone to."

She chuckled. It was also one of the only carnivals he'd ever gone to. Back home in Idaho, he and Gunnar dressed up in costumes purchased at the dollar store and trick-or-treated in their apartment complex. "I bet it is." She leaned over to tuck his goodies safely under her chair. "After we play bingo, we ought to think about getting you some supper, though. I think they're selling hamburgers or something in the cafeteria. Then you can bob for apples." Inhale whipped cream. Whatever.

"Hey, Dr. C!"

She jerked upright. Tyler was straining out of his chair, waving his cast wildly over his head at Caleb, who'd stepped up onto the stage and was taking a seat next to the bingo cage on top of a table.

He smiled and waved back at Tyler, giving him a thumbs-up. "Good luck," he said, then gave the crank on the side of the cage a whirl.

"All right, everyone." He raised his voice to be heard above the general din inside the gymnasium. "Ready to play some bingo? All you need are five numbers in a row. Get out that candy corn, and here we go! Our first number is—" he pulled out one of the balls from inside the cage "—twenty-two!"

"Where's my twenty-two, Mom?" Tyler pushed his bingo card in front of her. "Where is it?"

"Sorry, buddy. You don't have one." She glanced over her own card. "Neither do I."

He pushed out his lower lip.

"It's a game, Tyler. Sometimes you have the numbers. Sometimes you don't. But you can't pout. You have to be a good sport whether you're winning or losing. Remember?"

His narrow shoulders rose and fell as he let out an enormous sigh. "I 'member."

"Next number." Caleb drew out another ball. "Five. Everyone hear? The number is five."

"I got it," Tyler crowed.

Caleb heard and gave him another thumbs-up.

"Put a piece of candy corn on the spot where the five is," Kelly prompted.

"I never got to play bingo before." Tyler wriggled in his chair. "I'm gonna be the best bingo player *ever*!"

She laughed softly and brushed his hair away from his sweaty forehead. She made the mistake of glancing at Caleb, though, only to find him watching them. His gaze caught hers, and he smiled slightly.

Her face warmed. She wanted to squirm in her own chair pretty much the same way Tyler was. She was glad she hadn't bought two bingo cards. It was hard enough to keep track of her one.

When someone called out, "Bingo!" after several more draws, she was actually grateful. It had never occurred to her that Caleb might be at the carnival, much less that he'd be manning one of the entertainments.

"But I need another spot," Tyler said while the winner read back her numbers to Caleb.

"It's a game of chance. Sometimes you're luckier than others. And look." Kelly drew his attention to her card. "You have almost a full row, and I'm not even close. But the cool part of *this* bingo game is—" she popped one of the candy pieces she hadn't yet used in her mouth "—getting to eat the markers."

He giggled, happy enough with the explanation. "I

wanna go see Dr. C." Before she could stop him, Tyler hopped off his chair and darted toward the stage. Caleb had finished verifying the winner's numbers, and as she watched, he showed Tyler how to dump the numbered balls back into the round cage. When Tyler was finished, they high-fived. Tyler said something to Caleb that had him laughing, and then he was writing something on Tyler's cast.

Her son's smile was enough to light up the state of Wyoming, and her heart seized up.

He was still beaming as he hopped off the stage again and ran back to her. "I told Dr. C he should name his puppy Bingo, and guess what?"

Her chest tightened even further. "What?"

"He said that was the best name ever!" Tyler showed her where Caleb had scrawled his indecipherable doctor's signature on the cast. "And I get to go see Bingo again if you say I can."

"We'll—" She broke off. He was so happy she couldn't bear to offer a weak *we'll see*.

"We'll have to arrange that," she said instead.

Tyler was practically vibrating out of his robot costume. "Dr. C has to call more games. Can I play again?"

"Thought you wanted to bob for apples."

"I do. But Dr. C—"

"—would understand." They weren't just words. When it came to dealing with children, she had to give Caleb points. But mostly, she was the one who wanted an escape.

Cowardly? Sure.

Smart? Most definitely.

"Besides—" she retrieved their belongings from beneath the chair "—you still need to eat something for supper. Don't you want to see the cafeteria where *I* used to eat my lunches?"

Evidently, either that—or the prospect of supper— was enough of an enticement to lure him away from the bingo game.

It didn't seem possible, but when they reached the cafeteria, it was even more crowded than the gymnasium had been. Fortunately, the line they joined moved quickly, and before long, she'd paid for their selections. Then it was a matter of finding a place to sit.

"There's Lucas!" Tyler immediately darted down one row of tables.

Juggling the tray, Tyler's robot hat and his various prizes, Kelly swallowed her instinctive protest and followed.

Lucas, dressed like Superman, was indeed sitting at one of the long cafeteria tables. Along with about two dozen other familiar faces.

The little boy scooted over to make room for Tyler's boxy costume while Kelly was besieged by greetings from Lucas's parents, grandparents, great-grandparents and seemingly everyone in between.

She pasted a smile on her face that she hoped wasn't as wobbly as she felt inside and gave everyone a group hello.

"We're overwhelming her," Tabby said with a knowing smile. She was sitting at the far end of the adjacent table. "Come sit here, Kelly."

"Tyler will be fine," Leandra assured her. She was sitting directly across from the two boys. "Lucas has been asking when he'd get to see him again."

Sure enough, the two boys were already comparing their carnival adventures. Tyler barely even gave her a glance when she left his hamburger basket and carton of milk in front of him before she walked down to squeeze in beside Tabby.

She unwrapped her plastic fork and unfolded the thin napkin to spread on her lap. "Where's Justin?"

"Working at the lab tonight. Great costume for Tyler. He reminds me of the Tin Man from *The Wizard of Oz*."

Kelly couldn't help but chuckle. "We were aiming for futuristic robot. But I can see what you mean. I drew the line at painting his face silver, but he sure did beg." She squeezed a ketchup packet onto the waxy paper lining her hamburger basket and dragged a French fry through it before popping the fry into her mouth. "Good Lord, these haven't improved at all in ten years. Why did we once think they were so great?"

"Because we were teenagers?" Tabby laughed. "And it's the same cafeteria staff, far as I know." She waved suddenly at a slender brunette across the room, who waved back. "That's Abby McCray," Tabby said. "School nurse at the elementary school. You wouldn't remember her. She moved to Weaver after you'd already left."

"And snagged Tara's brother," Lucy said, walking up behind them. "Tara is Axel's wife."

"Leandra mentioned her," Kelly said. She looked over to check on Tyler. He was gesturing with his cast and talking with his mouth full. But then, so was Lucas. And Kelly was too far away to correct him anyway. "Abby looks too young to be a nurse."

Lucy laughed and patted her shoulder from behind. "So do you, yet we hear that's what you've become. Why is it that nobody is aging but me?"

"Please," Tabby said with a snort.

Kelly felt herself relaxing among them. She even finished the wilted French fries before she realized it. It wasn't too long, of course, before the children were clamoring to get back to the gymnasium for more fun. Tyler donned his butter tub hat long enough to be judged in the costume contest, then he shoved it into her hands and ran off with Lucas and a fistful of red tickets to try his luck bobbing for apples.

"Does he know how hard it is to find an apple lurking in a bowl of cream?"

She'd stiffened the moment she heard Caleb's voice. "He's five years old and faced with enough whipped cream to fill two pie pans. Do you really think he cares?" She slid a look Caleb's way. Despite everything that had happened since, it was impossible to stand there in the school gymnasium and *not* think about the past. Especially when he looked frustratingly appealing in his lumberjacky plaid shirt and blue jeans. "He told me about naming the dog."

He shrugged. "Bingo's a good name."

"Has she eaten any more pillows?"

"No. She's graduated to jumping on the counter now."

"Good thing you didn't seem to have anything on your counters last time I visited."

His lips twitched. "Silver lining, I guess."

She wasn't going to get drawn in by the man's appeal. "Aren't you supposed to be calling bingo? The games, not your puppy."

"Fortunately, my replacement arrived. You already ate?"

"Yes. If you're heading to the cafeteria, the French fries are as bad as they ever were. Just in case you were curious."

He smiled. "I wasn't, but thanks for the heads-up. No, I was thinking I'd give the cafeteria a pass, considering a good steak at Colbys is within walking distance. Want to come with me?"

Her lips parted but no words immediately emerged.

"I know you've already eaten, but the company would be nice."

"I can't," she finally managed to blurt. "Tyler—"

"—would be perfectly fine for an hour." Caleb gestured toward the line of children waiting their turn at the apple-bobbing booth. Behind them was a line of parents watching. "Lucy's there. Leandra's there. They're not going to mind keeping an eye out for one more for a little while. Hell, there's my mother, even."

Sure enough, Belle Buchanan had joined the adults. As if she'd heard her son, she looked their way, smiled and waved.

Kelly exhaled. "I don't think so."

"What're you afraid of?"

Her head jerked back. "Nothing! Just because I don't want to leave my son—"

"Go with me, you mean."

She closed her mouth, exhaling carefully. "It's not a good idea," she finally said.

"Why not? Is there someone in Idaho?"

"What?"

"Not the guy who never proposed. But someone else?"

She huffed. Her face felt flushed. "No, there's no one in Idaho." There'd never been. Only him.

"Then I fail to see the problem."

"Oh, for cryin'—" She broke off. "Why are you making an issue about this?"

"Why are you? We used to be friends."

She let out a snort. "Just because we couldn't keep our hands off each other doesn't mean we were friends!"

Her words suddenly sounded loud in the room, and she flushed even harder.

"We *were* friends," Caleb said evenly. If he felt embarrassed by the attention they were drawing, he hid it a lot better than she did. "And we were a lot more."

"Until you decided I wasn't what you wanted after all." Her throat suddenly ached. Which was infuriating, because she'd told herself she had stopped crying over Caleb Buchanan years ago.

"We were young," he said. "And young people make mistakes all the time."

So do adults.

She suddenly just wanted to gather Tyler up and go home.

Not to her mother's house and the difficult memories waiting for her there.

But to Idaho. Where her life was orderly. Where nothing unexpected ever occurred. Where she wasn't bombarded with her past everywhere she turned and it didn't feel as though she had to second-guess every decision she'd ever made.

The crowded gymnasium felt like it was closing in on her. She could feel a bead of sweat slowly crawling down her spine. "I don't want to talk about this."

"Right now? Or ever?"

Ever! The word silently roared in her head. She could see Tyler still waiting in line. He and Lucas were tossing a plastic pumpkin back and forth.

"Kelly—"

She shook her head, turning away from the hand Caleb put on her arm, and hurriedly made her way to the gymnasium doors, skirting around the booths and the people who stood in her way. But even when she made it out the doors and into the hallway, there were crowds of people there, too.

Had everyone in the entire darn county turned out for the carnival?

She ducked her head and made her way around them, too, until finally, she burst through the double doors leading outside.

Fresh air coursed over her hot cheeks, and she drew in a long breath. There was a couple approaching with three kids dressed like little pink pigs, and Kelly moved out of their way as they went inside, leaving the well-lit sidewalk altogether for the shadows alongside the building. She leaned her head back against the cold brick and slowly battled down the cloying, nauseating sense of panic.

She heard the distinctive sound of the doors and knew, even before she saw him, that it was Caleb.

He stopped on the sidewalk beneath one of the light poles, hands on his jeans-clad hips. She didn't make a sound, but that didn't stop him from turning her way.

He left the sidewalk for the shadows. "Are you done running?"

"Are you a bloodhound on the scent?"

"Maybe." He took a few more steps toward her.

She leaned her head back once more against the bricks. The clear sky they'd enjoyed so briefly that afternoon had been overtaken by thick, obscuring clouds, and the harsh bite of impending winter was in the air. Even though Kelly knew the weather wouldn't be that different back in Idaho Falls, she wished she were back there. "Why do you care, Caleb?"

He was silent for so long she wasn't sure he was going to answer. She pushed away from the brick. "I need to get back to Tyler."

"I've always cared."

His words washed over her. Instead of feeling like a balmy wave, though, it felt like being rolled against abrasive sand. "Right." She stepped around him.

"Dammit." His hand shot out and grabbed her arm.

She tried to shake him off. "Let *go*."

"You asked and I'm telling you. So now you're going to walk away?" He let her go. "I swear, you're as stubborn as your mother."

She flinched.

He swore again and thrust his fingers through his dark hair. "I didn't mean that."

Why not? Sure, she adored her son. She didn't regret his existence for one single second. In that, she was very different from her mother. But that didn't mean she wasn't Georgette Rasmussen's daughter with all the rest that that implied.

"I have to go." She tried stepping around his big body again.

"I'm sorry that I hurt you. I was always sorry, Kelly. Always."

She looked up at him. "But you did it anyway."

"And you're going to hate me forever because of it? It was nearly ten years ago!"

When he'd dumped her for another girl.

And only six years had passed since she'd impetuously, angrily put her mouth on his and set in motion a situation she still couldn't change.

Which was worse?

His actions or hers?

Her eyes suddenly burned. Because she was pretty sure keeping the existence of his son from him outweighed him falling in love with someone far better suited to him than simple little Kelly Rasmussen.

He made a rough sound of impatience. "If you're gonna hate me anyway—"

She barely had a chance to frown before his mouth hit hers.

She went rigid with shock, then yanked back. But she only got two inches away. Maybe three. Just far enough to stare into his dark eyes while her breath heaved in her chest.

Then his mouth was on hers again, and she wasn't sure if she'd moved first. Or if it had been him.

But what did it really matter?

Because they were once more standing in the shadows by the side of the high school, Caleb's weight pressing into her while his hands raced down her sides, delving beneath her short leather jacket. And she felt devoured by his kiss.

Why was it always that way? He put his lips on hers and she forgot all rhyme or reason. She'd forget every single thing but the taste of him, the smell of him, the weight of—

A burst of laughter accosted them, and they pulled apart. It was hard to tell who was breathing harder.

"Some things don't change, eh, Caleb?"

Kelly's cheeks burned. She turned her face away from whoever it was who'd noticed them, tugging her jacket back into place.

"Shut up, Marvin."

She cringed. Marvin Towers had been annoying when she was fourteen. So much so that she'd run her bicycle straight into a cement curb to get away from his incessant teasing about her crazy mama.

It was the day she'd gone over her handlebars. And Caleb had picked up the pieces.

Marvin, though, didn't take the hint. "That *is* you,

isn't it, Kelly?" He walked closer. "Heard you were back in town. Couldn't wait to hook up with your old boyfriend, I see. Maybe you ought to think about getting a room, seeing how the bleachers aren't available tonight."

Her shoulders stiffened. She couldn't look at Caleb's face again, so she turned on Marvin instead. "Maybe you ought to think about crawling back under your rock. You were a pain in the butt when we were in school. You want to talk about things not changing? Look in the mirror sometime, why don't you?" She shoved him out of her way and stomped back inside the gymnasium.

The sooner she and Tyler could leave Weaver, the better off they all would be.

Chapter Nine

The day after the carnival, Caleb did something he'd never done before in his life.

He had the office reschedule an entire afternoon's worth of appointments.

One way or another, he was going to have it out with Kelly.

But when he went to her mom's farm, the place was deserted. House locked up tight. Dusty car with the Idaho license plate nowhere to be seen.

He didn't want to think that she'd up and left town again, but he'd had the same knot in his gut when she'd done it before. Only back then, the knot had been caused by Georgette Rasmussen slamming the door of her house in his face after lying to him about her daughter being married.

What the hell kind of person did that? Who made up some damn pointless lie the way she had? It was as if she'd been afraid he'd go after Kelly or something.

Wouldn't you have?

It wasn't the first time the question had sneaked its way into Caleb's thoughts.

He'd never given it serious consideration, though. He'd been too focused on med school. Then his residency.

Yeah, he'd made a few stabs at locating her. But he hadn't tried hard enough. If he hadn't been so career driven, would he have tried harder? Fought for her?

He sat down on the front porch steps. While the puppy yanked on her leash, he stared at the land around him. The wind blew pretty constantly in these parts, and that afternoon was no different. It was kicking up little whirlwinds of dirt, flattening the weeds down against the sparse brown patches of grass and rattling the weathered wood of the abandoned coops.

When he and Kelly were teenagers, the farm hadn't looked this way. There'd been the chickens, of course. But there'd also been rows and rows of whatever crop was growing that season.

He scrubbed his face with his hands. Now the only thing surrounding him seemed to be the echoes of Georgette's dissatisfaction with life.

Which Kelly herself must have felt much more strongly.

Would it be any wonder if she'd had enough and had bolted?

Particularly after what had happened the evening before at the carnival?

And if she's gone back to Idaho now?

He suddenly yanked out his cell phone, startling Bingo into yipping. "Relax, dog." He reached out and rubbed his hand over her silky head while checking the signal on his phone. One bar. But it was enough, and he dialed the office. "Mary," he said when the receptionist answered, "I need you to pull Tyler Rasmussen's record for me. I need his mother's contact information."

"Sure. Hold on a second."

The nice thing about Mary was that she wouldn't pepper him with questions like some of the other people working for Doc Cobb. She was back in seconds. "She left a mobile number."

Thank you, God. "Text it to me, would you please? And I'll see you in the office as usual tomorrow after I'm finished at the hospital."

"You have three appointments here before your rounds," she reminded him. "Had to fit in those reschedules."

"Right. Thanks, Mary." He hung up. A moment later, the text arrived and he dialed the number.

It went straight to Kelly's voice mail. *Do not pass Go. Do not collect two hundred dollars.*

"It's Caleb. Call me."

Not that he had any expectation she would just because he'd asked.

He pushed to his feet and pocketed his phone. "Come on, Bingo." The puppy trotted after him to the truck, and he lifted her inside. She immediately hopped onto the passenger seat, propped one paw on the armrest and scratched at the window with her other.

Even though it was barely forty degrees out, he opened the window for her and drove away from the farm.

Not finding Kelly left him with an afternoon to fill. But if he spent it hanging around downtown, someone would be bound to notice and wonder why. Particularly if the rescheduled appointments started talking.

Pretty annoying when a man couldn't choose to take a break from work for an afternoon without people asking questions, but he'd known that was what he was getting into when he'd decided to come back to Weaver to practice.

In the end, he took refuge at his brother-in-law's office. Fortunately, Beck didn't ask questions the way Lucy would have. After raising his eyebrows a little at the unexpected sight of Caleb in the middle of the day, he filled a container of water for the dog and gestured for Caleb to sit in one of the office's cushioned chairs. He didn't ask questions about the black mood Caleb was in but just pulled out the latest version of his architecture plans.

After an hour of tweaking, Beck rolled the plans back up. "Would help if you'd decide where you want your house built. That's going to lead to some changes, too."

"I've got it narrowed down to a few spots." They'd been having this particular discussion for over a month.

"The Johansson place is your best bet," Beck told him. Which was also something he'd been saying for over a month. "Good location. You're looking at renovations versus a new build. Has the best view."

Caleb knew the Johansson place inside and out. It was perfect for the reasons that Beck said. He just hadn't been able to commit to it.

"Wait too long and someone's likely to buy it before you," Beck added.

"Yeah. I know. My Realtor's warning the same thing. I'll decide soon."

After that, Caleb gathered up Bingo and went back to his truck. He called Kelly again. And once again it went straight to her voice mail. This time he didn't bother with the message. She'd be able to see well enough that the calls were from him.

He was still sitting in his truck when someone banged on the window.

Pam Rasmussen.

He swallowed an oath and rolled down his window. "Hey, Pam."

"Just wondered if everything was all right. Saw you sitting here and all."

"Doing fine." If fine was feeling like he was standing at a train stop waiting on a train that no longer ran.

"S'pose you heard about all the excitement out toward Braden way."

The last thing he wanted was a dose of her gossip. "Nope." His voice was a little too curt.

Her eyebrows rose. "You haven't heard from Kelly?"

Why would he? "Pam—"

"Pretty bad accident." She kept speaking right over his visible jerk. "We had to send out the helicopter—"

He wanted to reach through the window and clamp his hand over her mouth. "What accident? Is Kelly hurt? Tyler?"

"Oh." Pam shook her head quickly. "No. No, I don't think so. But she was there. Rode with one of the victims in the helicopter. Pretty sure Tyler wasn't with her—"

He shoved the truck into gear. Pam had the good sense to back away quickly, or he might have run over her toes.

He didn't need to question where the helicopter would be heading. There was only one hospital in the region, and Weaver was it.

It took scant minutes to get there. As soon as he pulled into the parking lot, he could see the helicopter sitting in its usual spot. He left the dog in the truck with the window rolled halfway down and went straight in through the emergency entrance.

Courtney was on duty, and she gave him a surprised look.

"Where's Kelly? She came in with the helicopter."

"Ah." Comprehension dawned, and she gestured toward the curtained cubicles behind her. "Eight. Gown up first," she called after him as he strode across the tiled floor.

Halfway there, he snatched up a gown and a mask and yanked them on before he reached the eighth cubicle. He recognized what he was hearing even before he stuck his head around the curtain.

The woman in the bed was well into childbirth. Dan Yarnell was attending her, and Kelly was standing behind the laboring woman, holding her hand.

That wasn't the sight that rocked him.

It was seeing the blood on Kelly's pale blue gown that did that.

Aside from the first quick flare of shock in her eyes when she spotted him, she didn't give him another glance. All of her concentration was on the woman. "Come on now, Maria. You can do this. You're almost there," Kelly said through the mask covering half her face.

The woman in the bed was crying. Shaking her head. "I can't. I can't."

Kelly bent over her, giving the exhausted woman a shoulder to lean against. "I know how tired you are, Maria. But you've got a baby who needs you. And we're all here to help you." Her hands were white where the woman was squeezing them so tightly. "I'm here. Dr. Yarnell is here. You're not alone. Now let's do this together. *Push!*"

Caleb backed away from the curtain. He slowly returned to the nurses' station where his cousin was updating a chart, disposing of his gown and mask along the way. "Why didn't they take her up to labor and delivery?"

Courtney slid the chart into the appropriate slot on the wall behind her. "No time. Plus, they're already full upstairs." She looked back at him when the distinctive wail of a baby filled the air. "Nothing like a baby being born, but a terrible way for it to come about." She shook her head. "Head-on collision out on Bekins Road. Daddy was DOA."

"What was Kelly doing there? And where the hell is Tyler?"

Courtney gave him a wary look. "Criminy, Caleb. Take a breath. Tyler's fine. He's at Leandra's. Kelly had me call her to say she'd be late picking him up. All I know is that Kelly was there and tried to help. If you want to know more than that about the accident, talk to Sam Dawson. She was the officer on scene."

Caleb exhaled and pulled in a long, deep breath. He gave David Templeton a nod when he saw the physician head behind the curtain. He was a pediatrician based in Braden but did regular rounds in the afternoon at the hospital, the same as Caleb did in the morning.

Courtney's expression softened. "Heard the daddy didn't have a chance of making it. Bled out in a matter of minutes." Then she frowned. "Don't you usually have patients this time of day?"

He grimaced. "Usually. Give me an emesis basin, would you?"

"Planning to vomit on me?" She gave him a wry smirk before retrieving a kidney-shaped pink basin from her supply. "There you go. We charge twenty-two fifty per," she added, "but since you're a relative, I'll give it to you for twice that."

"Ha-ha. Put it on my tab. I left my dog in the truck. Last thing I need is some interested bystander accusing me of mistreating my animal." He filled the basin with water from the fountain in the waiting room and took it out to Bingo. The puppy was snoring away on Caleb's leather seat.

He left the water container on the passenger side floor and went back inside.

Kelly was standing outside the cubicle, slowly pulling off her paper gown. Even across the distance of the ER, Caleb could see the tears in her eyes.

"Here." Courtney shoved a plastic-wrapped bundle into his hands. "Take her some scrubs. She can clean up in the break room."

Caleb knew from experience that the break room was little more than a closet with a lumpy couch, a fridge and a hot plate. But it had a private bathroom and was better than nothing.

When he reached Kelly's side, she was holding the gown bunched in a ball at her waist. He recognized her dress as the one she'd been wearing that first day when she'd brought Tyler in for his cast.

He gestured toward the contaminated-waste container and held up the bundle. "Clean scrubs. Come on. I'll show you where you can change."

She didn't say a word but simply disposed of her gown and gloves in the container and followed him to the break room. "Bathroom's here." He pushed open the door, and she silently went inside.

He heard water running. A few thumps. Then she opened the door. The scrubs dwarfed her slender figure. Even with the high-heeled shoes she was wearing, she'd had to roll up the pant legs. The scrubs were also pale green, similar to the underlying tinge in her pale face. She'd wrapped her dress in the plastic bag the scrubs had come in. "I was supposed to pick up Tyler two hours ago."

"I'm sure he's fine with Leandra." He studied her face. "Did you get hurt in the accident?"

"No." She pressed her lips together for a moment. "I, uh, I was on my way back from Braden. The court gave me permission to have the auction, and I had to s-sign some paperwork for the auction house. The accident happened right in front of me." Her brows pulled together. "What are you doing here?"

"I heard *you* were here. Was there any blood exposure? Courtney told me the husband bled out."

She shook her head. "I had a first aid kit in my car. Gloves. An insulated blanket. I was careful. Maybe if I hadn't taken the time to be careful, that poor woman's husband would still be—"

"Don't." He took her arm. Whether she liked it or not, she wasn't looking particularly steady. "There's no point thinking that way. Come on. I'll take you home."

She didn't resist as he led her back through the ER. The curtains were still closed around Maria's cubicle, and the baby was still wailing. Kelly pulled away long enough to throw out her plastic-wrapped dress in the same waste container where she'd left her gown.

"I thought you didn't get his blood on you."

"I didn't," she whispered dully. "But I'll never want to wear that dress again."

Before they headed outside, Caleb shrugged out of his jacket and pulled it around her shoulders. She accepted it without reaction.

When she saw his truck, though, she stirred. "My car. It's still out on the highway."

"We'll get it later," he promised.

She made a faint sound he decided to take as agreement and pulled open the passenger door. Bingo popped up, wagging her tail. Caleb scooted her into the rear seat and closed the door once Kelly was inside.

He rounded the hood and got behind the wheel. She was staring at her shaking hands in her lap.

He started the engine, rolled up her window and turned on the heat. "You okay?"

"He died in my arms," she murmured. "All the classes, all the training, and I've never—" She broke off, shaking her head. "I'm a nurse. I should be better at this."

He squeezed her shoulder. "Don't forget you also just helped a woman bring her baby into the world."

Kelly's eyes flooded. She looked at him. "After she saw her husband die right beside her." Her voice was hoarse. "She didn't want me to leave her."

"And you didn't. So cut yourself a break. Boy or girl?"

"What? Oh. Boy. Seven pounds, eight ounces. Two ounces more than Tyler was." Kelly sniffed hard, blinking several times. "I want a shower." Her throat worked. "Before I have to pick him up."

Driving out to her mom's farm wasn't as easy as popping over to the corner store. Going back into town and out again to Leandra's would take even longer. "It'll be supper time at least before I can get you back to Leandra's. My place would be faster."

He expected a protest to that, too.

The fact that she didn't told him just how affected she was by the trauma she'd witnessed.

"Fine," she whispered.

He turned up the heater another notch. "Fasten your seat belt, honey."

She dutifully pulled the shoulder belt across her chest and pushed it into place. Then she leaned her head back against the headrest and closed her eyes.

He was glad he didn't pass any sheriff's vehicles on the way to his apartment.

He'd have gotten cited for speeding for sure.

* * *

Kelly rubbed the foggy mirror with the thick gray towel Caleb had provided.

She looked like a drowned rat.

But at least she no longer felt like she was swimming in that poor man's lifeblood.

She sniffed, willing away the weak tears that still threatened even after she'd already spilled them in a shower that smelled of Caleb.

If she'd been smart—if she'd been strong—she would have just asked him to take her straight to her car.

But she wasn't smart. And despite everything she'd accomplished with her life since leaving Weaver, she wasn't strong.

Not when it came to him.

"Hey." He knocked softly on the door. "How you doing in there?"

She had to clear her throat. "Fine." She briskly rubbed the towel over her wet head. "Sorry I've been taking so long."

"Take as long as you want. I'm not in any hurry."

But she should have been. Tyler was still out at Leandra's. Kelly had left him there that morning and only expected to be gone a few hours.

She'd taken the entire day.

She finished drying off. The idea of wearing anything she'd had on at the accident scene was anathema, including her bra and panties. She pulled on the scrubs without them, bundling them into a ball that she stuffed into the pants pocket, thanking her stars that the scrubs were well over a size too large. So long as she kept the V-neck of the top from sliding too far down, the only one who would know she was alfresco underneath was her.

She gave her bedraggled reflection a stern look.

She'd do well to keep it that way.

She hung the towel on the bar next to the one that had already been there. His. And when she realized her fingers were lingering, she snatched them away and yanked open the bathroom door.

She walked down the short hall, keeping her gaze from wandering through the open door of what could only be his bedroom, and went back into the living room. He'd turned on the gas fireplace. She was pretty sure it was for her benefit. When they'd gotten to his apartment, she'd been shaking so hard her teeth were chattering.

The sight of him standing in the kitchen at the stove, spatula in hand, was unexpected.

"I thought you couldn't boil water."

He glanced at her. "You think I'd get as many home-cooked meals as I do if I let anyone know otherwise?" He turned back to the stove, flipped whatever he was preparing, then turned to her again. "Your shoes are by the couch. I couldn't see any blood on them. But I pulled out a pair of my socks if you'd rather just use those for now."

Sure enough, a clean pair of thick white gym socks was sitting on the couch.

Her feet weren't particularly cold. If anything the apartment was feeling almost too warm.

It was possible that was a hangover from the lengthy shower. Or it could have been the fact that she was buck naked under her scrubs within touching range of Caleb Buchanan.

She sat on the couch and picked up the socks. "I don't think I left you any hot water."

"I'll live." He came around the breakfast counter with a plate containing a golden-brown sandwich cut in two. "Grilled cheese. It's about the only thing I had in the place." He set the plate on the side table next to the couch. Then he took the chair opposite her. "I talked to Leandra while you were in the shower. They were having supper. Evan took in another litter of animals. Kittens this time. Needless to say, the kids are having a great time."

"Perfect. More cute baby animals." She glanced around. "Speaking of—"

"Bingo's outside."

"It's not too cold for her?"

He looked amused. "If you're worried, I'll buy her one of those doggy sweaters."

Her cheeks warmed. She blamed it on the heat coming from the gas logs in the fireplace. "You were the one who grew up with dogs. My mother never allowed one. Said—"

"They'd scare the chickens out of laying eggs. I remember. I also called the hospital. Your Maria and her baby are doing well. Or as well as they can be under the circumstances." He held out the plate. "Eat."

Kelly didn't have the energy to argue. So she took half and nibbled on one corner, because she could see he wasn't going to give it a rest otherwise. "I pretty much lived on grilled cheese sandwiches when I first started nursing school. Tyler was still on baby food then." She took another bite of sandwich.

"What *did* spur the career choice?"

"Don't you mean what spurred a girl like me to pursue *any* sort of career?"

He gave her a look.

She polished off the first half of the sandwich. As far as grilled cheese went, his was better than some. "Well, it's true, whether you are too polite to say so or not."

"Jesus, Kelly."

She lifted her hand. "Until I left Weaver, my greatest ambition had been to be Doc Cobb's receptionist. I was the ultimate small-town girl with small-town dreams."

"There's nothing wrong with that."

"And you chose someone else over me. Someone who had aspirations just as big as yours."

He sighed. "Kelly—"

"I'm not trying to pick an argument."

"Oh, yeah?"

She couldn't blame him for his skepticism. She managed a faint smile. "Maybe tomorrow I'll have the energy to still hate you for that." Right now, her entire body—head to toe—smelled of his clean, spicy soap.

"Don't blame me if I don't want tomorrow to come, then." He smiled faintly, too. "So what changed? The guy you left Weaver for?"

God help her. "Having Tyler changed everything," she said finally. Truthfully. If it was only part of the truth.

"The advent of children always does."

There was a faint roaring in her ears. She opened her mouth to tell him. Just tell him. But she still couldn't make the words come.

"Here." He held out the plate again. "Finish that."

She shook her head. "I really can't."

He looked ready to argue. But then he just took the remaining half of the sandwich and ate it in two bites before taking the plate back into the kitchen. "If you're feeling better now, I'll take you back to get your car."

As a hint that he was ready to get rid of her, it was pretty plain.

She swallowed the unwanted pang of disappointment and bent over to pull on his socks. "I can find someone else to give me a ride." She glanced up at him when he came back into the living room. "You've already done a lot. I guess you must not have had any appointments this after—" She broke off, realizing he was staring at her a little fixedly.

Then she flushed, slapping her hand against the gaping vee of the top that had allowed him a straight-on view of her bare breasts. She sat upright and propped her foot on her knee to finish pulling on the second sock.

The corner of his mouth quirked. "You can't blame me for looking."

Nor could she blame him for the way her nipples had gone so tight they ached. But she wanted to.

She dropped her foot onto the floor and stood.

"And you don't need to find someone else to take you out to your car," he continued. "I'm gonna get the dog." He turned back toward the kitchen.

She snatched at the shoulders of her shirt, dragging them back as far as they'd go so as to draw up the neckline another inch.

The puppy tore through the kitchen and living room when Caleb opened the door, disappearing down the hall and then returning just as quickly to sniff around Kelly's feet, probably wondering why her master's socks were on someone else. Kelly started to lean over to pet the dog, only to feel her top gape again. So she scooped up the warm little body and stood, lifting her face away from Bingo's enthusiastic kisses. "Yeah, you're a good puppy, but the tongue's out of control."

"Here." Caleb dropped his jacket over her shoulders.

She held the collar closed beneath her chin, maneuvering the puppy from beneath the enveloping leather. "I started out the day with a coat," she told him. "I guess I left it in my car. And my purse," she realized suddenly. "The car keys." Dismay swamped her. "I left everything just sitting there." On the side of the highway where she'd pulled off at the scene of the accident. "Oh, my God. What if it's not even there? I left an open—"

His mouth covered hers.

"—invitation," she mumbled stupidly against his lips.

His hand cupped the back of her head. "It's going to be fine," he murmured.

Bingo was squirming between them.

"How do you know?"

His hand brushed hers as he took the puppy and let her jump down onto the couch. Then his arm slid behind Kelly's back, pulling her closer. So close that she could feel every hard inch of him against her. "Because I know Sam Dawson. She probably has your stuff safe and sound at the sheriff's station. Now will you be quiet for a minute?"

She huffed slightly, but that was all he needed. He angled her head slightly. And kissed her in earnest.

Her head whirled.

The whole world whirled.

"Caleb—"

He lifted his head just long enough for a soft "shh" before touching his lips to hers again.

Lightly. Teasingly.

Achingly.

"Caleb, we can't do this." So why were her fingers sifting through his rich, dark hair?

His lips worked their way toward her ear. "Feels like we can." His hand brushed over her breast, and desire swamped her. "I like the way you look in scrubs."

She shuddered. "They're too big."

"Easier to get under." His hand swept beneath the fabric of her top, and his palm found her breast. "See?"

She couldn't stop the sound that came out of her throat any more than she could stop the ripples dancing down her spine. Which got more intense as he loosened the tie at her waist.

She inhaled sharply when his fingers made their way inside her waistband, then slowly inched down her belly.

And lower still.

She groaned. Because nearly every cell inside her wanted him to keep going, to keep doing exactly what he was doing for about a hundred years. Except for a part of her brain that shrieked, "Oh, no, not again," so annoyingly loudly that she managed to plant her palm against his hard chest and push far enough away that she could yank the tie at her waist tight. "We can't go back to the past, Caleb. *I* can't go back to the past."

He lifted her chin, preventing her from escaping. His eyes—the only eyes she'd ever dreamed of looking into for a lifetime—stared into hers. "I don't want to go back." His voice was low. Deep.

Seductive.

She willed her knees against failing.

"We were just kids before," he continued. "Foolish kids who didn't know what the hell we were doing. Me, most of all."

He wasn't a kid now. And he knew exactly what he was doing: seducing her with nothing more than the deep, deep sound of his voice.

His thumb slowly stroked over her lower lip. "And now I don't want the past to stop us from going forward."

Something inside her yawned wide. And her knees did fail. The only thing keeping her upright was the gentle touch of his hands cradling her face.

He exhaled, closed his eyes and pressed his forehead against hers. "I went out to the farm this afternoon, and when you weren't there, I was afraid you'd gone again. Left."

Her eyes prickled. "I only had an appointment in Braden."

"I know that now." He lifted his head again. Looked at her. "But until I did, I didn't like the feeling. I just want more time with you. To figure this out. To see where we can go."

Her breath shuddered out of her chest. They could go nowhere.

Because all roads led to Tyler.

"There's so much you don't know," she whispered.

His mouth brushed over hers, feeling almost as light as air. "Then give me a chance to find out." He let go of her face, leaving her to feel like she was swaying in the wind. He grabbed the jacket from the carpet where it had fallen and put it around her shoulders again.

"You won't like me when you do." Her voice sounded raw.

"Pretty slim chance of that."

"Tyler is—"

"—waiting. I know."

"That's not what I meant. I—"

"Kelly, I get it. He's your priority. That's the way it should be."

She shook her head. "No. No, you *don't* get it. You don't get it at all, Caleb. Yes, Tyler is my priority." Her eyes flooded. "He's my world." She swallowed against the knot in her throat. "And he's your son."

Chapter Ten

He's your son.

The words circled in the air.

Inside Caleb's head.

Inside his chest.

Exhilaration. Shock. Disbelief.

He felt it all.

And then some.

He realized he was digging his fingers into Kelly's shoulders and abruptly let her go. He turned away, shoving his fingers through his hair.

Tyler was his son.

He suddenly turned back on her. "That's why your mom lied? Made up a damn husband for you that never existed?"

Kelly's eyes widened, looking darker than ever against her pale complexion. "No! My mother never knew."

He snorted. "Right."

"If she'd known I was pregnant with your child, she'd have pushed us both down the aisle with a shotgun at our backs, counting her good fortune every step of the way."

"What good fortune?"

"Getting her hooks into your family! 'Those people,'" she said in a harsh, mocking tone, "'those people take care of their own. They'll take care of all of us.' That's what she would have said." Kelly waved her arms and the jacket fell onto the carpet yet again. "Take care of *her*. That's what she would have really meant. She never wanted me, and she couldn't have given two figs about my baby."

"Our baby," he corrected. His legs abruptly gave out, and he sat down hard on the couch. *Our baby.* His throat felt tight. "How?" He didn't need to ask when. *When* was indelibly printed on his memory.

"How do you think?" Her eyes were glittering with tears. "The usual way. You were there. You ought to remember."

He remembered every moment. Every detail, from the time her headlights washed over him when she pulled up behind him on the side of the highway to the snow that piled on the outside of her windshield and the steam that clouded it from the inside.

He could recall every breath. Every touch. He could recall thanking God that she'd finally forgiven him, because if she hadn't, she wouldn't be pushing that little foil packet into his hands while she shimmied out of her jeans and pulled open his fly. If she hadn't, she wouldn't have sunk down on him, gloving him more perfectly than ever, obliterating everything else in the world but the feel of her body on his.

Oh, yeah, he remembered.

Every. Single. Moment.

From start to finish, when she was shutting her truck door in his face, telling him that now, *now*, it was her turn to walk away.

"We used a condom."

She grimaced. "And here we stand, discussing the very proof that condoms have been known to fail. We're a statistic. Just like a quarter of the patients my boss has." She laughed, but there was not a speck of humor in it. "The odds were against us, I suppose. After—how many times were we together in high school? Dozens?"

Hundreds.

He didn't say it, though.

She knew just as well as he did.

"We might as well have been playing Russian roulette."

"Except we got a son out of it. You should have told me."

She propped her hands on her slender hips. Hips that had carried *his* child. "What would you have done, Caleb?"

"Married you!"

She spread her hands. "And there's your answer."

"When you were eighteen you *wanted* to marry me!"

"And you wanted to marry me," she returned swiftly. Her cheeks were red, her eyes suddenly flashing. "At least that's what we talked about before you headed off to college. I'd wait for you. When you were finished, when the time was right, we'd be together until we were old and gray. Matching rocking chairs on the front porch," she finished harshly. "Only you changed your mind. You still wanted that. Just not with me. Tell me, Caleb, why, *why* would I want a proposal from you after that, when I knew it was only coming because I was pregnant!"

"You could have said no." God knew that by then he'd had practice having one marriage proposal tossed back in his face.

"Yes, you'd think, wouldn't you?" She swiped her cheeks and sat in the chair, wearily hunching over to rub her temples.

He looked away from the perfect view he had down the front of her loose shirt. Taking in the womanly shape of her pink-tipped breasts wasn't helping his situation any. Because even if he wanted to shake her, he still wanted her. Period.

"I never expected you to be here in Weaver." Her voice was husky. "I never expected—"

"To have to tell me the truth."

"To feel guilty that I hadn't told you in the very beginning." She sat up, and there were fresh tears on her cheeks. "I'm sorry. When I left Weaver—" She pressed her lips together for a moment. "When I left, I was only doing what I needed to do at the time. I couldn't stay under my mother's roof another moment. Couldn't bring my child—*our* child—into that world. I didn't know much." Her throat worked. "But I knew that."

"You didn't have to leave Weaver."

"Yes," she whispered. "I did."

A son. He and Kelly had a son.

A cute kid. Tall for his age.

Caleb pressed his palms into his eye sockets. "Doc Cobb? He knew?"

"No." Then she sighed. "I don't know. Maybe he suspected. Not about you, but about the baby. The day I left home, I drove as far as Billings."

"Why Montana?"

"It was the opposite direction of where you were in Colorado."

He dropped his hands, silently absorbing the sting of that.

"I had to call Doc Cobb to resign, though. He gave me the job in his office when the only thing I'd ever done was check groceries." She swiped her cheeks again and then stared at her fingers as if she couldn't figure out why they were wet. "He tried talking me into coming back. When I wouldn't, he told me to go to Idaho. He gave me the number of someone he knew. He said Dr. Maguire owed him a favor and would make sure I found a job. Doc Cobb made me promise to go there. He said I would be okay, and…and I was."

"So there was no guy." Her comments at the diner ran through his mind. "The one who didn't propose to you was me."

Her lashes lifted. Her eyes met his. "I ended up renting a room from one of the nurses at the complex where Dr. Maguire's practice was located. After Tyler was born, Dorothy and the other nurses helped watch him when I was in class. I became a nurse because of them. And I couldn't have done it without them. I got my license a couple years ago. I still work at Dr. Maguire's. Only now I don't clean bathrooms and mop floors. Tyler and I have an apartment. It's not as big as this—" she waved her arm "—but it's in a safe neighborhood and close to his school. His best friend, Gunnar, lives next door."

"The perfect life." His voice was flat.

"Not perfect," she said thickly. "But *good*. I made something good. For Tyler and for me. Doc Cobb put me in the right direction, but *I* did it."

And on any other day, in any other situation, he'd have applauded her for that.

"You should have told me," he repeated.

"Well, I didn't," she retorted. "But now I have. So now what?" Her brief spurt of attitude expended, she slumped back into the corner of the chair. Her hair was starting to dry in untidy waves around her pinched face, and the scrubs hung on her slender shoulders.

Bingo rubbed against her leg, suddenly hopping onto her lap. She circled once, plopped down and started licking Kelly's hand. Maybe just for the salty tears. Or maybe to offer the comfort that Caleb couldn't.

"I don't know what we do now. But you're not taking my son back to Idaho."

Her jaw tightened. "Is that a threat?"

He shoved to his feet. "I don't know what it is," he said. "Except a fact." He snatched up the jacket and tossed it over the arm of her chair. "Get up. I'll take you to your car."

She nudged Bingo to one side and stood. "I don't want your jacket."

"Well, that's too damn bad, Kelly. Put it on or I'll put it on for you."

Her jaw set and she stared him down. "I'm not scared of you, Caleb Buchanan."

"Then that makes one of us." He flipped the switch on the fireplace, extinguishing the flame in one quick motion.

It struck him as particularly fitting.

He yanked open the front door and gave a short, sharp whistle that had Bingo immediately bouncing from the chair to prance around his boots.

Giving Caleb a glare that would have done her mother proud, Kelly stomped past him wearing nothing on her feet but a pair of his white athletic socks. She went straight to his truck, which he'd left unlocked, yanked open the passenger door and climbed inside to sit with her arms crossed tightly over her chest.

And that's the way she was still sitting when they finally reached her car, still parked on the side of the highway outside town.

The vehicles involved in the collision had been towed away. The sun had given up the ghost, but his headlights showed that there was no leftover debris.

They also illuminated the puffy white flakes of snow that had started falling.

He signaled and pulled off, stopping a few feet behind her car.

She immediately unsnapped her safety belt and pushed open the door. Clearly she wasn't inclined to linger there and appreciate the parallels to that night six years ago when he'd been stranded. She clutched her purse against her waist as she hopped out. Just as he'd predicted, it had been safely waiting for her at the sheriff's station when he'd stopped there on the way out of town.

"I told you that you wouldn't like me."

Then she closed the door and strode to her car, somehow managing to look almost regal as she did so, even though she was wearing his socks instead of shoes and his jacket kept sliding off her shoulder.

There was no traffic on the highway, so he pulled up next to her car, rolling down the passenger window. "I'm following you to Leandra's."

She looked over her shoulder at him. "And then what?"

He wished to hell he knew.

Since he didn't, he just rolled up the window and

waited for her to get in her car. A moment later, her
headlights came on. She edged off the shoulder, then
hit the gas.

The Perry barn was nothing more than a dark shadow
in the night when Kelly passed it on the way to Leandra's
place. Caleb's headlights hadn't slacked off for a single
mile of the drive. She hadn't really expected that they
would.

The look of shock on his face when she'd told him
about Tyler was going to stay with her for the rest of her
life.

Shock.

And betrayal.

He would never forgive her.

Do you blame him? The caustic voice circling inside
her head taunted her mercilessly. *What did you expect?
For him to shrug his quarterback-size shoulders and
tell you no worries? Everything's just hunky-dory? Go
on about your life?*

She turned into the Taggarts' drive. Before she could
get out of her car, though, Leandra was hustling out
of her house. She darted across the drive and peered
through the car window Kelly rolled down. "Tried
phoning you but couldn't get through on your cell.
Tyler's sound asleep. Do you want to just leave him
here for the night?" She peered at the truck pulling up
on her tail. "I know Caleb's overprotective of you, but
he followed you here?"

It wasn't overprotectiveness at all.

Not of her, anyway.

"I don't want to impose more than I have already."

Leandra dismissed that with a wave of her hand.
"Don't be silly." She straightened again, swiping a

snowflake off her face as she watched Caleb get out of his truck. "You convince her," she said.

"Of what?"

Kelly hoped she was the only one who heard the dark tone in his voice.

"To let Ty spend the night. He's already asleep in Lucas's bunk bed." She shot Kelly a grin. "My son even gave up his top bunk for him. They have a total little-boy bromance going. Lucas is going to be completely bummed when you two go back to Idaho."

"They're not going back."

Kelly pushed open her car door. "Don't listen to him. Yes, we are." The gravel driveway poked uncomfortably into her stocking feet. "And it is nice of you to offer, but I really should take Tyler. I think he'd be upset in the morning when he realizes I didn't come to get him."

"Well, I understand that." Leandra angled her head, giving Kelly's feet a look. "Just wait here. Evan can carry him out."

"I'll do it." Caleb gave Kelly a hard look, forestalling her instinctive protest. She swallowed her misgivings for the nonsense that they were.

What did she think he was going to do?

Take him away from her right there at his cousin's house?

Leandra was frowning, turning her speculative attention from Caleb as he strode inside the house back to Kelly. "Everything all right?"

No. But she nodded anyway. "It's been a long day."

"I heard about the accident. Terrible thing. But the baby's okay. That's what Caleb told me. Horrible to have to grow up without his daddy, but—" She broke off suddenly and slipped her arm comfortingly around Kelly's shoulders. "Honey, don't cry."

"I'm sorry." She swiped away the tears that had escaped despite her best efforts, wishing the ground would open up and swallow her to put her out of her misery.

"You've had a hell of a day. On top of a hell of a week. And now you have the auction next week?" Leandra patted her shoulder comfortingly. "It's enough to bring a grown woman to her knees."

She'd actually managed to forget about the auction. She hadn't even told anyone yet that it was officially scheduled. "How'd you—"

"You know how word travels. Evan had a woman here picking out a kitten just before supper. Husband is one of the appraisers for the company you're using. You picked a good company," Leandra assured her. "They'll be fair."

The door to the house opened, and Kelly braced herself for the sight of Caleb carrying her sleeping boy.

But she needn't have, because Tyler was awake and walking under his own steam.

Stomping was more like it.

When he reached her, his lower lip was pushed out. "I wanted to spend the night, Mom."

So much for believing he'd be upset in the morning.

"Maybe another time." She was painfully aware of Caleb looming over them. "Tell Mrs. Taggart thank you."

For a moment, Kelly was afraid he was going to argue. Particularly when he set his jaw just so. But he looked up at Leandra. "Thank you, Mrs. Taggart."

She crouched down in front of him. "You're very welcome, Mr. Rasmussen. But next time, you can call me Leandra. Okay?" She tapped his nose lightly. "Maybe your mommy will bring you by tomorrow to play after Lucas is home from kindergarten. I'm sure he'd like that a lot."

He nodded, and Leandra rose. "Sunday dinner's at our place this weekend, too. Whole family will be here. You remember what that's like. Caleb should bring you guys on along whether we see you before then or not. It'll be fun."

Kelly opened her mouth to decline but never had a chance.

"We'll be here," Caleb said.

She could hear the inflexibility in his tone and hoped his cousin didn't, as well. Rather than argue with him about it, Kelly pulled open the rear door of the car. "In you go, Tyler. It's late."

"I wanna see the kittens again."

"You can see them another day."

"I wanna see them *now*."

Kelly's hand clenched over the top of the car door. "You're not going to see anything now. It's late. Get in the car."

"No!"

It wasn't Tyler's first willful display, and it certainly wouldn't be his last. But she wished to heaven and back again that this one could have happened without witnesses.

Particularly Caleb.

She gave her son a steady look. "Would you like a time-out?"

"No! I wanna see the kittens!"

"Tyler." Caleb's voice was firm.

Her son's head jerked up as he looked at Caleb.

"Listen to your mother."

Tyler's shoulders sank. He ducked his head a little and clambered into the car, wriggling onto his booster seat.

Her eyes stung. Sure. A few stern words and Caleb could accomplish miracles.

Knowing it was a childish thought didn't prevent her from having it. Once Tyler was strapped in, she closed the car door with a little more force than was necessary. She only had to take three steps and she could slide behind the wheel of her car, but they were enough to allow gravel to poke sharply into the soles of her stocking feet.

"Good night, Leandra. Thanks again for taking care of Tyler."

"My pleasure."

Then Kelly looked in Caleb's direction. "Good night, Caleb. We'll talk later." As an attempt to keep him at a distance, it was pretty weak. His cousin might be there watching all of this, but Kelly knew that meant nothing. A determined Caleb was not going to be held at bay. And he'd already made it quite clear that—where Tyler was concerned—he was very determined.

Wouldn't you be?

She ignored the voice and yanked the door closed, quickly starting the engine. Already, there was a thin coat of snowflakes on her windshield, and she flipped on the wipers before driving away.

She didn't relax until she was once again passing the old Perry place. So far, there hadn't been any headlights following her.

It was a reprieve.

The only question was, how long would that reprieve last?

Knowing Caleb, not long.

Chapter Eleven

"I'm afraid I have some bad news."

Kelly looked across the desk at Tom Hook, the attorney handling her mom's estate. Her lips twisted a little as she glanced at Tyler. He was sitting in the chair next to her, coloring in his robot book. She'd told Caleb the truth less than twenty-four hours earlier. And she hadn't heard from him since she'd driven away from Leandra's home the night before.

Maybe he'd given her a reprieve, but it was feeling more like a sentence.

She looked back at Tom. She'd come in to his office to give him the paperwork from the auction house. "Of course you do," she said with dark humor. Why would her luck change now?

"Your mother took out a mortgage on the house. We discovered it during the title search."

"A mortgage," Kelly parroted. It took a moment for

the man's words to penetrate. Then she sat up straighter. "A mortgage! What on earth for?" The house—and the land on which it sat—had been in her mom's family for three generations now. It had been paid for long, long ago.

"I would assume for the money," the attorney said, somewhat tongue-in-cheek.

She didn't take offense. It hadn't been one of her more intelligent questions.

He shuffled some papers on his desk, found one and handed it across to her. "Signed several years ago."

She studied the sheet of paper. It was a lot of mumbo jumbo to her. But one thing looked simple. There was, indeed, a mortgage on the house.

A staggering one.

She set the paper on the desk and smoothed it needlessly with her fingers. "Is the house *worth* that much?"

"I wouldn't think so." His sun-weathered face had a matter-of-fact expression that matched his tone. "Selling the land for a good price will help offset the mortgage. If the personal property—contents of the house, farm equipment and such—brings enough at auction, there should be enough to move things into the black. The good news in all of this is that it reduces the overall value of your mother's estate considerably. Which means I can try for a summary probate. If she'd left a will, it would have helped, but I'm afraid you're going to see even less of an inheritance than I'd initially thought."

"I never cared about an inheritance," she murmured. "Not for me." For Tyler, perhaps. It would have been nice to sock away a little extra for his education. "Is there at least going to be enough to pay your bill once all is said and done?"

His face creased in a faint smile. "Burial costs and administrative fees are paid out of the estate. I wouldn't worry about that if I were you. But estates are often tricky business. Your mother made hers more so simply by not being forthright with me. We have to wonder if there are other surprises out there."

"She wasn't forthright with anyone," Kelly said. "I wouldn't take it personally if I were you." She looped her purse strap over her shoulder and stood. "I don't want to take up any more of your afternoon, Mr. Hook. I appreciate everything you've been doing." She made a face. "I'm still not entirely sure why it's worth your time, but I'm grateful all the same." She nudged Tyler, opening her purse so he could dump his stuff inside. "Come on, buddy."

The attorney got up and came around his desk. His scuffed boots and jeans were more suited to the small ranch he also ran than the legal profession. "Well, Georgette and I went way back. I'm glad to help."

That information brought Kelly up short. The attorney hadn't even lived in Weaver six years ago when she'd left, yet they went "way back"?

"How'd you know my mother?"

"We met at summer church camp in Montana when we were teenagers," he said, looking reminiscent.

"Church camp!" Kelly tried to imagine. "I can count on one hand the number of times my mom stepped foot in a church."

He smiled slightly. "Well, at the time we were all more interested in fishing and swimming than saying our prayers. Georgette was quite something, though. You resemble her a lot."

"Not sure that's a good thing," Kelly murmured. "Was she happy then? When you knew her?" It suddenly seemed important to know.

His smile widened. "She always seemed to be. Your mother was very full of life." Then he opened the door for her and Tyler, escorting them into the room of his house that doubled as a waiting area. "I'll be in touch after the auction. You're still planning to return to Idaho Falls immediately afterward?"

That had been the plan.

Until last night, when she tossed everything into a bingo cage to be spun around and around and around.

"I am not sure," she admitted. "But you have my cell number regardless." She donned a smile she was far from feeling and grabbed Tyler's hand before he could go off exploring. "Though it works a lot better in Idaho Falls than it does in Weaver. Thanks again for your time." She nodded briefly at the woman sitting in one of the nail-studded leather chairs as they left.

Outside, the ground was dry with no sign left of last night's brief snowfall, but the wind felt icy. It was a needless reminder that she still had Caleb's jacket.

She tied the belt of her wool coat more firmly around her waist. "Zip up your coat, buddy."

Tyler did as he was told. "What're we gonna do now?"

She honestly didn't know.

But he wasn't talking about their lives.

Simply the afternoon.

"What would *you* like to do?" His attitude of the night before had dissipated under the weight of a good night's sleep, and he was his usual chipper self again. "Gunnar's probably home from kindergarten by now. Do you want to call and talk to him again?"

He shook his head. "I wanna visit Dr. C and Bingo."

Of course he did.

She managed to keep her smile in place. "Dr. C is at his office seeing patients this afternoon."

"With Bingo?"

"I doubt it, bud."

"Can we go see him?"

"Bingo?" She shook her head. "Not while Dr. C is at work."

"Then can we go see Dr. C?"

They'd reached the car, and she pulled open the rear door for him to climb inside. "You like him a lot, don't you."

Tyler nodded. He was sticking out his tongue slightly as he concentrated on fastening his safety belt.

A wave of love plowed through her, and she brushed her fingers lightly through his dark brown hair. She couldn't survive if she ever lost him. "Why?"

He shrugged. "'Cause he's nice. Can we have ice cream?"

"Sure."

He goggled. "*Really?*"

"Yes, really. We passed a new ice cream shop on our way here. We can stop in and have some there. But after ice cream, you have to finish some of your worksheets from your teacher."

He started to push out his lower lip but stopped. "Are you gonna marry Dr. C?"

She gaped. "*What?* Why would you think that?" The only opportunity Caleb would have had to say something to Tyler was the night before when he'd gone inside Leandra's house to get him. "What did he say to you?"

"Who?"

"Dr. C!"

"He didn't say nothing."

"Then why would you ask me that?"

This time, he did thrust his lip out. "Lucas said if you got married, then we could live in Weaver."

Kelly's outrage whooshed from her like a pinpricked balloon, and she leaned against the open car door for support. "Lucas."

"He says then I could go to school with him."

"Wouldn't you miss Gunnar?"

Tyler frowned as if it were a new consideration. "Gunnar could come and live with us."

"Gunnar has a family in Idaho. I think his mommy would miss him a lot." Her chest suddenly felt tight and she kissed his face. "Same way I would miss you a lot if you weren't with me."

He scrunched his nose. "Why do I gotta do worksheets?"

From marriage to homework. She wished she could switch her thoughts so easily. "So that when we get back home, you've done all the work that Gunnar and your other classmates have been doing while we've been here."

"If I went to school with Lucas, I bet I wouldn't have worksheets."

She wasn't going to get into that debate with him. "What kind of ice cream do you want?" It was a deliberate distraction on her part, but she wasn't going to feel guilty over it.

"Strawberry," he said immediately. "With sprinkles on top."

"Strawberry with sprinkles it is." She checked the buckle on Tyler's seat belt, got behind the wheel and set off.

They were just sitting down in a booth at the Udder Huddle when her cell phone rang. Her nerves tightened as she looked at the display. A local number, but not the one Caleb had used the day before. She thumbed the phone and answered.

"Is this Kelly Rasmussen?" The voice was unfamiliar. Male.

She leaned over to tuck a napkin in Tyler's shirt collar. "Yes."

"Dan Yarnell here."

She sat up straighter, surprised. "Dr. Yarnell. Hello."

"I got your number from one of the nurses here at the hospital. I apologize for disturbing your afternoon."

"Not at all." She tucked the phone against her shoulder. "How are Maria and her baby?"

"Physically, they're doing well. That's why I called. I wondered if you'd be willing to visit Maria. I know it's an imposition when I hear you're in town only briefly, but—"

"It's okay." After having grown up in Weaver, she didn't know why she still felt surprised that virtual strangers seemed to know her business. "I'd be happy to visit Maria. Are you releasing her soon?"

"Ordinarily, I would tomorrow. But she doesn't have any family, and given the circumstances of losing her husband, I hope to delay it a few more days. I think she'll benefit from the support."

"I'll go by today," Kelly promised. She couldn't say she knew exactly how Maria felt, but she did know what it was like becoming a brand-new mother.

He thanked her and rang off.

"Who was that?"

"Dr. Yarnell. I met him yesterday at the hospital when I helped that nice lady I told you about have her baby." She leaned over the table yet again and plucked a trio of rainbow-colored sprinkles out of Tyler's hair. "How do you manage to get your food everywhere?"

He shrugged and kept licking his sprinkle-dipped ice cream cone. "Are we gonna go visit her?"

Kelly wasn't sure of the wisdom of taking him with her to the hospital, but the alternative wasn't any better. "After you finish your ice cream. You're going to have to behave yourself there just like you did at Mr. Hook's. Okay?"

"If I do, *then* can I go see Dr. C?"

She brushed another sprinkle out of Tyler's hair. "We'll see."

She had no doubt that Caleb intended to see them, whether she liked it or not.

It was simply a matter of when.

Like most everything Kelly was dreading, when came sooner than she expected.

She'd stopped at the hospital nursery after visiting Maria to peek at the baby through the viewing window.

But it was the sight of Caleb's broad shoulders wedged into one of the rocking chairs with a baby cradled against his chest that had her catching her breath. She'd never given him the opportunity to hold Tyler like that. And in that moment, it felt like an unforgivable sin.

"There's Dr. C," Tyler was saying excitedly. Even though she tried to forestall it, he knocked on the window and waved his cast to get Caleb's attention.

Caleb looked up and smiled faintly at Tyler, but his gaze collided with Kelly's, and for a long moment, it felt like the world slowed.

He handed off the blanket-swaddled infant to one of the nurses and all too quickly appeared in the corridor where Kelly's feet still felt rooted in cement.

"Hey, Dr. C!" Tyler was bouncing on his toes. "Can I come and play with Bingo again?"

"Calm down, buddy. We're in a hospital, remember?"

He crouched down a little as he bounced, as if that helped. "Can I come and play with Bingo again," he repeated in a loud whisper.

Despite herself, Kelly couldn't help smiling a little.

"You can play with Bingo whenever you want," Caleb assured him. "It'll be easy once you and your mom move here."

Tyler's jaw dropped.

Kelly's jaw went rigid, her spurt of amusement disappearing like smoke. "Dr. C is being premature," she said through her teeth.

Her son looked from her to Caleb and back again, an astonished expression on his face. "What's premature?"

She took Tyler's hand in hers. "It means too early." She glared at Caleb. "Way, *way* too early. We're not moving here."

In response, Caleb's expression was set.

"But, Mom. I could go to school with *Lucas*."

"You already have a school," she reminded him. "Come on. We need to go."

"But, Mom—"

"Now!" She tugged his hand slightly and turned her back on Caleb.

Caleb's voice followed her. "You're not going to walk away from this, Kelly."

She inhaled an angry hiss. She couldn't remember the last time she was so abruptly, hotly furious. For that matter, she couldn't remember if she'd *ever* been so furious. She pointed at a chair in the hallway, which thankfully remained empty. "Tyler, please sit there while I talk to Dr. C."

He looked alarmed. "Am I having time-out?"

"No." She tamped down her ire. "I just need to have an adult talk for a minute. Here." She took his coloring book and the baggie of markers out of her purse. "A few minutes. Please?"

He still looked suspicious, but he grabbed his stuff and went over to the chair.

She watched him flip through his coloring book while she counted to ten.

She made it to five before her temper had her returning to Caleb. "*What* do you think you're doing?" Tyler's proximity was the only reason she was able to keep her voice low.

"Stating a fact."

She very nearly stomped her foot. "I'm not going to be manipulated into moving back to Weaver."

"Then you'll be in Idaho Falls on your own." His voice was flat. "I told you already, you are not taking him to Idaho."

"And how exactly do you intend to stop me?" Her face was so hot, she thought flames might shoot out her ears. "You think you have any legal rights at this point in time? Your name's not even on his birth certificate." Even when she'd wanted to list his name, she couldn't. Not without his knowledge. His consent.

"And whose fault is that? You know I have moral rights or you would never have said a damn word! But you really want to take me on in court? Say the word, Kelly. I'll get a DNA test and—"

Small arms suddenly wrapped around her waist from behind. "Don't yell at my mom!"

Dismayed, Kelly whirled around and picked up Tyler. "It's okay, baby. He's not yelling."

"Yes, he is. And he's got a mad face." Tyler's expression was fierce and, to her distress, an exact replica of Caleb's. His arms circled tight around her neck. "I don't wanna play with Bingo no more," he said.

Kelly's chest ached. This wasn't what she'd wanted. She rubbed his back. He was so young. So impressionable. "Mommy and Da—" *Dear God.* "Mommy and Caleb are just having a disagreement. That's all. It's going to be fine. We'll work it out." She looked up at Caleb.

His lips were tight. His expression pained.

"We'll work it out," she said again. Pointedly. "Isn't that right, Caleb?"

"Yeah." His voice was rough. Low. "We'll work something out."

Tyler wasn't having any of it, though. His arms and legs squeezed even more tightly around her. His cast felt like a block digging into her spine. "I wanna go."

"We're going to go," she assured him. "Right now." She carried him over to the chair where his coloring book and markers were scattered. Bending down to gather them up was hugely awkward with him hanging on to her the way he was. She'd only succeeded in grasping a few pens in her free hand when Caleb crouched next to her.

"I've got 'em," he said gruffly.

Tyler's arms tightened again.

She swallowed and straightened. Any mother who'd ever thought she needed a gym for working out just needed to do a few deep knee bends while carrying around a strapping five-year-old boy instead.

It took only a few seconds for Caleb to stuff the bag of pens and the coloring book into the purse hanging off her shoulder.

"Thank you." Her voice was stiff, but she'd be an example of politeness for Tyler if it choked her.

"I'm coming by your place tonight. Be there."

In other words: *Don't bolt back to Idaho.*

Her lips tightened. But she nodded once.

And then she carried their son away.

His parents were staring at him, speechless.

Caleb sat on a chair in the living room where he'd grown up and rubbed the back of his aching neck. "Tyler's my son," he said again. "And I don't know what to do about it."

His mother finally looked at his father. "Cage?"

"What do you *want* to do, son?"

"I want to be his father!"

"And Kelly?"

He shook his head. Clenched his hands together. "She's his mother. What about her?"

He saw the look passing between his mom and dad.

"Are you sure that's all she is to you?" Belle's voice was gentle.

Since Kelly had told him about Tyler, he'd stopped being certain about anything. "There's too much water under that bridge. Too many hurts to get over."

His dad closed his hand over his mom's. They shared another look. "Don't be so sure about that," he said.

They were talking about ancient history. When Cage Buchanan had had ample reason to hate Belle Day and her family. Before he'd ended up marrying her.

"That was different," Caleb dismissed.

"Forgiveness is forgiveness," Belle said simply. "You know that. You just have to give yourself a minute to remember."

"She *should* have told me." He pushed off the chair to pace. "Just because I couldn't locate her doesn't mean she didn't know how to locate *me*. She could have reached out to anyone here in Weaver to find me if she'd wanted."

"You tried to locate her?"

His mother's eyebrows had risen slightly, and he damned his tongue. "Once," he said grudgingly, looking away only to encounter his father's steady gaze. "Okay, more than once," he admitted. "But I gave up a long time ago. Georgette told me to my face that Kelly'd gotten married. She didn't give away squat besides that and the fact that they were living in Idaho. You know how little that is to go on? I even trawled all the social media sites. Only thing I found was that you can't find someone on the internet if they're not on the internet!" He realized he was yelling and linked his fingers behind his neck. He exhaled. "Kelly wants to settle this in court? We'll settle it, all right."

"Oh, Caleb," Belle sighed. "Surely you can avoid that. Kelly told you the truth, after all. It's plain as day to me that you still care about her."

"If she'd cared about me, she would have told me before he was born!"

His mother's lips formed a firm line. She pushed to her feet and propped her hands on her hips. "Now you sound like you're ten years old and in a snit. Put yourself in her shoes for a moment, Caleb. That girl never had one single thing handed to her. She didn't have the opportunities you had. She certainly didn't have a family who stood behind her no matter what. You broke her heart when you were twenty years old!"

"She wasn't twenty when she got pregnant with Tyler," he said through his teeth. "Damn sure her heart wasn't broken then."

"You're saying she did it deliberately? Seduced you? Got pregnant for the express purpose of telling you years later?" His mother raised her eyebrows again.

That hadn't been what happened six years ago. He knew it. But he didn't appreciate having his mother point it out to him.

His neck felt hot.

His father wasn't any help. He just sat there looking vaguely amused. Like he got a kick out of his wife putting a pin in Caleb's righteousness.

Belle's expression softened. She touched his cheek. "You're a good man, Caleb. You've wanted to heal everyone's hurts since you were a little boy. You'll find your way through this, too."

He grimaced. "That's *your* grandson she's going to take back to Idaho after she has the auction next week."

"Idaho isn't the end of the earth. It's one state away. Nor does it have to be permanent. And who knows what you can accomplish before next week if you put your mind to finding a solution that works for you both."

Her words were still hanging inside his head when he stood beneath the bare bulb lighting Kelly's doorstep later that evening.

He'd deliberately waited until a time when he figured Tyler would be long asleep. He had some ground to make up with him, and it would be easier once he and Kelly came to an agreement.

Late as it was, though, he only had to knock once before the door creaked open. Kelly leaned her cheek against the edge of the door, looking up at him.

"Are you going to let me in?"

Her lashes lowered for a minute, hiding her brown gaze. "Are you going to threaten taking my son away from me?"

"You know I wouldn't really do that."

She looked up again. "Really? Just how would I know that, Caleb?"

He exhaled, counting silently to ten.

She exhaled, too, and stepped back, opening the door wider in invitation. "I put Tyler to bed hours ago."

"Good." He stepped across the threshold and followed her into the living room. Unlike the last time he'd been there, the room now seemed nearly bare. Stripped down to only old furnishings and a few toys that were obviously Tyler's. "There's a simple solution to all of this."

She stood in the middle of the room, hugging her arms around her waist. "What?"

"Marry me."

Chapter Twelve

Kelly winced.

They were exactly the words she'd once longed to hear.

And ever since that stick had turned blue six years ago, they were exactly the words she still dreaded.

"No," she said. "That's not a solution at all."

He gave her an annoyed look. "Of course it is."

"Look. I'll—" She moistened her lips. "I'll consider… *consider*," she repeated for emphasis, "staying in Weaver." She'd been thinking of nothing else since running into him at the hospital. Since seeing him rocking that infant. "Because whether I like it or…or not, you are Tyler's father. And I don't want to deprive him of that. He should have a father."

"Big of you."

Her lips tightened. "Comments like that aren't inclined to make me want to stay here. You should want my cooperation. Otherwise you'll have to go to the trouble of proving paternity."

"You think I wouldn't?"

She sighed wearily and sank down on the corner of the lumpy couch. Because, of course, she knew that Caleb would do whatever it took. "I'm not marrying you."

"Why the hell not? We have a son together!"

"Mommy?"

Horrified, she bolted off the couch, turning to see Tyler—his hair sticking up like a rooster's tail—standing in the kitchen doorway.

"I woke up. My stomach was growly."

She quickly rounded the couch, going over to him. Maybe he *hadn't* heard. She was going to need to tell him, but not like this. She crouched down next to him. "Would you like some milk?"

The boy's gaze was locked on Caleb. He shook his head, so serious and solemn in his robot-patterned pajamas. "Are you my dad?"

Her heart sank through the floor. She'd never felt so helpless. Not even when she'd held a dying man's hand. "Tyler—"

"I am," Caleb said. His voice sounded impossibly deep. But it was calm. And the look he was giving Tyler was steady. "I didn't know that until last night, though."

"How come?"

Caleb's eyes met hers. "Because I wasn't around for your mommy to tell me."

A knot filled her throat.

"But I know now," he added, focusing on Tyler once more. "And that's what counts."

Tyler leaned against Kelly's shoulder. "I don't want a dad," he said.

She caught him in a hug. "Yes, you do," she said thickly. It was her fault this was happening. Her fault that her sweet, protective boy was even thinking such a thing. "It's just a lot to take in right now. But you want a father." Every child who didn't have one did. She knew that from personal experience. "And your father wants you," she said huskily, her eyes burning. She couldn't bear to look at Caleb as she kissed Tyler's forehead. "But it's very late and you should be asleep. Do you want some milk?"

He nodded wordlessly and looped his arms around her shoulders in a sure sign that he wanted to be carried.

She obliged, lifting him as she straightened.

She set Tyler on the counter in the kitchen and poured him a small glass of milk.

"Is he gonna stay?"

She didn't need to look to know that Caleb had followed them from the living room. "No."

"Yes," Caleb countered. He pulled one of the kitchen chairs out from the table and sat.

Her nerves jangled. But she contained the immediate knee-jerk reaction to argue. That could wait until Tyler was out of earshot. So she waited for him to finish drinking his milk and tried not to show any impatience when the process took about three times longer than it usually did.

But finally, he was handing her back the empty glass.

She rinsed it and left it in the sink, then lifted him off the counter and carried him up the narrow stairs.

At the top, she turned toward her old bedroom. Tyler buried his head against her neck. "I don't want Dr. C as a dad," he said.

"Shush," she whispered. "I know you don't really mean that. You like Dr. C. You like him a whole lot.

You told me so yourself. You're just upset right now. But you're going to get over that, the same way you get over it whenever you and Gunnar fight about whose turn it is to pitch when you're playing baseball." She lowered him onto the bed.

"He made you sad."

"That's not something I want you worrying about. That's for mommies to worry about. Not little boys."

"I'm a big boy."

"Getting bigger by the day," she whispered. She brushed his hair away from his forehead. "Do you want me to lie down with you until you fall asleep?"

He nodded.

"Scoot over, then."

He wriggled over several inches, and she stretched out beside him.

"Mommy?"

"What, buddy?"

"I wish Grandma Gette didn't die so we didn't have to come here."

She wished that, too. They'd been in Weaver a week now.

It felt like a year.

"Everything's going to be okay, Tyler. I promise."

"I don't like it when you're sad."

"I'm not sad." It was a lie, but she would live up to it somehow. There was no way she was going to let him feel any sort of burden like that. She kissed his forehead. "Now close your eyes. If you can't go to sleep, just pretend you're sleeping." It was an old trick. But it had never failed her before.

And that night, despite everything, it succeeded as usual. Before ten minutes had passed, he'd rolled away from her to sprawl across the mattress, snoring softly.

She carefully inched off the bed and left the room, pulling the door nearly shut.

Caleb was still in the kitchen when she went back down the stairs.

He'd found the bottle of whiskey that she'd opened only days ago.

His eyes roved over her when she sat down at the table. With one long finger, he pushed one of the two glasses he'd set on the table toward her.

She picked it up. Studied the amber liquid through the clear glass. "I'll marry you."

He gave a clear start of surprise, and she tossed back the whiskey.

It burned all the way down. But at least it gave her something on which to blame her tears.

"Why the change of heart?"

It was hardly a celebratory chant on his part.

She waited until the burning in her throat subsided enough to allow her vocal cords to work. "I don't want Tyler thinking he has to choose between me and you." She grabbed the bottle and poured another measure into her glass. "And don't kid yourself. He's my baby. He'd choose me." She blinked hard. "But he deserves more than that. He deserves everything." Her voice went hoarse, and she lifted the glass again to clink against his. "So cheers. You win. You'll get your son, whom you want, and a wife that you don't."

Caleb looked pained. "Kelly."

If she sat there any longer, she was going to be bawling like a damn baby.

She set down the whiskey that she had no interest in drinking and pushed out of the chair. "I haven't slept in my mother's room since we got here, but I guess it's time to start. If you're actually determined to stay, the couch is yours." She started up the stairs. "It's got lumps."

The couch did have lumps.

They weren't what kept Caleb awake all night, though. That was his conscience.

Ripping into him for pushing Kelly into a corner.

He withstood the lumps. And he withstood his conscience.

He waited the next morning until he heard sounds of movement upstairs before he scrawled a note on the backside of a page he pulled from Tyler's coloring book. He left it sitting on the kitchen table, weighted down by the bottle of whiskey that was nearly empty after he'd finished with it.

Then he let himself out the front door of the house. A bitter wind followed him to his truck and all the way back to town. He'd never believed in ghosts, but it felt as though Georgette herself was trying to chase him away.

Even though it was Saturday, he still had rounds at the hospital. He went to his place and let Bingo out. While she romped around the small yard, he showered and shaved. But he still couldn't wash off knowing he had somehow gotten what he wanted with Kelly without getting what he wanted at all.

He fed the dog. But when he started to leave for the hospital, she gave him such a sad, accusing look that he scooped her up, along with a blanket and the few toys she kept ignoring in favor of chewing on everything else, and carried her out to his truck. Instead of going straight to the hospital, though, he stopped off at Ruby's Café.

Sure enough, he found Tabby sitting at one of the tables, pregnant as pregnant could get, working on her payroll and her orders for the week. She agreed easily enough to watching the puppy for a few hours for him.

"Bingo and Beastie will keep each other entertained," she assured him.

So he left the puppy and her stuff in the recently fenced yard behind the restaurant, where Beastie was already romping around chasing a blowing leaf, and continued on his way to the hospital.

Not two hours had passed since he'd left Kelly's place when his cell phone rang.

He'd known she would call after she saw the note he'd left.

He stepped away from the nurses' station where he'd been updating a patient's chart and answered.

"I don't need an engagement ring," she said without preamble.

"You don't want one, you mean." Not from him. Not anymore.

"Isn't the wedding ring bad enough?"

The barb hit. "I told you in the note. I'll pick you and Tyler up this afternoon. We're driving to the jewelry store in Braden, getting rings and a marriage license."

"It's Saturday. What county clerk's office is open on a Saturday?"

"One that's run by the father of one of my patients."

"Nice to have connections." Her voice was tight. "So, license today? Marriage tomorrow? Is that your plan? Get it locked down tight before I try to escape with Tyler or something?"

The conscience he was ignoring said she wasn't far off. "When we're done in Braden, we'll stop and see a few properties I've been looking at."

"For what?"

"The house where we'll be raising our son."

He heard her shaky sigh. "Caleb, I said I'd marry you. I'm not going to run off. So there's no reason to rush like this."

"I have five years' worth of reason. I'll see you this afternoon." Before she could offer another protest, he ended the call and went back to his work.

Ever since he could remember, medicine had consumed him. Becoming a physician, then actually being one, crept into every personal thing he did. For the first time, though, it was his personal life that kept sidling into the forefront. Even when he should be wholly intent on his work.

It took him twice as long to finish his orders as it should have, because he kept picturing Tyler in place of his small patients.

"Everything all right, Dr. C?"

He glanced up to see Lisa Pope watching him curiously. As well she might, the way he was standing there staring blankly at the chart. "Fine, Lisa. I'm ordering an antibiotic for the Riley newborn." He finished off the chart with his scribbled signature and handed it back to her. "You know where to reach me if you need," he said before leaving the maternity unit.

He only had one patient in peds, a ten-year-old appendectomy who was recovering well. He played a game of Uno with him—which Caleb lost resoundingly—and left after promising to redeem himself at their next visit.

"Dr. C's so nice," he heard the boy's mom say once he left the room.

He doubted she'd think so if she were in Kelly's shoes.

He washed up in the doctor's lounge, grabbed a stale doughnut and a blistering cup of coffee that he drank on his way out to his truck. He retrieved Bingo from the diner—stopping only long enough for Tabby to see him through the window so she'd know that he was taking the pup again—and drove out to the farm.

Tyler was sitting on the porch steps, his chin in his hands. And even though he gave Caleb a wary look that held the power of a punch to his gut, the boy couldn't resist the lure of Bingo when Caleb set her on the ground.

Tyler had barely gotten down the steps, though, before Bingo raced across the dirt to jump on him.

Tyler giggled and caught the puppy up against the chest of his bright green coat.

"Hey, Ty," Caleb said as he neared him.

The boy watched him from the corners of his brown eyes. Eyes that Caleb now recognized were the same dark shade as his own. Kelly's eyes were brown too, but so much lighter. As different as day was from night. How could he not have noticed from the very beginning?

"Your mom inside?"

Tyler nodded against Bingo's head.

Caleb had never found it hard to deal with kids. Until life and circumstances taught them otherwise, they were unfailingly straightforward. It was one of the things that had drawn him to pediatrics.

But he found it hard now.

Instead of going inside to beard the lioness in her den, he sat on the porch steps a few feet away from her wary cub.

His cub.

"You're still upset with me."

Tyler's brows lowered. He didn't answer. But he was peeking at Caleb over the top of Bingo's silky blond head.

"I understand that." He propped his wrists on his

bent knees and spread his palms. "Anything I can do to make you not upset?"

"Mommy says when you're sorry you're supposed to say you're sorry."

"Mommy's right." He studied Tyler. "I'm sorry I upset you last night."

"You upset Mommy."

"I'm sorry I upset her, too."

Tyler lifted his head enough for Caleb to see his wrinkled nose. "You gotta tell *her*."

Caleb nodded, considering. Easier said than done when he still felt like he was reeling inside. "Right. The other part of saying you're sorry is accepting it." He reached out to rub Bingo's belly with his fingertips. "You know what that means?"

Tyler nodded.

"So if I tell you I'm sorry and I really mean it, you need to think about whether you can forgive me and really mean that."

"Forgiving means I can't be mad no more."

"Yup. You want to think about it for a while? Forgiving me?"

He nodded.

Caleb nodded, too. "That's fair. I'm going to go inside now and talk to Mommy. Okay?"

Again, Tyler nodded.

"Watch out for Bingo."

"I will. I gotta stay by the steps."

"Sounds like a plan." Caleb pushed to his feet.

"Do I gotta call you Dad?"

It was another slug to the gut. "You can call me whatever you want to call me." He waited a beat. "Except George. I don't usually answer to George."

Tyler ducked his head against Bingo again, but not quickly enough to hide his faint grin.

"Caleb. Cal. Cale. I've been called all of those."

"Kale is a vegetable," Tyler corrected, as if Caleb ought to know that.

"Better kale than carrots." Caleb shook his head. "I do *not* like carrots."

"I don't, *either*!" Tyler took a step forward. "Mommy says I don't have to eat 'em. Long as I eat the other stuff."

"Mommy's pretty cool that way."

"Mmm-hmm." Tyler put Bingo down on the ground, and she immediately started to dart off. He chased after her. "Bingo, we gotta stay by the steps."

"Maybe you should just bring Bingo inside."

Caleb turned on his heel to see Kelly leaning against the open doorway. "How long have you been standing there?"

"Long enough. George." She dropped her folded arms and straightened. She was wearing a gray turtleneck sweater and jeans tucked into tall, low-heeled boots. Her hair was slicked back from her oval face into a tight knot that his fingers wanted to untighten. "Tyler's already had his lunch, so we can go now."

"Go where?" Tyler slid around Caleb with the puppy right on his heels.

"For a drive."

"A *long* one?" The boy looked alarmed. "It took us a hundred hours when we came here for Grandma Gette's funeral."

"Not quite a hundred hours," Kelly corrected wryly. "And no, this won't be that long." She pushed his hair off his forehead. "We're going to Braden. I told you that while you had your sandwich."

"Yeah, but why?"

Kelly's gaze collided with Caleb's. "So your daddy and I can get married."

"We're not getting married today," Caleb said evenly. As much for Tyler's benefit as hers. "We're just getting the license that says we can get married."

"Why you gotta get a license?"

"Because the law requires it," Kelly murmured. She reached inside the house for a moment and then held out Caleb's leather coat. "Before I forget to give it to you again."

His fingers brushed hers when he took it, and she quickly looked away.

"Why's the law acquire it?"

"Require," she corrected and reached inside again, this time coming up with a black jacket she pulled on and a white scarf she looped loosely around her neck. "Because getting married is a serious thing."

"Like driving a car?"

"Something like that."

"Mommy, Dr. C—Caleb—don't like carrots, either."

Her gaze skidded over him again. "I heard that." She pulled the door closed behind her, focusing back on Tyler. "Does that make you just like him?"

Tyler's head fell back as he squinted up at Caleb. "I'm not as tall," he said matter-of-factly.

Kelly smiled slightly. "Not yet. But he didn't start out as tall as he is now, either. He was five years old once, too."

Tyler hopped down the porch steps. "Did you know my mommy when you were five?"

"Yeah. She was in the same class as me when we started kindergarten."

"All the way through high school." She followed him.

"And now Caleb's my dad." Tyler walked ahead of them, giggling when the puppy kept going between his feet. "'Cause you kissed and then bounced on the bed together."

Kelly's eyebrows shot up her forehead as she looked at Caleb. Her cheeks turned red. "Where did you get that idea, Tyler?"

The boy scuffed his shoe through the dirt, kicking a pebble. "Gunnar told me. He said that's how babies get made." Then he chased after Bingo, who'd chased after the pebble.

"Well," Caleb murmured. "I guess I had the facts of life wrong all this time. No wonder we ended up with him."

She stifled a laugh. But at least it was a laugh.

Chapter Thirteen

The diamond ring on her finger felt heavy. Kelly couldn't help twisting it nervously as she walked with Caleb into Leandra and Evan's house the next afternoon.

"Relax," Caleb muttered. "Everything's going to be fine."

"Easy for you to say." He'd told her that he'd already broken the news about Tyler to his parents. Which meant that was one task she could avoid, but it also left her not knowing what kind of reception she'd be getting from Cage and Belle when she came face-to-face with them.

Which she *would* be doing.

The pickup truck with the Lazy-B emblem on the side they'd just parked next to assured her of that.

Sunday dinner at Caleb's family members' homes meant anywhere from two people to twenty. She'd loved the days she'd been included when she and Caleb were teenagers.

Sometimes, she'd thought she loved his family as much as she loved him. Because she could pretend, for at least a few hours on a Sunday afternoon, that she was part of the Buchanan clan for real.

Of course, she'd always gone home afterward to the family that *was* real. To her mama. Who'd usually jeered at Kelly for acting as if she was good enough for the likes of them.

Caleb covered her fidgeting hands with his. "Relax," he said again. "You've known most of them nearly your whole life."

He meant it to be comforting. She knew that.

But she could still feel a bead of perspiration crawling down her spine. She wanted to turn around and leave. Or at least go outside, where Tyler was playing with Lucas and a handful of smaller, younger children.

She never had the chance to turn tail, though, because Leandra and Lucy both appeared, their faces wreathed in smiles. "Finally," Leandra exclaimed while Lucy snatched up Kelly's hand.

"Let me see the ring." Lucy's eyes were bright.

Caleb frowned. "Who told you?"

His sister laughed merrily as she squeezed Kelly's left hand and gave her a quick wink. "Our family grapevine spreads all the way to Braden these days. You know that. Yowza. Major sparkle." She looked up at her brother. "Didn't know you had it in you, Caleb."

"Everyone already knows?" From his tone, Kelly couldn't tell if he was annoyed or discomfited.

She was hoping for the latter. It made her feel slightly less alone.

"I'm so happy for you guys," Lucy said, wrapping her

arms around Kelly's neck for a quick hug. "And Shelby's over the moon." She let go of Kelly's neck but only to grab her arm and tug her farther into the house. "She figures it's her divine right to be in her uncle's wedding. Look who's here, everybody." Lucy raised her voice as they entered a great room crowded with bodies.

Kelly pinned a smile on her face that she was miles away from feeling. Everyone seemed to focus on the fact that she and Caleb were engaged, but not a single one of them mentioned the reason why.

Caleb had told his parents about Tyler, so they all surely had to know by now.

Across the room, Justin was pulling Tabby up to her feet, then she, too, was waddle-trotting toward them to add her congratulations. "Have you set a date?"

"Where are you planning to live?"

"Are you still going to sell the farm?"

"What kind of wedding do you want?"

"Izzy could make her dress!"

The bodies crowded around them. The questions and comments were flying, the voices seeming to get louder and louder as one person needed to speak above another.

"Give them some room to breathe, for heaven's sake." Belle Buchanan's calm order cut across it all, and suddenly, Kelly was face-to-face with Caleb's parents.

"Don't let them overwhelm you, Kelly." Belle wrapped her in a lightly fragranced hug. "They're like anxious calves getting at their mama's milk."

"You've been married to a cattle rancher too long," Cage joked. He nudged his wife aside to hug Kelly as well. "Welcome to the family, darlin'."

Belle and Cage's affection was so easy. So genuine. It made Kelly's throat tight and her eyes burn. "Mr. and Mrs. Buchanan—"

"Now, none of that. My wife told you before. It's Cage and Belle."

"Or Nana and Papa, depending on the generation," Lucy said humorously. Then her eyes widened at the look she received from her parents. "What? We're not pretending Tyler isn't Caleb's, are we?"

"Jesus, Luce," Caleb muttered.

"It's all right," Kelly said quickly, deciding it was a little like ripping off an adhesive bandage. No point in drawing out the process or the pain. "I'm sorry you all had to learn the way you did, but—"

"The point is we learned," Belle interrupted. "There's no need to say anything more. There's not a soul here who hasn't had a misstep before, or found themselves caught between a rock and a hard place. You're family now. That's what matters." She squeezed Kelly's arm. "And, of course, Tyler is perfect. I just saw him outside. I didn't say anything about being his grandma. I know this is all going to be very new for him. But he's just precious, Kelly." Her arm circled Caleb's waist, too. "And now that I know, I can see so much of both of you in his face."

"And before you get all weepy," Leandra interrupted, looking none too dry-eyed herself, "I've got a dozen boxes of pizza in the kitchen getting cold."

As quickly as Caleb and Kelly had first been engulfed by bodies, they were abandoned.

"Never underestimate the power of food when it comes to that group," Caleb said. "Told you everything was going to be fine."

Which it was.

If you considered having your immediate future pretty much planned out by committee.

By the time Caleb and Kelly left several hours later, that's the way she felt.

The wedding would be on Thanksgiving Day.

Which was two and a half weeks away.

It would be just a family affair out at the Lazy-B.

Which meant only half the town versus all of it.

And Isabella—Izzy—whom Kelly had never met until that afternoon but who was married to another one of Caleb's cousins and designed gowns, had insisted that two weeks was plenty of time to whip up the perfect dress.

"The only thing they didn't settle was where we were going to live," Kelly said when they finally left. "The farm. Your apartment. The Johansson place." She waved at Tyler through the window.

She'd finally given in to his pleas to stay with Lucas. Leandra had promised to drop him off at the farm when she took her son to school in the morning.

"Not the farm, that's for sure. You're selling it off, remember?"

As if she could forget.

"Would you rather have something different? A church wedding?"

When she was eighteen, she'd dreamed of the big white dress and their friends and family all crammed into the Weaver Community Church. But that was before her dreams turned to dust. Before she learned she wasn't what he wanted. And long before she'd run away from Wyoming to avoid this very thing.

"I don't see why we need a wedding at all when a trip to the justice of the peace would do just as well." She stared out the side window as they drove away from Leandra and Evan's place. "We could do it when you're between patients. No fuss, no muss." Maybe that way she could get through it without slipping into the fantasy that he truly wanted to marry *her*. That it wasn't a calculated decision on both their parts to give their son the parents he deserved.

"That's a good thing to show Tyler. His folks cared so much about becoming a family, they got hitched on a lunch break."

She closed her eyes as they neared the Perry place. "I don't know why it needs to be so fast, then. I still have the auction to get through. I have to figure out how to get our stuff from Idaho. Turn in my notice. I don't even have a job here."

"You don't need to have a job. I can afford—"

Her eyes snapped open. "I *want* a job. I worked hard to become a nurse! If you don't count the accident the other day, there are even some days when I think I'm pretty good at it."

He sighed noisily and suddenly turned off the road.

They were facing the Perry barn.

And he went just as silent as she did.

"Remember the first time we came here?" His deep voice finally broke the hush.

"How could I forget?" Her chest ached with memory. "Sixteen years old. You were the only boy I'd ever kissed. Much less—" She broke off, shaking her head. She'd kissed a few others in the years since. But he was still the only one she'd ever slept with.

That probably qualified her as an anachronism these days, but she didn't care. From the moment she'd known Tyler existed, her life had been all about him.

It had been easy, considering the only man she'd ever wanted was his father.

"I'm sorry I hurt you."

"I was a virgin, but I knew what I was doing."

His hand brushed her shoulder. "I don't mean that first time."

Her nerves were rippling. "I know that. It's just easier to think that you did."

"Are you ever going to forgive me?"

"For what?"

"For Melissa? For not being there when you were pregnant with Tyler? When he was born? A, B or C? All of the above? Take your pick. Volume discount."

She swallowed hard and looked at him. "Are you going to forgive *me*?"

His jaw canted to one side. "For what?" His voice was gruff. "Having my son?"

The sound of an engine grew louder, and a truck drove by, followed almost immediately by another that passed them with a short blow of its horn.

Kelly shifted in her seat, and Caleb's hand fell away.

He put the truck in gear, turning around in front of the barn and driving away.

She watched the barn grow smaller through the side-view mirror until he turned onto the highway and she lost sight of the Perry property completely.

They drove the rest of the way to the farm in silence, and it was nearly dark when he pulled up in front of the house. "Are you going to be okay here by yourself for the night?"

If she said she wasn't, he'd offer to stay.

And in her current mood, that would be a capital B-A-D idea. "I'll be fine."

"I'll stay if—"

"I know." She pushed open the truck door. "But I'm not ready to sleep with you again, and I'm afraid that's what will happen if you do. Things are complicated enough without that."

"Maybe that would uncomplicate things." He lifted his palm when she gave him a look. "Just a thought."

Despite herself, she let out half a laugh. "Good night, Caleb."

"Good night, Kelly."

He didn't drive away until she went inside the house.

She closed her eyes and leaned back against the door, the weight of his ring still heavy and unfamiliar on her finger.

The weight inside her chest, though? That was something infinitely familiar.

It was the feeling of still loving the one and only man she'd ever loved.

The one who would never be marrying her if not for their son.

The next morning, Kelly phoned Leandra and arranged to meet her and Tyler at the elementary school in Weaver. There was no point in the other woman making the drive out to the farm when Kelly needed to register Tyler for school anyway.

Once that was done and Tyler—wearing a clean outfit borrowed from Lucas that was only a hair too small—was settled excitedly in his new kindergarten class, she went over to the hospital and started the paperwork necessary to apply there before stopping in to see Maria and her baby.

They were both going home that day. To a life that was entirely different than Maria had planned.

The visit put things in perspective. Kelly's and Tyler's lives had taken a turn she hadn't planned for, but they were healthy. They were alive.

When Kelly was done, she sat in the hospital parking lot, where her phone signal seemed strongest, and called her boss in Idaho. He was shocked at the suddenness of her resignation. And gracious enough to tell her she'd always have a place there if she changed her mind.

Which just left her feeling weepy. Too weepy to contact her landlord, too, and start that ball rolling. Instead, she drove out of the hospital lot only to pull in a few minutes later at the sheriff's office, where Pam worked.

She'd thought to update her on everything, but she was too late. Pam already knew. About Tyler. About Caleb. Even about the glittering, unfamiliar stone on Kelly's finger. Pam also promised to be available on Thanksgiving. It was only right for her and Rob to represent the Rasmussen name at Kelly and Caleb's wedding, she said.

After that, with time still on her hands, Kelly drove out to Shop-World for a few groceries, stopped in at the Realtor's office to talk about getting the farm listed and met Izzy at Lucy's dance studio in town, because that was the most convenient place where they could get together to start on the dress.

Kelly held Izzy's sweet six-month-old baby, Tori, while her mama measured and sketched, and by the time Kelly left to pick up Tyler from school again, the other woman had created a vision that even Kelly—despite her misgivings about the entire wedding business—could love.

She figured Caleb would show up at the farm sooner or later that evening. And he did, though he spent most of the time sitting with Tyler as he shared every detail of his new kindergarten class. Then, when she was in the middle of preparing Tyler's bath, Caleb got an emergency call, and he left again.

She expected that it was an example of the evenings to come. And she was right.

The only thing that varied was the food she cooked

for dinner and whether or not Caleb got a call from some patient's parent who had his number on speed dial or a text from the hospital because he was on night call all that week.

Just as she'd known he would, Tyler reveled in the attention he got from Caleb. He was in seventh heaven.

By the night before the auction, though, Kelly's nerves were tighter than the overwound clock on her mama's fireplace mantel. "This thing is never gonna work again," she muttered to Caleb when he came downstairs after reading Tyler a bedtime story. She was polishing the wooden case. "It's not going to bring a dime at the auction tomorrow. I don't know why I'm bothering to polish it." It was just on the list of desirable items from the auction house. Same as the quilts. And a dozen other things that Kelly couldn't imagine bringing much money.

"I think you should go to Idaho."

She whirled, knocking the clock onto the floor. The solid thing didn't even have the common decency to break apart into pieces. It simply left behind a tiny dent on the wooden floor. Caleb bent down to pick it up.

"I knew you'd change your mind."

"About what?" He set the clock back on the mantel.

Her pulse pounded in her ears. "Marrying me."

"What?"

He was standing too close to her. She could actually feel the warmth radiating from him. "I'm glad I still haven't given notice on my apartment." She brushed past him to find some breathing space. "Bad enough I quit my job. Dr. Maguire's going to think I'm nuts when I tell him I changed my mind after all. If you think I'm going to leave Tyler here, though, you've got—"

Caleb covered her mouth with his hand. "Be quiet."

"—another think coming," she finished against his palm.

"I didn't mean you should go back to Idaho to *stay*. I meant for a few days. Dammit, Kelly." He turned away from her, shoving his fingers through his hair. "Are you always going to think the worst? Is that what's been bugging you all damn week? Here I figured it was the auction tomorrow, but it's really just been you waiting for some shoe to drop? For some new thing to use as a wedge between us?"

"I don't need a new wedge."

"No." His lips twisted slightly. "You've got the past to hold on to."

"I'm *trying*! You think this is easy?"

He shook his head. "Kelly, if we're to have a hope in hell of making this work, we've got to find a way to start fresh. Let go of the past."

"If it weren't for our past, we wouldn't even be here." She folded her arms tightly. "We wouldn't be getting married if not for Tyler. You'd never have proposed to me. I was the girl good enough to sleep with but not good enough to marry."

He pressed the palms of his hands to his eyes. "I swear to God, it's this house," he muttered and dropped his hands again. "That's your mother talking." His voice was flat. "And it's one more reason why you need to get out of this place. Take a break. Go to Idaho. *Move out of your apartment!* Or didn't you mean it when you agreed to marry me?"

She blinked hard, feeling the pain in her forehead pinch tighter than ever.

"Tom Hook can handle the auction tomorrow. When you come back in a few days—" he swept his arm out, encompassing the room around them "—all this could be—should be—gone. I'll put an offer in on the Johansson place. It's not a total new build—we could maybe be in before winter's over. And you liked it well enough when we drove by last week after we got your ring. Until then, you'll move in with me."

"Your one-bedroom apartment?"

"We'll rent something bigger. A bigger apartment. Bigger house. Whatever. But this place here?" He pointed at the floor beneath them. "I want us done with this place. *You* need to be done with this place. You are going to be my wife. My. Real. Wife. We *are* going to be a family. Stop hunting for signs that I'm changing my mind, because there are none!"

Her knees were shaking. "What do you mean, *real* wife?"

He looked exasperated. "What do you think I mean? In less than two weeks, we'll be married."

"You want to sleep with me?"

"Why do you sound surprised? Of course I want you in my bed!"

He shoved back his hair that had fallen over his forehead in the same way Tyler's always did. "You're a beautiful woman, Kelly. You're smart. You love that kid sleeping upstairs in a way that hits me in here—" he thumped his chest "—but I swear you're missing a screw if you honestly think we could be married on paper only. The only thing that's kept me from touching you this week has been you jumping a foot every time I come in the room."

Her stomach swooped, and her mouth felt suddenly dry. "I haven't been jumping a foot," she denied, even though he was more right than wrong. "But, say you, uh, you're right. Sex doesn't make a marriage *real*."

"It doesn't make it fake, honey."

"So sayeth the marriage expert. How many times have you made it down the aisle? *Love* makes a marriage real. Sex is not the root. Sex is the by-product!"

His eyes drilled into hers. "You think I don't love you?"

She laughed harshly. Which only seemed to prove he was right about the house, because even to her own ears, she sounded horribly like her mother. "I know you don't."

"And if I said you're wrong?"

"I wouldn't believe you." She couldn't let herself believe him. Because when it proved to be false, she wasn't sure she could survive.

"Why?"

Her mouth was dry. "We wouldn't be getting married if you did."

He waited a beat. "That's the most convoluted thing I've ever heard you say."

"We wouldn't be getting married like this," she amended. "It wouldn't be about Tyler. It would be…it would be about us."

"It *is* about us. It's about us being a family. Before I even knew about Tyler, I told you I didn't want the past stopping us from having a future. Remember that?"

How could she forget anything about that night? It hadn't even been a week ago, though it felt so much longer. "I remember. I also remember you never once mentioned marriage until after I told you about him."

"So I'm damned if I do and damned if I don't. Is that what we're down to?" Then Caleb swore and yanked his phone out of his pocket. He read the display and swore again. "I have to go. Tabby's in labor."

"Is she all right?"

"Baby's in fetal distress."

Kelly's knees went watery. But then she shook herself. Tabby and Justin were his dearest friends. She didn't need to add worry with her own distress. "Go." She snatched up his jacket and keys from where he'd left them and pushed them into his hands, following him to the front door. "Let me know more when you can."

He nodded. "It could be late."

"It doesn't matter how late." She opened the door for him. "Don't speed on the curves. They're going to need you there in one piece."

"Kelly—"

"Caleb, go do what you need to do."

His mouth covered hers in a hot, hard kiss that left her breathless. "I needed to do that, too."

Then he yanked on his jacket and strode out the door.

Chapter Fourteen

He didn't have a chance to call Kelly until the middle of the night. "Were you sleeping?"

"No. What's happening? How's Tabby?"

"C-section. She wanted a natural delivery, but it just wasn't going to happen. She's okay. Baby's doing better."

"Thank goodness." Her relief was palpable through the phone.

He leaned against the wall outside Tabby's hospital room. "Everyone's finally gone home except for Justin. It was a zoo here for a while." He could see his cousin through the door, sprawled on the chair beside Tabby's bed. Too wired to sleep, too drained not to.

"I can imagine. You're still at the hospital, then? You must be exhausted."

"I'll find an empty bed here somewhere. I don't want to get too far away just yet. The baby's stable, but—"

"You don't have to explain. Boy or girl?"

"A girl." He smiled slightly. "Justin's in for a ride, that's for sure." Silence, weighted by everything still unresolved between them, hung on the phone line for a moment.

"I'm not going to go to Idaho," she finally said abruptly. "But you're right about the auction. Not being here when it happens, I mean. I thought I'd take Tyler to Braden for the day. We can have lunch and there's a new movie out for the holidays and—"

"Sounds like a good idea." And even though it bugged the hell out of him that she was hanging on to her apartment, he couldn't say he actually wanted her to go there. What if she did and decided not to return? "Just pack up your stuff and go to my place when you get back. If I'm not there, I'll leave word with the manager to let you in."

She hesitated so long he braced for another argument.

"Okay," she finally said. "What do I do with Bingo for the day?"

Relief poured through him. "I'll call my sister in the morning." He glanced at the wall clock nearby. Which it technically already was, but—being the superior brother that he was—he'd wait until daylight. "She can dog-sit for a day in exchange for all the kid-sitting I've done for her." His phone pinged, and he glanced at the display. "The hospital is texting me. And I'm standing here in the hospital."

"Not Tabby's baby, I hope."

"Fortunately, no." He pushed away from the wall. "I'll see you tomorrow when you get back. Be careful on the drive."

"I will. Caleb?"

He put the phone he'd been ready to hang up back to his ear. "Yeah."

"I don't want to make another mistake." Her voice was soft.

"I don't, either, honey. I don't, either."

Then he pocketed his phone and made his way to the emergency room to deal with the next crisis.

Kelly smiled at the sight of Tyler throwing one of the red balls for the dog in Caleb's yard and waved through the window when he looked her way. Then she tucked her cell phone against her shoulder, listening while the auction house representative droned on about the results of the sale.

"Your mother's rings weren't particularly valuable, which we knew. The jewelry box was more so. The armoire in the master bedroom garnered quite a lot of interest, and of course the quilts, the farm equipment, the tools. We left the closing statement with Mr. Hook, as well. It takes a few weeks for the funds to settle, and they'll be deposited into your mother's estate account. I think you'll be quite pleased with the results," he said before finally ringing off.

She set the phone down and went back outside. She sat down on the porch step and pulled her sweater more closely around her. It was almost the middle of November, and the way the air felt, she wouldn't be surprised if snow was on its way again. "Tyler, are you warm enough?" There was little likelihood that he wasn't, considering the way he and Bingo were chasing each other around the yard.

"I'm fine, Mom." He snatched up the ball and threw it again, but it went right over the fence.

He looked so dismayed that she couldn't help laughing. "It's okay, buddy. I'll get it. Stay in the yard here, okay?"

He nodded and plopped on his knees to roll around with the dog.

She wished she had half his energy.

There was no gate on the fence. Going around it meant going out the front door and outside. And then it meant crawling under the bushes on the side of the fence to reach the darn ball. She finally managed to grab it and backed out, pushing to her feet. She brushed at the leaves sticking to her and turned to go back into the apartment only to find Caleb standing on the sidewalk.

She blushed. "I didn't know you were here."

He was smiling faintly. "Find anything interesting in the bushes?"

She held up the red ball. "Boys and toys. I've done a lot of chasing after them both in five years." She nodded toward the large paper-wrapped parcel Caleb was carrying. "What's that?"

"It's for you."

"What is it?"

The corner of his lip kicked up a little more. "Open it and see."

Her stomach squiggled around a little. "We never used to give each other gifts." A daisy from him here. A home-baked pie from her there. Nothing expensive in those days, simply because he'd always known she'd had no money.

"Consider it a new day then." He took the ball out of her hand, tossed it back over the fence and held out the bundle. "Well. Sort of."

"I don't know what that means."

"Stop being suspicious and just open it."

She pressed her lips together. She'd known him

nearly her entire life. A gift shouldn't make her feel so strange. But it did.

She slipped her finger beneath the edge of the brown paper and tore it back.

Then all she could do was stare at the pale pink-and-blue wedding-ring pattern of the quilt beneath.

"I ran into Lucy at the auction," he said after a moment. "She told me what you'd said about the quilt."

Kelly's vision blurred. She smoothed her hand over the soft cotton, pushing away the paper to reveal even more. "You went to the auction."

"A lot of people went to the auction. There were probably a hundred people when I got there."

"Did Lucy tell you to buy it?"

"No. But it seemed like you ought to keep one good memory from your childhood. If you don't want it, we'll just—"

"I want it," she whispered. "I want it very much." She wasn't sure if she meant the quilt or the sweetness behind the gift. She just knew she wanted it—wanted everything—as much as she ever had.

From the backyard, Bingo was barking and Tyler was laughing, and she looked up at Caleb.

She wanted everything even more than she ever had before.

"Thank you." She reached up and pulled his head down to press her lips to his.

He went still for a surprised moment. "If I'd known it only took a quilt—"

She kissed him again.

And his arms circled her back, pulling her close as his mouth opened over hers.

"Looking good, Dr. C," someone catcalled, and she sprang back to see a young man jogging past.

She flushed, glancing away from Caleb. She held the quilt against her chest, glad that the way her heart was pounding wasn't visible from the outside. "I…I should, um, probably see what Tyler's up to. Figure out some dinner for him. Is there anything you want?"

He didn't answer immediately, and she gazed back up at him, feeling her mouth go dry and her heart chug even harder at the steady look in his eyes.

"Whatever you're offering," he said.

She swallowed. "Steak," she said abruptly. He was the son of a cattle rancher. He'd always liked steak. He was sure to have one or two on hand.

He smiled faintly. "That'll do for a start."

His words hung in her head for the rest of the day. Through steaks that she broiled in the oven since he had no grill, through the bath she wrangled Tyler into and finally through the awkwardness of asking Caleb where Tyler should actually sleep.

"You two can take the bedroom," he said. He was sprawled on his couch wearing jeans and a T-shirt with an unexpected pair of reading glasses perched on his nose as he read a medical journal. He'd turned on the fireplace, and Bingo was sprawled over his bare feet. "I'll take the couch."

They were not exactly the words she'd expected, and she felt her shoulders droop a little. She was going to go through the rest of her life and not be able to predict the man.

When she'd come to Weaver in the first place, she'd intended it to be a couple weeks' time. Everything she'd brought to her mother's house she'd been able to pack up that morning and bring to Caleb's apartment. It amounted to two suitcases and a satchel full of Tyler's toys. She'd left them all stacked by the fireplace in the living room, but Caleb had moved them into the bedroom while she'd been busy supervising Tyler's bath. She searched through them until she found his pj's and tried not to think too hard about it when she shooed him up onto the middle of Caleb's wide bed and sat beside him. "Let me feel your cast again."

Tyler dutifully held up his arm. The cast was fiberglass with a water-repellent liner, but Kelly still preferred keeping it as dry and clean as possible, which was why bath time was such a joy. Tyler did not particularly care for having his arm wrapped in plastic and duct tape. "When do I getta get it off?"

She'd intended to be back in Idaho by now. "I have to get your records transferred here. Caleb can decide for sure, but probably in a few more weeks. That's when you'd have gotten it off if we were back home." By Thanksgiving.

She pushed away thoughts of the looming day.

"But home is here now. You said so."

"I did." She tapped his cast, which was satisfactorily dry. In the time since he'd gotten it, he'd amassed quite a collection of artwork and names on it. Particularly in the past week, when all of his new classmates had signed it.

"Can Caleb read me a story?"

"He can," Caleb's voice assured.

They both looked over at the doorway where he was standing. Bingo darted into the room, launching onto the blue comforter.

Kelly swallowed and slid off the bed. "His books are there in the bag." She didn't have to tell him which ones Tyler liked the best. He'd been discovering that all the past week.

"You stay, too, Mommy." Tyler wriggled under the

comforter and patted the bed on one side of him. "Right here."

She sat next to him where he wanted, and Bingo nosed her way onto Kelly's lap.

"You gotta lie down. Like you always do."

Her gaze skidded over Caleb. She moistened her lips, rearranged the puppy and stretched out next to Tyler.

"Now you, Daddy." Tyler patted the other side of the bed, innocently oblivious of the way Caleb had gone still.

Her throat tightened as she watched him grab the thick book of robot stories from the bag and tuck it under his arm before pulling off the black-framed reading glasses and polishing them on the hem of his shirt. Then he put them back on and cleared his throat before sitting on the bed next to Tyler. "Pick a page, buddy," he said huskily.

Bingo had wormed her way up the bed, and Kelly closed her eyes for a moment against the puppy's silky fur until the burning in them subsided.

"Here." Tyler flipped through the book, found the page he wanted and handed it back to Caleb. "Lie down like Mommy."

Caleb stretched out, his eyes meeting hers over their son.

Then he cleared his throat again and began to read. "'It was an exciting day for Sebastian the robot...'"

Kelly silently pulled the bedroom door closed on the soft snoring coming from both her son and his father. It had taken five stories, but the two of them were out like lights. As was Bingo, stretched out between them. None of them had even stirred when she'd unzipped her suitcase to pull out a few things or when she'd shut off the light. Considering the long hours that Caleb had put in the night before, she wasn't surprised that he'd dozed off, too.

In the bathroom, she cleaned up the mess Tyler had made, took a quick shower and pulled on her own pajamas. Then she finished cleaning up the kitchen, turned the fireplace down until it was a low blue glow and stretched out on Caleb's couch.

It was probably better this way. The two guys could share the bed. Caleb wouldn't be cramped on a too-short couch that fit her height perfectly well.

It wasn't perfect, just a one-bedroom apartment.

But it was better than the farmhouse.

And for the first time in weeks, when she closed her eyes, she felt peace.

It lasted for a few hours.

The sound of Caleb talking quietly woke her. She pushed aside the quilt that she couldn't remember covering herself with and peered over the back of the couch. She could see him standing shirtless in front of the open refrigerator, holding his phone to his ear.

Warmth spread through her, and she propped her chin on her arm, just watching.

"Of course I don't mind you calling me, Hildy. Make sure she drinks plenty of fluids, and if her temperature goes above one hundred, call me again. Uh-huh. Right. Perfectly all right. G'night, Hildy." He set his phone aside and pulled the milk jug out of the fridge, taking a sniff and then a swig.

Kelly smiled against her arm. "Asthma patient?"

He looked over his shoulder at her. "Sorry. Tried not to wake you."

"It's okay." The light from the refrigerator was giving his bare torso a very interesting halo. "Tyler still asleep?"

"Kid slept right through my cell phone ringing." He replaced the milk and closed the refrigerator door, leaving only the faint light from the fireplace. "I closed his door, so I hope he's not afraid of the dark."

"He's not."

"You should go take the bed."

Her heart seemed to skip a beat. She moistened her lips and stood. "Are you sure?"

"Yeah—" His voice broke off when she pulled her pajama top over her head.

"Are you still sure?" she whispered.

He slowly rounded the counter and came around the couch, not stopping until her tight nipples brushed against him.

It was too dark to see the expression in his eyes, but not too dark to feel. He slowly lowered his head and brushed his lips across hers. "Are you?"

She slid her fingertips down his abdomen until she reached his jeans, then pushed the button free and started on the zipper. She could hardly breathe, much less manage speech. "Yes."

His hands slid up her sides, setting off an avalanche of shivers. He brushed past her breasts much, much too quickly. Skirted her nipples, much, much too tantalizingly. Instead, his hands roved slowly up her neck to cradle her face. His thumb slowly rubbed across her lower lip. "I gave up stockpiling condoms a long time ago."

"I gave up trusting them a long time ago," she whispered. "I have an implant under my arm now. Easy peasy." Not that she'd ever needed it.

"You won't catch anything from me, either."

She pressed her forehead against his chest. "I worked

for an ob-gyn," she said. "I've talked to a lot of patients about the importance of having this very discussion, but I've never realized what a pain it is. You're safe. I'm safe. I would have had to actually be with someone since you for it to even be possible I'm not safe." Impatience was roaring through her bloodstream, making her feel more than a little crazy. "Now can you please put your hands on me?"

He inhaled sharply when she slid her hands inside his jeans, pushing them down. And his voice was gratifyingly raspy when she circled his length with her fingers. "No one?"

She shook her head, beyond caring what he would make of that information, and pressed her open mouth against his chest, tasting the saltiness of his skin. She started to work her way lower, then gasped when he pushed down her pajama pants. They fell right down to her feet. His arm went under her rear, lifting her out of them, and then he was turning, flipping her down on her back on the couch and putting his hands on her.

Everywhere.

His mouth covered hers, stifling the cry she couldn't contain when he finally, finally settled between her thighs and filled her.

His thumbs brushed her cheeks. Then his lips. "Don't cry."

She shook her head. "I'm not." Because she wasn't. Not really. There was just too much emotion, too much pleasure tightening inside her, and it only had so many places it could go.

Then he moved again, whipping the quilt from the couch onto the floor and pulling her down with him. His fingers threaded through hers as he rocked against her. Harder. Deeper. "One of these days we're going to do this in a bed." His voice was low. Rough.

She let out a sound—half sob, half laugh. "It's never mattered where." She buried a gasp against his hot neck as he surged inside her. "It's only mattered that it's you."

And then she arched against him, all that pleasure, all that emotion gathering together into the finest point there ever was. He was at the center of that point, and when it suddenly expanded again, blowing out into splinters of glorious perfection that went on and on and on, he was still the center.

No matter where she went. What she did.

She knew he always would be.

Twelve days later, Kelly stood in the master bedroom at the Lazy-B staring at herself in the big mirror on the wall while Lucy and Izzy fussed with her dress.

The entire house smelled like a Thanksgiving feast. But the food was waiting until *after* the ceremony. A fact about which Caleb's grandfather, Squire, had seen fit to complain loudly.

If Kelly hadn't seen the quick wink the old man gave her, she would have quailed even more about this whole thing.

"Your hands are cold as ice," Lucy said. "You're not having cold feet, are you? I love my brother, but I'll admit Caleb's hardly a great catch."

Kelly laughed despite herself, as Lucy had meant her to. Because they all knew Caleb was pretty much the ultimate catch. "I'm not having cold feet," she replied. "How could I be? I'm marrying the only man I've ever wanted to marry."

"And about time, too," Lucy said with feeling. She twitched the skirt of her own dress, which was a pretty russet-colored thing that showed off her lithe dancer's body to perfection. "I'm going to go see if Reverend Stone has gotten here yet."

Kelly nodded and inhaled deeply, trying to quell her nerves.

It was just hard. Knowing you were marrying a man who didn't love you the way you loved him.

Which wasn't a thing she could admit to any soul around.

"Dress feeling too tight?" Izzy asked.

"What?" She realized she was running her hands up and down the lace bodice of her dress. It was white, yet it wasn't white. It was ivory, yet it wasn't ivory. Every time she moved a muscle, the flowing, floaty layers of fabric that ended at her knees seemed to shift shades. "No, it's fine. Perfect, in fact. I've never worn anything so beautiful in my life."

"That's the way it should be on a girl's wedding day. A beautiful dress for a beautiful bride." Izzy smiled and set her pincushion and thread aside. "And I can't do a single thing more to improve on it."

"I don't know how to thank you for doing this."

Izzy's black-brown eyes, so startling in comparison to her white-blond hair, were sparkling. "You don't have to thank me at all. We women who marry into this big old crazy family have to stick together. Now, is there anything else I can do for you before this show gets on the road?"

Kelly started to shake her head. "Well, yes. Make sure that Tyler hasn't lost his clip-on tie already." Her son was downstairs somewhere playing with Lucas and the other kids.

Izzy grinned. "You bet." Then she, too, left the room.

Alone, Kelly stared at her reflection. She ought to

have left her hair down, but she'd pulled it back in a braid, which only seemed to magnify how pale her cheeks were.

She pinched them to put a little color into them and ordered her nerves to settle themselves back down.

She'd chosen this course knowingly. Just because Caleb's enthusiasm when they'd driven to his parents' ranch had been on par with hers—nonexistent—there was no reason to worry. Just because—aside from that first night they'd spent together in Caleb's apartment—he hadn't touched her again, there was no particular cause for concern.

They'd both been busy. Him with his patient load and rounds at the hospital and her with hiring a company to move their stuff from Idaho, working with the real estate agent who was listing the farm and dealing with Tom Hook and the seemingly endless tasks still necessary where her mom's estate was concerned. She'd been so busy the last few days, in fact, that she hadn't even had a chance to call the hospital back about the position they wanted her to fill. And of course there was Tyler. The constant presence of an active, inquisitive five-year-old boy who'd decided he liked sleeping in between his parents at night tended to put the brakes on things.

It would all be better once they got through this day. It had to be.

She exhaled again. Pinched her cheeks again. She should have put on more blush. When someone knocked on the door, she assumed it was Lucy. "Come on in. Is Reverend Stone finally here?"

But it was Caleb who stepped into his parents' bedroom.

When they'd driven to the Lazy-B earlier, he'd been

wearing his usual blue jeans and a black-and-gray-checked shirt.

The sight of him wearing a black suit, blinding white shirt and silver tie struck her nearly dumb. "Wow," she breathed. Even in her beautiful dress, she felt hopelessly outclassed. "You, uh, you didn't tell me you were going to wear a suit."

"You're wearing a dress, aren't you?" He had an envelope in his hand, and he held it up.

"Is that the license?" She'd told him that morning not to forget it. As if that were likely when he'd been the one to insist on getting it so quickly in the first place.

"No." His gaze roved over her face. "It's a prewedding gift, I guess you'd say."

He looked uncomfortable, though, and unease curdled inside her. "What do you mean?"

He pushed his fingers through his hair, rumpling the perfect way it had been brushed back from his face. "You were right. We shouldn't be getting married like this."

She felt the blood drain out of her head and swayed, knocking into the dresser with her knuckles when she reached out to steady herself. Somewhere inside her head she heard her mother's caustic laughter. "You decide this...*now*?"

His brows pulled together. "It has to be now. Otherwise it'll be too late."

"Too late because you'll be stuck married to me." She pressed her palm to her rolling stomach, and her diamond ring made a ray of light dance merrily in the mirror across from her.

"Because you'll be married to me and never believe me when I say I love you."

She gritted her teeth. He wasn't making any sense.

"I can't believe I gave up everything, *everything* I ever worked for. Everything I had to do to make a life for Tyler and me. In all these years I haven't learned anything. Not. One. Single. Thing. I suppose you think now you don't have to worry about Tyler. You're his daddy. The man he adores now. You don't have to tiptoe your way around a little boy's loyalty to his mother anymore."

"I am his daddy. And that's the damn problem!" His voice rose.

She straightened abruptly, her stomach clenched. "If you break his heart, I will haunt you to your grave."

"I'm trying not to break anyone's heart! Especially his." He shoved his hand through his hair again. She noticed almost absently that it was shaking.

"Here." He held out the envelope again. "Just take it. Then you can decide how long you want to haunt me."

She snatched it out of his hand, yanking out the sheet of paper inside. "What is it?"

"It's an authorization form for the state of Idaho, adding me to Tyler's birth certificate as his natural father. All you have to do is sign it."

"You've already signed it."

"And Mary Goodwin from my office notarized it about ten minutes ago when I bribed her to leave her family's holiday so she could save mine. She'll notarize your half of the form when you sign it. After it's submitted, Tyler will get a new birth certificate. I won't have to do one more thing for the world to know I'm his legal father. With all of the rights and the responsibilities that come with it."

He took a step closer to her. "And you won't have any more reason to keep believing that this marriage is only about our son." He took a deep breath and let it out slowly. "This marriage is about *us*, Kelly. I love you. Not like when we were fifteen. But not all that differently, either."

Her knees felt like water. She would have sat if there'd been a spot, but there was none, because Caleb just kept stepping closer and closer until she was well and truly backed up against the dresser behind her.

"You are the woman I can't get out of my head. You are the woman I don't want to get out of my heart. I can't lie and say that I don't love you more because you are the mother of my child. Because you *are* the mother of my child. I want us to be a family. And even if we didn't already have Tyler, I'd still want you for my wife."

"Why now?" she whispered. "Why couldn't you have done this yesterday? Last week? Why wait until today and—"

"Because I was afraid you'd change your mind about marrying me. You agreed for Tyler's sake."

Her eyes were wet. "And today?"

"I finally realized I need you to change your mind about marrying me for Tyler's sake."

She frowned. "And you tell me I've got convoluted thinking."

"It's as simple as it gets." He suddenly knelt in front of her.

Her heart climbed into her throat, and the form slid out of her nerveless fingers.

"Marry me, Kelly Rasmussen." He took her hands in his and kissed her fingertips. "Marry me because I'm the only man for you. Marry me because you're the only woman for me. Marry me because you believe I love you as much as I believe you still love me."

She pressed her lips together and pulled one hand free of his to brush his hair off his forehead. "That's quite a mouthful, Dr. C."

His eyes searched hers. And she finally recognized the uncertainty there. Recognized the love.

And it was like being bathed in warm, radiant light. "Is that a yes?"

She nodded. "I love you. Still." She leaned over him and slowly kissed his lips. "And I *do* believe you."

The bedroom door suddenly opened. "Reverend Stone's finally here—" Lucy stopped, taking in the sight of them. "*Okay.* Should I back up here? Yep. That's what I'm doing. Backing up. Reversing the truck. Beep, beep." She closed the door again.

"I don't know how my brother-in-law stands her." Caleb straightened. He set the form Kelly had dropped on the dresser and patted his lapel. "I had a pen—"

She slid her arms around him. "We'll find a pen soon enough. Right now we have something more important to do."

"Kissing you?" He obliged so slowly and thoroughly that she once again felt decidedly weak-kneed. But only in the best way possible.

"That *is* always important," she agreed. "But I was thinking more along the lines of our wedding."

"You're really sure?"

She looked into his eyes. "I've loved you since I went over the handlebars of my bicycle in front of you half my lifetime ago. I loved you even when I thought I hated you. And I loved you when I looked into our son's eyes for the first time. Yes, I am really sure."

He smiled the same smile she'd always loved and tucked her hand through his arm. "Then let's go get married."

And they did.

Epilogue

"Santa left you a present." Caleb dropped a thick envelope on Kelly's lap.

"Santa doesn't come until tonight," Kelly reminded him humorously.

"Yeah, well, Santa and I have a connection." Caleb sat down on the porch step beside her.

"A good thing, considering the length of Tyler's Christmas list."

Caleb grinned and her chest felt all fluttery. She wondered if that would ever go away. And hoped it wouldn't.

"Daddy, look! I'm making a snow angel."

"I see that." Caleb lowered his voice, leaning closer to her. "Does he know it takes more snow than we've got to make a decent snow angel?"

She laughed. There were barely two inches of snow covering their postage-stamp-size yard. "He's entertained," she said. "And he'll have plenty of snow when we go out to your sister's for dinner before the Christmas Eve service at church. How were things at the hospital?"

"Fine. Two newborns overnight. I don't know what's in the water around here, but people are having babies right and left." He gave her a sidelong smile. "Want to drink the water?"

She laughed softly. "Dr. Yarnell is taking out my birth control implant after New Year's. Who knows how long it'll take for me to get pregnant."

"My swimmers are pretty strong. He's proof." Caleb grinned and nodded toward the boy sprawled on the ground near the spruce tree. The tree boughs carried even more Christmas ornaments than the first time Kelly had seen it, thanks to Tyler's and Caleb's efforts.

She wasn't sure which one of her men was looking forward more to their first Christmas together.

"It's more about my hormones than yours, which you know perfectly well, Dr. C."

"Well, Mrs. B, we'll just have to keep practicing, then."

She didn't bother hiding her smile. Because even though she could hardly wait for the day when they gave Tyler a baby sister or brother, it *was* blissfully satisfying the way Caleb liked to practice. "So what's in the envelope?" It was catalog thick.

He shrugged and worked his fingers up the back of her winter coat beneath her shirt. "Open it and see."

She shivered and wriggled. "Your hands are cold. Put on gloves."

"Why? This is more fun."

She laughed softly. "You're impossible."

"And you love me anyway."

She rubbed her head against his shoulder for a moment. "That I do." Then she slid her gloved finger under the envelope flap and tore it open. She tipped out the contents onto her lap and then stared blankly at the documents. "What is this? A sales contract?" Not for her mother's farm. That was still tied up in probate and would be for months still. "I thought we agreed to wait on the Johansson place." Even though it meant remaining in the apartment for a while longer, neither one of them had been able to wholeheartedly plow forward on the property. It was definitely cozy, but they were making do.

"It isn't the Johansson place." He reached over and flipped a few pages until he came to one with a photograph.

She recognized it immediately, and her heart just sort of tumbled wide. "That's the Perry barn."

"If you agree. We could start building in the spring. Decide later if we want to replace the barn or not."

"Not," she murmured. "I didn't know the property was even for sale."

"It wasn't. I finally found the owners in Seattle. I can be persuasive when I try."

Her fingers traced over the photograph. "Yes, you can."

"So what do you think?"

She squirmed again as she felt his hand caress her back and begin to travel lower. "About what you're doing right now or buying the Perry place?" She set the papers aside.

"Either. Both. Take your pick."

She laughed and turned her lips to his. "I think they're both pretty darn perfect."

"You're pretty darn perfect," he said against her lips. Then he moved his hand and grabbed hers, pulling her to her feet.

She laughed. "Caleb." She looked toward their son meaningfully.

"Take your mind out of the bedroom," he murmured and tugged her toward the corner of the yard where Tyler was still vigorously swishing his arms and legs in the snow.

Caleb sat down next to their son and stretched out on the ground.

Delight bloomed inside her. Tyler was giggling wildly. "What are you doing?" Though it was perfectly obvious.

"Making snow angels." Caleb held out his hand. "You going to join us?"

She cherished the picture he and Tyler made and took his hand.

"Always."

* * * * *

Don't miss these other stories in
New York Times *and* USA TODAY
bestselling author Allison Leigh's long-running
RETURN TO THE DOUBLE C *series:*

THE RANCHER'S DANCE
COURTNEY'S BABY PLAN
A WEAVER PROPOSAL
A WEAVER VOW
A WEAVER BEGINNING
A WEAVER CHRISTMAS GIFT
ONE NIGHT IN WEAVER

Available from Mills & Boon.

1116/23

MILLS & BOON®

EXCLUSIVE EXTRACT

Crown Prince Armando enlists Rosa Lamberti to find him a suitable wife—but could a stolen kiss under the mistletoe lead to an unexpected Christmas wedding?

Read on for a sneak preview of
WINTER WEDDING FOR THE PRINCE
by Barbara Wallace

"Have you ever looked at an unfocused telescope only to turn the knob and make everything sharp and clear?" Armando asked.

Rosa nodded.

"That is what it was like for me, a few minutes ago. One moment I had all these sensations I couldn't explain swirling inside me, then the next everything made sense. They were my soul coming back to life."

"I don't know what to think," she said.

"Then don't think," he replied. "Just go with your heart."

He made it sound easy. Just go with your heart. But what if your heart was frightened and confused? For all his talk of coming to life, he was essentially in the same place as before, unable or unwilling to give her a true emotional commitment.

On the other hand, her feelings wanted to override her common sense, so maybe they were even. As she watched him close the gap between them, she felt her heartbeat quicken to match her breath.

"You do know that we're under the mistletoe yet again, don't you?"

The sprig of berries had quite a knack for timing, didn't it? Anticipation ran down her spine ceasing what little hold common sense still had. Armando was going kiss her and she was going to let him. She wanted to lose herself in his arms. Believe for a moment that his heart felt more than simple desire.

This time, when he wrapped his arm around her waist, she slid against him willingly, aligning her hips against his with a smile.

"Appears to be our fate," she whispered. "Mistletoe, that is."

"You'll get no complaints from me." She could hear her heart beating in her ears as his head dipped toward hers. "Merry Christmas, Rosa."

"Mer..." His kiss swallowed the rest of her wish. Rosa didn't care if she spoke another word again. She'd waited her whole life to be kissed like this. Fully and deeply, with a need she felt all the way down to her toes.

They were both breathless when the moment ended. With their foreheads resting against each other, she felt Armando smile against her lips. "Merry Christmas," he whispered again.

Don't miss
WINTER WEDDING FOR THE PRINCE
by Barbara Wallace

Available December 2016

www.millsandboon.co.uk

Copyright ©2016 Barbara Wallace

MILLS & BOON®

Why shop at millsandboon.co.uk?

Each year, thousands of romance readers find their perfect read at millsandboon.co.uk. That's because we're passionate about bringing you the very best romantic fiction. Here are some of the advantages of shopping at www.millsandboon.co.uk:

* **Get new books first**—you'll be able to buy your favourite books one month before they hit the shops

* **Get exclusive discounts**—you'll also be able to buy our specially created monthly collections, with up to 50% off the RRP

* **Find your favourite authors**—latest news, interviews and new releases for all your favourite authors and series on our website, plus ideas for what to try next

* **Join in**—once you've bought your favourite books, don't forget to register with us to rate, review and join in the discussions

Visit **www.millsandboon.co.uk** for all this and more today!